BOOKS BY GRAHAM SEAL

Great Australian Stories
Great Anzac Stories
Larrikins, Bush Tales and Other Great Australian Stories
The Savage Shore
Great Australian Journeys
Great Convict Stories
Great Bush Stories
Australia's Funniest Yarns

Praise for Graham Seal's books

Great Australian Stories

'The pleasure of this book is in its ability to give a fair dinkum insight into the richness of Australian story telling.'—*Weekly Times*

'This book is a little island of Aussie culture.'—*Sunshine Coast Sunday*

Larrikins, Bush Tales and Other Great Australian Stories

'. . . another collection of yarns, tall tales, bush legends and colourful characters . . . from one of our master storytellers.'—*Queensland Times*

Great Anzac Stories

'. . . allows you to feel as if you are there in the trenches with them.'—*Weekly Times*

'They are pithy short pieces, absolutely ideal for reading when you are pushed for time, but they are stories you will remember for much longer than you would expect.'—*Ballarat Courier*

The Savage Shore

'. . . a gripping account of danger at sea, dramatic shipwrecks, courageous castaways, murder, much missing gold, and terrible loss of life.'—*Queensland Times*

'Colourful stories about the spirit of navigation and exploration, and of courageous and miserable adventures at sea.'—*National Geographic*

Great Australian Journeys

'Readers familiar with Graham Seal's work will know he finds and writes ripper, fair-dinkum, true blue Aussie yarns. His books are great reads and do a lot for ensuring cultural stories are not lost.'—*The Weekly Times*

'Epic tales of exploration, survival, tragedy, romance, mystery, discovery and loss come together in this intriguing collection of some of Australia's most dramatic journeys from the 19th and early 20th century.'—*Vacations and Travel*

Great Convict Stories

'More than just a retelling of some of the most fascinating yarns, Seal is interested in how folklore around the convicts grew from the colourful tales of transportation and what impact that had on how we see our convict heritage.'—*Daily Telegraph*

'With a cast of colourful characters from around the country—the real Artful Dodger, intrepid bushrangers . . . *Great Convict Stories* offers a fascinating insight into life in Australia's first decades.'—*Sunraysia Daily*

Great Bush Stories

'This collection is Graham Seal at his best.'—*The Land*

'Takes us back to a time when "the bush" was central to popular notions of Australian identity, with the likes of Henry Lawson and "Banjo" Paterson serving to both celebrate and mythologise it.' —*Writing WA*

Australia's Funniest Yarns

'Aussies know how to spin a good yarn, and Graham Seal knows how to tell them.'—*Weekly Times*

THE BIG BOOK OF
GREAT AUSTRALIAN BUSH YARNS

GRAHAM SEAL

ALLEN&UNWIN
SYDNEY · MELBOURNE · AUCKLAND · LONDON

This edition published in 2020

Great Australian Stories first published in 2009
Larrikins, Bush Tales and Other Great Australian Stories first published in 2014

Allen & Unwin
83 Alexander Street
Crows Nest NSW 2065
Australia
Phone: (61 2) 8425 0100
Email: info@allenandunwin.com
Web: www.allenandunwin.com

A catalogue record for this
book is available from the
National Library of Australia

ISBN 978 1 76087 928 0

Set in 12.5/16 pt Adobe Caslon Pro by Bookhouse, Sydney
Printed and bound in Australia by Griffin Press, part of Ovato

10 9 8 7 6 5 4 3 2 1

The paper in this book is FSC® certified.
FSC® promotes environmentally responsible,
socially beneficial and economically viable
management of the world's forests.

Contents

Foreword

ONCE UPON A time, in a far different Australia, there was no television, no radio and no internet, so families, friends and even strangers entertained each other with stories. Hard to believe but young and old sat around the kitchen table, lounged on verandahs and even around crackling campfires as they swapped tales, recited poetry and maybe sang a song; such poems and songs being part of the storytelling tradition.

As a young country, its people living predominantly in what we now refer to as 'the bush', we were keen to hear stories about the 'old country', usually England, Ireland and Scotland, and be reminded of times gone by. We were also curious to hear stories about the people who lived down the road, even if they were two hundred or two thousand miles away.

The stories played several roles other than just entertainment. They provided an obvious romantic link with the past, fuelled the imagination of their audience, provided a creative outlet for the tellers and, in a country with a dubious past, an opportunity to relax. More often than not, they allowed us to laugh at ourselves—and pomposity in general.

A lot of our stories were born in the bush. It must be remembered that the nineteenth century was a male-dominated society with a definite class-consciousness where the majority of men worked either as shepherds, miners, bullockies or drovers. This is where the campfire ruled as a neutral territory where all men were equal. Over a mug of steaming black China tea men discussed the ways of the world and, as the fire dimmed, talk would often turn to storytelling as an opportunity for escapism. Old tales were told but new ones were also created, in many cases told in the first person and bringing in fellow workmates as members of the cast. Humour has always been a great leveller and there's no denying that Australia developed a unique sense of humour—often described as 'dry'. There are several reasons suggesting why our humour is so laconic, including the immense size and isolation of the country and the reality that Australia was so blatantly different from Europe. It was (and still is) dry, hot, brown and tough as old boots. Many of the stories reinforced our determination to survive against the odds: fighting floods, droughts, bushfires, pestilence and, more often than not, the banks and authorities. In some ways many of the old stories could be described as 'people's history' however, because the folk never let the truth get in the way of a good yarn, they are an unreliable history.

Back in the old days when we entertained each other rather than nowadays where we tend to get entertained, and mainly by the electronic media and fabricated popular culture, most people had a 'party piece'—often a story that they had made their own. We also had the accompanying skills to 'perform' in front of an audience, large or small. We are rapidly losing this ability in proportion to the advancement in technologically delivered entertainment and, sadly, this passivity has a high price resulting in far too many social problems.

This collection is much more than just a bunch of stories retold for the umpteenth dozen time. Graham Seal has provided us with valuable keys to our national identity: why we are unique as a people. He salutes our past, including a good swag of indigenous stories, tales from the back of Bourke, Woop Woop and beyond the Black Stump, stories from our soldiers on the front line and also some ripper yarns from the cities. As a folklorist and fellow 'road's scholar' my old 'China-plate', Graham Seal, has offered insightful observations on why certain stories were created, passed around and also down through the years. *Great Australian Stories* is true to its title as it wanders from bush track to spooky hollow, follows the path of yowies and bunyips, searches for Lasseter's Reef, meets Dad and Dave and, on a different path, Henny-Penny, and then rambles into the cities where just as many entertaining characters are ready to tell *their* stories.

Warren Fahey AM
Folklorist

Introduction:
Telling tales

As FAR AS we know, humans have always told stories. The first inhabitants of Australia created a vast oral archive of myth and legend that explained their origins, the landscape, and its plants, animals and spirits. Before settling the last continent, Europeans swapped fabulous tales about what they imagined it to be like—a land of hermaphrodites, strange winged beasts and people who walked upside down. When they finally did arrive in numbers, they found the reality was sometimes as extraordinary as the fables. As the colonists moved out across the country, they began to make and share new stories about the Australian experience, sometimes blending these with indigenous traditions.

Today, these processes have produced a rich legacy of story that reflects the distinctiveness of Australia's past and present. It is a legacy that includes the ancient stories of the first inhabitants, those tales brought here by settlers from many lands, and those that have developed from the historical experience of modern Australia. There are legends of the Dreaming, yarns of pioneering, the bush, war, work and play, tales of the unexplained, the heroic, the monstrous and the tragic. They reflect the deep beliefs, fears, hopes and humour of those who tell and re-tell them.

The stories in this book are not personal anecdotes, although they may occasionally be told in this way. They are part of a national conversation held by many voices, often over a number of generations and across the country. As a collective cultural possession, they are part of the repertoires of folklore shared between and within social groups. They originate in and spread through the informal interactions of everyday life. As they develop over time and move from place to place, the stories pick up new elements, drop details that are dated or otherwise unintelligible, and adapt to the needs and attitudes of their tellers and hearers. It is these adaptations that keep a story tradition alive from generation to generation and provide its inheritors with a powerful sense of connection with earlier tellers and hearers. These communities of story can be as small as a family or as large as an industry, an army, or spread across a whole nation.

Most tales are the cultural property of their tellers and hearers. The stories of a certain group may be unknown to outsiders. This often surprises those who are familiar with them; they assume that everyone has heard this or that 'old chestnut'. As communities change, so do their reservoirs of story. Some fall silent as their original sources dry up. Others are reshaped to suit new realities. Stories rarely die altogether. Like all forms of folklore, they may hibernate for decades, even centuries, before reappearing—as is the case with a number of ostensibly modern urban legends. Stories old and new are increasingly passed on through audio and video recordings and the internet, which vastly extends their staying power.

When it is possible to trace the evolution of particular tales, we often find out something about their meanings and their relationship to history and folklore. Stories not only tell what has been seen, heard or believed but also connect their hearers with the time, place, events and people about which they speak. They map real and imaginative landscapes, as well as documenting what happened, or is thought to have happened, in them. They help us, in other words, make sense of the world and of our place within it.

Part of the appeal of the stories Australians tell is the colour and vitality of their language. As well as a liberal sprinkling of profanity, there are typically shortened words like 'wharfie', 'bullocky' and 'swaggy', and uniquely Australian ones like 'bushranger', 'digger', 'Speewah', 'bunyip', 'redback' and 'drongo'. Traditional tales also contain many Australian placenames, some of indigenous origin, like Coraki or Min Min, and others which evocatively combine the indigenous and the European, such as Ooldea Soak or Top Bingera. While some tales are versions of those told elsewhere in the world, their local renditions are well and truly Australianised.

While segments of this tradition, particularly indigenous myths and bush yarns, have been collected before, relatively little attention has been given to other types of tales. This book presents, for the first time, a reasonably representative selection of Australian stories in all their variety. The collective tale they tell is one of down-to-earth realism, tragedy and heroism, dry and cutting humour, an unexpectedly wide supernatural streak, a strong sense of place, colourful truths and even the odd lie. It tells us a good deal about what Australians value; what they fear, dislike, laugh at and wonder about.

The stories have been sorted into chapters by theme. The first chapter presents a small selection of tales from the continent's indigenous tradition. These are all translations, of course, though many retain words and phrases from the original languages in which they were recorded. They explain the origins of people, animals and plants in the timeless spirit world usually known as the Dreaming. None of these stories are secret or sacred, so they can be freely told. Some of their themes recur in stories elsewhere in the book.

Pioneering was the central Australian experience of the nineteenth and early twentieth centuries. As settlers spread across the continent from landfalls on the coasts, a frontier was created along whose ever-moving edges Europeans and indigenous people came into often abrasive contact. In some frontier stories Aborigines appear as savage foes; in others they are saviours. Occasionally they appear in both roles in the same story.

Despite, or sometimes because of, these experiences, the story traditions of original occupants and incoming occupiers began to interact, creating such hybrids as the bunyip, the yowie, and other legendary creatures. Aboriginal belief and the actions of settlers merged in the mystery of the Min Min Lights.

The 'Legends on the land' chapter presents stories about particular parts of the country. Some tell how places got their names; others deal with strange events or treasure hunts. There may be different versions of how and when something important began or what happened—and why. Stories of this kind are part of a common fund of local knowledge that reflects the powerful bonds of shared experience.

Also closely linked with locality are Australia's many traditions of ghosts and the supernatural. Considering its small population, the nation has generated a very large number of ghost stories, and continues to do so. The variety of oddities and apparitions involved suggests that Australia is a powerfully haunted land. Its indigenous traditions are rich with spirits of many kinds, and its settler history adds European ghosts and gremlins.

As well as the supernatural, there is plenty of scope for the fantastic. So-called fairy tales were widely told to children by adults and by adults to each other until at least the early twentieth century. In versions mostly derived from British traditions, accounts of giant-killers, pumpkin coaches and magical beanstalks have proved remarkably durable. Although Australian fairy stories generally lack fairies, they do have witches. These come in imported form from the rich storytelling traditions of Ireland. 'The witch's tale', told by Simon McDonald, is a wonderful example of the Australian bush art of spinning tales.

A favourite bush tradition is the tall tale. Australia has giant mozzies (mosquitoes), hoop snakes and split dogs in abundance. Modern urban legends update the tall tale with funny fables that are highly unlikely to be true. Australians have generally taken their leisure at least as seriously as their labour, producing large numbers of leg-puller yarns about sport, pastimes and, of course, sex. They love a good lie, it seems, no matter what the subject might be.

All traditions contain heroes and villains, as well as a few figures who are a little bit of both. Outstanding men and women, mythical and historical, can be found in indigenous and settler lore. The bushranger is an especially ambivalent character, whose crimes—often violent—are cast in folklore as justified defiance of oppression. In this sense, Australia's handful of celebrated bushrangers are its tragic heroes. The digger is a hero of another kind. Originally the volunteer footsoldier of World War I, the digger has become part of the mythology of Anzac. His larrikin ways are balanced by his sense of humour, his sceptical attitude to authority, and his reputation as a fighter.

Colourful, eccentric and plain crazy characters abound in Australian stories. They include numbskulls like the drongo, Dave in the 'Dad and Dave' stories, and the Cornish-descended Cousin Jacks. There are tricksters aplenty, from Jacky Bindi-i to Snuffler Oldfield. These named identities jostle for our affection with stock figures like the three blokes at a bar and the racecourse doper, among many others.

The frontier experience also produced a string of hard cases, such as the notoriously stingy pastoralist Hungry Tyson and the helpful but deep-drinking Wheelbarrow Jack. These were real people, as were the tough Eulo Queen and the sad Eliza Donnithorne. Others, like the tight-fisted cocky farmer and the world's greatest whinger, are archetypes. Genuine or larger than life, their deeds and sayings are remembered and relished.

A sense of shared experience motivates many stories of working life. These are usually humorous, often with a sharp edge of anti-authoritarianism, satire or outright ridicule of those who are supposedly in charge. The examples given here range from the nineteenth-century frontier farm to the present-day office or factory. While the forms of working humour have changed, the values and attitudes that underlie them have remained substantially the same.

Australia's stories are of pioneering, farming, bushranging, war, hardship, triumph, loss and laughter. They are about the unexplained, the mysterious, the lost and the never-was. They tell of origins and endings, heroes and villains, ghosts and monsters. Some are humorous yarns and tall tales of tricksters, nongs and lucky ducks. Others speak of odd but believable things that might have happened to a friend of a friend. There are tales told by railway workers, soldiers, farmers, parents, sporting types, office workers and just about anyone else. We all have tales to tell. Some of them may even be true.

Whether these stories are fact, fiction or a little of both, it is important to note that tradition can preserve both the bad and the good. As well as humour, determination, resilience and healthy scepticism, Australian stories sometimes reflect attitudes—especially towards Aboriginal people and women—that we find distasteful today. As this book reproduces historical as well as more recent texts, readers should be prepared for occasional jarring notes. Understanding something of their context, however, may help us appreciate the role of stories in social change. The fusion between indigenous and settler traditions about bunyips and ghosts, for example, is a sign of positive engagement. On the other hand, the divergence between those traditions in stories about frontier clashes points to ongoing tensions.

In many of the stories here, it is hard to tell where fact ends and fiction begins. But the myths that form in the spaces between history and folklore exert a powerful spell. Many prefer to believe the myths because they speak to cherished ideals like mateship, freedom and the fair go. If these ideals are often dreams rather than deeds, they are no less beguiling for that. In the end, our stories tell us as much as we want them to.

1

Stories in the heart

She's got her stories in the heart, not on the paper.

Emily Munyungka Austin, Kupa Piti (Coober Pedy) elder,
speaking of her grandmother's Dreamtime traditions

THE CULTURES OF Australia's indigenous peoples, Aborigines
and Torres Strait Islanders, are rich in story. Together with song,
dance and art, stories were a principal means of preserving and
transmitting cultural knowledge from generation to generation.
Much indigenous story is related to secret and sacred ritual and
excluded from general circulation. But there is also an extensive
repertoire of legends and stories that may be told freely. The
very small selection of such stories given here demonstrates the
powerful connections between the land and all the living things
upon it that is the foundation of indigenous belief.

Wirreenun the rainmaker

Katherine Langloh-Parker (1856–1940) was the wife of a settler
near Angledool, New South Wales. She developed a close relationship with the Noongahburrah, a branch of the Yularoi people.
Her knowledge of their customs, beliefs and language helped
her compile a unique record of the indigenous traditions of the

Narran River region, even if filtered through the perceptions of an outsider and through various translations and retellings.

Wirreenun (meaning a priest or doctor) is a rainmaker who uses his magical abilities to help his people, despite the lapse of their belief in his powers. In this story, Wirreenun is also a name.

*T*he country was stricken with a drought. The rivers were all dry except the deepest holes in them. The grass was dead, and even the trees were dying. The bark *dardurr* (humpy) of the blacks were all fallen to the ground and lay there rotting, so long was it since they had been used, for only in wet weather did they use the bark *dardurr*; at other times they used only *whatdooral*, or bough shades.

The young men of the Noongahburrah murmured among them-selves, at first secretly, at last openly, saying: 'Did not our fathers always say that the *wirreenun* could make, as we wanted it, the rain to fall? Yet look at our country—the grass blown away, no *doonburr* seed to grind, the kangaroo are dying, and the emu, the duck, and the swan have flown to far countries. We shall have no food soon; then shall we die, and the Noongahburrah be no more seen on the Narran. Then why, if he is able, does not Wirreenun make rain?'

Soon these murmurs reached the ears of the old Wirreenun. He said nothing, but the young fellows noticed that for two or three days in succession he went to the waterhole in the creek and placed in it a *willgoo willgoo*—a long stick, ornamented at the top with white cockatoo feathers—and beside the stick he placed two big *gubberah*, that is, two big, clear pebbles which at other times he always secreted about him, in the folds of his *waywah*, or in the band or net on his head.

Especially was he careful to hide these stones from the women.

At the end of the third day Wirreenun said to the young men: 'Go you, take your *comeboos* and cut bark sufficient to make *dardurr* for all the tribe.'

The young men did as they were bade. When they had the bark cut and brought in, Wirreenun said: 'Go you now and raise with ant-bed a high place, and put thereon logs and wood for a fire, build the ant-bed about a foot from the ground. Then put you a floor of ant-bed a foot high wherever you are going to build a *dardurr*.'

And they did what he told them. When the *dardurr* were finished, having high floors of ant-bed and water-tight roofs of bark, Wirreenun commanded the whole camp to come with him to the waterhole; men, women, and children, all were to come. They all followed him down to the creek, to the waterhole where he had placed the *willgoo willgoo* and *gubberah*. Wirreenun jumped into the water and bade the tribe follow him, which they did. There in the water they all splashed and played about.

After a little time, Wirreenun went up first behind one black fellow and then behind another, until at length he had been round them all, and taken from the back of each one's head lumps of charcoal. When he went up to each he appeared to suck the back or top of their heads, and to draw out lumps of charcoal, which, as he sucked them out, he spat into the water. When he had gone the round of all, he went out of the water. But just as he got out, a young man caught him up in his arms and threw him back into the water.

This happened several times, until Wirreenun was shivering. That was the signal for all to leave the creek. Wirreenun sent all the young people into a big bough shed, and bade them all go to sleep. He and two old men and two old women stayed outside. They loaded themselves with all their belongings piled up on their backs, *dayoorl* (grinding) stones and all, as if ready for a flitting. These old people walked impatiently around the bough shed as if waiting a signal to start somewhere. Soon a big black cloud appeared on the horizon, first a single cloud, which, however, was soon followed by others rising all round. They rose quickly until they all met just overhead, forming a big black mass of clouds. As soon as this big, heavy, rain-laden looking cloud was stationary overhead, the old people went into the bough shed and bade the young people wake up and come out and look at the sky.

When they were all roused Wirreenun told them to lose no time, but to gather together all their possessions and hasten to gain the shelter of the bark *dardurr*. Scarcely were they all in the *dardurr*s and their spears well hidden when there sounded a terrific clap of thunder, which was quickly followed by a regular cannonade, lightning flashes shooting across the sky, followed by instantaneous claps of deafening thunder. A sudden flash of lightning, which lit a pathway from heaven to earth, was followed by such a terrific clash that the blacks thought their very camps were struck. But it was a tree a little distance off. The blacks huddled together in their *dardurr*s, frightened to move, the children crying with fear, and the dogs crouching towards their owners.

'We shall be killed,' shrieked the women. The men said nothing but looked as frightened.

Only Wirreenun was fearless. 'I will go out,' he said, 'and stop the storm from hurting us. The lightning shall come no nearer.'

So out in front of the *dardurr*s strode Wirreenun, and naked he stood there facing the storm, singing aloud, as the thunder roared and the lightning flashed, the chant which was to keep it away from the camp.

'*Gurreemooray, mooray, durreemooray, mooray, mooray,*' &c.

Soon came a lull in the cannonade, a slight breeze stirred the trees for a few moments, then an oppressive silence, and then the rain in real earnest began, and settled down to a steady downpour, which lasted for some days.

When the old people had been patrolling the bough shed as the clouds rose overhead, Wirreenun had gone to the waterhole and taken out the *willgoo willgoo* and the stones, for he saw by the cloud that their work was done.

When the rain was over and the country all green again, the blacks had a great corroboree and sang of the skill of Wirreenun, rainmaker to the Noongahburrah.

Wirreenun sat calm and heedless of their praise, as he had been of their murmurs. But he determined to show them that his powers were great, so he summoned the rainmaker of a neighbouring tribe, and after some consultation with him, he ordered the tribes to go to the Googoorewon, (a place of trees) which was then a dry plain with solemn, gaunt trees all round it, which had once been blackfellows.

When they were all camped round the edges of this plain, Wirreenun and his fellow rainmaker made a great rain to fall just over the plain and fill it with water.

When the plain was changed into a lake, Wirreenun said to the young men of his tribe: 'Now take your nets and fish.'

'What good?' said they. 'The lake is filled from the rain, not the flood water of rivers, filled but yesterday, how then shall there be fish?'

'Go,' said Wirreenun. 'Go as I bid you; fish. If your nets catch nothing then shall Wirreenun speak no more to the men of his tribe, he will seek only honey and yams with the women.'

More to please the man who had changed their country from a desert to a hunter's paradise, they did as he bade them, took their nets and went into the lake. And the first time they drew their nets, they were heavy with *goodoo*, *murree*, *tucki*, and *bunmillah*. And so many did they catch that all the tribes, and their dogs, had plenty.

Then the elders of the camp said now that there was plenty everywhere, they would have a *borah* that the boys should be made young men. On one of the ridges away from the camp, that the women should not know, they would prepare a ground.

And so was the big *borah* (ceremonial gathering) of the Googoorewon held, the *borah* which was famous as following on the triumph of Wirreenun the rainmaker.

Mau and Matang

Australia's northernmost extreme is the small island of Boigu, just six kilometres off the coast of Papua New Guinea. The six clans of the island began when a man named Kiba and his brothers settled there. Christian missionaries came to Boigu in 1871, an event commemorated today in the annual 'Coming of the Light' ceremony, which blends Boigu mythology with elements of Christian belief.

This important Boigu tale of impending doom, revenge and warrior honour highlights the importance of reciprocal relationships—even those of revenge and blood—and the high regard in which warrior skills were held by all the people of Torres Strait and beyond.

*L*ong ago there were two warrior brothers of Boigu, Mau and Matang. Mau was the elder brother. They fought for the love of fighting and very often for no reason.

One day they received a message from their friend Mau of Arudaru, which is on the Papuan mainland just across from Boigu. Mau bade them come quickly for yams and taro, which would otherwise be eaten by pigs.

Mau and Matang made ready to go to Arudaru.

Their sister wove the sails for their canoes. At mid-afternoon, just as she had completed them, she noticed a big stain of blood on one mat. She hurried to her brothers to tell them about it and so try to prevent them from setting out on their voyage.

Mau and Matang would not heed the warning sign, and they set off with their wives and children. They reached Daudai and spent the first night at Kudin. During the night Mau's canoe drifted away. The brothers sent the crew to search for it, and they came upon it at Zunal, the sandbank of *markai* (spirits of the dead).

As they drew close, they saw the ghost of Mau appear in front of the canoe. In its hand was a dugong spear decorated with cassowary feathers. The ghost went through the motions of spearing a dugong, then placed the spear in the canoe and vanished.

Next they saw Matang's ghost pick up the spear from the canoe, just as Mau's had done. It too made as if to spear a dugong. Then it replaced the spear in the canoe and faded from sight.

On reaching the canoe, the crew members found the spear in it.

On their return to Kudin they told Mau and Matang what had happened. The brothers refused also to heed this warning. They ordered the party to set out for Arudaru, which they reached after a day's walk.

The head man of Arudaru, whose name also was Mau, greeted them, with his own people and many others, gave them food, and said that he would give them the yams and taro the following day. With that, the Boigu people slept.

In the morning they woke to a deserted village. Only Mau of Arudaru remained. He gave them breakfast and then presented Mau and Matang with a small bunch of green bananas. It was a declaration of war.

Despite the friendship between Mau of Arudaru and the brothers Mau and Matang, the brothers had lightly killed kinsmen and friends of his, and his first duty as Mau of Arudaru was to avenge them. The invitation to come across for yams and taro had been part of a considered plan.

For days past, fighting men from the neighbouring villages had been gathering at Arudaru. There had been endless talking until the whole plan had ripened. With rage in their hearts, Mau and Matang herded their party together and set out on the return journey.

Mau of Arudaru had hidden his fighting men in two rows in the long grass so as to form two rows of unseen men. He allowed the brothers to lead their people back until they were halfway through the lines of fighting men. Then he gave the signal to attack.

The Boigu people were trapped. The women and children and the crew members fled. Mau bade his brother break the first spear thrown at him. He himself with his bow warded off the first spear that was hurled at him, splitting the end and throwing it backward between his legs, thus giving himself good luck in battle.

Matang warded off the first spear received by him, but did not break it as Mau had commanded.

Before long Matang was struck in the ankle by an arrow with a poisoned tip. 'I have been bitten by a snake,' he cried, and fell dead.

Mau continued to fight and kept backing towards his brother's body until he stood astride it. He fought until nearly all his assailants lay dead. The rest would have fled, but Mau signalled to them to put an end to him, so that he might join his brother. And this they did.

Mau and Matang did not have their heads cut off as would have been done were they ordinary men. Their courage and skill in battle were honoured by their opponents. They sat the brothers against two trees. They tied their bodies to the tree trunks, facing them south towards Boigu. On their heads they placed the warrior's headdress of black cassowary feathers and eagles' wings, so that when the wind blew from the south the eagles' wings were fanned backward and when it dropped, they fell forward.

Ungulla Robunbun

The anthropologist Baldwin Spencer (1860–1929) documented the complex oral traditions about ancestral beings and totemic relationships among the Kakadu people, publishing these in 1914 as *The Native Tribes of the Northern Territory of Australia*. The female entity in this story from Spencer's book creates birds, insects and human beings, giving male and female their physical characteristics. She is also the bringer of language. Pundamunga and Maramma, mentioned at the end of the story, are descended from the one great female ancestor of the Kakadu, Imberombera. Imberombera travelled all over the region, leaving her spirit children wherever she went and eventually sending them forth to take the different languages to the countries of Pundamunga and Maramma. Ungalla's naming of Pundamunga and Maramma's children confirms that this is the country of these two beings and their descendants. Once again, the story highlights the spiritual connections between country, ancestors, totems and language that are the basis of indigenous culture. Spencer recounts the following tale, including a reference to the tale being told to him.

A woman named Ungulla Robunbun came from a place called Palientoi, which lies between two rivers that are now known as the McKinlay and the Mary. She spoke the language of the Noenmil people and had many children. She started off to walk to Kraigpan, a place at the head of the Wildman Creek. Some of her children she carried on her shoulders, others on her hips, and one or two of them walked. At Kraigpan she left one boy and one girl and told them to speak the Quiratari (or Quiradari) language. Then she walked on to Koarnbo Creek, near the salt water at Murungaraiyu, where she left a boy and a girl and told them to speak Koarnbut. Travelling on to Kupalu, she left the Koarnbut language behind her and crossed over what is now called the East Alligator River, to its west side. She came on to Nimbaku and left a boy and a girl there and told them to speak the Wijirk language. From here she journeyed on across the plains stretching between the Alligator rivers to Koreingen, the place to which Imberombera had previously sent out two individuals named Pundamunga and Maramma. Ungulla Robunbun saw them and said to her children, 'There are blackfellows here; they are talking Kakadu; that is very good talk; this is Kakadu country that we are now in.'

Ungulla went on until she came near enough for them to hear her speaking. She said, 'I am Kakadu like you; I will belong to this country; you and I will talk the same language.' Ungulla then told them to come close up, which they did, and then she saw that the young woman was quite naked. Ungulla herself was completely clothed in sheets of *ranken*, or paper bark, and she took one off, folded it up, and showed the *lubra* how to make an apron such as the Kakadu women always wear now. She told the *lubra* that she did not wish to see her going about naked. Then they all sat down. Ungulla said, 'Are you a *lubra*?' and she replied, 'Yes, I am *ungordiwa*.' Then Ungulla said, 'I have seen Koreingen a long way off; I am going there. Where is your camp?' The Kakadu woman said, 'I shall go back to my camp if you go to Munganillida.' Ungulla then rose and walked on with her children. On the road some of them began to cry, and she said, '*Bialilla waji kobali*, many children are crying; *ameina waji kobali*, why are many children crying?' She was angry and killed two of them, a boy and a girl, and left them behind. Going on, she came near to Koreingung and saw a number of men and women in camp and made her own camp some little distance from theirs. She then walked on to Koreingung and said, 'Here is a blackfellows' camp; I will make mine here also.'

She set to work to make a shelter, saying '*Kunjerogabi ngoinbu kobonji*, I build a grass shelter; *mornia balgi*, there is a big mob of mosquitoes.' As yet the natives had not seen Ungulla or her children. There were plenty of fires in the natives' camps but no mosquitoes. They did not have any of these before Ungulla came, bringing them with her. She went into her shelter with her children and slept. After a time she came out again and then the other natives caught sight of her. Some of the younger Numulakirri determined to go to her camp. When she saw them coming she went into her *kobonji* and armed herself with a strong stick. She was Markogo, that is, elder sister, to the men, and, as they came up, she shouted out from her bush wurley, saying, 'What are you all coming for? You are my *illaberri* (younger brothers). I am *kumali* to you.'

They said nothing but came on with their hands behind their backs. As soon as they were close to the entrance to her shelter she suddenly jumped up, scattering the grass and boughs in all directions. She yelled loudly and, with her great stick, hit them all on their private parts. She was so powerful that she killed them all and their bodies tumbled into the waterhole close by. Then she went to the camp where the women and children had remained behind and drove them ahead of her into the water. The bones of all these natives are still there in the form of stones with which also their spirit parts are associated. When all was over the woman stood in her camp. First of all she pulled out her *kumara* (vagina) and threw it away, saying, 'This belongs to the *lubras*.' Then she threw her breasts away and a *wairbi*, or woman's fighting stick, saying that they all belonged to the *lubras*. From her dilly bag she took a *paliarti*, or flat spear-thrower, and a light reed spear, called *kunjolio*, and, throwing them away, shouted out, 'These are for the men.'

She then took a sharp-pointed blade of grass called *karani*, caught a mosquito (*mornia*) and fixed it on to his head (*reri*), so that it could 'bite' and said, 'Your name is *mornia*.' She also gave him instructions, saying, '*Yapo mapolio, jirongadda mitjerijoro*, go to the plains, close to the mangroves; *manungel jereini jauo*, eat men's blood; *kumanga kaio mornia*, (in) the bush no mosquitoes.' That is why mosquitoes are always so abundant amongst the mangroves. When she had done this Ungalla gathered her remaining children together and, with them, went into the waterhole.

There were a great many natives, and, after they were dead, their skins became transformed into different kinds of birds. Some of them changed into small owls, called *irre-idill*, which catch fish. When they hear the bird calling out at night they say 'dodo', which means wait, or, later on; 'tomorrow morning we will put a net in and catch some fish for you'. Others turned into *kurra-liji-liji*, a bird that keeps a look out to see if any strange natives are about. If a man wants to find out if any strangers are coming, he says to the bird, '*Umbordera jereini einji*? Are men coming to-day?' If they are, the bird answers, '*Pitjit, pitjit.*' Others changed into *jidikera-jidikera*, or willy wagtails, which keep a look out for buffaloes and crocodiles. Others, again, changed into dark-coloured kites, called *daigonora*, which keep a look out to see if any hostile natives are coming up to 'growl'. A man will say to one of these *daigonora*, if he sees it in a tree, *'Breikul jereini jeri?'* that is, 'Far away, are there men coming to growl?' If the bird replies to him he knows that they are coming, but if it makes no sound, then he knows there are no strangers about. Others changed into *moaka*, or crows, that show natives where geese are to be found; others into *tidji-tidji*, a little bird that shows them where the sugar-bags may be secured; others into *mundoro*, a bird that warns them when natives are coming up to steal a *lubra*. Some, again, changed into *murara*, the 'mopoke', which warns them if enemies are coming up in strong numbers. They ask the bird, and if it answers with a loud 'mopoke' they know that there are none about and that they have no need to be anxious, but if it answers with a low call, then they know that hostile natives are somewhere in the neighbourhood, and a man will remain on watch all night. Some of the women changed into laughing jackasses.

All these birds are supposed to understand what the blackfellows say, though they cannot themselves speak. While the men were explaining matters to us they spoke to two or three wagtails that came close up and twittered. The men said that the birds wanted to know what we were talking about, but they told them that they must go away and not listen, which they did.

Before finally going into the waterhole, Ungulla called out the names of the natives to whom she said the country belonged. They were all the children of Pundamunga and Maramma.

~

Ooldea Water

The colourful and enigmatic Daisy Bates (1863–1951) spent many years living with Aboriginal people in southwestern Australia. She claimed a special relationship with them that gave her unique access to indigenous traditions and insights into their significance. While these claims and many of her interpretations of the anthropological evidence she gathered have been strongly challenged, the stories she collected and preserved are of great value as records of traditions that have since fragmented or been completely lost.

In her book *The Passing of the Aborigines* Daisy Bates dramatically introduces the story of how the small marsupial Karrbiji brought water to Ooldea, in South Australia. The explorer Earnest Giles in 1875 was one of the first Europeans to discover this permanent water source, over 800 kilometres west of Port Augusta, on the eastern edge of the Nullarbor Plain. Bates lived at Ooldea from 1919 to 1934 and gave this description of the place:

> Nothing more than one of the many depressions in the never-ending sandhills that run waveringly from the Bight for nearly a thousand miles, Ooldea Water is one of Nature's miracles in barren Central Australia. No white man coming to this place would ever guess that that dreary hollow with the sand blowing across it was an unfailing fountain, yet a mere scratch and the magic waters welled in sight. Even in the cruellest droughts, it had never failed. Here the tribes gathered in their hundreds for initiation and other ceremonies.

In 1917 the Transcontinental Railway opened and the small settlement became a watering point for the railway line. By 1926 the water had been drained off in a process well described by Bates:

> In the building of the transcontinental line, the water of Ooldea passed out of its own people's hands forever. Pipelines and pumping plants reduced it at the rate of 10,000 gallons a day for locomotives. The natives were forbidden the soak, and permitted to obtain their water only from taps at the siding. In a few years the engineering plant apparently perforated the blue clay bed,

twenty feet below surface. Ooldea, already an orphan water, was a thing of the past.

Despite these events, Ooldea retained its special significance for local Aborigines, though access to the area was restricted during the 1950s in response to the atomic testing at Maralinga. By 1988, Ooldea was again Aboriginal land thanks to the *Maralinga Tjarutja Land Rights Act*.

This is the legend of Ooldea Water.

A long, long time ago in *dhoogoor* times, Karrbiji, a little marsupial, came from the west carrying a skin bag of water on his back, and as he travelled east and east there was no water anywhere, and Karrbiji said, 'I will put water in the ground so that the men can have good water always.'

He came to a shallow place like a dried lake. He went into the middle of it, and was just going to empty his water bag when he heard someone whistling. Presently he saw Ngabbula, the spike-backed lizard, coming threateningly towards him, whistling.

As he watched Ngabbula coming along, Karrbiji was very frightened, and he said, 'I can only leave a little water here. I shall call this place Yooldil-Beena—the swamp where I stood to pour out the water,' and he tried to hide the water from Ngabbula by covering it with sand, but Ngabbula came along quickly and Karrbiji took up his skin bag and ran and ran because Ngabbula would take all his water from him.

By and by he had run quite away from Ngabbula, and soon he came to a deep sandy hollow among high hills, and he said, 'This is a good place, I can hide all the water here, and Ngabbula won't be able to find it. He can't smell water.'

Karrbiji went down into the hollow and emptied all the water out of his bag into the sand. He covered up the water so that it could not be seen, and he said, 'This is Yooldil Gabbi, and I shall sit beside this water and watch my friends finding it and drinking it.' Karrbiji was feeling very glad that he had put the water in such a safe place.

All at once, he again heard loud whistling and he looked and saw Ngabbula coming along towards him. Karrbiji was very frightened of Ngabbula, and he quickly picked up his empty skin bag and ran away; but fast as he ran, Ngabbula ran faster.

Now, Giniga, the native cat, and Kallaia, the emu, were great friends of Karrbiji, and they had watched him putting the water under the sand where they could easily scratch for it and drink cool nice water always, and they said, 'We must not let Ngabbula kill our friend', and when Ngabbula chased Karrbiji, Kallaia and Giniga chased Ngabbula, and Ngabbula threw his spears at Giniga and made white spots all over Giniga where the spears had hit him. Giniga hit Ngabbula on the head with his club, and now all *ngabbulas'* heads are flat, because of the great hit that Giniga had given Ngabbula.

Then they ran on again and Ngabbula began to get frightened and he stopped chasing Karrbiji, but Kallaia and Giniga said, 'We must kill Ngabbula, and so stop him from killing Karrbiji,' and a long, long way north they came up to Ngabbula, and Kallaia, the emu, speared him, and he died.

Then they went to Karrbiji's place, and Kallaia, Giniga and Karrbiji made a corroboree, and Beera, the moon, played with them, and by and by he took them up into the sky where they are now *kattang-ga* ('heads', stars).

Karrbiji sat down beside his northern water. When men came to drink of his water, Karrbiji made them his friends, and they said, 'Karrbiji is our Dreamtime totem,' and all the men who lived beside that water were Karrbiji totem men. They made a stone emblem of Karrbiji and they put it in hiding near the water, and no woman has ever walked near the place where the stone emblem sits down.

Kallaia, the emu, 'sat down' beside Yooldil Water, and when the first men came there they saw Kallaia scraping the sand for the water, and they said 'Kallaia shall be our totem. This is his water, but he has shown us how to get it.' Giniga, the native cat, went between the two great waters, Karrbiji's Water and Kallaia's Water, and was always the friend of both. Ngabbula was killed north of Yooldil Gabbi, but he also had his water, and men came there and made him their totem, but Kallaia totem men always fought with Ngabbula totem men and killed them and ate them.

Karrbiji, after his work was done, went north, and 'sat down' among the Mardudharra Wong-ga (*wonga-ga*-speech, talk), not far from the Arrunda, beside his friends Giniga, the native cat, and Kallaia, the emu. And he made plenty of water come to the Mardudharra men, and by and by the men said, 'Karrbiji has brought his good water to us all. We will be brothers of Karrbiji.'

The woolgrum

This story is from the Weelman people of Australia's far southwest, now known broadly as Nyungar. It was told to Ethel Hassell, the wife of an early settler in the area during the 1870s. The woolgrum is half woman, half frog. This story, in one variation or another, was widely told. The possibility of winning a non-human wife is widespread in global tale tradition.

Far, far away in the west toward the setting sun there are three big rivers. The waters are fresh and flow down to the sea. Long, long ago, a *jannock* (spirit) lived between these rivers who had neither companions nor wives. He was very lonesome in this region but had to remain there for a certain time. To help overcome his loneliness he tamed all the animals in the region and they became fast friends with him. In the evening they used to sit around his fire. The *chudic* (wildcat) sat with the *coomal* (opossum), they told him stories of what was going on in the forest and on the plains.

In times of flood the rivers used to expand over a great expanse of territory, making many marshes, and, since the water was fresh, these became the breeding grounds for all kinds of *gilgie* (crayfish), fish and frogs [and] the *jannock* became friends with them too. There was one kind of frog, however, that he had difficulty in taming. This was *plomp*, the bullfrog. He coaxed the *plomp* to visit him and finally was able to persuade them to sleep under his cloak with him. He also tamed the *youan*, or bobtailed iguana. The *youan* made love to the *plomp* and this became very annoying to the *jannock*. He told the *plomp* that the *youan* made friends only that they might eat the young *plomp*. The *plomp* were grateful to him for this warning and showed their appreciation by surrounding his hut every night and singing him to sleep.

This kept up for some time, but finally it was time for the *jannock* to return to the other *jannock*. Just before he left, he breathed on the frogs and told them that in time they would be like himself.

The *jannock* had no business to say this, however, for he had not the power to cause them to change into beings like himself. The result was that every now and again the *plomp* brought forth a creature which is called a *woolgrum*. It is always half woman and half frog and never like a man. The *woolgrum*, being of *jannock* blood, were able also to make themselves invisible.

Now, when a man is an outcast from his tribe, no woman will live with him, even though the ostracism is not due to any fault of his own. As a last recourse to find a wife, he must travel towards the setting sun until he comes to the three great rivers which roll widely down to the sea through the broad marshes and between banks covered with thick-growing scrub. When he reaches this land he will hear the frogs croaking and on still nights he will hear the *woolgrum* calling. He will not be able to see them, however, because of their *jannock* blood, except on starlight nights in the winter when there is no moon. At that time the *woolgrum* come on shore and build a hut and a fire to warm themselves. On those occasions, men can sometimes see the figures of women camped by the fire. If they go too near to the fire or make a rush and try to grab the women, however, they find nothing but bushes, and the *woolgrum* disappear, never again to return to that camp. They make camp in another region where they may be seen again under the same conditions, but it is impossible to catch them in such a bold manner.

The only way by which a man can get a *woolgrum* for a wife is by following these directions. He must camp alone near the big marshy flats and live only on fish and *gilgie*. He must not tell anyone where he has gone or for what purpose. He must camp there until the marshes begin to dry up, at which time he must search for the *youan* and catch a female in the act of giving birth to her young. Just as the sun sets, but before it is dark, he must throw the newly born *youan* on the fire and watch until it bursts. As it burst, he must turn to the river marshes, and then he will see the *woolgrum*. As soon as he sees them he must seize the remains of the infant *youan*, throw it at the *woolgrum*, and run as fast as he can to the river.

If a portion of the *youan* touches a *woolgrum*, the lower or frog part disappears and a naked woman stands in the marsh. If he acts quickly he can catch her for his wife, but if he does not move hastily she will sink into the water and float down toward the sea. If this happens, there is nothing he can do to save her. He must commence his operations all over again in another region, for the *woolgrum* will never return to that part of the river. He will also have to wait until the next winter, when the *woolgrum* come to camp on the shore again.

However, should he be successful in catching the woman, he must take her to his camp and roll her up in his cloak and keep her warm by the fire all that night. The next day he can take her as his wife but must hurry away from the locality and remain constantly by her side until the moon is again in the same quarter. By that time she will have lost her power to make herself invisible and, once this is gone, she will never leave him no matter what his faults may be. She will bear him many children and they will be stronger and much more clever than any of the men or women of his tribe. They soon become bad men and women, however, and can never have any children, though the men take many wives and the women many husbands. Thus a man who gets a *woolgrum* for a wife knows that, although he may have many children, he will never have any grandchildren and his race will disappear completely. No *jannock* can harm his children because of their *jannock* blood, and they are always able to tell when the *jannock* are about.

The *woolgrum* herself is very beautiful, but her children are decidedly ugly, with big heads and wide mouths. They are capable of travelling very quickly, however, especially in the river beds and over marshy land, and they have a most highly developed sense of hearing. No native woman likes to think that her son would like to seek a *woolgrum* for a wife, for this is done only as a last recourse. No man likes to be told that his mother was a *woolgrum*, for that reflects on his father's character and implies that he will never have any children to fight for him in his old age.

The *woolgrum* are said not to belong to either moiety; hence, whether a man is a Nunnich or a Wording, he can take as a wife any *woolgrum* he can catch without questioning her relationship.

LOST IN THE BUSH.—[Drawn by Chevalier.]

2

Pioneer traditions

WHITE WOMAN! — There are fourteen armed men,
partly White and partly Black, in search of you . . .

Message to the 'captured white woman of Gippsland', 1846

THE EUROPEAN OCCUPATION of Australia brought mainly British settlers into a world for which they were totally unprepared. The trees and plants, animals, land forms and climate were difficult for them to comprehend, as were the original inhabitants. As settlement pushed into the interior from various parts of the continent's coastline, the frontier took on an increasingly colonial character that mingled the imported traditions of the newcomers with their sometimes dangerous and violent experiences in Australia. The consequences of the frontier's steady encroachment on indigenous lands were devastating for Aborigines and often confronting for settlers.

The uncertainties and fears of the colonists in this strange and harsh new land sometimes led to brutal acts and dark obsessions, even delusions. In many areas, people seized on stories that reflected common nightmares: the woman carried off by 'savages'; the children lost in the bush. And harking back to the fables, there were even stranger stories of Europeans stumbling onto Australian shores long before the arrival of the First Fleet.

The lost colony

The land we now call Australia was known from earliest times as 'the great south land' or 'the unknown southland'. It was the subject of wild speculations, rumours and fantasies about the people who might live in it, the beasts that might prowl across it and the wondrous riches that it might hold. Even before the official first settlement at Botany Bay in 1788, it is said, there was a mysterious Dutch colony deep in the Outback.

The tradition of lost or wandering peoples goes back to at least the Old Testament era with its stories of the lost tribes of Israel. Such tales are often linked with legends of lost or hidden riches or of utopias to be found in undiscovered or little-explored continents. A well-known late mediaeval example is the legend of Prester John, which involved a kingdom of lost Christians somewhere in the Muslim East. Rider Haggard made use of the it in his novel *King Solomon's Mines*, which popularised the idea of a lost white tribe of Africa for nineteenth-century British readers. There are also white Eskimo legends swirling around the tragic story of the ill-fated quest of Lord Franklin, one-time lieutenant-governor of Van Diemen's Land (Tasmania), for a northwest passage through Canada.

Australia also has traditions of secret or unrecorded colonies in the wilderness. For example, there is a well-documented story of a lost colony descended from Dutch mariners, shipwrecked generations before 1788. On 25 January 1834, an article appeared in the English *Leeds Mercury* newspaper under the headline, DISCOVERY OF A WHITE COLONY ON THE NORTHERN SHORE OF NEW HOLLAND. When it was reprinted in Australian papers, the unsigned item caused amazement and consternation.

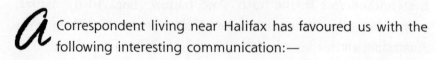 Correspondent living near Halifax has favoured us with the following interesting communication:—

TO THE EDITORS OF THE LEEDS MERCURY.

GENTLEMEN,—A friend of mine lately arrived from Singapore, via India overland, having been one of a party who landed at Raffles Bay, on the north coast of New Holland, on the 10th of April, 1832, and made a two months' excursion into the interior, has permitted me to copy the following extract out of his private journal, which I think contains some particulars of a highly interesting nature, and not generally known.

The exploring party was promoted by a scientific Society at Singapore, aided and patronized by the Local Government, and its object was both commercial and geographical; but it was got up with the greatest secrecy, and remained secret to all except the parties concerned. (For what good purpose it is impossible to conceive.)

Extract from an unpublished manuscript journal of an exploring party in Northern Australia, by Lieutenant Nixon:

*M*ay 15th, 1832—On reaching the summit of the hill, no words can express the astonishment, delight, and wonder I felt at the magical change of scenery, after having travelled for so many days over nothing but barren hills and rocks, and sands and parching plains, without seeing a single tribe of aborigines excepting those on the sea coast, and having to dig for water every day.

Looking to the southwards, I saw below me, at the distance of about three or four miles, a low and level country, laid out as it were in plantations, with straight rows of trees, through which a broad sheet of smooth water extended in nearly a direct line from east to west, as far as the eye could reach to the westward, but apparently sweeping to the southward at its eastern extremity like a river; and near its banks, at one particular spot on the south side, there appeared to be a group of habitations, embosomed in a grove of tall trees like palms. The water I guessed to be about half a mile wide, and although the stream was clearly open for two thirds of the distance from the southern bank, the remainder of it was studded by thousands of little islands stretching along its northern shores: and what fixed me to the spot with indescribable sensations of rapture and admiration was the number of small boats or canoes with one or two persons in each, gliding along the narrow channels between the little islands in every direction, some of which appeared to be fishing or drawing nets. None of them had a sail, but one that was floating down the body of the stream without wind, which seemed to denote that a current ran from east to west. It seemed as if enchantment had brought me into a civilized country, and I could scarcely resolve to leave the spot I stood upon, had it not been for the overpowering rays of a mid day sun, affecting my bowels, as it frequently had done, during all the journey.

On reaching the bottom of the hill in my return to our party at the tents, I was just turning round a low rock, when I came suddenly upon a human being whose face was so fair and dress so white, that I was for a moment staggered with terror, and thought that I was looking upon an apparition. I had naturally expected to meet an Indian as black or brown as the rest of the natives, and not a white man in these unexplored regions. Still quaking with doubts about the integrity of my eyes, I proceeded on, and saw the apparition advancing upon me with the most perfect indifference: in another minute he was quite near, and I now perceived that he had not yet seen me, for he was walking slowly and pensively with his eyes fixed on the ground, and he appeared to be a young man of a handsome and interesting countenance. We were got within four paces of each other when he heaved a deep and tremulous sigh, raised his eyes, and in an instant uttered a loud exclamation and fell insensible on the ground. My fears had now given place to sympathy, and I hastened to assist the unknown, who, I felt convinced, had been struck with the idea of seeing a supernatural being. It was a considerable time before he recovered and was assured of my mortality; and from a few expressions in old Dutch, which he uttered, I was luckily enabled to hold some conversation with him; for I had been at school in Holland in my youth and not quite forgotten the language. Badly as he spoke Dutch, yet I gathered from him a few particulars of a most extraordinary nature; namely, that he belonged to a small community, all as white as himself, he said about three hundred; that they lived in houses enclosed all together within a great wall to defend them from black men; that their fathers came there about one hundred and seventy years ago, as they said, from a distant land across the great sea; and that their ship broke, and eighty men and ten of their sisters (female passengers?) with many things were saved on shore. I prevailed on him to accompany me to my party, who I knew would be glad to be introduced to his friends before we set out on our return to our ship at Port Raffles, from which place we were now distant nearly five hundred miles, and our time was limited to a fixed period so as to enable the ship to carry us back to Singapore before the change of the monsoon. The young man's dress consisted of a round jacket and large breeches, both made of skins, divested of the hair and bleached as white as linen; and on his head he wore a tall white skin cap with a brim covered over with white down or the small feathers of the white cocatoo [sic]. The latitude of this mountain was eighteen degrees thirty minutes fourteen seconds south; and longitude one hundred and thirty-two degrees twenty-five minutes thirty seconds east. It was christened Mount Singapore, after the name and in honour of the settlement to which the expedition belonged.

A subsequent part of the journal states further, 'that on our party visiting the white village, the joy of the simple inhabitants was quite extravagant. The descendant of an officer is looked up to as chief, and with him (whose name is Van Baerle), the party remained eight days. Their traditional history is, that their fathers were compelled by famine, after the loss of their great vessel, to travel towards the rising sun, carrying with them as much of the stores as they could, during which many died; and by the wise advice of their ten sisters they crossed a ridge of land, and meeting with a rivulet on the other side, followed its course and were led to the spot they now inhabit, where they have continued ever since. They have no animals of the domestic kind, either cows, sheep, pigs or any thing else; their plantations consist only of maize and yams, and these with fresh and dried fish constitute their principal food, which is changed occasionally for Kangaroo and other game; but it appears that they frequently experience a scarcity and shortness of provisions, most probably owing to ignorance and mismanagement; and had little or nothing to offer us now except skins. They are nominal Christians: their marriages are performed without any ceremony: all the elders sit in council to manage their affairs; all the young, from ten up to a certain age, are considered a standing militia, and are armed with long pikes; they have no books or paper, nor any schools; they retain a certain observance of the Sabbath by refraining from their daily labours, and perform a short superstitious ceremony on that day all together; and they may be considered almost a new race of beings.'

While the story seems to have passed out of the colonial newspapers, it never quite faded away in folk tradition. Recent researchers have been unable to identify a likely Lieutenant Nixon, nor have any other verifiable facts about the claimed expedition or lost colony been found. The man who sent the report to the *Leeds Mercury* was Thomas J. Maslen, an Australia enthusiast who, like many others at that time, had never actually visited the place. This did not stop him publishing a book on the subject, titled *The Friend of Australia*, in 1827. The book included a map that, in accord with one of the persistent nineteenth-century delusions about Australia, showed an inland sea at the continent's centre. Much of the book, like the story of the lost colony, must be considered another one of the fables about the great south land.

The battle that was a massacre

Australia's colonial history produced many stories of violence between indigenous people and settlers. Controversial and elusive though the details may be, it is undeniable that there were numerous confrontations, sometimes followed by massacres. Such events are known, or believed, to have taken place at Myall Creek, New South Wales, in 1838, at Mundrabilla Run, on the Nullarbor Plain, in the 1870s, and in dozens of other places on the edge of the frontier. As late as 1928, a massacre of Walpiri people took place at Coniston, 300 kilometres northwest of Alice Springs. Many of these events are remembered in stories told among both black and white people. Not surprisingly, these accounts often reflect very different points of view. On the settler side, they emphasise the fear that pervaded isolated outposts, and just retribution for Aboriginal misdeeds. On the indigenous side they reflect anger over settlers' violence and their invasion of traditional lands.

Events on the Murray River, Western Australia, in late 1834 remain the subject of intense local controversy: direct descendants of participants in the battle—or massacre—still live near the town of Pinjarra, where it took place. One of the earliest sources for what happened that day is the diary of a local settler, George Fletcher Moore, writing just a few days after the chilling events he describes.

*T*HURSDAY—A strange rumour has reached us here that the party who went to the Murray River have fallen in with the natives there, and killed 35 of them. Captain Ellis being slightly wounded, and another soldier grazed by a spear. This is important if true . . .

Saturday, Nov. 1—Went to Perth yesterday, and got from the Governor an account of the battle of Pinjarra. They came upon the offending tribe in a position which I dare say the natives thought was most favourable for their manoeuvres, but which turned into a complete trap for them. In the first onset, three out of five of the small party which went to reconnoitre were unhorsed, two being wounded. The Governor himself came up with a reinforcement just in time to prevent the natives rushing in upon and slaughtering that party. The natives then fled to cross a ford, but were met and driven back by a party which had been detached for the purpose. They tried to cross at another ford, but were met there also, when they took to the river, lying hid under the overhanging banks, and seeking opportunities of casting their spears, but they were soon placed between two fires and punished severely. The women and children were protected, and it is consolatory to know that none suffered but the daring fighting men of the very tribe that had been most hostile. The destruction of European lives and property committed by that tribe was such that they considered themselves quite our masters, and had become so emboldened that either that part of the settlement must have been abandoned or a severe example made of them. It was a painful but urgent necessity, and likely to be the most humane policy [in] the end. The Governor narrowly escaped a spear. Captain Ellis was struck in the temple and unhorsed. Being stunned by the blow he fell.

Tuesday night—Poor Captain Ellis has died in consequence of the injury he received at the time of the conflict with the natives; but it is supposed that it was from the concussion of the brain by the fall from his horse, rather than by the wound from the spear (which was very trifling), that he died. The natives here are uneasy, thinking that we mean to take more lives in revenge.

Appended is a more detailed report of the encounter with the natives in the Pinjarra District, to which I briefly referred the other day. I was not one of that party.

The party consisted of His Excellency Sir Jas. Stirling, Mr. Roe, Cap. Meares and his son (Seymour), Mr Peel, Capt. Ellis, Mr Norcott with five of his mounted police (one sick), Mr Surveyor Smythe, a soldier to lead a pack horse, Mr Peel's servant, two corporals and eight privates of H.M.'s 21st Regiment (to leave at Pinjarra)—in all, 25 persons. On the night of October 27, the party bivouacked at a place called by the natives 'Jimjam', about ten or eleven miles in the direct line E.N.E. from the mouth of the Murray, where is abundance of most luxurious feed for cattle, at a broad and deep reach of the river flowing to the N.W., and at this time perfectly fresh. After an early breakfast, the whole encampment was in motion at ten minutes before six the next morning. Steered South Eastward for Pinjarra—another place of resort for the natives of the district, and situated a little below the first ford across the river, where it was intended to establish a town on a site reserved for the purpose, and to leave half of the party including the military, for the protection of Mr Peel and such other settlers as that gentleman might induce to resort thither.

Crossing the ford, where the river had an average depth of 2½ feet, and was running about 1½ miles an hour to the north, an Easterly course was taken for the purpose of looking at the adjoining country, but the party had not proceeded more than a quarter of a mile over the undulating surface of the richest description, covered with nutritious food for cattle, when the voices of many natives were heard on the left. This being a neighbourhood much frequented by the native tribe of Kalyute, which had long been indulging in almost unchecked commission of numerous outrages and atrocious murders on the white people resident in the district, and which had hitherto succeeded in eluding the pursuit of the parties that had been searching for them since their treacherous murder of Private Nesbitt of the 21st Regiment, and the spearing of Mr Barron only a few weeks ago—the moment was considered propitiously favourable for punishing the perpetrators of such and other diabolical acts of a similar nature, should this prove to be the offending tribe. For the purposes of ascertaining that point, His Excellency rode forward 200 or 300 yards with Messrs. Peel and Norcott, who were acquainted both with the persons of the natives and their language, and commenced calling out and talking to them for the purpose of bringing on an interview. Their own noise was, however, so loud and clamorous, that all other sounds appeared lost on them, or as mere echoes.

No answer being returned, Captain Ellis, in charge of the mounted police, with Mr. Norcott, his assistant, and the remaining available men of his party, amounting to three in number, were dispatched across the ford again to the left bank, where the natives were posted, to bring on the interview required. The instant the police were observed approaching at about 200 yards distance, the natives, to the number of about 70, started on their feet, the men seized their numerous and recently made spears, and showed a formidable front, but, finding their visitors still approached, they seemed unable to stand a charge, and sullenly retreated, gradually quickening their pace until the word 'forward' from the leader of the gallant little party brought the horsemen in about half a minute dashing into the midst of them, the same moment having discovered the well-known features of some of the most atrocious offenders of the obnoxious tribe. One of these, celebrated for his audacity and outrage, was the first to be recognized at the distance of five or six yards from Mr. Norcott, who knew him well and immediately called out, 'These are the fellows we want, for here's the old rascal Noonar,' on which the savage turned round and cried with peculiar ferocity and emphasis, 'Yes, Noonar me,' and was in the act of hurling his spear at Norcott, in token of requital for the recognition, when the latter shot him dead.

The identity of the tribe being now clearly established, and the natives turning to assail their pursuers, the firing continued, and was returned by the former with spears as they retreated to the river. The first shot, and the loud shouts and yells of the natives, were sufficient signal to the party who had halted a quarter of a mile above, who immediately followed Sir James Stirling, at full speed and arrived opposite Captain Ellis' party just as some of the natives had crossed and others were in the river. It was just the critical moment for them. Five or six rushed up the right bank, but were utterly confounded at meeting a second party of assailants, who immediately drove back those who escaped the firing. Being thus exposed to a cross fire, and having no time to rally their forces, they adopted the alternative of taking to the river and secreting themselves amongst the roots and branches and holes on the banks, or by immersing themselves with the face only uncovered and ready with a spear under water, to take advantage of any one who appeared within reach. Those who were sufficiently hardy or desperate to expose themselves on the offensive, or to attempt breaking through the assailants, were soon cleared off, and the remainder were gradually picked out of the concealments by the cross fire from both banks, until between 25 and 30 were left dead on the field and in the river. The others had either escaped up and down the river, or had secreted themselves too closely to be discovered except in the persons of eight women and some children, who emerged from their hiding places (where, in fact, the creatures were not concealed), on being assured of their personal safety, and were detained prisoners until the determination of the fray. It is, however, very probable that more men were killed in the river, and floated down with the stream.

Notwithstanding the care which was taken not to injure the women during the skirmish, it cannot appear surprising that one and several children were killed, and one woman amongst the prisoners had received a ball through the thigh. On finding the women were spared, and understanding the orders repeatedly issued to that effect, many of the men cried out they were of their sex; but evidence to the contrary was too strong to admit the plea. As it appeared by this time that sufficient punishment had been inflicted on this warlike and sanguinary tribe by the destruction of about half its population, and amongst whom were recognised, on personal examination, fifteen very old and desperate offenders, the bugle sounded to cease firing, and the divided party reassembled at the ford, where the baggage had been left in charge of four soldiers, who were also to maintain the post. Here Captain Ellis had arrived, badly wounded in the right temple, by a spear at three or four yards distance, which knocked him off his horse, and P. Heffron, a constable of the police, had received a bad spear wound above the right elbow. No surgical aid being at hand, it was not without some little difficulty the spear was extracted, and it then proved to be barbed at the distance of five inches from the point.

Having recrossed the river in good order with the baggage on three horses the whole party formed a junction on the left bank, fully expecting the natives would return in stronger force, but in this were disappointed. After a consultation over the prisoners, it was resolved to set them free, for the purpose of fully explaining to the remnant of the tribe the cause of the chastisement which had been inflicted, and to bear a message to the effect that, if they again offered to spear white men or their cattle, or to revenge in any way the punishment which had just been inflicted on these for their numerous murders and outrages, four times the present number of men would proceed amongst them and destroy every man, woman and child. This was perfectly understood by the captives, and they were glad to depart even under such an assurance; nor did several of their number, who were the widows, mothers and daughters of notorious offenders shot that day, evince any stronger feeling on the occasion than what arose out of their anxiety to keep themselves warm.

Nyungar tradition tells a substantially similar tale as far as the details of the encounter are concerned, though the numbers killed are often said to have been much larger. Descendants of the Pinjarra settlers continue to believe that Stirling and his men were reacting to the justifiable fears of their ancestors about the threat of a concerted Aboriginal attack. In settler tradition it was a battle. In Nyungar belief, what happened in 1834 was a massacre. The discrepancy between these views is poignantly reflected in a memorial of the incident in the park just south of Pinjarra township. Never completed, it is the victim of warring stories about the past.

The White Woman of Gippsland

The White Woman of Gippsland legend was widely circulated in Australia and beyond during the nineteenth century. It is part of a class of stories in which settlers are captured by the people they are displacing. Frequently the captives are women. While there were certainly well-authenticated instances of European women living with indigenous groups in America and Australia, many other such stories are folklore rather than fact. And like much folklore, they reveal deep truths about fear and prejudice.

The first mention of the white woman was in a letter published in the *Sydney Herald* in October 1840. A Scots settler in Gippsland named Augustus McMillan claimed that he and a small group of colonists had frightened a band of twenty-five Kurnai people, mostly women, into the bush. The settlers found European clothes, weapons, medicines and a range of other goods in their hastily abandoned camp, even newspapers, dated 1837. They also discovered, in a kangaroo-skin bag, the corpse of a two-year-old boy who was later identified as European.

While the pioneers of this only recently settled region were rummaging through this cache, they noticed that one of the women being herded to safety by the Kurnai men seemed unusually curious about them and what they were doing. Putting together their puzzling find and her interest, McMillan and his companions came to the conclusion 'that the unfortunate female is a European—a captive of these ruthless savages'. They thought the woman, perhaps with a small child, might be a survivor, probably the only one, of a 'dreadful massacre' of settlers. Two years later there surfaced in the newspapers another—anonymous—account of a sighting of

Aborigines driving a white person, probably female, before them as they fled from a surveying party. The surveyors found a pile of European objects in the abandoned camp, as well as a giant heart shape drawn in the ground with a sharp object. The letter claimed that other settlers had also seen Aboriginal groups with white captives.

By 1845, these rumours had developed into a storyline in which the white captive was always female. Sightings were reported frequently throughout Gippsland and beyond. In every case, the white woman was supposedly being herded away from the Europeans but looking desperately to them for rescue. By the following year, claimed sightings were so common that people began demanding government intervention. A settler with the pen-name Humanitas wrote a windy letter to the editor of the *Port Phillip Herald* on 10 March 1846, concerning the alleged fate of a missing white woman known as Miss Lord.

> Sir: About twelve months ago, I addressed a letter to one of the newspapers shewing that this lady was a captive of a tribe of blacks in the Portland Bay district, and although that letter was calculated to call forth all the sympathies and at the same time the energies of man on her behalf, yet what has been done?

The letter berated Governor La Trobe for his failure to act and pointed out that a £1000 reward had been offered by the public. Nonetheless, 'The blood of every true Briton boils with indignation at witnessing the utter indifference, the utter barbarity in respect of this lady...'

Although the government had been making inquiries into the stories, it took no further official action. Instead, in October that year a private expedition was mounted under the command of Christian De Villiers and James Warman. They carried white handkerchiefs printed with a message of rescue:

WHITE WOMAN! — There are fourteen armed men, partly White and partly Black, in search of you. Be cautious and rush to them when you see them near you. Be particularly on the lookout every dawn of morning, for it is then the party are in hopes of rescuing you. The white settlement is towards the setting sun.

The message was printed in both English and Scots Gaelic, as many of the early Scots settlers spoke only that tongue.

Although the expedition failed to locate the lost woman, it did add a new slant to the story. Dispatches published in the *Port Phillip Herald* suggested that the white woman was a shipwreck survivor, a theory bolstered by the discovery that the Aborigines possessed a wooden ship's figurehead around which they reportedly performed corroborees.

Finally the government mounted its own rescue expedition, led by the head of the Port Phillip Native Police, Henry Dana. There were now two expeditions roaming the same area in search of the elusive white woman. Both focused on capturing a Kurnai chieftain named Bunjaleene, suspected of being the woman's abductor. But after Dana's party murdered a large number of Kurnai people in the Gippsland lakes district, it was recalled. The De Villiers/Warman party's supplies were withheld, forcing it too to return.

Rumour and speculation continued to run wild, however, and the government felt it wise to dispatch another expedition in March 1847. It captured Bunjaleene and held members of his family hostage while he led the would-be rescuers to the Snowy Mountains, where most of the Kurnai had retreated. It was now thought that Bunjaleene's brother was holding the white woman. Winter forced the abandonment of the search, and Bunjaleene and his family were (illegally) detained pending the white woman's return. Mumbalk, one of Bunjaleene's two wives, died in captivity, and the old chieftain, having been told that he and his people would be shot and hanged, died the following year.

Late in 1847, the bodies of a European woman and a part-Aboriginal child were discovered at Jemmy's Point. It was widely speculated that Bunjaleene's brother had murdered them, and the local newspaper concluded that the remains were indeed those of the lost white woman and her child. The sightings, then, had been real, or so the paper declared:

> Death though regarded as a mishap by others, must have descended as a blessing upon this poor woman, who has undergone a trial far more harrowing and terrible than even Death's worst moments.
>
> She is now no more—and it is a melancholy gratification that the public suspense has been at length relieved, by her discovery even in death.

While this should have marked the demise of the White Woman legend, some people still persisted in the belief that at least one white woman was in the hands of the Kurnai. The story, reinforced by persistent Kurnai traditions of the massacres and related injustices that took place as a result of the search for the white woman, lived on, finding its way into artworks and even local histories.

Was there a White Woman of Gippsland? It is possible that there were several. Kurnai tradition holds that there were at least two European women living among them at this period, including one, known as Lohan-tuka, who had long red hair—a feature that appeared in several of the early settler accounts. A number of European women did live with indigenous people, often after surviving shipwrecks. Eliza Fraser, who spent several months with Aborigines on and near what is now Fraser Island in 1836, is the best known of these enforced cultural crossovers. True or not, these stories owed their longevity to their theme's strong hold on the popular imagination.

Raising the Southern Cross

The bloody events at the Eureka Stockade of 3 December 1854 involved men, women and children from many nations, including Italy, Germany, the United States, Canada and Britain. They came in search of wealth and a better life, but they found what some considered to be an inflexible and oppressive system of taxation without representation in the form of expensive gold digging licences sold by the government. Hundreds of these 'diggers', as they were known, initially took up arms against the Victorian authorities within a hastily erected wooden stockade near Ballarat. Subsequent events, involving around one hundred and twenty defenders of the ramshackle assemblage of wooden mine supports and carts, have created an enduring colonial narrative.

One of the miners involved in the Stockade was the colourful Italian who called himself Rafaello Carboni. Under that name he authored a compelling memoir of the revolt. *The Eureka Stockade* was published in 1855, shortly after Carboni and twelve of his Eureka comrades had been acquitted of treason. It provided a point of view, strongly biased towards the diggers, of the events leading up to the battle and of the fight itself. It included not only Carboni's recollections but those of other participants and observers. In this extract, Carboni describes the first raising of the Southern Cross flag among a crowd said to number twelve thousand. Peter Lalor (pronounced Lawler) was the leader of the Stockade miners. The scene is 'Lalor Stump' on Bakery Hill where the 'flag of stars' was first raised on 29 November 1854. Carboni begins with a short verse that echoes the tone of the revolt:

*B*rave LALOR—
Was found 'all there',
With dauntless dare,

His men inspiring;
To wolf or bear,
Defiance bidding,
He made us swear,
Be faithful to the Standard,
For Victory or Death!

On that Thursday, November 30th, more memorable than the disgraced Sunday, December 3rd, the SUN was on its way towards the west: in vain some scattered clouds would hamper its splendour—the god in the firmament generously ornamented them with golden fringes, and thus patches of blue sky far off were allowed to the sight, through the gilded openings among the clouds.

The 'SOUTHERN CROSS' was hoisted up the flagstaff—a very splendid pole, eighty feet in length, and straight as an arrow. This maiden appearance of our standard, in the midst of armed men, sturdy, self-overworking gold-diggers of all languages and colours, was a fascinating object to behold.

There is no flag in old Europe half so beautiful as the 'Southern Cross' of the Ballarat miners, first hoisted on the old spot, Bakery-hill. The flag is silk, blue ground, with a large silver cross, similar to the one in our southern firmament; no device or arms, but all exceedingly chaste and natural.

Captain Ross, of Toronto, was the bridegroom of our flag, and sword in hand, he had posted himself at the foot of the flag-staff, surrounded by his rifle division.

Peter Lalor, our Commander-in-chief, was on the stump, holding with his left hand the muzzle of his rifle, whose butt-end rested on his foot. A gesture of his right hand, signified what he meant when he said,

'It is my duty now to swear you in, and to take with you the oath to be faithful to the Southern Cross. Hear me with attention. The man who, after this solemn oath does not stand by our standard, is a coward in heart.

'I order all persons who do not intend to take the oath, to leave the meeting at once. "Let all divisions under arms 'fall in' in their order round the flag-staff."'

The movement was made accordingly. Some five hundred armed diggers advanced in real sober earnestness, the captains of each division making the military salute to Lalor, who now knelt down, the head uncovered, and with the right hand pointing to the standard exclaimed a firm measured tone:

'WE SWEAR BY THE SOUTHERN CROSS TO STAND TRULY BY EACH OTHER, AND FIGHT TO DEFEND OUR RIGHTS AND LIBERTIES.'

An [sic] universal well rounded AMEN, was the determined reply; some five hundred right hands stretched towards our flag. The earnestness of so many faces of all kinds of shape and colour; the motley heads of all sorts of size and hair; the shagginess of so many beards of all lengths and thicknesses; the vividness of double the number of eyes electrified by the magnetism of the southern cross; was one of those grand sights, such as are recorded only in the history of 'the Crusaders in Palestine'.

The famous battle of the Eureka Stockade took place a few days later as poorly armed miners were swiftly defeated by a combined force of the police and military on the morning of 3 December 1854. The aftermath of the encounter is described in Chapter 8.

Although the Eureka Stockade has been the subject of much literary and political romanticisation, curiously there is little general folklore about the event. There are traditions within the families of descendants of those who fought on either side of the brief but bloody encounter at Ballarat, but there are no stirring folk ballads of defiance and injustice, as there are about Ned Kelly and Ben Hall, for example. The goldfields minstrel, Charles Thatcher, wrote popular satires of the event and Henry Lawson and other poets later celebrated it, but these have only been collected in oral tradition, and only then on rare occasions. Few tales are publicly told about the event, apart from some fragmentary anecdotes about the sewing of the Southern Cross flag by goldfields women. Despite this, the Eureka Stockade, its emblem and the opposition to injustice and oppression that they signify are well and truly embedded in Australian mythology.

The lost children of the Wimmera

On the morning of 12 August 1864, seven-year-old Jane Duff and her brothers Frank and Isaac went searching for broom in the bush near their home at Spring Hill Station. Spring Hill was about fifty kilometres from Horsham, Victoria, in the maze of scrub known as the Wimmera. Jane and Frank were the children of Hannah Duff by her previous husband. Isaac was the child of Hannah and her second husband, John Duff, a shepherd. The family lived in a slab hut, and one of the children's chores was to collect twigs for their mother's brooms.

On this Friday, though, the children strayed too far into the bush. When they did not come home, Hannah went looking for them. She found no trace, nor could her husband when he joined the search. On Saturday morning, the Duffs contacted their neighbours and thirty men hunted all through that day and into the next two. At last, on Tuesday, the children's tracks were sighted. Searchers followed them until a storm washed away all traces on the Thursday night.

Now desperate, the searchers made a wise decision. They called on an Aboriginal elder named Wooral, also known as Dick-a-Dick, a noted tracker. (He was destined to be a member of the Aboriginal cricket side that toured England a few years later.) By the time Wooral and two other Aboriginal men arrived, the searchers had found the children's tracks again. The Aborigines were able to follow them much more quickly than the settlers, and soon detected signs that the children had become very weak.

Eventually, however, they were found—huddled together beneath a tree with Jane's dress covering them all for warmth. Fearing the worst, their father rushed to the children and was overjoyed to find them still alive, though only just. The children were returned home and nursed back to health, having miraculously survived eight winter nights in the open with few clothes and hardly any food. They had eaten a few quandong berries but feared that these might be poisonous. 'We used to suck the dew off the leaves at night to ease our thirst and dry throats,' Jane Duff recalled in later life.

The news of their rescue and Jane's heroism—she had helped carry the younger boy as well as sharing her clothing—spread fast through Victoria and beyond. Aside from its local significance, the story resonated with British tales of lost babes in the woods, which had been popular since at least the sixteenth century, and with European fairy tales like that of 'Hansel and Gretel'. General rejoicing over the children's survival combined with these echoes of history and legend to infuse the story with great emotional power. Large donations were made to assist the rescued children and reward the Aboriginal trackers. Jane became a celebrity, and a local squatter later paid for her education. At the age of nineteen she married and settled in Horsham, eventually having eleven children. She died in 1932, still a heroine. Showing how she is remembered in local tradition, the inscription on her gravestone reads:

In sacred memory
of
Jane Duff
Bush Heroine
who succoured her brothers
Isaac and Frank
nine days and eight nights
in Nurcoung Scrub in August 1864
died 20th Jan. 1932 aged 75 years

The story of the lost children became a staple in Victorian school readers and was continuously updated for new generations, still appearing in these books as late as the 1980s. The following version comes from a Victorian school reader from the 1960s. It uses some inaccurate terms—there were no Aboriginal 'monarchs' or 'subjects', for example—and some unrealistic quotations of Aboriginal English, as well as mixing up some minor details of the rescue. But it is a good example of how the story of the Duff children was reworked as a moral tale, at first emphasising Christian virtues and later highlighting self-sacrifice and strength of character. Through all these adaptations, Jane's heroism remained pivotal.

Three children—Isaac, nine years old; Jane, seven and a half; and Frank, a toddler, not four—helped their mother, and filled in the long day as best they could, playing about the hut, for there was no school for them to attend.

Well, one day, their mother called them, and said, 'Now, children, run away to the scrub, and get me some broom to sweep the floor and make it nice for father when he comes home.'

It was a fine day in August—spring was early that year—and the children, who had been to the scrub on the same errand before, liked going: so they set off merrily.

They had a fine time. Isaac amused himself by climbing trees, and cutting down saplings with his tomahawk; he found a possum in a hollow in the trunk of a tree, and poked at the little creature with a stick, but without doing it much harm. Jane chased butterflies, picked flowers, and tried to catch the lizards that Frank wanted so much. When they felt hungry, they all had, in addition to their lunch of bread and treacle, quite a feast of gum from a clump of wattle-trees.

In laughter and play the time passed pleasantly and quickly; and, when half a dozen kangaroos bounded away from them through the bush, their delight knew no bounds. But, by and by, Jane thought of going home; so they gathered each a bundle of broom for Mother, and turned, as they thought, homewards.

After they had walked some distance, Isaac began to think it was farther to the edge of the scrub than he had expected, so he urged his sister and little brother to go faster. In an hour or two the scrub grew thicker, and it looked strange to him. He thought that he might have taken a wrong turn, and started off in another direction, and then tried another, and another; but no remembered spot met his straining eyes.

Then deep dread seized them all. They stopped, and cooeed, and shouted—'Father! Mother!' but there was no answer—only the sad 'caw! caw!' of a crow, winging its homeward flight, came to their ears.

On they pressed once more. Soon little Frank began to cry; and his sister said, 'Don't cry, Frankie dear; don't cry. We'll soon be home, and you shall have a nice supper. Let me carry your broom, it's too heavy for you.'

She took the bundle of tea-tree twigs; and forward again they went with wildly beating hearts, sometimes stopping to cooee and look about; and then on, on till the sun set, and the bush, except for the dismal howl, now and then, of a dingo in the distance, grew gloomy and still.

Tired out and hungry, they huddled together at the foot of a big tree, and said the prayers their mother had taught them. Then they talked of home, wondering if Father would be vexed, and if Mother knew that they were lost. Frank soon cried himself to sleep; and his sister put some of the broom under his head for a pillow. Poor, dear little things! They little thought how glad Mother would be to see them, even without their broom.

As the night went on, it grew cold; and Jane, who was awake, took off her frock to wrap around her little brother, and crept close to him to keep him warm. For hours, she lay listening to the cry of the curlew, and the rush of the possum as it ran, from tree to tree, over the dead leaves and bark. At last, she fell asleep, and slept till the loud, mocking, 'Ha, ha! ho, ho! hoo, hoo!' of the laughing-jackass roused her at dawn. What a waking it was! Tired and cold, hungry and thirsty, and lost.

The mother had grown anxious as the day wore on, and the children did not return; and so, late in the afternoon, she went into the scrub, and cooeed for them till she was hoarse. As she got no answer, she became really alarmed, and, at length, hurried back to tell her husband, who, she expected, would return home from his work just before nightfall. He also searched through the scrub, and cooeed till long after dark, but in vain.

Before daybreak next morning, they were up, and, as soon as it was light enough, were hurrying to tell their nearest neighbours what happened, and ask their help in the search. Before dinner-time, a score of willing people—men and women—were scouring the scrub in various directions.

All that day, and the next, and the next, they searched, but found nothing; and the poor mother began to lose hope of ever seeing her darlings again. A messenger had been sent to a station some distance off to bring two or three blackfellows, who were employed there as boundary-riders.

The Australian blacks can find and follow a trail with wonderful skill. They have sharp eyes; and their training in searching for the tracks of the game they hunt causes them to note signs to guide them in places where a white man, even with good eyesight, sees nothing.

The children had been lost on Saturday; and the black trackers—a monarch, King Richard (better known as Dicky), and two subjects, Jerry and Fred—arrived on Wednesday. The three, taking positions some distance apart, began to look about for the trail of small footsteps. They had worked for some hours, when a yell from Dicky brought them to his side. 'What is it?' asked the father. 'There! there!' exclaimed the black, with a broad smile, pointing to a faint mark of a little boot.

Forward now they went, with the father and some of his neighbours. Sometimes the blacks ran; sometimes they walked; and sometimes they had even to crawl. In rocky places, they had to search carefully for traces, working from one point to another. Whenever this happened, it was a trying time for the poor father, as he felt that every minute's delay lessened the small chance there was of finding his children alive.

The blacks led on so many miles into the bush that the white men began to think their tracking was all a sham. At last, however, they stopped at the foot of a big gum-tree; and, pointing to three bundles of broom, Dicky said, 'Him been sleep there, fus night.'

The father was astonished to find that the children had travelled so far in a day, and much troubled at the thought of the long distance they might yet be from him; but he was comforted, too, for he felt that he could trust his guides.

There was no time to stop; but onward the party pressed still faster, till night came and put an end to their efforts for some hours, in spite of their wishes. How the father must have suffered through those hours, and how eagerly he must have watched for the first streaks of the coming dawn!

We can fancy how anxious the poor mother was, also, as day by day passed without any news of the finding of her children. Her fears slowly grew into the belief that they were dead; and her only hope was that their bodies would not be torn to pieces by dingoes, or eaten by ants.

As Dicky was leading next day at a trot, he was seen to halt, and begin looking around him. An anxious 'What is the matter?' from the father caused only a sad shake of the head from Dicky; and two fingers held up showed too well what was in his mind. Making a sign to his mates to look about for the dead body, he cast himself on his hands and knees to study the ground. A cry from him soon brought the party together. 'Here three,' he said, 'here two. Big one carry little one'; and he went through the motions of one child taking another on its back.

When the next sleeping-place of the little wanderers was found, the blacks pointed out that the smallest had lain in the middle. 'Him not get cold,' they said.

Their third day's tramp had not been so long as the others had been; and the blacks said again and again. 'Him plenty tired; not go much longer.' The tired little feet could not get over the ground so quickly now.

Another camping-place was reached, and 'Here yesterday!' exclaimed Dicky. On that fourth day's journey, the children had been passing through a patch of broom like that near their home; and the blacks, pointing to some broken twigs, showed that some branches had been broken off. Had they been gathered for a bed? No, there was no sign of that. Dicky turned to the father, and said, 'Him t'ink it him near home.' Yes; the children had supposed that they knew where they were when they reached that spot, and their first thought was of mother's broom. They were weary and starving; but they had been sent for the broom, and they would not go home without it.

'Him run now,' said the blacks; 'Him t'ink it all right'; and they pointed to the signs of haste. But, alas! what a blow to their hopes! By and by a bundle of broom was found. It had been thrown away—a sure sign of despair. 'Him been lose him. Him been sit down. Mine t'ink it him plenty cry.' Thus ran Dicky's history of the event.

Another camping-place was passed; and the blacks became doubly earnest, and kept saying, 'Him walk slow, slow, slow.' Soon Dicky whispered, 'Him close up.' And then he stopped and pointed before him in silence at something stretched on the ground.

'They must be dead,' groaned the father, and rushed forward with drawn face and straining eyes. Though all were living, only one was able to greet him, and that was little Frank, who raised himself slightly, held out his feeble arms, and cried in a weak, husky, voice, 'Daddy, Daddy, we cooeed for you, but you didn't come.' Jane had wrapped her frock around her little brother whenever they lay down to rest; and she and Isaac had carried him for miles, so that he had not suffered so much as they had. All alive, but very near death! Think of it: eight days and eight nights in the bush without food to eat or water to drink!

When they were found, the blacks laughed and cried, and rolled on the ground for joy; and Dicky (we may well call him King Richard now), springing on a horse that belonged to one of the party, gave his last order, 'Me tak gal home'; and Jane was handed up to him.

For some weeks, the children were between life and death, but kind attention and loving care brought them back to health. The story of their suffering and heroism spread far and wide. Jane's motherly attention to her little brother has won for her a place among the world's noble girls.

$\frown$

The theme of the child missing in the bush has lost none of its power, and real disappearances periodically recharge it. Henry Lawson wrote poems and short stories on the subject; country singer Johnny Ashcroft had a national and international hit in 1960 with a song titled 'Little Boy Lost' in the wake of another search and rescue drama involving a four-year-old boy in northern New South Wales. And the disappearance of baby Azaria Chamberlain in 1980—and the now notorious trial of her parents—gripped the public imagination and led to a best-selling book and a Hollywood movie.

J. Macfarlane

ABORIGINAL MYTHS.—THE BUNYIP.

3

Making monsters

The old world has her tales of ghoul and vampire, of Lorelei,
spook and pixie, but Australia has ... her bunyip.

Mrs Campbell Praed on the bunyip, 1891

EUROPEAN STORIES BEGAN mingling with Aboriginal ones within
a few years of the first settlement. Just as towns, rivers and
mountains were given often-mangled indigenous names, so new
hybrid legends arose, including that of the fearsome bunyip, the
human-like yowie and the Min Min lights.

The bunyip

Bunyips are creatures of Aboriginal mythology; a few groups called
them something like *banib*. They were usually said to be hairy,
though sometimes feathered, and to live in deep water holes and
ponds from where they attacked unwary passing humans. The
figure of the bunyip quickly merged with stories of European
water monsters such as the northern English Jenny (or Ginny)
Greenteeth.

The earliest substantial description of a bunyip was provided
in 1852 in the reminiscences of William Buckley, an escaped
convict who lived with Victorian Aborigines from 1803 to 1835:

I could never see any part [of the bunyip] except the back, which appeared to be covered with feathers of a dusky-grey colour. It seemed to be about the size of a full-grown calf. When alone, I several times attempted to spear a Bun-yip; but had the natives seen me do so it would have caused great displeasure. And again, had I succeeded in killing, or even wounding one, my own life would probably have paid the forfeit; they considering the animal something supernatural.

But accounts of water-dwelling monsters had surfaced some thirty years earlier in the Sydney press. Perhaps the earliest serious appearance of the bunyip in European records is found in the 1821 minutes of the Philosophical Society of Australasia. Three years before, the explorer Hamilton Hume had found bones of apparently amphibious animals near Lake Bathurst, in New South Wales. The society resolved to give Hume a grant 'for the purpose of procuring a specimen of the head, skin or bones'.

The *Melbourne Morning Herald* of 29 October 1849 reported a bunyip at Phillip Island. One was also reported in a lagoon near Melrose, South Australia, in the early 1850s. It was described as 'a large blackish substance advancing towards the bank, which as I approached raised itself out of the water. I crept towards it ... It had a large head and a neck something like that of a horse with thick bristly hair ... Its actual length would be from 15 to 18 feet.' There were several alleged sightings in the 1870s, from Tasmania to central Queensland. In the 1890s a bunyip was seen in the Warra Warra Waterhole near Crystal Brook, South Australia. The newspaper report of this incident neatly sums up the ongoing problem with bunyip sightings: 'Although seen during the last ten days by no less than six different persons, none of them can give an intelligent description of what the bunyip is like.'

In New South Wales, Katherine Langloh-Parker documented stories of water-dwelling monsters among the Euahlayi: 'Several waterholes are taboo as bathing-places. They are said to be haunted by Kurreah, which swallow their victims whole, or by Gowargay, the featherless emu, who sucks down in a whirlpool any one who dares to bathe in his holes.'

In his *Bunjil's Cave: myths, legends and superstitions of the Aborigines of south-east Australia*, Aldo Massola recorded stories of bunyips and many other monsters and bad spirits, including the mindie, which was 'greatly feared by all the tribes in north-western and central Victoria', and was described as 'a huge snake, very, very long, very thick and very powerful. He was visible, yet not visible.'

This story of a bunyip causing a deluge or great flood was probably collected in Victoria in the 1890s:

> ... a party of men were once fishing in a lake, when one man baited his hook with a piece of flesh and soon felt a tremendous bite. Hauling in his line, he found that he had caught a young *bunyip*, a water monster of which the people were much afraid; but though his companions begged him to let it go, because the water monsters would be angry if it were killed, he refused to listen to them and started to carry the young *bunyip* away. The mother, however, flew into a great rage and caused the waters of the lake to rise and follow the man who had dared to rob her of her young. The deluge mounted higher and higher, until all the country was covered, and the people, fleeing in terror, took refuge upon a high hill; but as the flood increased, gradually surmounting it and touching the people's feet, they were all turned into black swans and have remained so ever since.

The Ngarrindjerie people of South Australia preserve stories of bunyip-like mulgewongks. These creatures live in rivers and drag unsuspecting swimmers down to their caves. Dangerous as mulgewongks are, it is unlucky to kill one. In a story told by Ngarrindjerie man Henry Rankine in 1990, a riverboat captain unwise enough to kill such a creature sickened and died two weeks later. 'He did not listen to the old people who said to him, "Don't do that",' Rankine said, adding that his people still warn their children not to swim in the river at night.

Similar tales of water-dwelling monsters were told by the Nyungar people of southwestern Australia. The marghett, a male figure, was round but very long, with a large head and a great many teeth. It travelled by night, so was rarely seen. If an unwary Nyungar ventured into a marghett's waterhole, the creature would softly seize its victim's legs and drag him or her to a watery death.

So widespread and common were such stories that by 1891 it was possible for Mrs Campbell Praed to write: 'Everyone who has lived in Australia has heard of the bunyip. It is the one respectable flesh-curdling horror of which Australia can boast. The old world has her tales of ghoul and vampire, of Lorelei, spook and pixie, but Australia has . . . her bunyip.'

By this time the bunyip had become routinely used by white Australians to discipline their children. In his *Life in the Australian Backblocks* (1911), E.S. Sorenson wrote:

The average youngster has a horror of darkness, and talks in awe-struck whispers of hairy men, ghosts and bunyips. This fear is inculcated from babyhood. The mother can't always be watching in a playground that is boundless, and she knows the horror that waits the bushed youngster. So she tells them there is a bunyip in the lagoon, and gigantic eels in the creek; and beyond that hill there, and in yonder scrub, there is a 'bogey-man'. Those fairy tales keep the children within bounds—until they are old enough to know better.

Aboriginal parents also used monster stories to warn and control their children.

The figure of the bunyip became deeply embedded in Australian popular culture—it has found its way into children's stories, art, plays and verse. It also travelled to Britain, from where it was reimported in new versions, such as this one from Andrew Lang's *The Brown Fairy Book* (1904), elaborating on the tradition collected in Victoria a decade or so earlier:

*L*ong, long ago, far, far away on the other side of the world, some young men left the camp where they lived to get some food for their wives and children. The sun was hot, but they liked heat, and as they went they ran races and tried [to see] who could hurl his spear the farthest, or was cleverest in throwing a strange weapon called a boomerang, which always returns to the thrower.

They did not get on very fast at this rate, but presently they reached a flat place that in time of flood was full of water, but was now, in the height of summer, only a set of pools, each surrounded with a fringe of plants, with bulrushes standing in the inside of all. In that country the people are fond of the roots of bulrushes, which they think as good as onions, and one of the young men said that they had better collect some of the roots and carry them back to the camp. It did not take them long to weave the tops of the willows into a basket, and they were just going to wade into the water and pull up the bulrush roots when a youth suddenly called out: 'After all, why should we waste our time in doing work that is only fit for women and children? Let them come and get the roots for themselves; but we will fish for eels and anything else we can get.'

This delighted the rest of the party, and they all began to arrange their fishing lines, made from the bark of the yellow mimosa, and to search for bait for their hooks. Most of them used worms, but one, who had put a piece of raw meat for dinner into his skin wallet, cut off a little bit and baited his line with it, unseen by his companions.

For a long time they cast patiently, without receiving a single bite; the sun had grown low in the sky, and it seemed as if they would have to go home empty-handed, not even with a basket of roots to show; when the youth, who had baited his hook with raw meat, suddenly saw his line disappear under the water. Something, a very heavy fish he supposed, was pulling so hard that he could hardly keep his feet, and for a few minutes it seemed either as if he must let go or be dragged into the pool. He cried to his friends to help him, and at last, trembling with fright at what they were going to see, they managed between them to land on the bank a creature that was neither a calf nor a seal, but something of both, with a long, broad tail. They looked at each other with horror, cold shivers running down their spines; for though they had never beheld it, there was not a man amongst them who did not know what it was—the cub of the awful bunyip!

All of a sudden the silence was broken by a low wail, answered by another from the other side of the pool, as the mother rose up from her den and came towards them, rage flashing from her horrible yellow eyes. 'Let it go! Let it go!' whispered the young men to each other; but the captor declared that he had caught it, and was going to keep it. 'He had promised his sweetheart,' he said, 'that he would bring back enough meat for her father's house to feast on for three days, and though they could not eat the little bunyip, her brothers and sisters should have it to play with.' So, flinging his spear at the mother to keep her back, he threw the little bunyip on to his shoulders, and set out for the camp, never heeding the poor mother's cries of distress.

By this time it was getting near sunset, and the plain was in shadow, though the tops of the mountains were still quite bright. The youths had all ceased to be afraid, when they were startled by a low rushing sound behind them, and, looking round, saw that the pool was slowly rising, and the spot where they had landed the bunyip was quite covered. 'What could it be?' they asked one of another; there was not a cloud in the sky, yet the water had risen higher already than they had ever known it do before. For an instant they stood watching as if they were frozen, then they turned and ran with all their might, the man with the bunyip running faster than all. When he reached a high peak over-looking all the plain he stopped to take breath, and turned to see if he was safe yet. Safe! Why, only the tops of the trees remained above that sea of water, and these were fast disappearing. They must run fast indeed if they were to escape.

So on they flew, scarcely feeling the ground as they went, till they flung themselves on the ground before the holes scooped out of the earth where they had all been born. The old men were sitting in front, the children were playing, and the women chattering together, when the little bunyip fell into their midst, and there was scarcely a child among them who did not know that something terrible was upon them. 'The water! The water!' gasped one of the young men; and there it was, slowly but steadily mounting the ridge itself. Parents and children clung together, as if by that means they could drive back the advancing flood; and the youth who had caused all this terrible catastrophe, seized his sweetheart, and cried: 'I will climb with you to the top of that tree, and there no waters can reach us.'

But, as he spoke, something cold touched him, and quickly he glanced down at his feet. Then with a shudder he saw that they were feet no longer, but bird's claws. He looked at the girl he was clasping, and beheld a great black bird standing at his side; he turned to his friends, but a flock of great awkward flapping creatures stood in their place. He put up his hands to cover his face, but they were no more hands, only the ends of wings; and when he tried to speak, a noise such as he had never heard before seemed to come from his throat, which had suddenly become narrow and slender. Already the water had risen to his waist, and he found himself sitting easily upon it, while its surface reflected back the image of a black swan, one of many.

Never again did the swans become men; but they are still different from other swans, for in the night-time those who listen can hear them talk in a language that is certainly not swan's language; and there are even sounds of laughing and talking, unlike any noise made by the swans whom we know.

The little bunyip was carried home by its mother, and after that the waters sank back to their own channels. The side of the pool where she lives is always shunned by everyone, as nobody knows when she may suddenly put out her head and draw him into her mighty jaws. But people say that underneath the black waters of the pool she has a house filled with beautiful things, such as mortals who dwell on the earth have no idea of. Though how they know I cannot tell you, as nobody has ever seen it.

Lang's version of the bunyip story represents the children's end of the tradition. The other end focuses on the creature as killer. According to a version told to author Roland Robinson by an Aboriginal man named Percy Mumbulla, a 'clever man' or sorcerer of his acquaintance who once had a bunyip in his power; the creature was 'high in the front and low at the back, like a hyena, like a lion. It had a terrible bull head and it was milk white. This bunyip could go down into the ground and take the old man with him. They could travel under the ground. They could come out anywhere.' But for ordinary men, Mumbulla said, there was no making friends with a bunyip. 'When he bites you, you die.'

Yaramas, jarnbahs, jannocks and yowies

Indigenous mythology is full of spirits, monsters and usually loathsome creatures, some of which, like the bunyip, have also fused with monsters of European legend.

The yarama (or yaroma) is tall, hairy and has very sharp teeth in a large and hungry mouth, as in this early twentieth-century account:

*O*n one occasion a blackfellow went under a large fig-tree to pick up ripe figs, which had fallen to the ground, when a Yaroma, who was hidden in a hollow place in the base of a tree, rushed out, and catching hold of the man swallowed him head first. It happened that the man was of unusual length, measuring more than a foot taller than the majority of his countrymen. Owing to this circumstance, the Yaroma was not able to gulp him farther than the calves of his legs, leaving his feet protruding from the monster's mouth, thus keeping it open and allowing air to descend to the man's nostrils, which saved him from suffocation. The Yaroma soon began to feel a nausea similar to what occurs when a piece of fishbone or other substance gets stuck in one's throat. He went to the bank of the river close by, and took a drink of water to moisten his throat, thinking by this means to suck into his stomach the remainder of his prey, and complete his repast. This was all to no purpose, however, for, becoming sick, the Yaroma vomited the man out on the dry land, just as the whale got rid of Jonah. He was still alive, but feigned to be dead, in order that he might perhaps have a chance of escape. The Yaroma then started away to bring his mates to assist him to carry the dead man to their camp. He wished, however, to make quite sure that the man was dead before he left him, and after going but a short distance he jumped back suddenly; but the man lay quite still. The Yaroma got a piece of grass and tickled the man's feet and then his nose, but he did not move a muscle. The Yaroma, thinking he was certainly dead, again started away for help, and when he got a good distance off, the man, seeing his opportunity, got up and ran with all his speed into the water close by, and swam to the opposite shore, and so escaped.

In his description of the yarama, under the name *Yara ma tha who*, the Aboriginal writer David Unaipon suggests that the creatures were common along the east coast and explains: 'This is one of the stories told to bad children: that if they do not behave themselves the *Yara ma tha who* will come and take them and make them to become one of their own.'

In his memoir *Wyndham Yella Fella*, Reg Birch tells of his terrifying encounters with the jarnbah, 'an ugly, hairy, smelly little muscular dark man' who invaded dreams and sleep to torment and degrade boys and men. He was not the only Aboriginal male in the district to suffer this way.

The Nyungar of the southwest speak of jannocks, small, evil beings that lurk after dark. Often manifested in puffs of wind, they are especially dangerous to humans—all the more so because they are easily offended. Even referring to them the wrong way can bring trouble.

More widely known and feared is the yowie, a fierce animal of uncertain shape and features. An army officer in 1832 recorded hearing about a wawee, as it was called by the Eurambone people of the Liverpool Plains, west of Sydney. This was a tortoise-like creature that lived in rivers and fed on unwary humans. The officer, a Captain Forbes of the 39th Regiment of Foot, thought the story might be an indigenous joke at the settlers' expense. Others thought it and similar tales were concocted by the Aborigines to frighten settlers away. Some colonists used 'yowie' interchangeably with 'Yahoos', the fantastical savages invented by Jonathan Swift in his 1726 book *Gulliver's Travels*. Yahoo also sounds like the term for 'dream spirit' in the Yuwaalaraay language of northeastern New South Wales. Whatever its origins, the term has stuck, and yahoo is frequently used as a variation on yowie.

The earliest documented mention of this creature, referred to as both a 'Yahoo' and a 'Devil-Devil', seems to have been in 1835. The *Australian and New Zealand Monthly Magazine* provided this description in 1842:

The natives of Australia have, properly speaking, no idea of any supernatural being; they believe in the imaginary existence of a class which, in the singular number, they call Yahoo, or, when they wish to be anglified, Devil-Devil. This being they describe as resembling a man, of nearly the same height, but more slender, with long white straight hair hanging down from the head over the features, so as almost entirely to conceal them; the arms are extraordinarily long, furnished at the extremities with great talons, and the 'feet turned backwards', so that, on flying from man, the imprint of the foot appears as if the being had travelled in the opposite direction. Altogether, they describe it as a hideous monster, of an unearthly character and ape-like appearance. On the other hand, a contested point has long existed among Australian naturalists whether or not such an animal as the Yahoo existed, one party contending that it does, and that from its scarceness, slyness, and solitary habits, man has not succeeded in obtaining a specimen, and that it is most likely one of the monkey tribe.

Long before the term yowie came into general use, variants of it were used by indigenous Australians to denote what David Unaipon described as 'the most dreadful animal in existence'. He was referring to the Riverina whowie, a large reptile or goanna with six legs, a tail and an enormous frog-like head. The whowie would devour whatever creatures it came across, including humans—and in large numbers. It lived in a cave on the river bank and its footprints were said to have formed the sandhills along the river. Unaipon retells a story in which the whowie is eventually killed by the animals, birds and reptiles. As with the yarama and bunyip, fearsome tales of the whowie's doings were used to caution disobedient children.

About 1903, William Telfer, a stockman who spent his life around Tamworth, New South Wales, wrote down his memories. These included, from the 1840s, a graphic description of his encounter with a man-like beast on the Liverpool Plains, said in local Aboriginal tradition to have once been a vast lake or inland sea.

*T*he Aborigines have a tradition that it is three hundred miles long, a large lot of islands in the middle of it. One Aboriginal told me his grandfather told him big fellow water all about the plains. He said they used to have canoes and go fishing from one island to the other making a stay at each place as they went across from one side to the other. His story must have some truth in it as Mr Oxley, Surveyor General, when he came over Liverpool Plains had to cross large marshes or swamps . . . I said [to the Aboriginal man] at the time there was the river. He said no river, all water and ridges and mountains all round the outside . . . There came a very wet season and his people shifted away to the mountains. He said they heard great noise at different times, like thunder. He said they were very frightened. When they came back all the big water was gone. Nothing but mud and swamps where the Plains are now, plenty of fish in different waterholes . . . he said the ridges about Gunnedah were swept away by the great rush of water in its course down the Namoi . . .

Then they have a tradition about the yahoo. They say he is a hairy man like a monkey. Plenty at one time, not many now. But the best opinion of the kind I heard from old Bungaree, a Gunnedah Aboriginal. He said at one time there were tribes of them and they were the original inhabitants of the country. He said they were the old race of blacks. He was of Darwin's theory that the original race had a tail on them like a monkey. He said the Aboriginals would camp in one place and those people in a place of their own, telling about how them and the blacks used to fight and the blacks always beat them but the yahoo always made away from the blacks, being a faster runner, mostly escaped. The blacks were frightened of them. When a lot of those were together the blacks would not go near them as the yahoo would make a great noise and frighten them with sticks. He said very strong fellow, very stupid. The blacks were more cunning, getting behind trees, spearing any chance one that came near them. This was his story about those people.

I have seen several stockmen in the old times said they had seen this hairy man. His feet [were] reversed—when you thought he was coming towards you he was going away. I had an experience myself of this gorilla or hairy man. In the year 1883 I was making a short cut across the bush from Keera to Cobedah via Top Bingera. It was a very hot day. I was on foot when, after crossing those steep hills, being tired, camped for about two hours. This left me late. The sun was only an hour high. Having to go about ten miles [I] went about five miles. Getting dark, [I] came on a creek of running water. Had to camp for the night. Made a camp on a high bank of the creek, lit a fire and made myself comfortable, my dog laying down at the fire alongside me. I sat smoking my pipe. The moon rose about an hour after, when you could discern objects two hundred yards away from the camp. I heard a curious noise coming up the creek opposite the camp. Over the creek I went to see what it was about one hundred yards away. He seemed the same as a man only larger. The animal was something like the gorilla in the Sydney Museum, of a darkish colour and made a roaring noise going away towards Top Bingera, the noise getting fainter as he went along in the distance.

I started at daylight, getting to Bell's Mountain about 9 o'clock. Mr Bridger lived there; stopped and had breakfast. I was telling them about the night before. They said several people has seen the gorilla about there. He was often seen in the mountains towards the Gwyder and about Mt Lyndsay. I was thinking how easily this animal could elude pursuit, travelling by night, camping in rocks or caves in the daytime. After those blacks, the Governors [brothers, who murdered five white people in July 1900], so many out after them I do not think it wonderful those wild animals should escape being caught, as they are faster than the Aboriginal by his own account. Some people think they are only a myth, but how is it they were seen by so many people in the old times fifty years ago?

In referring to the search for the Governor brothers, Telfer was making the point that a yahoo could hide away in the bush as easily as they could.

The doolagarl, or hairy man, was also well known and feared in southeastern New South Wales. Percy Mumbulla, who told Roland Robinson about the bunyip and the 'clever man', described this creature as 'a man like a gorilla. He has long spindly legs. He has a big chest and long swinging arms. His forehead goes back from his eyebrows. His head goes into his shoulders. He has no neck.'

In 1989, folklore collectors in Queensland recorded fading rumours of a 'wowey-wowey', a creature 'that is supposed to run around the bushes'. Nor was that the end of the yowie legend's career. In September 2000, a bushwalker claimed to have filmed a large creature he believed could be a yowie in the Brindabella ranges near Canberra. The Brindabellas have long been a favourite yowie lair, with reported sightings dating back to pioneer days (one claimed an eyewitness spoke of 'a man-like thing whose coat was as hairy as that of a gorilla'). News reports quoted the bushwalker as saying, 'I was filming what I thought was a large kangaroo in a gully, when I realised it was far too big for a roo.' People who viewed the film, including 'hominid researcher' Tim the Yowie Man, said it seemed to show a large, hairy creature walking upright through the bush but that the footage was too dark to draw any conclusions.

Alien cats

The study and pursuit of mythical animals, including yaramas and bunyips, is known as cryptozoology. Australian folklore is rich in what cryptozoologists call 'Alien Big Cats' or 'ABCs'.

One of the best-known of these is the Tantanoola Tiger, said to have been attacking stock in that region of South Australia since the early 1890s. Scant though the evidence is, many people genuinely believe in ABCs and spend a great deal of time and money looking for them.

In an extended study of weird animal traditions in Australia, folklorist Bill Scott noted: 'There is certainly a very strong folk belief in this country of the existence of such an animal, which is usually described by witnesses as a "panther" or a "big cat".' Scott went on to identify a number of these beasts from his own fieldwork and reports by others. These included the Emmaville Panther and the Kangaroo Valley Panther (New South Wales), the Waterford Panther (Queensland), the Dromana Mountain Lion (Victoria), the Marulan Tiger (New South Wales), and the Guyra Cat (New South Wales). To these could be added the Tasmanian Tiger, the Nannup Tiger (Western Australia), and the Kyneton Cat (Victoria), among many others. In Queensland, there are said to be cougars around Townsville, Mount Spec and Charters Towers. In September 2008, a leopard was reported on the northwestern edge of Sydney, the latest of many similar sightings in the Blue Mountains and along the Hawkesbury River.

Most reports of this type involve, as well as descriptions of some variety of 'big cat', an explanation, often venerable, of how such a creature came to be prowling the Australian bush. Often, the animals are said to have escaped from a circus. Another common theme is that a pair of panthers (or cougars, or mountain lions) were brought to Australia as mascots for American troops during World War II and released into the bush after the war. Convincing documentation of such animals, however, has yet to be produced. Big cat sightings nowadays are often 'irrefutably proven' by a photograph or video footage. As with the yowie video of 2000, these invariably turn out to be murky snaps that could show almost any animal at all.

Another feature of big cat (and yowie) lore is outsized, backward-pointing or otherwise odd tracks. Plaster casts are often made of these prints for examination by 'experts' whose task seems to be to vindicate the claims of the cat seekers. The experts' findings, however, rarely see the light of day.

Naturally, farmers who find their stock mauled to death want to know what did it. Reports of big-cat attacks on sheep and cattle have surfaced regularly since the nineteenth century. Around Busselton, south of Perth, for example, a series of unexplained sheep losses in 1997 and 1998 were blamed by some locals on a wild cougar. A cast of a suspected paw print was given to Perth Zoo for inspection. Its specialist was 'unable to determine what had left the print, but said it was not large enough to be a cougar', according to a report in Perth's *Sunday Times*. 'The claws have the characteristics of a cat,' the specialist said. 'But I would not like to put my money on it being a big cat, it could even be a large dog.'

In the mid 1970s, reports of pumas in Victoria's Grampian Ranges were investigated by environmental science students at Deakin University, who collected casts of footprints, fur, bone, and even faeces. Puma experts in Colorado who examined the specimens found them consistent with pumas. The outcome 'was tantalising but not conclusive', Professor John Henry, who had been in charge of the investigation, later said.

Henry decided to probe further. He had heard the story that the US Air Force had released big cats into the Grampians during World War II. Now he tracked down six former members and quizzed them about it in writing. Some of the ex-servicemen recalled hearing stories along those lines, but that is as far as any of them would go. Henry's final (2001) report on the case for pumas found there was 'sufficient evidence from a number of intersecting sources to affirm beyond reasonable doubt the presence of a big-cat population in western Victoria'.

In 2000, there was another sighting of a mysterious creature in the area, and this time video 'evidence' was screened on television. Officials in Victoria's Department of Natural Resources thought the animal was probably a feral cat. A spokesman told *The Weekend Australian*: 'We remain sceptical of the exotic cat theory until field evidence comes along rather than hearsay of sightings.'

The Tasmanian Tiger, *Thylacinus cynocephalus* (pouched animal with a dog's head), became extinct in 1936, but many have hunted in vain for it since. A descendent of the carnivorous marsupial is widely believed to roam the mainland's far southwest and is still pursued in Tasmania. Reports of the beast, known as the Nannup Tiger (or some variant of that name), seem to date back almost to the earliest European settlement of Western Australia, but were especially frequent in the late 1960s and early 1970s, when wet winters supposedly forced it into the wooded areas around Nannup. Various attempts were made to capture the Nannup Tiger, without success. As with the bunyip and the yowie lack of evidence has not prevented this and other Alien Big Cats from taking up residence in Australia's monster menagerie.

The Min Min lights

The Min Min lights are a Queensland version of an eerie phenomenon reported elsewhere in Australia and around the world. Ghost lights were reported by explorers in southeastern Australia from the 1830s. The Wongagai people of Australia's northwest believe the night lights they sometimes observe on the plains are spirits luring humans into the desert with evil intent. Several of these apparitions, as they were often called in the nineteenth century, are associated with tales of haunting. People in Hay, New South Wales, for example, used to see a light that appeared to be on a mail coach travelling across One Tree Plain. No matter how fast men rode after the light, no one was ever able to catch up with it. But while the Phantom Mail is a legend known mainly to locals, the story of the Min Min lights has become widely told.

Min Min was the Aboriginal-derived name of an inn built in the late nineteenth century, about 100 kilometres east of the town of Boulia, in the channel country of north-central Queensland. The pub thrived as the Queensland frontier expanded, and a small township grew up around it, but the population gradually dwindled, and during World War I the pub burned down. Since at least the time the hotel was built, however, there have been reports of strange lights dancing through the night skies in the area. The lights are described in a bewildering variety of ways: as small, large, single, numerous, of one colour, changing in colour, standing still, moving slowly, moving fast, or sometimes following startled travellers.

There are many scientific and pseudo-scientific explanations for the Min Min lights. Probably the most frequent is that they are a form of marsh light, or *ignis fatuus* (Latin for foolish fire). Also known as will o' the wisps, these are caused by phosphorescent gases rising from swampy ground. Min Min lights have also been attributed to mirages, weather effects, the ghosts of massacred Aborigines and, inevitably, UFOs. One sceptical scientist has even managed to reproduce the lights in his laboratory in a probably futile attempt to quash the notion that they are somehow supernatural. The legend of the Min Min lights arose from a mingling of Aboriginal, British and Australian settler traditions, with a romantic gloss provided mostly by the press.

Even before European settlement, Aborigines seem to have witnessed the lights; a number of the local Pitta Pitta people averred that they were or of unearthly origin, in some cases associated with the spirits of stillborn children. They have also been said to be linked to an Aboriginal burial ground. A variation on this theme is that the lights first appeared after a number of Aborigines were killed by settlers. This is possibly a reference to the incident at Battle Mountain near Mount Isa in 1884, when as many as several hundred Kalkadoon people may have been killed; or it may refer to other reprisal killings of Kalkadoons by settlers. Queensland oral tradition contains many massacre stories that have never been historically confirmed.

When settlers first saw the lights, they generally interpreted them as marsh lights. These are often explained in British folklore as ghosts or disembodied souls, sometimes referred to as 'corpse candles'. Similar phenomena around the world are also widely associated with ill luck, evil and death.

The earliest accounts of the Min Min lights generally have them arising from the cemetery behind the hotel. This establishment apparently gained a bad reputation for encouraging bush workers to 'lamb down', or drink down, their pay cheques, giving no change and plying them with rotgut alcohol. In some versions of the Min Min tale, patrons of the hotel were sometimes drugged and robbed or murdered. This embellishment added an extra dimension of spookiness to the legend; perhaps the lights were the vengeful ghosts of murdered men.

The first coherent account of the lights comes from Henry Lamond, a station manager, who saw them in 1912:

During the middle of winter—June or July—I had to go to Slasher's Creek to start the lamb-marking. I did not leave the head station until about 2 a.m., expecting to get to Slasher's well before daylight . . .

After crossing the Hamilton River, 5 miles wide with 45 channels, I was out on the high downs . . . 5 or 6, or 8 or 10, miles out on the downs I saw the headlight of a car coming straight for me . . . Cars, though they were not common, were not rare. I took note of the thing, singing and trotting as I rode, and I even estimated the strength of the approaching light by the way it picked out individual hairs in the mare's mane.

Suddenly I realised it was not a car light—it remained in one bulbous ball instead of dividing into the 2 headlights, which it should have done as it came closer; it was too green-glary for an acetylene light; it floated too high for any car; there was something eerie about it. I ceased to sing, though I kept the mare at the trot. She stopped that: she propped her four legs wide, lifted her head, pricked her ears, and she snorted her challenge to the unknown!

The light came on, floating as airily as a bubble, moving with comparative slowness—though I did not at the time check its rate of progression. I should estimate now that it was moving at about 10 m.p.h. and anything from 5 to 10 feet above the ground . . . Its size, I would say, at an approximate guess, would be about that of a new-risen moon. That light and I passed each other, going in opposite directions. I kept an eye on it while it was passing, and I'd say it was about 200 yards off when suddenly it just faded and died away. It did not go out with a snap—its vanishing was more like the gradual fading of the wires in an electric bulb. The mare acknowledged the dowsing of the glim by another snorting whistle: it must have been at least five miles or so ere I lifted up my voice again in song.

Lamond's recollection of this incident was not published until twenty-five years later, on 1 April 1937—not a date to engender confidence in the veracity of the story. But many other people also reported seeing a similiar light, or lights.

In May 1981, Detective Sergeant Lyall Booth, of the Police Stock Investigation Squad at Cloncurry, was camped at a waterhole about 60 kilometres east of Boulia. Waking at around 11 p.m., he saw what looked like a car's headlight on the road. Police Commissioner Norriv Bauer later published a report of Booth's statement on the sighting. He quoted Booth as saying the light 'appeared to be moving but it did not seem to get any closer

(I know that's hard to grasp, but that is how it appeared)'. He described the light as 'white in colour, similar to the light thrown by a quartz iodide headlight'. He went back to sleep but woke about 1 a.m., and saw another light about 1000 metres southwest of where he'd seen the earlier one.

> It was not as bright as the first light and had a slightly yellow colour to it. It was about the colour of a gas light which is turned down very low and is about to go out, but it was of much greater intensity than that type of light.
>
> It appeared to be slightly bigger than the gas light used in the cook's camp. It seemed to be from 3 to 6 feet from the ground, and moved only several yards from west to east and then remained stationary. It illuminated the ground around it, but I was too far away from it to see any detail. I could, however, see the cook's camp.

Booth watched it for another five or six minutes, 'and then it suddenly dived towards the ground and went out. It may even have gone out on contact with the ground. I did not see it again.' Bauer quoted Booth as saying he was 'at a loss to explain in physical terms the lights that I saw. My enquiries lead me to believe that they were not caused by man.'

Despite the inconsistencies among (and within) reported sightings, the scepticism of scientists and the existence of a number of possible natural explanations, the notion that the Min Min lights are supernatural in origin lives on. Tourism promoters refer to them, and UFOlogists investigate them. Whatever their origin, the lights have become one of Australia's most persistent tales of the unexplained.

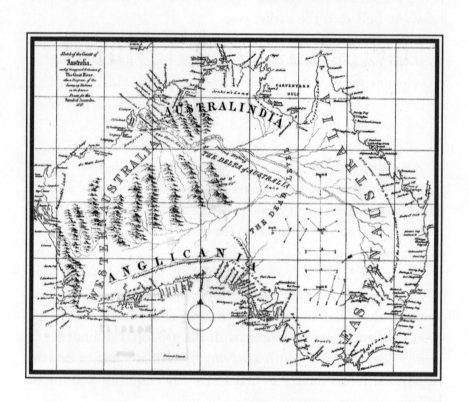

4

Legends on the land

These stories belong to us.

Bob Turnbull

MUCH LORE AND legend is closely tied to places. Such stories often help to forge and maintain a common sense of identity. They may not be widely known outside the locality where they arose, though some are local variants of tales told around the world. A few, however—like that of the Min Min lights—manage to spread widely without losing their links with the places of their birth.

Place-specific stories often contain explanations for the names of local landmarks or for local customs. A large group of these type of legends concerns buried, or otherwise lost, treasure.

The man who sold his Dreaming

Australia's earliest local tales are, of course, those of the first Australians. And as this next one shows, they are not necessarily set in the mythological world before European settlement. Collected by Roland Robinson from an Aboriginal man named Bob Turnbull, it is a good example of the way indigenous and settler traditions often coalesce. As well as explaining how the local town got its name, it is a cautionary tale about giving up what is most important to you. The term jurraveel, introduced near the end of the story, means 'a sacred place', to which Frank Jock was connected by his totem, a bird similar to a bantam rooster.

*Y*ou know that water-hen with the red beak? He sings out 'Kerk', and 'Kerk', well, that bird is my totem. Every dark feller has a totem. It's his spirit. It looks after him and warns him of any danger. In my tribe, the Bunjalung tribe of the Richmond River, his name is *geeyarng*. And our native name for a totem is *barnyunbee*.

I want to tell you about a totem that belonged to a dark feller named Frank Jock. Frank Jock had a totem that was something like a little bantam rooster. Everyone would hear this bird singing out. They'd go to look for him, but they could never find him.

Away on the mountain in the lantana, he'd be singing out. He was sort of minding that place, looking after it, you'd say.

Well, the mayor of Coraki wanted to make a quarry in that mountain. There was the best kind of blue metal there. He sent the men of the council to that place. They put three charges, one after another, into the rock. But not one of those charges would go off.

There was a dark feller in the gang by the name of Andrew Henry. He told the mayor of Coraki that he'd have to go and have a talk to Frank Jock. The mayor would have to ask Frank if he could do something so that they could blow up this mountain and make a quarry in it.

The mayor sent for Frank Jock, he said he wanted to see him. 'Look,' the mayor said to Frank, 'can you let us blow this mountain up?'

'All right,' Frank said, 'but you'll have to pay me.'

So the mayor gave Frank five gold sovereigns and two bottles of rum to let the council blow up the mountain.

The council men went back to the mountain and they put in one big charge. When it went off, it blew the side right out of the mountain. The explosion shook Coraki. A big spout of black water rushed up out of the mountainside. The council had to wait a long time until all the water cleared away before they could work the quarry.

The little bantam rooster, he disappeared. He didn't sing out any more. *Jurraveel* I can see you know all about this black-feller business.

Well, after the mountain was blown up, Frank Jock, the owner of that *jurraveel*, began to get sick. In three weeks he was dead. You see, like it says in the Bible, he'd sold his birthright. It was the same as killing him. He sold his *jurraveel* to the mayor of the town.

That's why we call it in our language Gurrigai, meaning 'blowing up the mountain'. That's how Coraki got its name.

———

After Bob Turnbull had finished telling the story, he said to Roland Robinson, 'You know, I've been looking for years for a feller like you to write these stories down. These stories are dying out. They're lost to the young people. I'd like to think that one day the young people will read these stories and say, "These stories belong to us."'

Naming places

The American humorist and travel writer Mark Twain visited Australia in the late 1890s. A master yarn spinner and teller of tall tales himself, Twain was mildly sceptical when told by a local liar that the Blue Mountains of New South Wales had been thrown up by the rabbits then plaguing the country. Tongue in cheek, Twain wrote that the rabbit plague 'could account for one mountain, but not for a mountain range, it seems to me. It is too large an order.' Whether this was the origin of the long-running joke about Australians outdoing Americans in the size of their lies, the rabbit-pile theory certainly fits into it.

In 1989, folklorists collected at least six different stories about the origins of the Queensland town of Ravenshoe. These included the suggestion that someone had once seen some ravens or crows playing with an old shoe on the creek bank—despite the fact that the name is pronounced Ravens-hoe. (Hoe, or Hoo, is the name of a place in Norfolk). There was also an elaborate story about how local streams, when viewed from the air, meet in the shape of a crow's foot. Many of the people who supplied these stories thought the town's original name, Cedar Creek, was a much better choice.

Locals say Crows Nest, Queensland, is so named because Aborigines called the place something like 'home of the crows'. A more colourful version of this story holds that during the early days of settlement, an Aboriginal man lived in a hollow tree in the town, from which vantage point he provided directions to bullock drivers and cedar getters as well as acting as an unofficial post office. It is said that the settlers called him Jimmy Crow and his tree Jimmy Crow's Nest, a contraction of which became the town's name.

Whipstick, near Bendigo in Victoria, is an area of mallee scrub first encountered by gold diggers. As some locals told folklorist Peter Ellis, the scrub was almost impenetrable, twisted about with creepers that whipped back into men's faces as they struggled through it or tried to cut it down. Other people claimed that Whipstick was named after the whip handles made from the scrub by bullock drivers.

Another story from the goldfields explained how Dunolly got its name. A couple were driving their horse-drawn cart along a track. The woman, whose name was Olive, asked her husband to stop and went to squat behind a bush. After a while, her husband became impatient and called out, 'Are you done, Ollie?'

Leatherass Gully is another goldfields name that cries out for a foundation legend. In this case, it's based on an old fossicker who had a leather patch on the seat of his worn-out trousers. The original spelling was Leatherarse, but that was deemed vulgar, so it was replaced by Leatherass.

Walkaway, near Geraldton, Western Australia, was established in the 1850s and now has a population of 612. Some say its name is derived from *waggawah*, an Aboriginal word meaning either camping place, a break in the hills, or the hill of the dogs. One tradition has it that some of the earliest settlers in the district left when their wheat crop failed. When the Aborigines were asked what happened to them, they replied: 'Him walk away.' Another version that alludes to these early farmers' struggles is heartbreakingly succinct: 'If you saw the place, you'd walk away too!' Yet another version involves the railway line that for a time terminated near Walkaway: passengers who wanted to go further north were told they would have to walk a way.

The dramatic legend of Govetts Leap, in the Blue Mountains of New South Wales, tells of an escaped convict turned bushranger named Govett who, pursued by troopers, found himself trapped on the edge of a 300-metre cliff. Preferring death to capture, he wheeled his horse around and rode it over the edge. In fact, the place was named after a colonial assistant surveyor, William Govett, who discovered the site in 1831. It is possible that the more romantic version originated from the observations of the English novelist Anthony Trollope, who travelled through Australia during the early 1870s. In his sometimes abrasive account of that trip, *Australia and New Zealand*, Trollope wrote:

> ... there is a ravine called Govett's Leap. Mr. Govett was, I believe, simply a government surveyor, who never made a leap into the place at all. Had he done so, it would certainly have been effectual for putting an end to his earthly sorrows. I had hoped, when I heard the name, to find that some interesting but murderous bushranger had on that spot baffled his pursuers and braved eternity—but I was informed that a government surveyor had visited the spot, had named it, and had gone home again. No one seeing it could fail to expect better things from such a spot and such a name.

The Lone Pine seedlings

The heroism and slaughter of the Gallipoli campaign in World War I gave rise to one of Australia's most enduring national stories: the legend of Anzac. Closely bound up with it are tales related to Lone Pine. This was, on the day of the landings at Gallipoli, part of a ridge officially named 400 Plateau. Australian troops called it Lonesome (later Lone) Pine for a single, stunted tree that rose above the scrub. In August 1915, Lone Pine was seared into Australian memory when a terrible battle took place there. More than 2000 Australians were killed or wounded, and seven won the Victoria Cross. Each Anzac Day, Lone Pine cemetery is the site of the official Australian memorial service at Gallipoli.

Today, Australia is dotted with trees said to be descended from the original lone pine. There are various stories about the origins of these symbolic trees. According to one of these, a Lance Corporal Benjamin Smith witnessed the death of his brother at Lone Pine and later pocketed a cone from the by-then felled pine tree that the Turks had used to cover their trenches. He sent it home to his mother who kept the cone for some years, eventually growing two seedlings from it. One of these was sent to Inverell, New South Wales, the place where her dead son had enlisted. Here it was planted and grew until it had to be cut down in 2007. In 1929, Smith's mother sent another seedling to Canberra, where it was planted in the Yarralumla nursery. In 1934, the visiting Duke of Gloucester planted this tree in the grounds of the Australian War Memorial.

Although the War Memorial's Lone Pine is not often featured in official ceremonies, its existence is well known in the Australian community. When the tree was damaged by a storm in December 2008, the incident received nationwide media coverage. Memorial staff also report that 'small wreaths, home-made posies and the occasional red poppy are sometimes seen resting at its base'.

Another story has it that a Sergeant Keith McDowell of the 24th Battalion also souvenired a Lone Pine cone and kept it with him until the war's end when he returned safely to Victoria, giving the cone to his aunt, Mrs Emma Gray, who lived near Warrnambool. Mrs Gray kept the cone for a decade or so until she too propagated four seedlings. These were planted variously throughout Victoria from 1933, in Wattle Park and the Shrine of Rememberance in Melbourne, and the Soldiers Memorial Hall, The Sisters, and at Warrnambool Botanic Gardens. However, researchers say they have found no such digger as Sergeant Keith McDowell and the battalion to which he supposedly belonged did not reach Gallipoli until a month after Lone Pine. Nor, it seems, were any Smiths involved in the Lone Pine battle. Nonetheless, the legend of the Lone Pine seedlings is now deeply rooted, and the trees so widely distributed (two seedlings were planted at Gallipoli for the 75th anniversary of the battle) that no amount of historical fact will weaken it.

Like most such legends, the Lone Pine story arises from a powerful national desire for tangible connections to long-ago tragedies. If the connections are incomplete, explanatory tales are spun to bridge the gaps. While the Lone Pines are an unusually stark example of the process, similar needs underlie many national traditions, including the Anzac dawn service.

The first dawn service

Australia's single most important national ritual is Anzac Day. Before sunrise each 25 April, people gather at memorials all over the country to begin the day with prayers for the fallen of all wars. This dawn service varies in form from place to place and has evolved over time to suit a variety of local needs and traditions. Its basic meaning, however, remains the same. In the years immediately after World War I, the services were relatively simple, spontaneous ceremonies. Over time they have become more elaborate as Anzac Day has developed into what is arguably a more consensual expression of national identity than Australia Day, the anniversary of the first settlement. Given its significance and its emotional resonance, it is not surprising that there are a number of different versions of the dawn service's origins.

The military version is that the ceremony is derived from the 'stand-to', in which soldiers were put on full alert to guard against a pre-dawn (or post-sunset) attack. Great War veterans are said to have remembered stand-to as a peaceful moment of the day in which the bonds of comradeship were keenly felt. Some began to hold informal stand-to ceremonies on Anzac Day, their significance increased by the dawn timing of the first Gallipoli landings. The order to stand-to would be given. Then there would be two minutes' silence, after which a lone bugler would play the Last Post call and finally the Reveille. It is unlikely that these events were referred to as services, as there were no clergy present and no sermons or speeches. These elements of formality crept in from 1927, when the first official dawn service was held at the Cenotaph in central Sydney.

This event has its own foundation legend. According to the story, five members of the Australian Legion of Ex-Service Clubs were on their unsteady way home in the early hours of Anzac Day after a celebratory evening. As they rolled past the Cenotaph they saw an elderly woman laying a wreath in memory of a lost soldier. The roisterers were so shamed and sobered by this dignified act of commemoration that they joined the woman in silent tribute and prayer. Inspired by this experience, the men decided to conduct a wreath-laying ceremony at the Cenotaph at dawn the following year, 1927. More and more people began to join them, including government dignitaries and representatives of the clergy and the military.

In Albany, Western Australia, the first dawn service took a

different form. At 4 a.m. on the day the first Anzac convoy left the town, the Anglican reverend Arthur Ernest White conducted a service for members of the 44th Battalion, AIF. After serving in the war, White returned to Albany. There, at dawn on 25 April 1923, he led a small group of parishioners up nearby Mount Clarence. As they watched the sun rise over King George Sound, a man in a boat threw a wreath onto the water. White recited the lines: 'As the sun rises and goeth down, we will remember them'—*a fusion of a Biblical verse and poet Laurence Binyon's 'At the going down of the sun and in the morning/We will remember them.'* News of this simple but moving observance—again with no strong religious overtones, despite a clergyman's presence—is said to have spread rapidly, and the ritual was adapted and adopted in many other communities.

Though well attested, this version does have a rival in Queensland. There, it is said that the first dawn service took place at 4 a.m. on Anzac Day, 1919. A small party led by a Captain Harrington placed flowers on the graves and memorials of World War I soldiers in Toowoomba, then drank to the memory of their fallen comrades. The observance was repeated, the Last Post and Reveille bugle calls were added, and other communities followed suit.

These different accounts of the origins of the dawn service have many features in common, but each is adapted to its own locality. Like the dawn service itself, they have become part of the edifice of legend that has formed around the Anzac tradition.

Lasseter's Reef

Many of Australia's wilder places have a tale of lost treasure. It may be in a reef, a cave, a river or under the ground; sometimes it involves secret maps, indigenous custodians or even pirates. Despite varying details, these legends are suspiciously similar—suggesting that they are more likely to be rooted in folklore than fact. The best known of all is the legend of the ill-fated Lasseter.

In Billy Marshall-Stoneking's book *Lasseter: the making of a legend*, he quotes the observation of a Papunya man named Shorty Lungkarta that Australians' obsession with Lasseter's 'lost' gold reef is just 'a whitefella dreaming'. It's a perceptive judgement. Marshall-Stoneking said he was inspired to investigate Lasseter's story by memories of the 1956 movie *Green Fire*—about a 'lost' South American emerald mine—in which Stewart Granger's character mentions 'Lasseter's Reef'. *Green Fire* is only one of innumerable films and novels that deal with the El Dorado get-rich-quick theme of the quest for a fabulous treasure.

The 'mystery', the history and the folklore of Lasseter's Reef have been kicking around Australia for over a century. They—and the numerous books, articles and fruitless expeditions the legend has spawned—are a revealing insight into human acquisitiveness.

In 1929 a man named Lewis Harold Bell Lasseter claimed that, years before, he had become lost in central Australia. During his wanderings, he said, he had discovered a reef of gold with nuggets 'as thick as plums in a pudding', but had been unable to mark or otherwise document its location. He said he had been saved from certain death by an Afghan cameleer. He claimed that three years later, in partnership with another man, he had managed to locate the reef. Because their watches were slow, however, the bearings they took were wrong and the reef was lost again.

In 1930, with backing from a trade union leader and other investors, Lasseter formed the Central Australian Gold Company, which mounted a large expedition. It was plagued with mishaps almost from the first. Eventually, after considerable strife and bickering, the party split up. Lasseter was stranded in the desert, and died in the Petermann Ranges, southwest of Alice Springs, probably in January 1931. The famous bushman Bob Buck was commissioned by the company to find Lasseter. After considerable hardship and danger, he found and, allegedly, buried Lasseter's remains, and retrieved the dead prospector's diary and some letters.

These papers, which included a map of the supposed location of the reef, triggered a futher series of expeditions. The fact that these ended in failure did nothing to quash the legend. At least eight books have been written about Lasseter and his treasure, the best known of which is Ion Idriess's semi-fictional and often-reprinted *Lasseter's Last Ride* (1931).

In 1957, the American explorer Lowell Thomas made a television documentary on the story that included interviews with the ageing Bob Buck and the opening of Lasseter's grave. This was intended to settle speculation that the remains Buck buried were not those of Lasseter and that the prospector had made his way to safety, only to disappear into either an obscure but wealthy life or anonymous shame. Whatever the truth, a number of people claimed to have seen or met Lasseter in Australia or overseas after the date of his death.

And there is a curse. One of the expedition members took a *churinga*, a sacred Aboriginal artefact, back to England. Almost immediately, he was plagued by misfortune; there were deaths in the family and he fell into a depression. Finally, he destroyed the precious but cursed object.

In some ways a uniquely Australian legend, the story of Lasseter's Reef neatly fits the template common to 'lost treasure' folklore around the world: an intrepid male explorer stumbles on a fabulous trove but loses its location in his struggle to return to civilisation alive. Perhaps he has a sample of the find. Invariably he has a map or a diary, or some other clue, either too cryptic to be useful or itself mislaid. These scant signs and indications entice others to embark on vain—even fatal—searches. Disturbing the treasure or coming too close to it may arouse its native guardians or trigger some dreadful curse. The treasure remains lost.

Yet the story lives on. We don't want to let go of Lasseter and his reef. The story is a variant on El Dorado, a universal beacon for the greedy. But it also stirs specifically Australian feelings: the awe and fear that, even in the jet age, the 'dead heart' still provokes.

The carpet of silver

On 5 July 1834, the *Perth Gazette* carried an intriguing report of a shipwreck.

a strange report has just reached us, communicated to Parker, of Guildford, by some natives, that a vessel had been seen wrecked on the beach, a considerable distance to the northward. The story has been handed from tribe to tribe until it has reached our natives and runs as follows. We give it of course without implicitly relying on its accuracy, but the account is sufficiently authenticated to excite well-founded suspicions that some accident has happened. It appears the wreck has been lying on shore for 6 moons, or months, and the distance from this is said to be 30 day's journey, or about 400 miles. When the water is low, the natives are said to go on board, and bring from the wreck 'white money'; on money being shown to the native who brought the report, he picked out a dollar, as a similar piece to the money he had seen. Some steps should be immediately taken to establish or refute this statement: the native can soon be found. He is said to be importunate that soldier man, and white man, with horse, should go to the wreck, volunteering to escort them. We shall look with anxiety for further information upon this point.

This news was met with some scepticism, but the following Saturday the paper published a fresh version of the story. In this rendition, the wreck, or 'broke boat', as the Aborigines called it, also had survivors.

The report we gave publicity to last week respecting the supposed wreck of a vessel to the northward, has met with some farther confirmation, and has attracted the attention of the local Government. A Council was held on Wednesday last (we believe) expressly for the purpose of taking this subject into consideration, and, after a diligent inquiry, it was thought expedient to make arrangements for despatching an expedition to the northward, which will be immediately carried into effect. This, the winter season, rendering a land expedition both dangerous, and, in every probability, futile, it has been determined to charter the *Monkey* (a small vessel, now lying in our harbour) to proceed immediately to Shark's Bay, somewhere about the distance described at which the wreck may be expected to be fallen in with, where Mr. H. M. Ommanney, of the Survey Department, and a party under his directions, will be landed to traverse the coast north and south, the *Monkey* remaining as a depot from whence they will draw their supplies, to enable them to extend their search in either direction . . .

. . . The following we believe to be the substance of the information conveyed to the Government: about a week or ten days since, Tonguin and Weenat came to Parker's and gave him and his sons to understand, that they (Tonguin and Weenat) had recently learned from some of the northern tribes (who appear to be indiscriminately referred to under the name of Waylo men, or Weelmen) that a ship was wrecked ('boat broke') on the coast to the northward, about 30 (native) days walk from the Swan—that there was white money plenty lying on the beach for several yards, as thick as seed vessels under a red gum tree. On some article of brass being shewn, they said that was not like the colour of the money; but on a dollar being shewn, they recognized it immediately as the kind of money they meant: but laid the dollar on the ground and drawing a somewhat larger circle round it with the finger, said 'the money was like that'. They represented that the wreck had been seen six moons ago, and that all the white men were dead: none, as it is supposed, having been then seen by their informants, the Weelmen. They added that, at low water, the natives could reach the wreck, which had blankets (sails) flying about it: from which it is presumed that the supposed vessel may not have entirely lost her masts on first striking, and they stuck up three sticks in a manner which led Parker's sons to understand that the wreck they were attempting to describe had three masts, but Parker himself did not infer the same meaning.

A day or two after Tonguin's visit, Moiley Dibbin called at Parker's with further information on the same subject, but derived from the same distant source; namely, the Weelmen. Moiley had been informed by some of the latter that there were several white men, represented to be of very large stature, ladies and 'plenty piccaninnie'—that they were living in houses made of canvas and wood (pointing out these materials, among several shewn to him)—that there are five such houses, two large and three small—that they are not on a river but on the open sea ('Gabby England come')—that the sea coast, at the site of the wreck, takes a bend easterly into an apparent bay (as described by Moiley on the ground)—that the spot where the white money is strewed on the beach is some (indefinite) distance from the spot where the houses are and more within the bay—that the gabby (surf) breaks with very great noise where the money is, and as it runs back, the Weelmen run forward and pick it up—that the white men gave the Weelmen some gentlemen's (white) biscuit, and the latter gave in return spears, shields, &c.—that they, Moiley, Tonguin, and Weenat, had never seen the wreck or the white men, and were afraid to go through the territories of the Weelmen, who are cannibals: but that they intend to go as far as the Waylo country, and then coo-ee to the Weelmen, who will come to meet them and give them some of the white money—and that the white men then could walk to the houses at the wreck in ten days—but though the word walk be used, there can be little doubt that Moiley alludes to a 'walk—on horseback'.

The prospect of rescuing white people from the aftermath of ship-wreck and perhaps the depredations of the 'natives', together with the lure of money, electrified the small settlement. A few months before, some other Aborigines from the north had brought a few British coins into Perth, claiming that they had received them from the fearsome 'Wayl men'. This only increased people's eagerness to find out more, and plans were made for a boat to sail north in search of the wreck.

At this point, a local Aboriginal leader named Weeip enters the story. He had recently been outlawed for his resistance to colonial rule, and his son had been taken as, in effect, a hostage by the administration of Governor James Stirling. Hoping to win his son back, Weeip volunteered to travel north to see what he could discover. He returned in early August, claiming he had been told by the northern people that there were definitely no survivors of the mysterious wreck, but that there was plenty of 'white money'. The settlers were sceptical, but the Governor released Weeip's son all the same in return for Weeip's promise of good behaviour. The *Monkey* returned in October, having found nothing but some worm-eaten teak and fir wreckage on reefs off Dirk Hartog Island.

Meanwhile, however, other odd stories had begun to circulate. In July, soon after the *Perth Gazette*'s first story on the 'wreck', some Aborigines reported that they had contact with a party of whites living about eighty kilometres inland from the Perth colony. As there was no known settlement at that distance from the colony, this was astounding news. Who these people might have been, if they ever existed, is a mystery. Although highly unlikely, it is conceivable that a group had landed unnoticed and trekked inland to settle in the wilds.

It was eventually determined that the shipwreck stories were old. They had been passed from one generation to the next for perhaps a century or more. Stories passed on in this way tend to compress time spans. In this case, the 'broke boat' and the 'white money' did have a basis in fact, but that did not become clear until 1927, when the wreck of the Dutch East Indiaman *Zuytdorp* was first located. She had foundered in 1712, and perhaps thirty survivors had mysteriously disappeared into the continent's vast emptiness. The only evidence of their coming was the wreckage of their craft and a sandy bottom carpeted in silver coins—a scene that bore out the Aboriginal story of 1834.

The stories of Lasseter's Reef and the carpet of silver are local legends that have travelled far from their points of origin. Australia has many other tales of hidden, sunken, buried or otherwise 'lost' treasures that are little known outside their local regions and perhaps to a few enthusiastic treasure hunters.

The dead horse treasure

One frontier lost-treasure yarn has no map, but involves luck, human frailty and the skeleton of a horse.

Brock's Creek is about 160 kilometres southwest of Darwin. A group of men made a lucky strike on a very rich find there in 1880. Swearing off the grog, they worked hard to get as much of the gold into the saddle-packs of one of their horses, before the wet season and lack of food overcame them. Within a week they had the horses saddled and ready to go with a fortune in the saddle-packs. They decided to have one drink to celebrate their good fortune. The one became two and then too many. Their drunken merrymaking frightened the horses away, including the one carrying the gold. Despite months of desperate searching, the men never found the horses which would have perished fairly quickly.

It is said that prospectors in the Northern Territory still look closely at any bones they find in the hope that they may stumble again across the dead horse treasure.

The silver reef

The silver reef is a fabulously rich lode said to be located somewhere in the remote north between Wyndham and King Sound in Western Australia's Kimberley region.

According to one version of the tale, the reef was discovered by a Malay merchant called Hadji Ibrahim some time before European colonisation took place in the area in 1829. After selling a load of silver ore from the trove in Macassar, in what is now Indonesia, Ibrahim returned for more, only to be shipwrecked and drowned. But the merchant had kept a journal of his voyages and recorded all the details of his find—minus its location.

But the story continues. A colourfully named local—'Mad Jack'—was found dead in his cutter in 1909 near Yampi Sound. Several spear wounds had pierced his body and his head had been split open with a tomahawk. The discoverers of the body found a few ounces of gold in the cabin as well as a kerosene tin full of silver ore.

Some years later, an employee of Ibrahim's great grandson became obsessed with the legend of the silver reef and made many visits to the area to find it. He was last seen in 1939 travelling through the Kimberley with a group of Aborigines. As far as anyone knows, the reef is still lost.

Black Jack's booty

Another story in the lost-treasure vein has elements of the classic buccaneer's trove, a staple element of pirate lore.

Long before the permanent European settlement of Western Australia's Swan River Colony in 1829, the southern coasts of Australia attracted mainly American whalers and sealers. The whalers usually based themselves on islands where there were supplies of fresh water, establishing semi-permanent settlements and stocking the islands with livestock, including rabbits. They were often, at least in part, responsible for the subsequent hostilities between the indigenous inhabitants and the settlers who arrived later as they terrorised many of the coastal Aboriginal groups. The oral traditions of these communities still hold tales of narrow escapes from one such identity known as Black Jack.

An African-American, Jack was leader of a gang of sealers and whalers operating during the 1830s. He and his crew of cutthroats were based on Middle Island in the Recherche Archipelago, off what is now Esperance. Piracy was also part of Jack's repertoire and he and his gang were rumoured to have carefully hidden away a horde of treasure for future use. Despite the softening influence of an English lover named Dorothea, Jack was almost as brutal towards his own men as he was to his victims. Eventually, the gang members became sufficiently aggravated by this ill treatment and to shoot Jack in the head while he slept.

But despite frantic searching, the murderers were unable to find where Jack had stashed his loot, and so another lost treasure tradition began, attracting at least one modern day hunt for Black Jack's booty.

FISHER'S
GHOST
POOL.
CAMPBELLTOWN.

1768. K & Co.

5

The haunted land

She'll cross the moonlit road in haste
And vanish down the track;
Her long black hair hangs to her waist
And she is dressed in black...

Henry Lawson, 'The Black Lady of Mount Victoria'

MORE PEOPLE BELIEVE in ghosts than don't, according to researchers. Certainly, stories of hauntings and other ghostly visitations are no less widely told in Australia than anywhere else, and they appear in both European and indigenous traditions.

In Aboriginal lore, as in European, spirits caught between this world and the next are said to trouble the living. Some groups believe ghosts can move between worlds for a time, but must finally separate from the living. Some believe that ghosts have certain places where they await the right moment to leave the living and join their ancestors. Aboriginal people often treat ghosts as everyday realities rather than as unusual or frightening ones.

Stories of European-style ghosts also tend to be associated with particular places. Famous apparitions include the headless ghost of Berrima, New South Wales, and a blue nun who is said to disturb locals from time to time in the monastic town of New Norcia, Western Australia. Haunted houses can be found at Bungaribee, New South Wales; Drysdale, Victoria; and on the River Esk, near Fingal, Tasmania.

Other favoured ghost haunts include shipwrecks, hotels, theatres, jails and other old buildings. A headless diver is said to lurk beneath the Sydney Harbour Bridge—the ghost of a worker who died there. The explorer Robert O'Hara Burke, bushranger Johnny Gilbert and navigator William Dampier are all said to linger in ghostly form.

Fisher's ghost

Australian ghost stories, like many others, often involve violent or unusual deaths. The first such death to produce a ghost in Australia seems to have been that of ex-convict Frederick Fisher, who was murdered and secretly buried at what is now Fishers Creek, New South Wales.

On 17 June 1826, Fred Fisher, the proprietor of the Horse and Groom Hotel near Campbelltown, west of Sydney, was released from prison. He had knifed a customer in a fight at the hotel and been jailed for six months. Fisher had been transported in 1816, at the age of twenty-two, for possessing forged banknotes. He had worked hard in the colony, obtained a ticket-of-leave, and now owned considerable property. After his release, Fisher returned to his hotel—and almost immediately disappeared.

Fisher's neighbour, George Worrall, said he'd returned to England. Since Fisher had expressed no interest in leaving the colony where he was doing so well, locals found this unconvincing. Then Worrall, to whom Fisher had given power of attorney over his farm while serving his sentence, began selling the vanished man's belongings. Documents he produced to prove ownership were shown to be forged, and Worrall was arrested on suspicion of murder. No body, however, was found.

At this point the legend begins. Here is one of its earliest versions, from 1863. The writer has mistakenly named a Mr Hurley as the sighter of the ghost; it was actually a man named Farley.

*A*bout six weeks after Fisher's disappearance, Mr Hurley, a respectable settler in the vicinity of Campbelltown, was returning thence to his residence; he had long been acquainted with Fisher, and it is by no means improbable that his mind reverted to his sudden disappearance, when passing the place where he had so long resided; be that as it may, however, no doubt as to Worrall's statement ever entered his mind.

It was about ten o'clock at night when he left Campbelltown; the moon had risen, but her brilliance was obscured by clouds. After he had passed the late residence of Fisher, about from five to eight hundred yards, he observed the figure of a man sitting on the top of the fence on the same side of the road as the house. On approaching nearer, what was his surprise to recognize distinctly, the features of Fisher, whom he had supposed then far on his way to England. He approached the figure with the intention of assuring himself that he had not been deceived by a fancied resemblance.

The ghastly appearance which the features presented to his view on his nearer approach, struck such a chill of terror to his heart, as chained him motionless to the spot. The figure, as he gazed, rose from the fence, and waving its arm pointed in the direction of a small creek, which crosses the paddock at the place, and disappeared gradually from his view, apparently following the windings of the creek. The terror which overpowered the faculties of Hurley at this sight, defies all powers of description; in a state of stupefaction he left the spot, and endeavoured to obtain an entrance into the nearest house. How he managed to find his way to the house he has no recollection, but just as he approached it, his senses totally forsook him. The noise caused by his head striking the door as he fell, alarmed the inmates, who on opening it found him lying in a death-like swoon; he was carried into the house, where he lay for a whole week in the delirium of a brain fever.

The frequent mention of the name of Fisher in his ravings, attracted the attention of those who attended him, and conjecture was soon busy at work to ascertain what had driven him into such a state; his known character for sobriety, as well as the testimony of those who had parted from him only a few minutes before, forbade the supposition that he had been caused by drunkenness; and rumour, with her thousand tongues, turned the villagers' heads with vain conjectures as to its probable cause.

On the morning of the ninth day of Hurley's illness, he awoke after a long and refreshing sleep, in full possession of his senses, and expressed a wish to those around him that the Police Magistrate should be sent for.

William Howe, Esq., of Glenlee, who then filled the situation of Superintendent of Police for Campbelltown and the surrounding districts, was sent for, and came immediately on being made aware of the circumstances. To him Hurley disclosed what he had seen, and the suspicion of Fisher's having met with foul play, which that sight had impressed on his mind. As soon as Hurley was able to leave his bed, Mr. Howe, accompanied by a few constables, among whom was a native black man named Gilbert, went, conducted by Hurley, to the place where the apparition had been seen. On closely examining the panel of fencing pointed out, Mr Howe discovered spots of blood. An active search was commenced to discover further traces of the supposed murder, but nothing more was observed.

It was thought advisable to trace the course of the creek, in the direction to which the apparition had pointed, and in which it had disappeared. Some small ponds of water still remained in the creek, and these Black Gilbert was directed to explore with his spear; he carefully examined each as he approached it, but the shake of his head denoted his want of success. On approaching a larger pond than any of those he had before searched, the standers by observed his eyes sparkle, as he exclaimed in a tone of triumph, while yet at some distance from the pool, 'white man's fat sit down here'; as soon as he reached the bank of the pond he thrust his spear into the water, and after some search, he pointed to a particular spot in the water, saying 'white man there'. The constables were immediately set to work to clear away the water, which was soon effected—and on digging among the sand the remains of a human being in advanced stage of decomposition were discovered.

It became now obvious to all that Fisher (if the remains which had been found were really his) had met with an untimely end. Suspicion alighted on Worrall, who was the only person who had reaped any benefit from Fisher's death; and it was remembered also that he it was who had first propagated the story of Fisher's return to England. Many circumstances, corroborative of this suspicion, flashed on the minds of the neighbours, which until now had escaped their notice. Mr Howe caused Worrall to be arrested, and the suspicion being confirmed by the body of circumstantial evidence, he was committed to take his trial before the Supreme Court for the murder.

The conviction that retributive justice was now about to overtake him, had such an effect on his mind that he confessed his guilt. His reason for so barbarous a proceeding arose from the transaction mentioned in the former part of the narrative. Fisher, overjoyed at the success of the scheme by which he had defrauded his creditors, forgot to regain possession of the deed of conveyance by which he had made over his property to Worrall. The thought occurred to Worrall, that if he could only get Fisher quietly out of the way, he would be able to claim possession of the property in right of that conveyance; this project had repeatedly occurred to him while Fisher was in jail: and he had resolved even then, either to regain possession of the private agreement which compelled him to restore the property whenever it might be required, or to get rid of him entirely. Foiled in his scheme to obtain possession of this document by Fisher's unexpected liberation, he formed the diabolical scheme, which he ultimately accomplished.

Under the mask of friendship, he was Fisher's companion during the day—and night after night he watched Fisher's motions from the time of this return from jail, but had accidentally been foiled in every attempt he made, until the one on which the murder was committed. On that night he was as usual prowling about Fisher's cottage, looking out for an opportunity to attain his ends, when Fisher, tempted by the beauty of the evening, left his house to take a walk, followed at some distance by Worrall. At the place where the blood was afterwards discovered, Fisher stopped and leant against the fence, apparently wrapped in deep thought. The assassin had now before him the opportunity he had so long waited for, and taking up a broken panel of fence, he stole quietly behind him, and with one blow of his weapon stretched him lifeless on the ground; he carried the body from the scene of the murder to the place where it was afterwards discovered, and buried it deep in the sand. A few weeks after he had made the confession he expiated his crime on the scaffold, imploring with his last breath the forgiveness of his Maker.

No mention of the ghost was made at Worrall's trial, but the story had already gained its own momentum. While there was considerable speculation about whether the helpful ghost had really appeared, the story quickly escaped the confines of local gossip to become one of the nineteenth century's best-known tales. An anonymous ballad version appeared as early as 1832 in a colonial guidebook, quickly followed by articles in colonial periodicals, and even an early history. The story soon made the British and French newspapers, and in 1879 a play based on it was performed at the Sydney School of Arts.

The Scots folklorist Andrew Lang made an exhaustive

investigation of the evidence in the early twentieth century, by which time, he wrote 'Everybody has heard about "Fisher's Ghost". It is one of the stock "yarns" of the world ...' Through some impressively researched comparisons between the Fisher's Ghost tales (whose origins had by then been lost in time), and a number of similar British cases, Lang convincingly argued that the story of the ghost developed rapidly in the locality of the murder. The tale was probably included in the initial evidence put before local magistrates but suppressed, for sound legal reasons, when the case was tried in the Sydney criminal courts. Despite this official silencing (for which Lang also provides some interesting British parallels), the story of the ghost leading authorities to its own murdered body continued to enthral common folk and scholars alike, chiming as it did with other tales and ballads involving ghostly messengers. Campbelltown hosts an annual Fisher's Ghost Festival and enthusiastically promotes the area's connections with the tale. There have also been more plays, an early Australian feature film, even an opera televised by the Australian Broadcasting Corporation in 1963.

The ghost on old Pinjarrah Bridge

One of Western Australia's earliest recorded ghosts died of an apoplectic fit some time during the 1860s. This account is from the early-1870s journal of settler Thomas Scott.

I had occasion during my stay in Pinjarrah to see Mr. C. on some small business transactions. Mr. C. was a near relation of the nocturnal visitant of which we are about to speak. On the third evening of our stay at Mr. Greenacre's Mr. C. paid me a visit. He was a man of firm resolution and would laugh trifles in the face. And a thorough unbeliever in such things as disembodied spirits. On my remarking how unwell he looked he only shook his hand and said, 'No wonder, Sir, for we have seen her again. And this makes the sixth time of her reappearance, and more distinct she appeared than she has on the former occasions.'

'Seen who? may I ask,' said I.

'Seen who?' reiterated Mr. C. 'Why surely, Mr. Margrave, you have not been in Pinjarrah these three days and heard nothing of the Ghost of the old Bridge?'

'Indeed then I have,' I replied. 'But you really don't mean to tell me that you believe in the story? Why, it was only last night, rather late that I came across the old Bridge and met none save one solitary individual, an elderly lady to all appearance who was attired in a light loose dress.'

'My poor Aunt, Mrs. C.,' exclaimed my friend, 'who has been dead for the last seven years, and this is the anniversary of her mysterious death. Why, Mr. Margrave this is the veritable ghost of the old Bridge of which I was just speaking to you, and which makes its nocturnal appearance on the old Bridge every year about this time. Whether it is the disembodied spirit of my aunt, which carries her feature and is recognised by us all, or whether it is but a phantom of the mind, God only knows, for it is very mysterious.'

'Strange, no doubt, as you say,' I ejaculated, 'but I rather think you are labouring under some illusion.'

'No illusion whatever,' said Mr. C., 'it is too true. She walks that old Bridge towards midnight nine days in each year just before and after the anniversary of her death. She has been recognised by her two sisters, her brother John, and Mr. Koil, my uncle.'

'You say she has been dead for the last seven years. May I ask in what manner she met her death?'

'Certainly, Sir,' answered Mr. C. 'She was found dead seven years ago on the old Bridge. She was supposed to have died from an apoplectic fit, but whatever the cause of death was she was interred next day as the weather was too oppressive to keep her any longer than that short time. On the 1st July, one year from the date of her demise, she, or rather her apparition, for I cannot be convinced to the contrary, was first seen by my uncle at midnight walking the old Bridge like a silent sentinel from the place of departed spirits.

'My uncle came home—I remember the night well—just as he had finished telling us what he had seen, three distinct, loud knocks were heard at our back door. It was a beautiful moonlit starry night—not a cloud was seen in the vast blue firmament; and bewildering stillness seemed to reign supreme. There was no time for anybody to have made off nor was there any place of concealment near at hand, as instantaneously we all ran to the door—but there was nothing to be seen and there was not a breath of air stirring. With palpitating hearts and big drops of perspiration on our foreheads we returned to the house. The door was hardly closed when three more knocks louder than the first was heard again, and at the same time we heard as distinctly as possible my uncle's Christian name repeated two or three times outside the door. The sound or voice was that of my aunt, which was recognised by all present. We all stood looking at each other in mute fear and astonishment—terror seemed to sway every heart now beating thrice three times as fast.

'My uncle was the first to break the spell. He rushed to the door, closely followed by myself, as if ashamed of his momentary fear, to behold a tall stately figure of a female clad in a light loose dress similar to that she had on at the time she was found dead on the old Bridge. 'Yes,' said my uncle, in a tremulous hoarse voice, 'Yes, that is my sister Kate or her apparition which I saw on the old Bridge.' She was walking or rather slowly gliding as it were in the direction of the old Bridge, which is about a quarter of a mile from our farm. My uncle instinctively shouted out 'Kate,' his sister's name. But, as if by magic, on her name being called she immediately disappeared from our view. We all proceeded to the old Bridge with the expectation of seeing the apparition there, for we were all fully convinced now that the figure was nothing else, but we were disappointed. None of us slept that night but kept a vigil till morning.

'On the third night after this the apparition was seen again but could not be approached by my uncle. Finally it disappeared altogether until the following year, about the same time, it made its reappearance again. Each succeeding year to the present one has brought us the ghostly visits of my deceased aunt, and for what purpose is to us as yet a mystery.'

'You say', said I, 'that the apparition is to be seen on the old Bridge but will not be approached; must I understand by that it disappears on your approach to it?'

'Precisely so,' answered Mr. C. 'And', he went on, 'if you, Mr. Margrave, have no objection you are welcome to join our little private party who are going to watch for it to-night.'

'I shall be too glad to accept your offer,' I replied; 'and I only hope I shall have a glimpse of your nocturnal visitant. May I bring a friend?'

'Certainly, with pleasure—half a dozen if you like—the more the merrier.'

The hour appointed by the C. party for apprising the apparition was fixed at midnight, that being the accustomed time of its first appearance. On my informing Mr. M. of our midnight adventure and the object it had in view, he most readily assented to accompany me, saying at the same time, 'And, by my soul, if it were a ghost we'd better be after letting the poor creature rest, faith, or may be it will be giving us a turn as well as its own people, sure. But no matter, go we will and if it should turn out to be some spalpeen night-walking, that wants waking, faith an' we'll give him a good ducking in the river that runs under the old Bridge.'

According to previous arrangements, half-past eleven that night found our small midnight party, comprising five in all, at our respective positions. The night was beautifully starlit with a full moon coursing in the heavens above. To the right of the Bridge was a burying ground and on either side of this lay nothing but the dark, dense forest, that looked in this lonesome hour the very place for a ghost scene.

Twelve o'clock came and—no apparition appeared—a quarter-past twelve—half-past—and now five-and-twenty minutes to one and yet no appearance. We were literally counting the minutes after twelve but to no effect.

'Bad luck to it,' exclaimed Mr. M. 'I believe after all it will turn out nothing more than a hoax, sure.'

'Well,' said I, 'never mind, Mr. M., we will keep it up till one o'clock, then we'll give it up as a—————.'

'Hist. Look!' interrupted Mr. M. 'By my soul, but there's somebody coming over the Bridge.'

On looking at my watch I found it was just twenty minutes to one. Scarcely had the last word died on Mr. M's lips when from four different quarters we advanced as previously arranged, with stealthy step (like 'stealing a march') toward the Bridge. A slight thrill ran through me as I clearly recognised the same figure I had seen the night previous. The old Bridge was a wooden construction about 50 yards long, with railing on each side as a protection to the dark waters beneath. We were not twenty yards from the apparition when on the deathly stillness of the surrounding dark-looking forest broke the prolonged and mournful howl of a dingo or native dog, causing us to fairly start. But it was only momentarily. Mr. M. and myself arrived at one end of the Bridge whilst at the other end appeared at the same time the C. party.

The apparition was in the centre of the Bridge and seemed to be on the move. It was quite recognisable by all parties and the same that has already been described. We instinctively stopped to watch it for a few minutes. The signal was given by the other party to apprise it, and simultaneously we all rushed to the spot where the apparition stood, visible as plain as day, and—aghast, we stood gaping at each other scarcely believing our own eyes. The figure whether earthly or spiritual had vanished. Five men whom I am in a position to prove were in their sane senses witnessed the mysterious—what shall we call it?—a delusion?—a phenomenon?—or what the world in the nineteenth century laughs at as gross superstition, viz., a ghost or spirit of the departed.

⌒

Although Scott doesn't say, it seems this was the last time that Kate was seen walking the old bridge, which was washed away in a flood some years later.

A Vice-Regal haunting

Yarralumla, the Governor-General's official residence in Canberra, was already said to be haunted when it became government property in the early twentieth century. As the recounter of this chronologically confused version of the tale puts it, 'Here is all the material for a five-reel movie drama.'

*W*hen the Governor-general goes into residence at Yarralumla House, his temporary home at Canberra, he will find that with the old house goes a tale of mystery. According to more or less conflicting versions of the tale, a ghost, a real Australian blackfellow ghost, has been known to walk, but—well, ghosts are rather out of date, anyway.

The story begins with a jewel robbery, tells of a big diamond passed to the robber's friend, and afterwards to the friend's son, and ends with bushrangers, and the murder of a trusty blackfellow. Here is all the material for a five-reel movie drama.

The skeleton of the blackfellow, so the story goes, lies at the foot of a big deodar, nearly a hundred years old, which is the pride of Yarralumla.

The record of the mystery is an old letter or manuscript, unsigned, dated 1881, 'written near Yarralumla', and it was left, no doubt overlooked and forgotten, by the former owners when the place was handed over to the Government. The homestead has been a hostel for members of Parliament, Government officials, and approved visitors, since the Canberra project has been in hand and many visitors have read the tale. It is a rambling story, and you may believe or not, as you like. Here it is :—

'In 1826, a large diamond was stolen from James Cobbity, on an obscure station in Queensland. The theft was traced to one of the convicts who had run away, probably to New South Wales. The convict was captured in 1858, but the diamond could not be traced; neither would the convict (name unknown) give any information, in spite of frequent floggings. During 1842 he left a statement to a groom, and a map of the hiding-place of the hidden diamond.

'The groom, for a minor offence, was sent to Berrima gaol. He was clever with horses, and one day, when left to his duties, plaited a rope of straw and then escaped by throwing it over the wall, where he caught an iron bar. Passing it over, he swung himself down and escaped. He and his family lived out west for several years, according to the Rev. James Hassall who, seeing him live honestly, did not think it necessary to inform against him. I have no reason to think he tried to sell the diamond. Probably the ownership of a thing so valuable would bring suspicion and lead to his re-arrest.

'After his death his son took possession of the jewel, and with a trusty blackfellow set off for Sydney.

'After leaving Cooma for Queanbeyan they met with, it was afterwards ascertained, a bushranging gang. The blackfellow and his companion became separated, and finally the former was captured and searched, to no avail, for he had swallowed the jewel.

'The gang, in anger, shot him. He was buried in a piece of land belonging to Colonel Gibbes, and later Mr. Campbell. I believe the diamond to be among his bones. It is of great value.

'My hand is enfeebled with age, or I should describe the trouble through which I have passed. My life has been wasted, my money expended, I die almost destitute, and in sight of my goal.

'I believe the grave to be under the large deodar-tree. Being buried by blacks, it would be in a round hole. I enclose my dwindling fortune . . .'

⌒

It is said that the ghost of the murdered Aboriginal haunts the grounds of Yarralumla looking for the lost diamond. Some accounts claim that he has been seen digging at the roots of the ancient deodar tree, thought to be the finest example of its type in the country.

The Black Lady of Mount Victoria

In 1841 Caroline Collits, of Little Hartley in the New South Wales Blue Mountains, left her husband William and went to live with John Walsh and his wife. Caroline and Walsh had been lovers before her marriage and, with the apparent blessing of Walsh's wife, resumed their relationship. Early the next year, Caroline and the two men met for a drink at a local tavern in an attempt to reconcile their differences. But the meeting did not go well. The men fought, and William ran off into the night, leaving Walsh and Caroline alone together. The next morning the postman found her battered body by the roadside, her skull smashed in with a large rock. Walsh was arrested and protested his innocence, but he was hanged for the crime at Bathurst a few months later.

Caroline's ghost has since been seen many times near Mount Victoria. She is said to be dressed in black, often with blazing eyes and outstretched arms and is sometimes followed by a hearse drawing four black horses. At least one report claimed the ghost had laid a curse upon the village of Mt Victoria. Today, the ghost is often sighted by truck drivers on the Victoria Pass road.

Henry Lawson became well acquainted with the story of the Black Lady when he lived in the area during the 1880s, and used it in his poem 'The Ghost at the Second Bridge'. His tongue-in-cheek tone, however, suggests he was more than a little sceptical. The 'Second Bridge' refers to a convict-built, stone-lined section of the road through Victoria Pass.

You'd call the man a senseless fool,
    A blockhead or an ass,
Who'd dare to say he saw the ghost
    Of Mount Victoria Pass;
But I believe the ghost is there,
    For, if my eyes are right,
I saw it once upon a ne'er-
    To-be-forgotten night.

'Twas in the year of eighty-nine—
    The day was nearly gone,
The stars were shining, and the moon
    Is mentioned further on;
I'd tramped as far as Hartley Vale,
    Tho' tired at the start,
But coming back I got a lift
    In Johnny Jones's cart.

'Twas winter on the mountains then—
    The air was rather chill,
And so we stopped beside the inn
    That stands below the hill.
A fire was burning in the bar,
    And Johnny thought a glass
Would give the tired horse a spell
    And help us up the Pass.

Then Jimmy Bent came riding up—
    A tidy chap was Jim—
He shouted twice, and so of course
    We had to shout for him.
And when at last we said good-night
    He bet a vulgar quid
That we would see the 'ghost in black',
    And sure enough we did.

And as we climbed the stony pinch
    Below the Camel Bridge,
We talked about the 'Girl in black'
    Who haunts the Second Bridge.
We reached the fence that guards the cliff
    And passed the corner post,
And Johnny like a senseless fool
    Kept harping on the ghost.

'She'll cross the moonlit road in haste
    And vanish down the track;
Her long black hair hangs to her waist
    And she is dressed in black;
Her face is white, a dull dead white—
    Her eyes are opened wide—
She never looks to left or right,
    Or turns to either side.'

I didn't b'lieve in ghosts at all,
    Tho' I was rather young,
But still I wished with all my heart
    That Jack would hold his tongue.
The time and place, as you will say,
    ('Twas twelve o'clock almost)—

Were both historically fa-
    Vourable for a ghost.

But have you seen the Second Bridge
    Beneath the 'Camel's Back'?
It fills a gap that broke the ridge
    When convicts made the track;
And o'er the right old Hartley Vale
    In homely beauty lies,
And o'er the left the mighty walls
    Of Mount Victoria rise.

And there's a spot above the bridge,
    Just where the track is steep,
From which poor Convict Govett rode
    To christen Govett's Leap;
And here a teamster killed his wife—
    For those old days were rough—
And here a dozen others had
    Been murdered, right enough.

The lonely moon was over all
    And she was shining well,
At angles from the sandstone wall
    The shifting moonbeams fell.
In short, the shifting moonbeams beamed,
    The air was still as death,
Save when the listening silence seemed
    To speak beneath its breath.

The tangled bushes were not stirred
    Because there was no wind,
But now and then I thought I heard
    A startling noise behind.

Then Johnny Jones began to quake;
    His face was like the dead.
'Don't look behind, for heaven's sake!
    The ghost is there!' he said.

He stared ahead—his eyes were fixed;
    He whipped the horse like mad.
'You fool!' I cried, 'you're only mixed;
    A drop too much you've had.
I'll never see a ghost, I swear,
    But I will find the cause.'
I turned to see if it was there,
    And sure enough it was!

Its look appeared to plead for aid
    (As far as I could see),
Its hands were on the tailboard laid,
    Its eyes were fixed on me.
The face, it cannot be denied
    Was white, a dull dead white,
The great black eyes were opened wide
    And glistened in the light.

I stared at Jack; he stared ahead
    And madly plied the lash.
To show I wasn't scared, I said—
    'Why, Jack, we've made a mash.'
I tried to laugh; 'twas vain to try.
    The try was very lame;
And, tho' I wouldn't show it, I
    Was frightened, all the same.

'She's mashed,' said Jack, 'I do not doubt,
    But 'tis a lonely place;

And then you see it might turn out
    A breach of promise case.'
He flogged the horse until it jibbed
    And stood as one resigned,
And then he struck the road and ran
    And left the cart behind.

Now, Jack and I since infancy
    Had shared our joys and cares,
And so I was resolved that we
    Should share each other's scares.
We raced each other all the way
    And never slept that night,
And when we told the tale next day
    They said that we were—intoxicated.

The Murdering Sandhill

A perhaps now worn-out legend from the gold-rush days is known by the chilling title of 'The Murdering Sandhill'. It is said that during the 1860s two brothers named Pohlman or Pollman were murdered in the sandhills near Narandera—as the name of the town was spelt in those days—in New South Wales. The victims were carrying a large amount of money, perhaps from gold-mining activities, and were robbed and killed by a number of men who were hawking goods in the area.

In the *Town and Country Journal* of 23 April 1881, a correspondent named 'The Raven' described his journey by Cobb & Co coach from Narandera to the town of Hay, which was located about one hundred and eighty kilometres to the west.

*N*arandera being on the high road from Sydney to the Mount Brown diggings via Hay, I took the precaution to give in my name for a seat in the coach two or three days beforehand, as every train to Narandera brings in numbers of eager travelers, whose first words on stepping on to the platform are, 'Where is Cobb and Co's booking office?' and although the coach leaves for Hay three times a week, the proprietors have had occasion once or twice to put on an extra vehicle.

At 1.30 p.m. we were being slowly dragged through the Narandera sand by four fine greys. With the exception of myself, the passengers were diggers, off for Mount Brown, regardless of warning, most of them having come away from Temora in disgust, and having left tons weight of unwashed dirt behind, which, however, they did not leave without registering. By-the-bye, going from Temora to Mount Brown, seems to me very like the proverbial jumping from the frying pan into the fire, as reports from the latter are, up to the present, anything but cheerful, the water being exhausted, and not much prospect of any more just yet; but the Australian digger is, and always will be, a roving kind of investigator, who would rather do anything than sit still and wait.

On leaving Narandera the coach track takes a parallel course midway between the river and the railway, until we get to a place known as 'The Murdering Sandhill', where the terrible tragedy of the Pohlmann Brothers' murder took place some 12 or 13 years back; it will be remembered that after the murder the bodies were burnt, and only a few ashes were recovered; the spot is marked by an enclosure. Here the coach road diverges from the railway line.

∽

Although 'The Raven' reported no sounds, the rumoured hauntings were mainly auditory in nature, consisting of the creaking and rumbling sounds of the ghostly hawker's wagon used by the murderers to transport their victims, whose bodies were then burned to ashes.

Another auditory haunting—known as 'the ghost cattle of Yallourn'—still occurs in the Gippsland Hills in Victoria. During the middle of the nineteenth century, a cattle stampede almost destroyed the town of Moe. Since then, many have heard the sounds of cattle moving around but no cows can be seen. Local explanations of these sounds include earth movements associated with the open cut coal mines at Yallourn, adjacent to Moe.

The rabbi and the roseate pearl

Broome, in Western Australia's north, has a history that is romantic but violent and which is one of greed, exploitation and oppression. The pearling trade was established there from the 1860s and governed the growth of the town and its restless multicultural population for decades.

With such an exotic history it is not surprising that Broome also has a rich tradition of lore and legend, including ghost stories. One of these is known as 'the pearler's light'. According to the tale there is a beacon on the Broome foreshore that dims unaccountably from time to time. No cause of this mysterious phenomenon has ever been found, despite the light having been overhauled on many occasions. No natural occurrence, such as mist, appears to be the reason behind the light's dimming and it is said that the ghosts of drowned pearlers creeping around the beacon on certain nights of the year cause the light to fade.

Broome has an even more romantic tradition about a possibly mythical but highly valuable yet cursed red pearl, going by the name of 'the roseate pearl', and the ghost of a rabbi. Abraham Davis was a prominent Jewish entrepreneur in the pearling industry around the turn of the nineteenth century with a substantial home in Broome. He was drowned off Port Hedland, along with all other passengers and crew in the wreck of the *Koombana*, on 20 March 1912. His fine house later became the grand residence of the first Anglican Bishop of the northwest, Bishop Gerard Trower (1860–1928).

One night, Bishop Trower awoke to see a ghostly figure standing in a pool of light. The figure was dressed in the garments of a rabbi. When the Bishop called to the figure it promptly vanished. The same figure was seen by others on numerous occasions, usually late in the afternoon or early in the evening. In 1957 the house was demolished, and there have been no sightings reported since.

A link between this particular haunting and another item of pearling folklore was suggested by the writer Ion Idriess. In his book *Forty Fathoms Deep* (1937), Idriess puts forward the possibility that the ill-fated Davis was carrying with him the allegedly priceless 'roseate pearl'. According to the legend, this pearl had been secured in Broome by Davis for the enormous sum of twenty thousand pounds. It is said to be still with his bones at the bottom of the sea in the wreck of the *Koombana*.

As with many other precious stones and minerals, as well as priceless treasures of antiquity and lost gold mines, it is believed that this pearl has a curse upon it that brings ill-luck to its possessor and there are stories that it has been implicated in several deaths. Ion Idriess made an excellent living for many years as the writer of romantic adventure stories. He had a vivid imagination.

It is often the case with supernatural traditions that the number of ghosts present at any haunted site seems to increase over the years, along with the details of the legend. This is very much in accordance with the growth of folk traditions generally, and even a casual reader of ghost tales and hauntings will have noticed the similarities between them. In the case of the Davis house at Broome, there is also a tradition that it was haunted by the ghost of a Portuguese sea captain.

The ghosts of Garth

On the banks of the River Esk, near Fingal, are the ruins of
Tasmania's most haunted house: a mid-nineteenth century residence
named Garth. In and around the remains of the house many claim
to have heard the moans of troubled spirits, and the place has a
number of well-documented, if confused, hauntings. One concerns
a spurned lover, the other a terrified child.

The sad history of Garth is one of early hope, and eventual
tragedy and decay. The house was constructed by Charles Peters,
who had been the tenant of a small farm in Scotland of the same
name. Peters arrived in Tasmania in 1823 and began to make a
new life for himself. He married Susan Wilson in Launceston and
in 1830 was granted 320 acres of land near Fingal. They named
the property and began to build a large stone house. In 1840, the
couple's two-year-old daughter Ann died and was buried on the
property, where her grave can still be seen. By 1843, Garth was a
substantial landholding with eight workers and their families. In
later years the property suffered a number of fires that severely
damaged the house. Today, only suitably spooky ruins remain,
attracting ghost hunters and tourists.

The earliest ghost is said to be that of a young settler who
purchased the still-unfinished house at Garth for his intended
bride waiting in England. When he returned from the antipodes
to marry his fiancée he found she had jilted him for another.
Desolate, the man returned to the house and hanged himself
in the courtyard. Ever since then, the disappointed young man's
shade has wandered through the remains of the courtyard crying
out for his inconstant love.

Some years after the settler hanged himself, a young girl died
in a well near the abandoned house. The girl was in the care of
a convict woman who had apparently threatened her with being
thrown into the well if she misbehaved. On this occasion the

girl did something wrong and, fleeing from her convict nanny in unreasoning fear of the threatened punishment, fell into the well. Trying to save her, the convict woman was drowned along with the child. Both lie buried at Garth and the cries of the girl and her would-be saviour can still be heard on dark nights.

Over the years, the details of what were different characters and separate events have twined together. What remains is a bush gothic tradition of lost love, tragedy and destruction.

'Mad Dog' Morgan's ghost

Stories of headless apparitions are usually associated with British hauntings, but Australia has adapted the tradition to the bush experience. A headless horseman who rides through the ranges around Woodend in Victoria is said to be the ghost of the notorious bushranger 'Mad Dog' Morgan.

Daniel Morgan (thought to be Jack Fuller c. 1830–1865) carried out robberies and murder along the Victorian–New South Wales border between 1863 and 1865. His wildly unpredictable behaviour careened between extreme violence and tender care for his victims, leading to the unenviable nickname of 'Mad Dog'. His more considerate acts also earned him the contradictory title of 'the traveller's friend' as he would occasionally stand workers a drink of their boss's grog and inquire whether they were being properly treated. He was also considerate to women and was said to have occasionally returned part of the money he had stolen from his victims to help them complete their journey.

Morgan met his end at Peechelba station, north of Wangaratta, on 9 April 1865 when he was gunned down from behind by John Wendlan. The body was publicly displayed, photographed, shaved and then beheaded. At that time, medical interest in the shape of a criminal's head—the new 'science' of phrenology—meant that many were decapitated for study after their execution, as occurred with Ned Kelly. The treatment of Morgan's corpse, though, was an act of savagery that led to heavy censure of the police involved and also helped establish the legend of Morgan's headless rides through the bush.

Most bushrangers who have entered our folklore have a range of standard stories associated with their lives and afterlives. These include their buried loot, places where they allegedly hid out from pursuers and even the belief that they were not really killed or executed but somehow managed to elude these fates and escape to a faraway region or country to live out their lives in respectable obscurity. 'Mad Dog' Morgan is the subject of similar local speculation.

At the anniversary of Morgan's death, a woman dressed in black placed flowers on the bushranger's grave in Wangaratta cemetery. After her supposed death, the tradition was kept up by two local women, though now using plastic flowers. His stolen treasure is believed to have been buried at the bottom of Glenholm Hill. As far as anyone knows, it has never been found. It is said that Morgan's hideout was at Hanging Rock in Victoria, where a rust red underground stream runs. The water from the stream is known as 'Morgan's blood'.

The headless drover

Another headless horseman is the shape of a drover named Doyle who died of unknown causes at the Black Swamp in the Deniliquin–Moulamein–Bourke region of New South Wales sometime in the 1850s. Since then, overlanders camping there reported seeing his ghost, wrapped in a cloak but without a head, mounted on a short-legged horse. The phantom rode through the drovers' camp at night, terrifying dogs, men and cattle, usually causing a stampede. As well as the inconvenience caused by the stampedes, the belief grew that a sighting of the headless drover foretold their own fates and so the overlanders stopped camping in the area.

A further element of the story is that a Moulamein butcher, in cahoots with local publicans, sensed a business opportunity in these strange tales. Whenever the butcher heard that a mob of cattle was on the way through the area he would kit himself out to look like the ghostly drover, complete with a light wooden frame, cloak and concealed head. Wearing this contraption, he would ride into the cattle camp at night and cause a stampede. Disappearing into the darkness and confusion, he would dispose of his disguise, pick out a few choice beasts from the scattered herd and drive them to a secure location to be butchered for future sale. So well connected was the butcher that his duffing operation was never troubled by the police. It could, perhaps, be said that he had a head for business.

6

Tales of wonder

...and if they didn't live happy, we may.

Simon McDonald concluding 'The Witches Tale'

WHAT WE NOW call fairy tales did not exist until the seventeenth century, when French writers invented the form for the entertainment of an increasingly literate middle class. Many fairy tales were based on more down-to-earth folk tales, which had generally been told aloud rather than written down.

In an 1852 issue of Charles Dickens' magazine *Household Words*, a writer—clearly of middle-class background—reflected on his experiences as a convict in Australia, including the way he and fellow inmates whiled away the hours after lock-up each night:

> It was a strange thing, and full of matter for reflection, to hear men, in whose rough tones I sometimes recognized the most stolid and hardened of the prisoners, gravely narrating an imperfect version of such childish stories as 'Jack the Giant-Killer', for the amusement of their companions, who with equal gravity, would correct him from their own recollections, or enter into a ridiculous discussion on some of the facts.

By the start of the twentieth century, Australia had its own tales of fairies flitting, often rather unconvincingly, through the bush. More successful were works that invested the country's native plants and animals with magical qualities, such as Ethel Pedley's *Dot and the Kangaroo* and the lovable gumnut babies of *Snugglepot and Cuddlepie*, by May Gibbs, in which the villians were big, bad Banksia Men.

Henny-Penny

Children have always delighted in word play, in stories propelled by repetition and rhyme. The fable of Henny-Penny is a perennial favourite. Australian folklorist Joseph Jacobs transcribed this version he'd heard in Australia during the 1860s. It is still popular today.

*O*ne day Henny-penny was picking up corn in the cornyard when—whack!—something hit her upon the head. 'Goodness gracious me!' said Henny-penny; 'the sky's a-going to fall; I must go and tell the king.'

So she went along, and she went along and she went along, till she met Cocky-locky. 'Where are you going, Henny-penny?' says Cocky-locky. 'Oh! I'm going to tell the king the sky's a-falling,' says Henny-penny. 'May I come with you?' says Cocky-locky. 'Certainly,' says Henny-penny. So Henny-penny and Cocky-locky went to tell the king the sky was falling.

They went along, and they went along, and they went along, till they met Ducky-daddles. 'Where are you going to, Henny-penny and Cocky-locky?' says Ducky-daddles. 'Oh! we're going to tell the king the sky's a-falling,' said Henny-penny and Cocky-locky. 'May I come with you?' says Ducky-daddles. 'Certainly,' said Henny-penny and Cocky-locky. So Henny-penny, Cocky-locky, and Ducky-daddles went to tell the king the sky was a-falling.

So they went along, and they went along, and they went along, till they met Goosey-poosey. 'Where are you going to, Henny-penny, Cocky-locky, and Ducky-daddles?' said Goosey-poosey. 'Oh! we're going to tell the king the sky's a-falling,' said Henny-penny and Cocky-locky and Ducky-daddles. 'May I come with you?' said Goosey-poosey. 'Certainly,' said Henny-penny, Cocky-locky, and Ducky-daddles. So Henny-penny, Cocky-locky, Ducky-daddles, and Goosey-poosey went to tell the king the sky was a-falling.

So they went along, and they went along, and they went along, till they met Turkey-lurkey. 'Where are you going, Henny-penny, Cocky-locky, Ducky-daddles, and Goosey-poosey?' says Turkey-lurkey. 'Oh! we're going to tell the king the sky's a-falling,' said Henny-penny, Cocky-locky, Ducky-daddles, and Goosey-poosey. 'May I come with you, Henny-penny, Cocky-locky, Ducky-daddles, and Goosey-poosey?' said Turkey-lurkey. 'Oh, certainly, Turkey-lurkey,' said Henny-penny, Cocky-locky, Ducky-daddles, and Goosey-poosey. So Henny-penny, Cocky-locky, Ducky-daddles, Goosey-poosey, and Turkey-lurkey all went to tell the king the sky was a-falling.

So they went along, and they went along, and they went along, till they met Foxy-woxy, and Foxy-woxy said to Henny-penny, Cocky-locky, Ducky-daddles, Goosey-poosey, and Turkey-lurkey, 'Where are you going, Henny-penny, Cocky-locky, Ducky-daddles, Goosey-poosey, and Turkey-lurkey?' And Henny-penny, Cocky-locky, Ducky-daddles, Goosey-poosey, and Turkey-lurkey said to Foxy-woxy: 'We're going to tell the king the sky's a-falling.'

'Oh! But this is not the way to the king, Henny-penny, Cocky-locky, Ducky-daddles, Goosey-poosey, and Turkey-lurkey,' says Foxy-woxy; 'I know the proper way; shall I show it you?'

'Oh, certainly, Foxy-woxy,' said Henny-penny, Cocky-locky, Ducky-daddles, Goosey-poosey, and Turkey-lurkey. So Henny-penny, Cocky-locky, Ducky-daddles, Goosey-poosey, Turkey-lurkey, and Foxy-woxy all went to tell the king the sky was a-falling.

So they went along, and they went along, and they went along, till they came to a narrow and dark hole. Now this was the door of Foxy-woxy's cave. But Foxy-woxy said to Henny-penny, Cocky-locky, Ducky-daddles, Goosey-poosey, and Turkey-lurkey, 'This is the short way to the king's palace: you'll soon get there if you follow me. I will go first and you come after, Henny-penny, Cocky-locky, Ducky-daddles, Goosey-poosey, and Turkey-lurkey.' 'Why of course, certainly, without doubt, why not?' said Henny-penny, Cocky-locky, Ducky-daddles, Goosey-poosey, and Turkey-lurkey.

So Foxy-woxy went into his cave, and he didn't go very far, but turned round to wait for Henny-penny, Cocky-locky, Ducky-daddles, Goosey-poosey, and Turkey-lurkey. So at last at first Turkey-lurkey went through the dark hole into the cave. He hadn't got far when 'Hrumph,' Foxy-woxy snapped off Turkey-lurkey's head and threw his body over his left shoulder. Then Goosey-poosey went in, and 'Hrumph,' off went her head and Goosey-poosey was thrown beside Turkey-lurkey. Then Ducky-daddles waddled down, and 'Hrumph,' snapped Foxy-woxy, and Ducky-daddles' head was off and Ducky-daddles was thrown alongside Turkey-lurkey and Goosey-poosey. Then Cocky-locky strutted down into the cave, and he hadn't gone far when 'Snap, Hrumph!' went Foxy-woxy and Cocky-locky was thrown alongside of Turkey-lurkey, Goosey-poosey, and Ducky-daddles.

But Foxy-woxy had made two bites at Cocky-locky, and when the first snap only hurt Cocky-locky, but didn't kill him, he called out to Henny-penny. But she turned tail and off she ran home, so she never told the king the sky was a-falling.

The witch's tale

Simon McDonald was a bushman-musician who lived in a slab hut in rural Victoria and performed traditional songs and folk tales. In 1967, folklorists Hugh and Dawn Anderson recorded him spinning, from many Irish wonder tales, this magical saga, which he Australianised as he went with bush slang and interspersed comments. By turns serious and tongue-in-cheek, McDonald mixed shape shifting, cannibalism and sorcery to make something entirely new. Stories like this are a hint of what fairy tales were in the days when they were still adult entertainments.

*I*n the Underworld—well, what that means I don't even know, because there was no underworld in those days, but these witches lived underground, that's how it was called, and the underworld these days is a crook business, isn't it? But not those days, and there was a great horse there called Black Entire. He was worth a thousand pounds, and that was a lot of money. And no one could get it and they were all out trying to pinch him.

There was an old woman there—I don't know what her name was, but she had three sons, Pat and Jack and Jim. They lived with her and she used to go out scrubbing and washing every day till she said, 'Well, I can't feed you no longer, you got to go out in the world and earn your own living.' So they said, 'Well, we don't know, Mother, we don't like leaving you.' 'Oh, well,' she said, 'we'll play a game of cards.' Those days you played a game of cards and if you had a wish, whoever had the wish won and you'd have to carry out that wish—oh, yes, it would be disgraceful—whatever the wish was, it had to be carried on.

So they put the cards on the table, and I think Jim won the first wish. 'Right!' he said. 'I won this,' he said. 'Plenty to eat and drink on the table.' That was his wish. The old mother was sitting there with them. Anyhow, the next game of cards they played again, Pat won. 'Plenty to eat and drink on the table' was his wish. Jack won the third and Jack said, 'I'll leave my wish till last, if you don't mind.' There was a law them days that you could leave your wish till last.

Then the fourth one, the old woman won, the mother. She said, 'Look, I wish that you never sleep two nights in the one place or have two feeds on the one spot till you bring back to me the Black Entire from Bryan O'Ville in the Underworld.' It was the most famous horse was ever known in Ireland. It was owned by three witches, and nobody ever come back alive that ever went for it, you see, or tried to get it off them.

So 'Righto, Mother,' they said. Well, Jack said, 'Now I've left my wish till last.' He said, 'Now, what I wish [is] you'd get up on that steeple there in the church and you'd stand there with a sheaf of hay on one side of you and a needle the other side and all you'll eat is what blows through the eye of that needle till we bring back the Black Entire from Bryan O'Ville in the Underworld.' It had to be carried out—all the wishes them days—oh, it was legal.

She got up on the tower saying, 'You bring with you a horse, a hawk and a hound. You'll all have a horse, hawk and a hound, you know, to go with you.' Where they got the horse, hawk and a hound, I don't know. Anyhow, she got up on the tower, and they seen her get up there. And they put a sheaf of hay on the other side of her, and she had a needle in the other hand, and that's the last they seen of her the other side. And they said, 'Well, she's not getting much till we get back.'

They went along the road and they took them, the horse, hawk and hound—and, of course, as far as the hawk, the hawk would perch upon their shoulder in them days; that was part of a man's protection. They didn't have rifles, guns or anything else. And the first man that went along the road was Pat, you see. He went along on his horse with his hawk and his hound, and it went day on and day on, and he hadn't had a bite to eat. And it come towards night and he said, 'I'll camp in this patch of the woods tonight.' There's an old hut there, sort of empty, and he said, 'I'd better camp here anyhow, and I'll tie my horse up.' He got in and he said, 'I'll light a fire. I've got nothing much to eat.' But all of a sudden there was a man come along with a mob of sheep, and as soon as he lay down and went to sleep, Pat said, 'I'll have one of his sheep.'

He come out with his knife and he cut a sheep's throat and he roasted a bit, fair on the fire—there was no cooking pots or anything there. He just got it half roasted when he heard a knock on the door—knock, knock. 'I'm old, cold and feeble, will you let me in?' Anyhow he said, 'Yes. Come in, well, old lady, come in quick, you'll die of the cold.' 'Oh! But I'm frightened of your horse, hawk and hound. Here's three bits of cord to tie them up with.' And she pulled three hairs out of her head. 'Oh,' he said, 'They won't touch you.' 'Well, just tie them up to please me,' she said. So he tied them up, much to his own misfortune after, because they were magic hairs.

Then she said, 'I'm starving with the hunger, will you give me something to eat?' 'Oh, righto,' he said. 'Poor old lady, I've got a sheep on the fire I'm just cooking, and you can have a bit off that.' Anyhow, he could see she was getting a bit restless and as he had it half-cooked he said, 'Well, there's a forequarter, you can have that.' She gulped it down as fast as she could and she said, 'Oh, I feel strong now.' He hadn't time to have a bite, hardly, so he said, 'What did you do with that?' 'Oh, I ate it and I'm still starving with hunger. More meat!'

'Look,' he said, 'I just give you a forequarter, but you can have another one.' So he cut another off the grilled sheep that he's got on the fire still cooking, and he watched her devouring that, and he said, 'Madam, my God! That's awful, I never seen a woman eat like that in my life.' She said, 'More meat!' She was getting stronger and stronger and he got a bit suspicious then. He thought, this is a queer business, this.

'Well,' she said, 'more meat, or else fight.' 'I don't like fighting women,' he said, 'and I've only got one leg left for myself and you're not getting that—you've ate the rest of the sheep.' 'Well,' she said 'more meat, or else fight.' Pat said, 'Fight you must have, then.' And they pulled out their swords—them days they fought with swords—but it wasn't long till she chopped his head off. She was a witch, you see, she had a magic sword and she cut his head clean off. That was the end of poor old Pat.

Jim come along and he met the same fate. The same mob of sheep and everything. But when Jack come along the road the next day, he was looking along and he seen a bit of grass growing like rope, and he thought he'd put these few bits in his pocket, as they might do to tie the horse up and that, you see. He's a wary man, Jack was. He had a look along there and he came to the same place on the same night somehow—you know, days after it. And he slept there and he saw the same man coming with the same mob of sheep, and then he was inside cooking this sheep as usual and he heard a knock at the door.

'I'm old, cold and feeble, will you let me in?' 'Yes,' Jack said, 'come in.' 'No, but I'm frightened of your horse, hawk and hound. Here's three little bits of cord to tie them up with.' 'All right,' he said, 'but they won't touch you.' 'Oh yeah, but just do it to please me.' 'Right,' he said, 'I'll do it to please you.' And he threw the three hairs in the fire—he was a bit suspicious of witches, you see. In them days there were numerous witches in Ireland, hundreds of them perhaps, we don't know. They've died out, I think, to the present day. Anyhow, he threw hers in the fire and he tied them up with his own three bits of rope—the rushes what he brought along the road. He just tied them up to please her, you know.

So while he was cooking his sheep and that, you know, she starts screaming with the hunger and wanting meat and everything. And he says, 'All right.' It come down that she ate three-quarters of the sheep. She said, 'More meat, or else I'll fight you.' Now, you don't often hear an old woman saying that, at her age. Those days, though, they were tough, you see. And he could see her getting stronger and stronger. Jack said to himself, 'That's a witch. I know,' he said. 'That's one of the rottenest witches in this land!' And she screamed out again.

'Look,' he said. 'I've only got one forequarter left for myself, and you're not getting it and that's that.' 'More meat, or else fight,' she said again. 'Well,' he said, 'fight you must have.' 'Right! Take that sword,' she said. 'There's the sword that killed your two brothers, and this'll kill you too.' She thought she had him well tied up. 'You see,' she said, 'I'm the most famous witch in the land. I kill and eat men.' Anyhow, Jack didn't like to do it, but out they went. She flew around in the air and she was hopping about ten feet here and there and coming down on him with the point of the sword, and he was getting beat quick and lively. So he called, 'Help, horse!' 'Ah!' she said, 'hold fast hair.' And the hair said, 'How can I when I burn behind the fire?' 'Ah!' she said, 'you tricked me.'

Out come the horse with his front paws and all, and he come bashing at her, but she was beating the two of them with her sword. Anyhow, Jack said, 'She's doing the two of us, better sing out for the hound. Help, hound!' And she cried, 'Hold fast, hair.' The hair said, 'How can I, when I burn behind the fire?' Out came the hound. She's doing the hound too; she's doing the three of them. And the last thing was the hawk. I don't know where they got the hawk from, but he was always in—one of their famous compatriots them days, you know. 'Help, hawk,' cried Jack. 'This is the last, I'm done.' He's bleeding to death, you see. She's stabbing them in all directions. The horse was done, he was falling down. Anyhow, 'Hold fast, hair' again. The hair said, 'How can I when I burn behind the fire?' And out come the hawk. He picked her two eyes out.

Soon as the eyes went out, Jack up with his sword and he hit a sidelong blow and he cut her head clean off. It flew up in the air about twenty feet. It was coming down again, and he could see it was going to stick on again so he give it a side-swipe with his sword then. 'Ah,' she said, 'if I'd have got me head on again that time you'd have never got it off again'. She said, 'Strike them two stumps there and you'll find your brothers, they'll get up again.' So with the magical sword of hers he struck them two butts of wood, and up jumped Pat and Jim. And they never seen much of the old woman after because she just disappeared in a vanish of smoke.

So they said, 'Well, we might as well all go along the road together'—they were all after the same mission you see—'we've got to bring back that horse.' The mother is still up on the steeple, still waiting there with a sheaf of hay on one side of her and a needle on the other.

They go along the road a bit, and there's a bloke come along on a black horse. And he said, 'Where are you going?' And Pat said,

'Mind your own business, we're not talking to you at all.' He said to Jim, 'Where're you going, what are you doing?' 'Nothing to do with you at all.' And he said to Jack, 'Do you mind telling me where're you going?' And Jack, he was a level-headed sort of fellow and he thought he might even find some information. 'We're going to find the great horse called the Black Entire.' He said, 'I'm just the man that can help you, I'm Gothy Duff.'

Now what that man was like I don't know, but that was his name in Ireland. He said, 'I can turn myself into a rooster. There are three witches own that horse and they're the worst kind of women that ever lived in the underground. Just on account of you being friendly. I'll go along with you.'

So they all tramped along the road and they come into the dark woods and then they went into the deep gullies—one way or another—until they came into what they used to call the underworld. It was all undermined out of the earth, y'know, with caves and everything. [Gothy Duff] says, 'You fellows better stop out here for a minute, and I'll get in and I'll get the horse. I'll get him out, I know the witches that own him. Oh, no,' he said, 'I can turn myself into a rooster anytime and they can't catch me.'

He went down and he was getting in the stable where the horse was, and he just started to put the halter on when the horse give a neigh that shook the world. The witches were inside, and the old mother, she said, 'Go out, there's someone stealing the horse!' When they rushed out, old Gothy just turned himself into a rooster, flew up on the beam, and they couldn't find him. 'Oh, there's nobody there, Mother, at all. Not a soul.'

They went back inside again, and after a while everything was quiet. He thought, 'I'll go back and I'll get this horse out this time,' but he just got the bridle half on him when the horse neighed and shook the world again. The witch said, 'Go out, there's someone stealing the horse.' They went out. Nobody there. He had turned himself into a rooster again. He didn't even crow; he was too cunning to crow. He flapped up on the beam. Anyhow, the third time it happened the old woman put on her thinking cap—she had a thinking cap and once she put that on she could think out anything in the world—and she said to the young witches, 'See if there's a strange rooster in the fowlhouse.'

He was perched up on the roost. They went out and they got him. 'We've got you, Gothy,' they said, 'we've got you at last. Come in, we've got you by the neck!' He was squawk, squawk, squawk. 'Turn yourself back into a man. You've got mates around here.' The old woman said to the young witch, 'Put on the cloak of darkness and the shoes of swiftness and scour the world till you find them.' Out they went. They wasn't long till they came back with Jack and Pat and Jim, bound and gagged. 'We've got them, Mother,' they said. 'You've come stealing our horse.'

As it went on, then they said, 'Well, you're all prisoners, we've got you down.' Gothy said to her, 'Can't you let me and my friends there off? We did come to steal your horse, all right, but we haven't got it.' 'Well,' she said, 'can you tell us a story?'

'Oh yes.' This story goes on and it says: 'One time there was a king. This king was going out every day to the hills and he comes home and he wants to eat meat. He always wanted to eat human meat, and he wanted to cook his own child this day. His wife was living with him, and he said, "I'll have to have the little girl in the pot tomorrow night." His wife didn't like it and said I don't think I can do it. He said, "You got to do it, wife. If I say kill her, kill her and put her in that pot. I've got to eat her." She always knew that he wanted toes first, fingers after. She was just crying along the road one day when she met this Gothy Duff, and he said to her, "What's wrong?" and she said, "Oh, my husband wants to kill the little girl and eat her." "Oh," he says, "it can't be done. You've got a little dog at home, haven't you?"

'"Yes."

'"Well, you cook the little dog. Put him in the pot, don't put in the little girl at all, and when he sings out for the toes, tell him you longed for the toes and you ate them. And when he sings out for the fingers tell him you longed for the fingers and you ate them."

'That night, this king, he was really a giant you know, comes home. "Where's me tucker, wife? I'm longing to eat this little girl." And she said, "All right, husband, I've got her cooked there in the pot in the oven." "Well, dish it out, I want the toes." She said, "I longed for the toes and I ate them." "Well, I want the fingers!" "I longed for the fingers and I ate them. There you are, you can have the rest of it." The giant was very happy after he ate the little dog, because he thought it was the little girl. And he said, "Thanks, wife, you're a good wife. After that I'll sleep happy."'

When the witch asked for that tale, Gothy said, 'I can't give it while that poor man's all tied up with chains in the corner. If you let him go, he won't run away—it'll be OK.' 'All right,' said the old woman to Gothy. 'I want another tale.' So he said, 'No, you'll have to let one of the other men go every time I tell a story.' Anyhow, he told it, and in the finish she said, 'Do you know who that little girl was? It was my little daughter, she's a big grown-up now. Thanks, Gothy, you saved her life, and I think that youse can have the horse.' And she gave them three girls to go home with and take them for their wives then.

The three horses were found, and they went home leading the black horse along the road. And the old Gothy Duff just disappeared into the bushes the way he come about. But when they were getting near to the town where they lived, and where their poor old mother was still standing on the steeple with a sheaf of hay one side and a needle on the other, she was that overjoyed to see them that she fell off the steeple and broke her neck. Anyhow they stuck three spoons in the wall and they drank tea until they was black in the face, and if they didn't live happy, we may.

7

Bulldust

He's the man who drove the bull through Wagga
and never cracked the whip.

Traditional saying

LYING—IN ITS CREATIVE form—is common in stories told out
loud. Tall tales are staples of the frontier traditions of Australia
and the United States, which have produced some stupendous liars,
boasters and yarn-spinners, among them Davy Crockett and Mike
Fink in the US and Crooked Mick and Lippy the Liar in Australia.

Tall tales may be told about anyone and anything, of course,
though Australians have tended to focus on unusual animals.
Modern forms of bulldust, such as the urban legend, include
almost-believable tales about sex as well as the dreadful things
that might happen to you on the dunny.

What a hide!

This story is attributed to a famous northwestern yarn-spinner
known as 'Lippy the Liar'. Lippy was a shearer's cook. He'd grown
up, or so he said, living with his mother on a cockatoo farm.

*W*e was so poor we lived on boiled wheat and goannas. The
only thing we owned was an old mare. One bitter cold

night Mum and me was sittin' in front of the fire tryin' to keep from turnin' into ice blocks, when we hear a tappin' on the door. The old mare was standin' there, shiverin' and shakin'. Mum said, 'It's cruel to make her suffer like this; you'd better put her out of her misery.'

Well, I didn't want to kill the old mare, but I could see it was no good leavin' her like that. So I took her down to the shed. We was too poor to have a gun, so I hit her over the head with a sledgehammer. Then I skinned her and pegged out the hide to dry.

About an hour later, we're back in front of the fire when there's another knock on the door. I open it, and there's the old mare standin' there without her hide. Me mother was superstitious and reckoned that the mare wasn't meant to die and that I'd better do somethin' for her. So I took her back down the shed and wrapped her up in some sheep skins to keep her warm.

And do you know, that old mare lived another six years. We got five fleeces off her and she won first prize in the crossbred ewes section of the local agricultural show five years runnin'.

The split dog

One of Australia's most popular bush tall tales—and one also widely told in Britain and America—involves a hunter and his dog. In the local version, one day, the hunter wounds a kangaroo, and his dog tears off to locate it. The dog either runs through some barbed wire or across an opened tin left by some careless camper, and is cut in half from head to tail. Unperturbed, the hunter puts the two halves of the dog back together. In his haste, however, he connects them the wrong way round, leaving the dog with two legs on the ground and two sticking up in the air. This does not slow down the dog. It continues chasing down the roo until he gets too tired, whereupon he simply rolls over and continues running with the other two legs. When it finally catches the roo, it bites both ends of the animal at once.

Drop bears

Drop bears are mythical creatures of Australian tall-tale tradition that fall from the trees onto unsuspecting bush walkers. They are often described as koala-like, with large heads and sharp teeth. They serve as a peg around which brief yarns can be spontaneously spun, usually cautionary tales for tourists and new migrants. This is not unique to Australia, though Australians do seem to relish giving new arrivals a hard time. This particular drop-bear yarn includes parenthetical comments by the teller on exactly how to tell the tale for maximum effect.

I was working at . . . the hardware shop in 1987 when some Pommy backpackers came in to get some fly screen to cover the bull bar of their Dodge van to stop the insects clogging the radiator. A bit of a slow day, so I helped them attach it. When I was finished, I stood up and stated, 'That'll stop anything from a quokka to a drop bear.'

'A what?'

'Well, a quokka is a small wallaby looking thing from Western Australia.'

'Yeah, but what's a drop bear?' (Made them ask.)

'You guys don't know what a drop bear is?' (Disbelief at their lack of knowledge.) 'OK, they are a carnivorous possum that lives in gum trees but then drops out of the branches, lands on the kangaroo or whatever's back, and rips their throat out with an elongated lower canine tooth. Sort of looks like a feral pig tusk. Then laps the blood up like a vampire bat.' (A couple of references to existing animals with known characteristics.)

'My God. Have you ever seen one?'

'Well, not a live one. During the expansion of the 1930s the farmers organised drives because they were killing stock. There is a stuffed one in the museum in town.' (Offering verification if they want to stay another day. But they had already established they were heading for Mount Isa as soon as I was finished.) 'They're not extinct but endangered; just small isolated groups now.' (More believable that there are only limited numbers as opposed to saying they are everywhere.)

'Really, whereabouts?'

'Here in Queensland; well the western bits at least.' (Which direction are they heading? Townsville to Mt Isa, i.e. west.)

'But how will we know if it's safe to camp?' (Concern now; they can't afford motels.)

'Oh, well, it's a local thing. As you're going through the last town before you're gunna stop for the night, just go into any pub and ask what the drop-bear situation is like. Bye . . . have a nice trip.'

(Jeez, there are some bastards in this world.)

⌒

In one drop-bear story from Queensland, the creature is said to have size 10 feet, which it uses to kick in the head of its unfortunate victims. There have been a band and an online gaming sports team named the Drop Bears, and the dangerous little beasts also lead a busy life on the internet.

Hoop snakes

Hoop snakes inhabit the same mythical dimension as drop bears and giant mosquitoes. Said to put their tails in their mouths and roll after their intended victims, they have been rolling through Australian tradition since at least the mid nineteenth century. Here's a typical example:

*W*ell, there I was, slogging through this timber country, and just as I gets to the top of the hill I almost steps on this bloody great snake. Of course, I jump backwards pretty smartish-like, but the snake comes straight at me, so off I went back down the hill, fast as I could go. Trouble was, it was a hoop snake. Soon as I took off, the bloody thing put its tail in its mouth and came bowling along after me. And it was gaining on me, too—but just as I reached the bottom of the hill, I jumped up and grabbed an overhanging branch. The hoop snake couldn't stop. It just went bowling along and splashed straight into the creek at the bottom of the hill and drowned. Well, of course it's a true story. I mean—if it weren't true the snake would have got me and I wouldn't be telling you about it, would I?

Hoop snakes are also native to North America, where they sometimes wriggle into tales of Pecos Bill, the superhuman cowboy who bears some resemblance to the Australian shearers' hero Crooked Mick.

Giant mozzies

Australia is also inhabited by mosquitoes that wear hobnailed boots, carry off cows and bullocks, and may be seen later picking their teeth with the beasts' bones. This anonymous twentieth-century ballad tells of a particularly vicious New South Wales variety.

Now, the Territory has huge crocodiles,
Queensland the Taipan snake
Wild scrub bulls are the biggest risk
Over in the Western state.
But if you're ever in New South Wales,
Round Hunter Valley way

Look out for them giant mozzies,
The dreaded Hexham Greys.

They're the biggest skeetas in the world,
And that's the dinkum truth
Why, I've heard the fence wire snappin'
When they land on them to roost.
Be ready to clear out smartly
When you hear the dreaded drone—
They'll suck the blood right out ya' veins
And the marrow from ya' bones.

Now some shooters on the swamp one night,
Waiting for the ducks t' come in,
Loaded their guns in earnest
At the sound of flappin' wings.
As the big mob circled overhead
They aimed and blasted away,
But by mistake they'd gone and shot
At a swarm of Hexham Greys.

And a bullocky in the early days,
Bogged in swampy land,
Left his team to try and find
Someone to lend a hand.
When he returned next morning,
He found to his dismay,
His whole darn team had perished,
Devoured by Hexham Greys.

Oh his swearin' they say was louder
Than any thunderstorm
When he saw a pair of Hexham Greys

Pick their teeth with his leader's horns.
And ya' know, twenty men once disappeared—
To this day they've never been found—
They'd been workin' late on a water tank
By the river at Hexham town.

The skeetas were so savage,
The men climbed in that tank's insides,
Believin' they'd be protected
By the corrugated iron.
When the skeetas bit right through that tank,
Determined to get a meal,
The apprentice grabbed his hammer,
Clinched their beaks onto the steel.
Well, it wasn't long before they felt
That big tank slowly rise,
Them skeetas lifted it clear from the ground
Then carried 'em into the sky.

Well, they're just a few of the facts I've heard,
Concernin' the Hexham Greys
Passed on to me by my dear old dad,
Who would never lie they say.
So if you are in New South Wales,
Round Hunter Valley way
Look out for them giant mozzies,
The dreaded Hexham Greys.

There is a three-metre-tall statue of a grey mosquito outside the Hexham Bowling Club, near Newcastle. The locals say it is a life-sized model.

Dinkum!

A perennial favourite is the yarn in which an Australian one-ups an American skiter—often quite a feat. This example is from World War I:

*I*n a London café last month a soldier who hailed from the other side of Oodnadatta fell into a friendly argument with an American, as to the relative greatness of the two countries.

'Wal,' said the Yankee, 'that bit o' sunbaked mud yew call Australia ain't a bad bit o' sile in its way, and it'll be worth expectoratin' on when it wakes up and discovers it's alive, but when yew come to compare it with Amurrica, wal, yer might 'swell put a spot o' dust alongside a diamond. Y'see, sonny, we kinder do things in Amurrica; we don't sit round like an egg in its shell waitin' fer someone tew come along and crack it; no, we git hustling' till all Amurrica's one kernormous dust storm kicked up by our citizens raking in their dollars. Why, there's millions of Amurricans who 'ave tew climb to the top of their stack o' dollars on a ladder every morning, so's they ken see the sun rise. We're some people!'

The Australian took a hitch in his belt, put his cigarette behind his ear, and observed:

'Dollars! Do yer only deal in five bobs over there! We deal in nothin' but quids [pounds] in Australia. Anything smaller than a quid we throw away. Too much worry to count, and it spoils the shape of yer pockets. The schoolboys 'ave paperchases with pound notes. Money in Australia! Why, you can see the business blokes comin' outer their offices every day with wads of bank notes like blankets under each arm. I remember before I left Adelaide all the citizens was makin' for the banks with the day's takin's, when a stiff gale sprung up pretty sudden. Them citizens let go their wads ter 'old their 'ats on and immediately the air was full of bank notes—mostly 'undred quidders. Yer couldn't see the sun fer paper. The corporation 'ad to hire a thousand men ter sweep them bank notes in a 'eap and burn 'em. Dinkum!'

The exploding dunny

This is an update of an old bush yarn from the days before septic tanks and sewers. Back then, the dunny was a hole in the ground. Every week or two, as the hole began to fill, kerosene would be poured in to disguise the smell and aid decomposition. As the yarn used to go, one day someone mistakenly poured petrol down the hole and the next person to use the dunny dropped his still-lit cigarette butt. The resulting explosion blew up the dunny, its contents and the smoker too.

In the modern version, the woman of the house is trying to exterminate an insect, often a cockroach. She throws it into the toilet bowl and gives it a good spray of insecticide. Her husband immediately uses the loo, drops his cigarette butt and gets a burned backside when it ignites the flammable mix of gases and chemicals.

With badly burned rear and genitals, the husband is in need of hospitalisation. When the ambulance arrives, the ambulance men are so amused that they cannot stop laughing. They get the husband on to the stretcher, but on the way out their laughter becomes uncontrollable. They drop the stretcher. The burned husband hits the concrete floor and breaks his pelvis.

The continued popularity of this fable is perhaps due to its message that even the most mundane activities can be dangerous.

The well-dressed roo

There are a good many bush yarns about kangaroos mimicking the actions of humans. This one was probably not new when it was published in a 1902 book of humour titled *Aboriginalities*. It was still being told in the 1950s about visiting English cricket sides and in the mid-1980s about an Italian America's Cup team in Western Australia. It has been frequently aired in the Australian press.

a group of tourists is being driven through the Outback. The bus runs down a kangaroo, and the driver stops to assess the damage. The tourists, excited by this bit of authentic Australiana, rush out to have a look. After the cameras have clicked for a while, someone gets the bright idea of standing the dead roo against a tree and putting his sports jacket on the animal for a novel souvenir photo.

Just as the tourist is about to snap his photo, the roo, only stunned by the bus, returns to consciousness and leaps off into the scrub, still wearing the tourist's expensive jacket—with his wallet, money, credit cards and passport in the pocket.

This tale of a supposedly dumb animal meting out poetic justice to a dumb human has many international variations, including the American bear that walks off into Yellowstone Park carrying a tourist's baby, and the deer hunter who loses his rifle after placing it in the antlers of a deer he has just shot. Versions are also told in Germany and Canada. But Australia's is better, of course.

Loaded animals

The ancestry of the 'biter bitten' yarn goes back at least as far as the Middle Ages. It's known in Europe and in India. Probably Australia's best-known version is Henry Lawson's 'The Loaded Dog':

*D*ave Regan, Jim Bently, and Andy Page were sinking a shaft at Stony Creek in search of a rich gold quartz reef which was supposed to exist in the vicinity. There is always a rich reef supposed to exist in the vicinity; the only questions are whether it is ten feet or hundreds beneath the surface, and in which direction. They had struck some pretty solid rock, also water which kept them baling. They used the old-fashioned blasting-powder and time-fuse. They'd make a sausage or cartridge of blasting-powder in a skin of strong calico or canvas, the mouth sewn and bound round the end of the fuse; they'd dip the cartridge in melted tallow to make it water-tight, get the drill-hole as dry as possible, drop in the cartridge with some dry dust, and wad and ram with stiff clay and broken brick. Then they'd light the fuse and get out of the hole and wait. The result was usually an ugly pot-hole in the bottom of the shaft and half a barrow-load of broken rock.

There was plenty of fish in the creek, fresh-water bream, cod, cat-fish, and tailers. The party were fond of fish, and Andy and Dave of fishing.

Andy would fish for three hours at a stretch if encouraged by a 'nibble' or a 'bite' now and then—say once in twenty minutes. The butcher was always willing to give meat in exchange for fish when they caught more than they could eat; but now it was winter, and these fish wouldn't bite. However, the creek was low, just a chain of muddy water-holes, from the hole with a few bucketfuls in it to the sizable pool with an average depth of six or seven feet, and they could get fish by baling out the smaller holes or muddying up the water in the larger ones till the fish rose to the surface. There was the cat-fish, with spikes growing out of the sides of its head, and if you got pricked you'd know it, as Dave said. Andy took off his boots, tucked up his trousers, and went into a hole one day to stir up the mud with his feet, and he knew it. Dave scooped one out with his hand and got pricked, and he knew it too; his arm swelled, and the pain throbbed up into his shoulder, and down into his stomach too, he said, like a toothache he had once, and kept him awake for two nights—only the toothache pain had a 'burred edge', Dave said.

Dave got an idea.

'Why not blow the fish up in the big water-hole with a cartridge?' he said.

'I'll try it.'

He thought the thing out and Andy Page worked it out. Andy usually put Dave's theories into practice if they were practicable, or bore the blame for the failure and the chaffing of his mates if they weren't.

He made a cartridge about three times the size of those they used in the rock. Jim Bently said it was big enough to blow the bottom out of the river. The inner skin was of stout calico; Andy stuck the end of a six-foot piece of fuse well down in the powder and bound the mouth of the bag firmly to it with whipcord. The idea was to sink the cartridge in the water with the open end of the fuse attached to a float on the surface, ready for lighting. Andy dipped the cartridge in melted bees'-wax to make it water-tight. 'We'll have to leave it some time before we light it,' said Dave, 'to give the fish time to get over their scare when we put it in, and come nosing round again; so we'll want it well water-tight.'

Round the cartridge Andy, at Dave's suggestion, bound a strip of sail canvas—that they used for making water-bags—to increase the force of the explosion, and round that he pasted layers of stiff brown paper—on the plan of the sort of fireworks we called 'gun-crackers'. He let the paper dry in the sun, then he sewed a covering of two thicknesses of canvas over it, and bound the thing from end to end with stout fishing-line. Dave's schemes were elaborate, and he often worked his inventions out to nothing. The cartridge was rigid and solid enough now—a formidable bomb; but Andy and Dave wanted to be sure. Andy sewed on another layer of canvas, dipped the cartridge in melted tallow, twisted a length of fencing-wire round it as an afterthought, dipped it in tallow again, and stood it carefully against a tent-peg, where he'd know where to find it, and wound the fuse loosely round it. Then he went to the camp-fire to try some potatoes which were boiling in their jackets in a billy, and to see about frying some chops for dinner. Dave and Jim were at work in the claim that morning.

They had a big black young retriever dog—or rather an overgrown pup, a big, foolish, four-footed mate, who was always slobbering round them and lashing their legs with his heavy tail that swung round like a stock-whip.

Most of his head was usually a red, idiotic, slobbering grin of appreciation of his own silliness. He seemed to take life, the world, his two-legged mates, and his own instinct as a huge joke. He'd retrieve anything: he carted back most of the camp rubbish that Andy threw away. They had a cat that died in hot weather, and Andy threw it a good distance away in the scrub; and early one morning the dog found the cat, after it had been dead a week or so, and carried it back to camp, and laid it just inside the tent-flaps, where it could best make its presence known when the mates should rise and begin to sniff suspiciously in the sickly smothering atmosphere of the summer sunrise. He used to retrieve them when they went in swimming; he'd jump in after them, and take their hands in his mouth, and try to swim out with them, and scratch their naked bodies with his paws.

They loved him for his good-heartedness and his foolishness, but when they wished to enjoy a swim they had to tie him up in camp.

He watched Andy with great interest all the morning making the cartridge, and hindered him considerably, trying to help; but about noon he went off to the claim to see how Dave and Jim were getting on, and to come home to dinner with them. Andy saw them coming, and put a panful of mutton-chops on the fire. Andy was cook to-day; Dave and Jim stood with their backs to the fire, as Bushmen do in all weathers, waiting till dinner should be ready. The retriever went nosing round after something he seemed to have missed.

Andy's brain still worked on the cartridge; his eye was caught by the glare of an empty kerosene-tin lying in the bushes, and it struck him that it wouldn't be a bad idea to sink the cartridge packed with clay, sand, or stones in the tin, to increase the force of the explosion. He may have been all out, from a scientific point of view, but the notion looked all right to him.

Jim Bently, by the way, wasn't interested in their 'damned silliness'. Andy noticed an empty treacle-tin—the sort with the little tin neck or spout soldered on to the top for the convenience of pouring out the treacle—and it struck him that this would have made the best kind of cartridge-case: he would only have had to pour in the powder, stick the fuse in through the neck, and cork and seal it with bees'-wax. He was turning to suggest this to Dave, when Dave glanced over his shoulder to see how the chops were doing—and bolted. He explained afterwards that he thought he heard the pan spluttering extra, and looked to see if the chops were burning.

Jim Bently looked behind and bolted after Dave. Andy stood stock-still, staring after them.

'Run, Andy! Run!' they shouted back at him. 'Run!!! Look behind you, you fool!' Andy turned slowly and looked, and there, close behind him, was the retriever with the cartridge in his mouth—wedged into his broadest and silliest grin. And that wasn't all. The dog had come round the fire to Andy, and the loose end of the fuse had trailed and waggled over the burning sticks into the blaze; Andy had slit and nicked the firing end of the fuse well, and now it was hissing and spitting properly.

Andy's legs started with a jolt; his legs started before his brain did, and he made after Dave and Jim. And the dog followed Andy.

Dave and Jim were good runners—Jim the best—for a short distance; Andy was slow and heavy, but he had the strength and the wind and could last. The dog leapt and capered round him, delighted as a dog could be to find his mates, as he thought, on for a frolic. Dave and Jim kept shouting back, 'Don't foller us! Don't foller us, you coloured fool!' but Andy kept on, no matter how they dodged. They could never explain, any more than the dog, why they followed each other, but so they ran, Dave keeping in Jim's track in all its turnings, Andy after Dave, and the dog circling round Andy—the live fuse swishing in all directions and hissing and spluttering and stinking, Jim yelling to Dave not to follow him, Dave shouting to Andy to go in another direction—to 'spread out', and Andy roaring at the dog to go home.

Then Andy's brain began to work, stimulated by the crisis: he tried to get a running kick at the dog, but the dog dodged; he snatched up sticks and stones and threw them at the dog and ran on again. The retriever saw that he'd made a mistake about Andy, and left him and bounded after Dave. Dave, who had the presence of mind to think that the fuse's time wasn't up yet, made a dive and a grab for the dog, caught him by the tail, and as he swung round snatched the cartridge out of his mouth and flung it as far as he could: the dog immediately bounded after it and retrieved it. Dave roared and cursed at the dog, who seeing that Dave was offended, left him and went after Jim, who was well ahead. Jim swung to a sapling and went up it like a native bear; it was a young sapling, and Jim couldn't safely get more than ten or twelve feet from the ground. The dog laid the cartridge, as carefully as if it was a kitten, at the foot of the sapling, and capered and leaped and whooped joyously round under Jim. The big pup reckoned that this was part of the lark—he was all right now—it was Jim who was out for a spree.

The fuse sounded as if it were going a mile a minute. Jim tried to climb higher and the sapling bent and cracked. Jim fell on his feet and ran. The dog swooped on the cartridge and followed. It all took but a very few moments. Jim ran to a digger's hole, about ten feet deep, and dropped down into it—landing on soft mud—and was safe. The dog grinned sardonically down on him, over the edge, for a moment, as if he thought it would be a good lark to drop the cartridge down on Jim.

'Go away, Tommy,' said Jim feebly, 'go away.'

The dog bounded off after Dave, who was the only one in sight now; Andy had dropped behind a log, where he lay flat on his face, having suddenly remembered a picture of the Russo–Turkish war with a circle of Turks lying flat on their faces (as if they were ashamed) round a newly arrived shell.

There was a small hotel or shanty on the creek, on the main road, not far from the claim. Dave was desperate, the time flew much faster in his stimulated imagination than it did in reality, so he made for the shanty. There were several casual Bushmen on the verandah and in the bar; Dave rushed into the bar, banging the door to behind him. 'My dog!' he gasped, in reply to the astonished stare of the publican, 'the blanky retriever—he's got a live cartridge in his mouth—'

The retriever, finding the front door shut against him, had bounded round and in by the back way, and now stood smiling in the doorway leading from the passage, the cartridge still in his mouth and the fuse spluttering. They burst out of that bar. Tommy bounded first after one and then after another, for, being a young dog, he tried to make friends with everybody.

The Bushmen ran round corners, and some shut themselves in the stable. There was a new weather-board and corrugated-iron kitchen and wash-house on piles in the back-yard, with some women washing clothes inside. Dave and the publican bundled in there and shut the door—the publican cursing Dave and calling him a crimson fool, in hurried tones, and wanting to know what the hell he came here for.

The retriever went in under the kitchen, amongst the piles, but, luckily for those inside, there was a vicious yellow mongrel cattle-dog sulking and nursing his nastiness under there—a sneaking, fighting, thieving canine, whom neighbours had tried for years to shoot or poison. Tommy saw his danger—he'd had experience from this dog—and started out and across the yard, still sticking to the cartridge. Half-way across the yard the yellow dog caught him and nipped him. Tommy dropped the cartridge, gave one terrified yell, and took to the Bush. The yellow dog followed him to the fence and then ran back to see what he had dropped.

Nearly a dozen other dogs came from round all the corners and under the buildings—spidery, thievish, cold-blooded kangaroo-dogs, mongrel sheep- and cattle-dogs, vicious black and yellow dogs— that slip after you in the dark, nip your heels, and vanish without explaining—and yapping, yelping small fry. They kept at a respectable distance round the nasty yellow dog, for it was dangerous to go near him when he thought he had found something which might be good for a dog to eat. He sniffed at the cartridge twice, and was just taking a third cautious sniff when—

It was very good blasting powder—a new brand that Dave had recently got up from Sydney; and the cartridge had been excellently well made. Andy was very patient and painstaking in all he did, and nearly as handy as the average sailor with needles, twine, canvas, and rope.

Bushmen say that that kitchen jumped off its piles and on again. When the smoke and dust cleared away, the remains of the nasty yellow dog were lying against the paling fence of the yard looking as if he had been kicked into a fire by a horse and afterwards rolled in the dust under a barrow, and finally thrown against the fence from a distance. Several saddle-horses, which had been 'hanging-up' round the verandah, were galloping wildly down the road in clouds of dust, with broken bridle-reins flying; and from a circle round the outskirts, from every point of the compass in the scrub, came the yelping of dogs. Two of them went home, to the place where they were born, thirty miles away, and reached it the same night and stayed there; it was not till towards evening that the rest came back cautiously to make inquiries. One was trying to walk on two legs, and most of 'em looked more or less singed; and a little, singed, stumpy-tailed dog, who had been in the habit of hopping the back half of him along on one leg, had reason to be glad that he'd saved up the other leg all those years, for he needed it now. There was one old one-eyed cattle-dog round that shanty for years afterwards, who couldn't stand the smell of a gun being cleaned. He it was who had taken an interest, only second to that of the yellow dog, in the cartridge. Bushmen said that it was amusing to slip up on his blind side and stick a dirty ramrod under his nose: he wouldn't wait to bring his solitary eye to bear—he'd take to the Bush and stay out all night.

For half an hour or so after the explosion there were several Bushmen round behind the stable who crouched, doubled up, against the wall, or rolled gently on the dust, trying to laugh without shrieking. There were two white women in hysterics at the house, and a half-caste rushing aimlessly round with a dipper of cold water. The publican was holding his wife tight and begging her between her squawks, to 'hold up for my sake, Mary, or I'll lam the life out of ye.'

Dave decided to apologise later on, 'when things had settled a bit', and went back to camp. And the dog that had done it all, Tommy, the great, idiotic mongrel retriever, came slobbering round Dave and lashing his legs with his tail, and trotted home after him, smiling his broadest, longest, and reddest smile of amiability, and apparently satisfied for one afternoon with the fun he'd had.

Andy chained the dog up securely, and cooked some more chops, while Dave went to help Jim out of the hole.

And most of this is why, for years afterwards, lanky, easy-going Bushmen, riding lazily past Dave's camp, would cry, in a lazy drawl and with just a hint of the nasal twang—

"El-lo, Da-a-ve! How's the fishin' getting on, Da-a-ve?'

~

This is a modernised version of Lawson's yarn:

*a*rabbito, new to the job, was not having much luck. No matter what he did, he couldn't seem to bag a single rabbit. The old hands were doing well, so the new bloke asked them for advice. They told him to get himself a rabbit, tie a stick of gelignite to its tail, light the 'gelly' and send the rabbit down the nearest burrow. This would guarantee a big, if messy, haul.

The new bloke thought this was a fine idea. The only trouble was, he couldn't catch a rabbit in the first place. So he decided to buy one at the pet store in town. Back in the bush, he got the rabbit out of its cage, tied the explosive to it, lit the fuse and pointed the rabbit towards the burrows. Off it went, but, being a pet-shop rabbit, it didn't know what to do in the wild. It circled round, ran back towards the bloke, and scurried, fuse still sputtering, straight under his brand new ute, blowing the whole thing to buggery.

In other recent versions, it is a couple of cruel blokes out hunting who tie the gelignite to the rabbit. The wild rabbit, terrified, does the same thing as the pet-shop one, running under—and duly blowing up—their $50,000 four-wheel drive. There is also an exploding fish—or shark—variant. In Queensland they seem to prefer exploding pigs.

The blackout babies

The subject of sex is often avoided in the lore of the bush. Not so in urban legends, where it's a staple—and where wild exaggeration is the norm (though presented as true, of course).

One such tale is the perennial explanation for an unusual surge in the number of babies born at a certain time of the year. The reason: there was a blackout nine months earlier, and telly-less couples were forced to amuse themselves in more traditional ways. A more inventive reason, as in this story collected by folklorist Bill Scott in Canberra in 1978, is the noisy passing of the night train.

*T*he Census Office was puzzling over the latest figures from Kyogle, New South Wales. The staff couldn't work out why this place had a birth rate three times the national average. They sent an officer to investigate. He found the school crammed with kids and a new wing added to the maternity hospital. After a few days, the officer worked it out.

The Kyogle Mail used to pass through town about 4.30 every morning, blowing its whistle first at the level crossing on the north side of town and waking everyone up. Just as they were dozing off again, the train would cross the crossing on the south side of town and blow its whistle again. By then just about everyone in town was wide awake. It was too early to get up, but . . .

In South Africa the story is so well-known in one particular town that the local offspring are known far and wide as 'train babies'.

The Head

A favourite with teenagers is an urban legend usually called 'The Head' or 'The Escaped Maniac':

*T*his couple went parking in the bush around town one night, and when they went to go home they couldn't get the car started. So the guy went to get help, and the girl waited in the car for him. She waited and waited and waited, but he didn't come back. Then she hears this strange *thump, thump, thump* on the roof of the car. She's terrified. She doesn't move. She sits there all night hearing this weird *thump, thump, thump*. Then suddenly all these bright flashing lights surround the car—it's the police! And they tell her to get out of the car when they count to three, and to run towards them as fast as she can, but not on any account to look back at the car. So they count: one, two, three! And she gets out and runs over, but she looks back to see what was making the thumping noise. And there's this maniac sitting on the roof of the car banging the boyfriend's severed head: *thump, thump, thump.*

~

An oft-included detail is that while the couple are doing whatever they are doing in the car, a news bulletin comes on the radio, saying that a dangerous maniac has escaped from a local lunatic asylum.

Readers familiar with the Bible will recognise the order to the girl not to turn around as similar to that given to Lot's wife, Sarah. She was told not to look back at the doomed city of Sodom, but she did—and was instantly turned into a pillar of salt.

The sex life of an electron

This tale, a feast of electronics puns and double entendres, is particularly popular with computer geeks. As with urban legends, this story circulates the world in photocopied or email forms and is as popular in Australia as elsewhere.

*O*ne night when his charge was high, Micro Farad decided to seek out a cute coil to let him discharge. He picked up Milli Amp and took her for a ride on his mega cycle. They rode across a Wheatstone bridge, around the sine waves, and stopped in a magnetic field beside a flowing current.

Micro Farad was attracted by Milli Amp's characteristic curve and soon had her fully charged and excited her resistance to a minimum. He laid her on the ground potential and raised her frequency and lowered her inductance. He pulled out his high frequency probe and inserted it into her socket, connecting them in parallel and short-circuiting her resistance shunt so as to cause surges with the utmost intensity. Then, when fully excited, Milli Amp mumbled, 'Ohm, ohm, ohm.' With his tube operating at a maximum and her field vibrating with current flow, it caused her to shunt over and Micro Farad rapidly discharged, drawing every electron. They fluxed all night, trying different connections and sockets until his magnet had a soft core and lost its field strength.

Afterwards, Milli Amp tried self-induction and damaged her solenoids in doing so. With his battery discharged, Micro Farad was unable to excite his field, so they spent the night reversing polarity and blowing each other's fuses . . .

Authorship of this piece is often attributed to one Eddy Current.

Do not break the chain

The chain letter probably existed since postal services were first established. In its standard form, it claims that good luck and riches will be showered on the recipient if only he or she mails the letter to a number of others. Failure to do this will bring disaster. Chain letters have become chain emails, but they've been joined by some playful parodies, including this 'Chain Letter for Women':

*D*ear Friend,
    This letter was started by a woman like yourself, in the hope of bringing relief to the tired and discontented. Unlike most chain letters, this one does not cost anything. Just send a copy to five of your friends who are tired and discontent. Then bundle up your husband or boyfriend and send him to the woman whose name appears at the top of the list.

When your name comes to the top you will receive 16,374 men, and some of them are bound to be a hell of a lot better than the one you already have.

Do not break the chain. Have faith. One woman broke the chain and got her own husband back.

At the time of writing, a friend of mine had already received 184 men. They buried her yesterday, but it took three undertakers 36 hours to get the smile off her face!!!

"Damn yer explosive bullets! You've gone & bust the pocket I 'ad me cigarettes in!"

8

Heroes

'Ave a cup o' tea, Mr Birdwood.

Gallipoli Anzac, on meeting General Birdwood

EVERY COUNTRY HAS its heroes, real and mythic. Australia's include bushrangers, diggers and sportsmen. Even a racehorse can be a hero.

Though most heroes are men, Australia has heroines too, like Grace Bussell, rescuer of shipwreck victims, and Caroline Chisholm, the friend of colonial immigrant women. There are also female heroic types, such as 'the little Irish mother' and military nurses. One of numerous indigenous heroines is Wungala.

Wungala and the wulgaru

The story of Wungala is told by the Waddaman people, whose country is southeast of the Katherine River, in the Northern Territory. This story concerns her encounter with an evil creature known as a wulgaru, which resulted from a botched attempt by a man named Djarapa to make a man from wood, stone, red ochre and magic songs. A little like Frankenstein's monster, it is a shambling mess of twisted limbs, with eyes that blaze like stars. Ever since its misbegotten creation, the wulgaru has menaced Waddaman people as keeper and judge of the dead. Although it is evil, however, the wulgaru is also the caretaker of the spirits and regulator of the rules governing everyday life.

*W*ungala took her young son, Bulla, seed gathering after the wet season. Bulla ran around happily, finding the best mounds of seeds, but when a dark cloud passed across the sun Wungala told him to be quiet. Along with the shadows might come the evil big-eyed one who lived in a cave in the nearby hills. If this being, known as a *wulgaru*, heard Bulla he would come out of his cave and bring evil upon them. But Bulla kept up his chatter, and a *wulgaru* did appear, creeping toward them through the shadows.

Wungala knew that the only way to avoid a *wulgaru*'s power was to ignore it and to show no fear. When Bulla ran to her in terror, pointing at the *wulgaru*, she told him it was only the shadows of the swaying bushes. Trusting his mother, Bulla calmed down and went on gathering seeds. This enraged the *wulgaru*, who gave a fierce yell. Bulla ran to his mother again, saying that he had not only seen the *wulgaru* but heard it. He wanted to run away, but Wungala calmed his fears again, saying that it was just a cockatoo.

She began grinding the seeds on a large flat stone to make flour for bread, as if nothing had happened. This only further angered the *wulgaru*, who began to jump around. He thrust his evil face into Wungala's, but she calmly continued her baking. When the damper, or bush bread, was baked nice and hot, Bulla, who had gone to sleep, awoke and told his mother that the evil one was still there. 'No,' said his mother, 'that is just the smoke from the fire.' Hearing this, the monster pounced, its claws ready to tear Wungala apart. But she jumped straight at him, pushing the hot damper into the *wulgaru*'s face. It screamed in pain and tried to brush the hot mass from its mouth and eyes. That gave Wungala her chance to snatch up Bulla and to run back to camp.

Aftermath of the Eureka Stockade

The Eureka Stockade of 1854, introduced in Chapter 2, was a bloody affair. Its immediate aftermath was described by a correspondent to the local newspaper, the *Geelong Advertiser and Intelligencer*. The correspondent woke up on the Sunday morning after the violence and saw the condition of the defenders, some of whom were known to him. He wrote the events down and his account was reproduced in Rafael Carboni's book, *The Eureka Stockade*, together with some bracketed comments from Carboni when some of his mates are mentioned.

*T*he first thing that I saw was a number of diggers enclosed in a sort of hollow square, many of them were wounded, the blood dripping from them as they walked; some were walking lame, pricked on by the bayonets of the soldiers bringing up the rear. The soldiers were much excited, and the troopers madly so, flourishing their swords, and shouting out—'We have waked up Joe!' and others replied, 'And sent Joe to sleep again!' The diggers' Standard was carried by in triumph to the Camp, waved about in the air, then pitched from one to another, thrown down and trampled on.

The scene was awful—twos and threes gathered together, and all felt stupefied. I went with R---- to the barricade, the tents all around were in a blaze; I was about to go inside, when a cry was raised that the troopers were coming again. They did come with carts to take away the bodies, I counted fifteen dead, one G----, a fine well-educated man, and a great favourite ... I recognised two others, but the spectacle was so ghastly that I feel a loathing at the remembrance.

They all lay in a small space with their faces upwards, looking like lead, several of them were still heaving, and at every rise of their breasts, the blood spouted out of their wounds, or just bubbled out and trickled away. One man, a stout-chested fine fellow, apparently about forty years old, lay with a pike beside him: he had three contusions in the head, three strokes across the brow, a bayonet wound in the throat under the ear, and other wounds in the body—I counted fifteen wounds in that single carcase. Some were bringing handkerchiefs, others bed furniture, and matting to cover up the faces of the dead. O God! Sir, it was a sight for a Sabbath morn that, I humbly implore Heaven, may never be seen again. Poor women crying for absent husbands, and children frightened into quietness.

I, sir, write disinterestedly, and I hope my feelings arose from a true principle; but when I looked at that scene, my soul revolted at such means being so cruelly used by a government to sustain the law. A little terrier sat on the breast of the man I spoke of, and kept up a continuous howl: it was removed, but always returned to the same spot; and when his master's body was huddled, with the other corpses, into the cart, the little dog jumped in after him, and lying again on his dead master's breast, began howling again. ---- was dead there also, and ----, who escaped, had said that when he offered his sword, he was shot in the side by a trooper, as he was lying on the ground wounded. He expired almost immediately. Another was lying dead just inside the barricade, where he seemed to have crawled. Some of the bodies might have been removed—I counted fifteen. A poor woman and her children were standing outside a tent; she said that the troopers had surrounded the tent and pierced it with their swords. She, her husband, and children, were ordered out by the troopers, and were inspected in their night-clothes outside, whilst the troopers searched the tent. Mr. Haslam was roused from sleep by a volley of bullets fired through his tent; he rushed out, and was shot down by a trooper, and handcuffed. He lay there for two hours bleeding from a wound in his breast, until his friends sent for a black-smith, who forced off the handcuffs with a hammer and cold chisel. When I last heard of Mr. Haslam, a surgeon was attending him, and probing for the ball.

R----, from Canada, [Captain Ross, of Toronto, once my mate] escaped the carnage; but is dead since, from the wounds. R---- has affected his escape. [Johnny Robertson, who had a striking resemblance to me, not so much in size as in complexion and colour of the beard especially: Poor Johnny was shot down dead on the stockade; and was the identical body which Mr. Binney mistook for me. Hence the belief by many, that I was dead.] V---- is reported to be amongst the wounded [Oh! No his legs were too long even for a Minie rifle]. One man was seen yesterday trailing along the road: he said he could not last much longer, and that his brother was shot along-side of him. All whom I spoke to were of one opinion, that it was a cowardly massacre. There were only about one hundred and seventy diggers, and they were opposed to nearly six hundred military. I hope all is over; but I fear not: or amongst many, the feeling is not of intimidation, but a cry for vengeance, and an opportunity to meet the soldiers with equal numbers. There is an awful list of casualties yet to come in; and when uncertainty is made certain, and relatives and friends know the worst, there will be gaps that cannot be filled up. I have little knowledge of the gold-fields; but I fear that the massacre at Eureka is only a skirmish.

I bid farewell to the gold-fields, and if what I have seen is a specimen of the government of Victoria, the sooner I am out of it the better for myself and family. Sir, I am horrified at what I witnessed, and I did not see the worst of it. I could not breathe the blood-tainted air of the diggings, and I have left them forever...

A commission of inquiry was subsequently held, the results of which largely upheld the diggers' complaints. Reforms were swiftly made and Peter Lalor became the representative of Ballarat in the Victorian parliament and, soon after, Speaker of the Legislative Assembly.

Ben Hall

The bushranger is a paradox: a criminal who is seen as a hero. Like Robin Hood, Australian bushrangers are often depicted as helping the poor against the powerful—including the police.

Benjamin Hall (1837–1865), a respected free selector smallholder in the Forbes district of New South Wales, was arrested in early 1862 on suspicion of having participated in a minor highway robbery led by the notorious Frank Gardiner. After a month in prison, Hall was acquitted, but when he returned home he found that his wife had deserted him, taking their baby son with her. The story goes that Hall then joined with the Gardiner gang. He was later arrested over a gold robbery, but soon released for lack of evidence. While he was in jail, the police burned his house and left his cattle to die, penned in the mustering yard.

Hall now became a bushranger, committing highway robbery and attacking wealthy properties. In October 1863 he took part in a raid on Bathurst. Financially it was a failure, but it panicked the population and the colonial government. The bushrangers were officially outlawed and hunted down. Hall was betrayed and shot dead by police—according to legend, while he slept—on 5 May 1865.

The many ballads and stories about Hall portray him as the victim of injustice and unfortunate circumstances. He is shown as courteous to women, even-handed and kind. He robs a wealthy squatter but reportedly gave £5 back to his victim to see him to the end of his journey. One of the ballads about him contains the line: 'He never robbed a needy man', and his local reputation was that of a decent man wronged by circumstances and the law.

In the 1920s, John Gale recalled meeting Hall nearly sixty years earlier, before his bushranging career began:

*I*n the fifties of the last century I was tutor to the children of a squatter on Bland Plains. The sparse population thereabout at the time had never been visited by parson or priest, so in my spare time, from Friday evening to the following Monday morning of each week, I did what in me lay to supply this defect. Amongst the homesteads thus periodically visited was that of Bland Plains. It was here I first became acquainted with Hall, who was the station overseer—of fine physique, courteous bearing, and but newly married. Gardiner's gang of bushrangers were disturbing the country, and had committed some of their most daring raids.

Saddle-swapping was an ordinary practice amongst stockmen in those days. Ben Hall had indulged in this saddle-swapping business. One day the police found in his possession, thus acquired, a saddle which had been stolen by Gardiner's gang from one of their victims. It had without question passed through several hands before it came into Hall's possession. But that possession was enough to justify the police in effecting his arrest. Justices of the peace were then few and far between out in these parts, and consequently Ben was remanded again and again until his case could be heard. This eventually took place, and resulted in his discharge from custody. But that detention was his ruin, and that of his domestic life.

His wife had been seduced during her husband's incarceration, and lived with her paramour, who was well known to me, but whose name for obvious reasons I prefer not to disclose. Ben made it no secret that he would take the life of the betrayer of his wife's honour. From time to time he watched his home, which was also now that of the misguided woman. One day he saw his quarry enter his home, which was on the margin of an extensive plain, overshadowed by large yellow-box trees. Ben followed his quest. He met his wife at the door.

'Where's —?' he queried, 'I've a bullet for him.'

'He saw you coming, Ben, and went out into the bush through the back door-way.'

'Tell him that I'll do for him sooner or later. I don't blame you, Norah, in the least; you are young and foolish, though you ought to have known better.'

Her two-year-old little boy was clinging to his mother's skirts during the colloquy. Turning to the tall fellow conversing with his mother, and clasping him by the knees, 'Don't you shoot my dada,' said he pleadingly, looking up into Hall's face.

That was the determining factor in Ben Hall's career. The pleading child was his own offspring—was clasping his own father's knees—and he had spoken of his mother's seducer as 'my dada'. Then and there Ben broke away from all restraint from all regard for the sanctities of society, saying, 'I've been accused of being in sympathy with the bushrangers: from this out I'll play the game.'

Often and often did I earnestly wish to meet with this deluded man whilst he was operating hereabouts, for I entertained the hope that an interview with him might be productive of some measure of good. But it was a forlorn hope.

Tales of Ben Hall often recount what happened after he died. The wife of the man who betrayed him was pregnant. When she heard that Hall had been shot and that it was her husband who had told the police where to find him, she took it very badly. When her baby (sometimes said to have been Hall's) was born, he was covered in spots on exactly the same places as the shots that had killed Hall. In some versions of the story, the marked child is said to have been that of Hall's estranged wife.

A continuation of this legend has it that the baby grew up to be 'the Leopard Boy', so-called because of the bullet marks on his body, from which he made a living by exhibiting himself in travelling shows.

Thunderbolt

Frederick Ward, who called himself Thunderbolt, began his bushranging exploits in 1865, less than eighteen months after breaking out of the supposedly escape-proof prison on Sydney's Cockatoo Island. He and his fellow escapee, Frederick Britten, were helped by Ward's wife Maryanne, a part-Aboriginal woman. Ward turned to bushranging in New England, but developed a reputation for using minimal violence—he claimed he had been driven to bushranging—and for being kind to women and the poor. On one occasion, he is said to have refrained from stealing a watch when its owner told him it was her only momento of her dead mother, and to have returned gold after stealing it from some children. A verse sometimes attributed to him goes:

My name is Frederick Ward, I am a native of this isle;
I rob the rich to feed the poor and make the children smile.

There was a large price on Ward's head, but his bush skills and strong local sympathy kept him at large for nearly seven years, until he was killed by a policeman in May 1870. In an echo of many other outlaw stories, it was long claimed that it was another man—Frederick Britten or a Fred Blake—who had been killed, and that the real Thunderbolt was living safely elsewhere in Australia, or in New Zealand, Canada or even the United States.

Contemporary accounts of Thunderbolt's robberies tend to support his Robin Hood image, as in this letter by one of his victims, hotel manager James Neariah Roper, in May 1867:

*O*n the 3rd May I sent the Hosteler to Tenterfield on business, but he could not find the horse he intended to ride, which at once excited my suspicion that he was stolen, in consequence of a boy the previous evening, purchasing 20 lb of flour with other goods, to go on a journey to Grafton. I wrote a note to Constable Langworthy. He arrived the same evening and has been in and about the neighbourhood till now.

On the 8th (this morning) I sent the mail off to Tenterfield and Constable Langworthy kept it in sight as far as Maidenhead, they had been gone about half an hour (half past 10 o'clock a.m.) when Thunderbolt and boy rode up, both well mounted. I was making up my accounts. Old Dick and Archie Livingstone in my company, immediately recognized the boy that I suspected of stealing my horse. We at once said, that is Thunderbolt. Archie slipped out of the back door and hid his watch under the kitchen bed. I walked into the bar, threw open all the doors and prepared to serve him if he called for grog. When he came in he presented a horse pistol at me and stated his business. I told him I could not resist, being at the moment unarmed, and he then mustered the lot of us, asked for the key of the store and marched us all into it, locked us up and the boy kept guard over us with a small pistol. He then went over the premises and finding a drawer locked, he sent the boy to fetch the key. I went back with the boy and unlocked the drawer, his pistol disagreeably close to my head. I told him he need not be frightened (he appeared to be very nervous) as I did not intend to show fight, the balance of power being against me. He took several cheques and small orders and about £2 worth of silver. I asked him to leave the silver as I could not carry on the business without it, then he gave me back about a dozen shillings, I told him 23 [shillings] belonged to the Hosteler, the price of an accordion I sold for him, he said he would not take the Hosteler's money and left it.

I told him my mates were getting tired of their confinement, he ordered the boy to let them out, and then keeping us in conversation on the verandah whilst the boy selected what ever they fancied in the store. After getting all they wanted, he called for glasses all round and paid me for them. I told him my stock was very low so he only took a couple of bottles of brandy away with him. We had a long conversation after it was over. I tried to persuade him to give over his present calling and take a stockman situation, where he was not known. He thanked me for my advice but said he tried that before but it was no answer.

They left here 10 minutes to 12 a.m. and rode by a few minutes afterwards leading two horses, all in fine condition. Three hours after they left, Constable Langworthy came back from Maidenhead, his horse considerably faded and extremely vexed. He wanted to follow, I told him 'twas no use with the horse he had by him, he went to the station for another, but I don't think he succeeded. I must say Mister Langworthy had exerted himself to the utmost, but will never succeed until he is furnished with better horses. When he borrowed a horse 'tis a 2nd or 3rd rate animal, whereas Thunderbolt is riding the finest horse I have seen in the district. John Macdonald, Esquire is an exception to the rule and furnishes a good horse if one is to be convenient to the place.

May 9th. Thunderbolt and boy went through Ashford today with five horses.

～

Thunderbolt's gentleman-thief image lived on long after his death. It was recalled in 1939 by James Roper's son, then around 90 years old:

*O*f course we often heard of Thunderbolt's doings. It was often rumored that he would stick up Tenterfield, but he never did. Once he was supposed to have paid the town a visit and to have mixed with the people and to have at length been recognized by somebody, but as he was far from being unpopular, he got away from the town without trouble.

My father was stuck up by him when managing a store at Bonshaw for C A Lee. The bushranger took all the cash from the till and made my father have dinner with him. They sat at opposite ends of the table and Thunderbolt had two revolvers and placed one at each side of his plate and watched my father like a cat all the time. My father said to him, 'You need not be afraid of me. I have no gun at all, and you have two. I'm not such a fool as to try anything with you.' The dinner passed off pleasantly enough. Apart from his mission at [that] moment, my father said Thunderbolt was a very nice chap and took a liking to him. Of course, Thunderbolt never took life.

When he was leaving my father said to him. 'Look, you are putting me in a fix, taking all the change. When people come along with only notes or cheques, I won't be able to do business with them.' Thunderbolt agreed it was not quite playing the game and handed him back a good handful of silver, although when he had first taken the money he had said, 'It's not enough.' But my father had been warned that Thunderbolt was about and had previously hidden the bulk of the money in an old boot hidden above the door.

Today, Thunderbolt the gentleman bushranger is like many other bushrangers, proudly advertised by tourism bodies in New England.

Grace Bussell

In September 1838, the steamship *Forfarshire* was wrecked on the Farne Islands, off Britain's northeast coast. The lighthouse keeper William Darling and his daughter, Grace, mounted a heroic rescue effort, rowing a small boat through mountainous seas to save the lives of five passengers. The country was agog with admiration and gratitude. Grace and her father were both awarded gold medals by the Royal Humane Society and an admiring public subscribed 1700 pounds for them. Twenty-three year-old Grace became a national sensation, but she shunned all attempts to turn her into a heroine. She died of tuberculosis at the age of twenty-seven but her story would have a lasting echo in Australia.

*T*hirty-eight years after the *Forfarshire* was lost, Grace Bussell, a sixteen-year-old living in the Margaret River region of Western Australia, had a strange dream. She saw a smoking sailing ship shattered on jagged rocks, with screaming passengers hanging desperately to the rigging. The following night, the ship *Georgette*, bound for Adelaide with a cargo of jarrah wood, ran aground twenty kilometres from the Bussells' home. With the boiler room flooded, the captain had deliberately wrecked his sinking ship to give its passengers and crew, some sixty people in all, a chance to survive. A lifeboat was launched, but the stormy seas capsized it, drowning five children and two women. The others in the lifeboat were then rescued by four crewmen, eventually reaching shore after a twelve-hour battle against the wind and waves. The rest of the *Georgette*'s crew and passengers were unable to escape. Any lifeboats they launched capsized in the crashing seas, drowning their occupants.

On shore, an Aboriginal employee of the Bussells' named Sam Isaacs saw the ship and galloped to the homestead with the news. Grace Bussell took a spyglass, ran to the top of a nearby hill and spotted the wreck. She and Sam found some ropes, mounted their horses and rode to the sea.

At a rocky place called Calgardup, they were able to get down a cliff and into the swirling water. They swam the horses out to the ship, and carried or towed the survivors to shore. After four hours, they had saved most of the *Georgette*'s remaining passengers and crew. Grace then rode back to the homestead and alerted her father. He and a rescue party arrived at the scene the following morning. The passengers and sailors were all taken to the family home, where they were cared for by Grace's mother, Ellen.

When news of the rescue reached Perth, and then the world, Grace Bussell was pronounced 'the Grace Darling of the West'. In 1878, she was awarded the silver medal of the Royal Humane Society. Sam received the Society's bronze medal and a grant of 100 acres. Ellen Bussell, already in poor health, died just a few weeks after the disaster. Her last words were supposedly, 'Fetch them all. I can take them in.'

❦

Grace Bussell's legend lives on, though mostly in Western Australia. At Redgate Beach, where the *Georgette* foundered, the rock that brought the ship to disaster is known as Isaacs Rock after Sam Isaacs. Grace is commemorated in the town names Lake Grace and Gracetown, and the city of Busselton is named after the Bussell family. No one seems to have recognised the bravery of the horses.

Diggers

From Gallipoli on, the Australian experience of war has produced a rich trove of anecdotes, legends and yarns, which commonly stress the diggers' wit, lack of pretension, and refusal to kowtow to their presumed betters.

One particularly popular group of stories dealt with Lieutenant-General Sir William Birdwood, the commanding officer at Gallipoli, whom the Anzacs affectionately nicknamed Birdie. One day Birdwood was nearing a dangerous gap in a trench when the sentry called out, 'Duck, Birdie; you'd better —— well duck.' 'What did you do?' asked the outraged generals to whom Birdwood told the story. 'Do? Why, I —— well ducked!'

Most Birdie yarns present the general as a 'digger with stripes', a leader who has—and appreciates—the qualities his men themselves esteem. Set in central London, this story neatly combines Australian anti-authoritarianism with a wariness of the English class system. In it, Birdwood explains to the class-bound English generals that he would be abused by the low-ranking Australian soldiers if he had the temerity to discipline him for failing to observe the military etiquette of saluting officers, thus affirming the egalitarian character of the AIF, as opposed to that of the British army.

*W*hilst General Birdwood was chatting in the Strand with two or three Tommy officers, an Aussie strolled by, characteristically omitting the salute.

'Notice that Digger go by, Birdwood?' asked a Tommy officer.

'Yes, why?'

'Well, he didn't salute. Why didn't you pull him up for it?'

'Look here,' said Birdie, 'if you want to be told off in the Strand, I don't.'

A number of the Birdwood yarns play on the general's 'common touch'. When a naive sentry fails to recognise him, for example, Birdwood jovially shakes his hand. At Gallipoli, Birdwood seldom wore his insignia of rank. In one story, a digger addresses him a little too casually. 'Do you know who I am?' asks Birdwood. 'No,' says the digger. 'Who are you?' 'I'm General Birdwood.' 'Struth,' says the digger, springing to attention. 'Why don't you wear your feathers the same as any other bird would?'

There is also the Gallipoli reinforcement who mistakes the general for a cook, and the digger who, when told Birdwood's name, asks him to "ave a cup o' tea, Mister Birdwood.'

Birdwood sees an Anzac pushing a wheelbarrow, an unusual sight at Gallipoli. 'Did you make it yourself?' he asks. 'No, Mister Birdwood, I bloody-well didn't,' pants the digger, 'but I'd like to find the bastard who did!'

Later, on the Western Front, Birdwood says to a digger, 'Come on, let's go for a run.' 'Too right,' replies the digger, and off they go. After a while, the panting digger draws level with Birdwood. 'Hey, where's that bloody rum you promised me?'

In another tale, Birdwood sees a digger trying to wash from a tin half-full of water. 'Having a good bath?' he asks. 'Yes,' says the digger, 'but I could do much better if I was a blinking canary.'

One digger, flat broke, decides to write to God and ask for a ten-pound note. He addresses the letter 'per General Birdwood, Headquarters'. The general, much amused, takes the letter into the officers' mess. 'We will collect amongst us and raise the tenner for this fellow,' he says. The laughing officers put together seven pounds, and Birdwood sends it to the digger. Next day there arrives a receipt as follows: 'Dear God, Thanks for sending me the tenner; but the next lot you send, don't send it through Headquarters, as Birdie and his mob pinched three quid of it.'

In another anti-authoritarian Aussie tale, Lord Herbert Horatio Kitchener, the British War Minister, visits the Anzacs at Gallipoli and tells them they can be proud of what they've achieved. To which one digger replies: 'My oath we are, Steve.'

Another tale that understood Australians' irreverence towards rank appeared in the *British Australasian* in 1920 under the title 'The Digger and the Colonel':

*A*n 'Aussie' story has to do with a sentry who stopped an English colonel, who was trying to get to his own lines. The officer was without a passport so the sentry would not let him pass.

'But I am an English colonel, and I must get to my lines,' the officer said.

'I don't care a damn,' said the Aussie, as he shouldered his rifle.

The colonel continued his expostulations until he heard a drowsy voice from the trench say: 'Don't argue, Bill; shoot the tinted cow, and let's get to sleep.'

In a variant on this story, a captain draws the fed-up cry from a nearby tent: 'Don't stand there argufying all night, Dig, shoot the blighter.' Variations of this one were still being told by Australian troops in the Western Desert during World War II.

The toughness and nonchalance of the digger under fire was another common theme. In a typical story, four Aussies have settled down to a game of cards in a quiet corner of the Western Front trenches when a great commotion is heard. One of the players jumps up to the look-out step. 'Hi, you fellows!' he calls to his mates. 'A whole enemy division is coming over!' Another digger gets up, looking bored. 'All right,' he says. 'You get on with the game. I'm dummy this hand; I'll go.'

Similar stories are told of diggers who are so little bothered by enemy fire that they play two-up by the light of the barrage flares, or who are so intent on their game that others think they are praying. Then there are the diggers who blast an enemy position, then, meeting no resistance, run up to it—and find a fellow digger inside, nonchalantly cooking a meal and wondering what all the noise is about.

Other tales underscore the diggers' bravery by gently mocking awards like the Victoria Cross. In one, a soldier is carrying a mate across No Man's Land under heavy fire.

''Ere,' the wounded soldier suddenly exclaims, 'what about turnin' round and walkin' backwards for a spell? You're gettin' the V.C., but I'm gettin' all the blinkin' bullets.'

The same kind of casual iconoclasm features in the yarn in which a digger is taken to see a sacred flame (usually in Bethlehem) that has burned for two thousand years. The puzzled Australian looks at it for a moment, fills his lungs and blows. 'It's about time someone put it out,' he says.

The alleged vulgarity of ordinary Australians—alleged by British visitors, at least—became a popular theme of digger yarns, which often combined a proud use of Aussie vernacular with a tilt at perceived British pretensions.

An officer, inspecting the front lines, calls down, 'What soldiers are in this trench, my man?' 'First Sussex Regiment, Sir.' A few yards on, he repeats, 'What soldiers are in this trench, my man?' 'What the ———— has it got to do with you?' comes the reply. 'Oh, this is the Australian trench,' the officer says.

Or, in another version: 'Halt! Who goes there?' asks a sentry. 'Auckland Mounted Rifles,' or some such. 'Pass, friend.' Next, 'Halt, Who goes there?' 'What the ———— has that got to do with you?' 'Pass, Australian.'

The diggers' egalitarianism and sense of humour went home with them after the war. This tale dates from World War II:

a traveller stopped to chat to a farmer who had a large number of men at work in the fields.

'Are those men ex-soldiers?' he asked.

'Most of them,' the farmer said. 'One was a private; he's a first-class worker. The chap over near the fence was a corporal; he's pretty good. The chap driving the harrow was a major; he's only so-so; and the man over there stacking the weeds used to be a colonel.'

'And how do you find him?'

'Well, I'm not going to say anything against no man who used to be a colonel,' the farmer said; 'but I've made up my mind about one thing—I'm not going to hire no generals.'

Sportsmen

Australia is widely recognised as a sports-loving nation, and one of the largest troves of heroic tales centres on hall-of-famers like

Don Bradman, Roy Cazaly, Cathy Freeman, Evonne Goolagong and Dawn Fraser.

In many cases, sporting heroes' life stories are impressive enough to serve as quasi-legends. Les Darcy is just one example.

Born near Maitland, New South Wales, in 1895, Darcy was apprenticed to a blacksmith. As a teenager, he started making money by entering boxing matches, and eventually caught the attention of managers in Sydney. He lost his first three bouts there, but from early 1915 he won twenty-two fights in a row, including thirteen successive Australian middle-weight titles, and seemed well on the way to fame and fortune.

In October 1915, Darcy stowed away on a ship headed for the US. This not only breached the *War Precautions Act* but brought accusations that he was a shirker who was afraid to enlist. When promised American matches did not eventuate, he was reduced to performing in vaudeville. He became a US citizen and joined the army, but his call-up was deferred so he could train for a bout in Memphis, Tennessee. On the eve of the fight, he collapsed from septicaemia, which was later blamed on poor dental work he'd received in Australia. His fiancée flew to his side, but he died at the age of twenty-one.

Already a popular favourite in Australia, Darcy now became a tragic hero. His distant and apparently inexplicable death sparked rumours (still extant) that he had been poisoned by the 'Yanks', who were afraid their own hero would be beaten by an upstart nobody from Down Under, as a contemporary ballad about his death had it:

Way down in Tennessee
There lies poor Les Darcy
His mother's pride and joy
Yes, Maitland's fighting boy.

All I can think of tonight
Is to see Les Darcy fight,
How he beats them,
Simply eats them
Every Saturday night.
And people in galore
Said they had never saw
The likes of Les before
Upon the stadium floor.
They called him a skiter
But he proved to them a fighter
But we lost all hope
When he got that dope
Way down in Tennessee.

When his casket was brought back to Sydney, an estimated half a million people turned out to farewell Darcy. Outside sporting circles, his popularity has waned, but on the fiftieth anniversary of his death flags were flown at half-mast in New South Wales and a memorial was built at his birthplace.

Racehorses

As might be expected in a country where people are known to enjoy a bet on the 'gee-gees', Australian horseracing is a mine of stories. As well as its own argot ('ring-in', 'mug punter' and so on), the turf boasts legends, yarns and songs about great—and not-so-great—horses, jockeys, punters, trainers and other characters, many with colourful nicknames like Perce 'The Prince' Galea, Harry the Horse and Hollywood George.

Melbourne Cup Day is almost a national holiday: millions of Australians stop work to watch or listen to the race, and many place bets on that day alone.

The country's best-known racing legend by far is the story of Phar Lap. The chestnut gelding was initially thought to be a loser, not even placing in its first four races. But between 1928 and 1932 it won thirty-seven of fifty races, including the 1930 Melbourne Cup. As the hardships of the Great Depression began to weigh on Australians, Phar Lap became a national hero.

On a wave of adulation, Phar Lap travelled to the US, but on the eve of his first race, in April 1932, he suddenly and mysteriously died. People immediately thought of Les Darcy, and rumours quickly spread that the horse too had been poisoned—still a widespread folk belief.

The remains of the fabled horse were parcelled out: the hide to the National Museum of Victoria, the heart initially to the National Institute of Anatomy in Canberra, and the skeleton to the National Museum of New Zealand, where Phar Lap was born. The unusually large heart is the most popular exhibit at the National Museum of Australia, where it now resides, and the expression 'a heart as big as Phar Lap's' has passed into the vernacular.

Phar Lap embodies the culturally powerful image of the battler, the underdog who struggles against adversity—and sometimes triumphs. Such is the popular interest in his story that Australian governments have spent considerable sums investigating the rumours that the horse was poisoned. Tests done in 2006 found abnormal levels of arsenic in Phar Lap's remains. How it got there has yet to be determined.

9

Characters

Mum: Dave's gone and broke his leg, Dad!
Dad: D'yer think we ought to shoot 'im?

Dad and Dave

THE ODD AND the eccentric, those who stand out from the crowd, are popular folk figures in all countries. They might be noted for their stupidity, their idleness, their cleverness or their cheek.

In the idiot category, the French have Jean Sot (Foolish John), the Italians have Bastienelo, and the English have Lazy Jack. Sandy the Shearer is an Australian member of this low-wattage family. When told that some lambs are for sale at five shillings each, he complains bitterly that this is far too expensive. When the seller says he can have them for £3 (sixty shillings) a dozen, Sandy is overjoyed and buys the lot. Interestingly, fools are almost always male.

Tricksters—also mostly male—use their intelligence to hood-wink and manipulate others. Typical examples include the Javanese Pak Dungu, Germany's Till Eulenspiegel, and Turkey's Hodja. Australian Aboriginal tradition has many mythical trickster figures, as well as the more modern character usually known as Jackie Bindi-i.

Dopey or smart, characters are usually humorous figures.

The drongo

The fools of folklore are more than ordinarily dumb, so stupid that they acquire an almost heroic aura. The Australian version of this folk type includes—along with Sandy the Shearer—the ubiquitious drongo. (The name is said to commemorate a racehorse of the 1920s who was famous for losing.) The drongo is a congenitally naive figure who interprets literally whatever he is told. When the boss tells him to hang a new gate, the drongo takes the gate to the nearest tree and puts a noose on it. Asked to dig some turnips about the size of his head, the drongo is found pulling up the entire turnip patch and trying his hat on each uprooted turnip for size.

When the drongo goes fishing, he has no luck. He asks another fisherman who is catching plenty what he uses for bait. 'Magpie,' the man says. The drongo gets his gun, shoots a magpie and returns to the riverside. He hooks the bird to his line and casts it into the water, but still he has no luck. The other fisherman cannot understand it and asks to have a look at the drongo's line. He reels it in, revealing a sodden mess of feathers. 'You didn't pluck the bird!' he says. The drongo replies that he was going to pluck it but thought that if he did the fish would not be able to tell what kind of bird it was.

In another story, the drongo is working for a farmer when the boss decides it is time to build another windmill. The drongo agrees to help but asks the farmer if he thinks it really makes sense to have two windmills. 'What do you mean?' the farmer asks. 'Well,' says the drongo, 'there's barely enough wind to operate the one you already have, so I doubt there'll be enough to work two of them.'

Snuffler Oldfield

Queensland's own drongo is the stockman Snuffler Oldfield, about whom there are said to be thousands of stories. One goes like this:

*S*nuffler Oldfield was droving one time. He always seemed to be the one who ended up rounding up the cattle each night, while the boss and the jackaroos took it easy or slept back at the camp.

One night the cattle rushed and headed straight through the camp. The drovers had to clamber up trees to avoid being crushed. The boss called out, 'Where are you, Snuffler?'

From just above the boss's head came Snuffler's voice: 'One limb above you.'

Once, when Snuffler's wife was giving birth, the nurse came out to tell Snuffler that he had a child. She returned to the birthing room but returned a short while later saying that he now had a second baby. 'Christ, nurse,' said Snuffler, 'don't touch her again, she must be full of them!'

Tom Doyle

Tom Doyle is said to have been the publican and mayor of Kanowna, in Western Australia's goldfields. An Irishman, he didn't always understand colloquial expressions. In one of the many yarns told about him, he attends a function for a visiting dignitary. For the first time in his life, he is confronted with olives. He gingerly picks one up and is alarmed to discover that it is moist. Just as the dignitary rises to speak, Tom cries out that someone has pissed on the gooseberries.

In Tom's days as a member of the local council, a debate is held on a proposal to enlarge a local dam. Tom declares that the existing dam is so small he can piss halfway across it. When a councillor tells him he is out of order, Tom says, 'Yes, and if I was in order I could piss all the way across it.'

Commenting on a dispute over whether to fence the town cemetery, Tom says, 'Why worry? Them that's in don't want to get out, and them that's out don't want to get in.' He also describes prospectors as 'people who go into the wilderness with a shovel in one hand, a waterbag in the other and their life in their other hand'.

The widow Reilly's pigs

The Irish influence on Australian folklore has been profound. Irish people themselves are almost always portrayed as fools, albeit funny ones. This story first appeared in print in the 1890s, but was probably old by then.

The widow Reilly had eight children. She struggled to provide for them by raising cows and pigs.

One of her sows gave birth to ten piglets. As the piglets grew, the widow's neighbor, whose name was Patrick, would admire them as he passed by on the way to work.

One morning, the widow Reilly discovered that one of the piglets was missing. She informed the local priest, who, based on her suspicions, asked Patrick whether he had seen the pig. Pat, squirming a little, said no. The priest reminded Patrick that on Judgment Day, when all men would stand before the Good Lord, someone would have to answer for the theft of the widow Reilly's piglet.

Pat thought for a moment. 'Will the widow be there on Judgment Day too?' he asked. 'Yes,' said the priest, 'and so will the pig. What will you have to say then?'

Pat replied brightly, 'I'll say to Mrs Reilly, "Here is your pig back, and thanks very much for the lend of it."'

Dad, Dave and Mabel

Perhaps the best-known forms of Australian yokel lore are the Dad and Dave yarns. An invention of Australian author 'Steele Rudd' (Arthur Hoey Davis, 1868–1935), Dad, Mum and their foolish son Dave first appeared in *The Bulletin* in 1895. Four years later the sketches appeared in book form under the title *On Our Selection*, which spawned many sequels and subsequent editions. The books were best-sellers, also having stage, film and radio adaptations, and have inspired numerous humorous folktales which concentrate on portraying Dad, Dave and the family as country hicks.

The other important aspect of the Dad and Dave yarns is the portrayal of Dave as a gormless fool, very much in the tradition of the popular 'numbskull' stories. In one typical exchange, Dave is leaving home to join the army. Mum, worried about her son in the big city, prevails on Dad to give him a fatherly lecture about the perils of drink, gambling and women. Dave is at pains to let Dad know that he doesn't have any truck with such things. Dad returns to Mum and says: 'You needn't worry. I don't think the army will take him anyway, the boy's a half-wit!'

In another tale, Dave gets a job driving a truck in the city. On the first day the boss asks him to deliver three bears to the zoo. Hearing nothing from Dave for a very long time the boss decides to find out what has happened to him. He drives along the route that Dave would have taken and sees him buying tickets to the cinema for himself and the bears.

'I told you to take those bears to the zoo,' the angry boss yells at Dave. 'What are you doing at the cinema with them?'

Unperturbed, Dave slowly replies that the truck broke down and as he couldn't take the bears to the zoo he decided to take them to the 'pitchers' instead.

Many Dad and Dave yarns involve Dad, Dave and Dave's mother, but there are also others involving Dave's wife, Mabel. In one of these Dave comes into a bit of extra money and decides to buy Mabel a present. He goes into the dining room, picks up the table and carries it down the street. On the way he meets a mate who asks him if he is moving house. 'Oh no,' Dave replies cheerfully, 'I'm just going out to buy Mabel a new tablecloth.'

The theme of yokel stupidity that lies at the heart of the Dave character continues in a number of stories about Dave and Mabel's escapades in the hospitality business. Dave and Mabel decide to make some money by opening an outback roadhouse. The locals and truckies are quite happy with Mabel's basic but sustaining cooking but the restaurant fails to attract any tourists. Eventually an American comes in. Dave sits him down and asks him what he would like to eat. The American looks around and notices a truckie demolishing a meal of steak, salad, chips and eggs. 'I'll have what he's eating, but eliminate the eggs.'

Dave bustles back to the kitchen to prepare the order but after a few minutes' discussion with Mabel he returns to the American's table. 'Uhh, sorry, but we've had an accident in the kitchen and the 'liminator's broke. Would you like your eggs fried instead?'

In another story from the sequence, Dave and Mabel open a bed and breakfast. The rooms are pretty basic but eventually a couple arrive from the city to stay the night. When they see the room they complain that there is no toilet. Dave assures them that this is just the way things are done in the bush and provides them with a bucket to use if they need to relieve themselves during the night.

Next morning Dave knocks on their door and asks what they would like for breakfast. They order a full bush breakfast and coffee. Dave dashes off but is back in a minute asking if they would like milk in their coffee. 'Yes, please,' chorus the couple. 'Alright,' says Dave, 'but could you give us the bucket back so's the missus can milk the cow?'

When Dave and Mabel finally get married, Dave asks Dad for a quiet word before they leave for their honeymoon. 'Could you do me a favour, Dad?' he asks.

'Of course, Dave,' Dad replies, 'what is it?'

'Would you mind going on the honeymoon for me, you know a lot more about that sort of thing than I do.'

Published Dad and Dave stories are mostly in this style, although there is a considerable number that rarely appear in print due to their overtly sexual nature. By modern standards, the bawdy element is quite mild, although many older Australians consider such tales unsuitable for telling in public or in mixed company. Folklorist Warren Fahey recalls being told 'hundreds' of obscene Dad and Dave jokes in the 1970s and '80s, though believes they are now dying out in oral tradition.

But Dad and Dave are alive and well in the small Queensland town of Nobby. This is 'Dad and Dave Country', where visitors can find 'Rudd's Pub', named after the the author, who allegedly wrote there.

Cousin Jacks

Groups on the periphery of a community are often portrayed as stupid, whether the community is a city or a nation. This mocking of the marginal was perhaps more common before the twentieth century, when such groups were often physically separate from the mainstream. Just as America had its Okies and Canada its Newfoundlanders, Australia had Tasmanians— and Cousin Jacks, Cornish people who migrated to work in the tin mines of South Australia in the nineteenth century. While Cousin Jacks were not portrayed as inbred like 'Taswegians', they were endowed in folklore with the kind of idiocy city folk have long associated with yokels. Many Cousin Jack yarns poke fun at the Cornishmen's distinctive accent.

a Cornishman hires a carpenter, a fellow Cousin Jack, to erect a fence. When it is done, the boss Cousin Jack complains that it's a bit crooked in the middle.

'It be near enough,' says the carpenter.

'Near enough be not good enough. 'E must be 'zact.'

'Well, 'e be 'zact,' replies the carpenter.

'Oh well, if 'e be 'zact, 'e be near enough,' says the employer, walking away satisfied.

~

Tom'n'oplas

The central character of a series of tales told around Sydney during the 1980s is an Australian version of the trickster, a staple of folk tradition around the world. The teller in this case acted out the antics he described:

T he bank manager is sitting at his desk, round about lunchtime, when the assistant manager comes in and says, 'Look, he's done it again. Tom'n'Oplas—he's put a thousand dollars in the bank. I can't work it out.'

And the manager says, 'Well, what should we do? Do we have a responsibility to dob this guy in? Is he getting his money legally, or . . . ? What do you think?'

The assistant manager said, 'Well, why don't we call him in and find out?'

So come next Monday Tom'n'Oplas arrives, puts a thousand dollars in the bank. And the assistant manager says, 'Mr Tom'n'Oplas, the manager would like to see you.'

He goes into the office. The manager sits him down, says, 'Mr Tom'n' Oplas, you're one of our best customers, but I can't work out why every Monday morning you put a thousand dollars in the bank.'

Tom'n'Oplas laughs. He says, 'Oh yes. Well, I'm a gambler.'

The manager says, 'What do you mean? Is it something you can let me in on? A thousand dollars a week—that's fifty grand a year. I could retire on that.'

Tom says, 'Well, I tell you what I'll do. I'll bet you a thousand dollars that this time next week you'll have hair growing all over your back.'

And the manager thought, 'Ha, ha, ha. Obviously this fellow's gone off the rails a little bit under a bit of pressure from me.' He said, 'Mr Tom'n'Oplas, that's a bet.'

Next day the manager checks his back. No hair. This is wonderful, he thinks. That night he sleeps on his back so it won't grow because he's putting pressure on it.

Wednesday he wears a sweater because he thinks the only way Tom'n'Oplas can get him is to tape something on his back, or put something on his shirt, or whatever. It's the middle of summer, and all the staff think he's a little bit crazy, but he's thinking 'a thousand dollars'.

Thursday, he doesn't wear a shirt, just a jumper, in case Tom gets to his laundry and puts hairs in his shirt.

Friday he's getting a little bit toey. Saturday and Sunday he just locks himself away in the house.

Monday morning arrives. He checks his back in the mirror and he can't see anything there. 'A thousand dollars,' he thinks.

Tom'n'Oplas arrives at the bank, and he's got a Japanese fellow with him. The manager says 'Mr. Tom'n'Oplas, in here.' Tom says, 'I thought you'd be wanting to see me. I suppose you think you've won your bet.' The manager whips his shirt off and turns around—and the Japanese fellow faints. 'Look, look,' the manager says. 'No hair. But . . . what's happened to your mate?'

Tom says, 'Oh, that's simple, I bet him $2000 that within thirty seconds of getting in here I'd have the shirt off your back.'

Jacky Bindi-i

An Aboriginal stockman or roustabout known as Jacky Bindi-i, Jacky-Jacky or just Jacky, features in a number of bush yarns, and even in song. Jacky is generally distinguished by his sharp retorts, often undercutting the authority of the boss, the policeman or the magistrate. As the folklorist John Meredith points out:

> There are literally dozens of these stories, all concerned with situations involving Jacky-Jacky, his lubra Mary, black sheep, white sheep, the white boss and his station-hands and his wife. In this series of folk-tales, 'Jacky-Jacky' generally, but not always, comes out on top, scoring a victory over the white boss.

One day Jacky and his boss needed to cross a flooded river but the only boat was on the far bank. The boss told Jacky to swim across and bring the boat back. Jacky protested, saying that there may be crocodiles in the river. The boss said that he need not worry as crocodiles never touch blackfellas. Jacky replied that the crocodiles might be colour-blind and that it would be better to wait until the flood subsided.

On another occasion Jacky was in a distant part of the property minding a mob of sheep and he needed his rations and other necessities delivered to him by the boss each week. One week the boss forgot to bring Jacky's food. Jacky was not too happy and told the boss that he only had a bone left from last week's rations and that it would be another week before any more meat came. The boss laughed and told him not to worry, saying 'The nearer the bone the sweeter the meat.' When the boss returned the following week the sheep were in a terrible condition as Jacky had kept them where there was no grass to eat. The boss turned on Jacky and angrily asked him what he thought he was doing. Jacky just laughed and said 'The nearer the ground, the sweeter the grass.'

Jacky Bindi-i's other main activity is stealing sheep or cows, for which he is frequently brought before the courts. At one of his hearings the judge gave Jacky three years in prison and asked him if he had anything to say. 'Yes,' said Jacky angrily, 'You're bloody free with other people's time.'

In another court, this time for being drunk and disorderly, the magistrate fined Jacky and gave him twenty days in prison. 'I'll tell you what I'll do, boss,' said Jacky. 'I'll toss you—forty days or nothing.'

Jacky is caught red-handed by a trooper one day as he catches him butchering a stolen bullock. He ties Jacky to his horse and leads the way on the lengthy journey back to town. As they ride, Jacky asks the trooper how he had tracked him down. 'I smelled you out,' replies the trooper proudly.

They ride on and as darkness falls, so does the rain and it is not too long before the trooper loses his way. 'Do you know the way to town, Jacky?' he asks his prisoner at last. Jacky is ready with his answer: 'Why don't you smell the way back to town the same as you smelled out Jacky?'

Jacky-Jacky also features in a modern Aboriginal song sung in many versions around the country:

Jacky Jacky was a smart young fellow
Full of fun and energy.
He was thinkin' of gettin' married
But the lubra run away you see.
Cricketah boobelah will-de-mah
Billa na ja jingeree wah.

Jacky used to chase the emu
With his spears and his waddy too.

He's the only man that can tell you
What the emu told a kangaroo.
Cricketah boobelah will-de-mah
Billa na ja jingeree wah.

Hunting food was Jacky's business
'Til the white man come along.
Put his fences across the country
Now the hunting days are gone.
Cricketah boobelah will-de-mah
Billa na ja jingeree wah.

White fella he now pay all taxes
Keep Jacky Jacky in clothes and food.
He don't care what become of the country
White fella tucker him very good.
Cricketah boobelah will-de-mah
Billa na ja jingeree wah.

Now Australia's short of money
Jacky Jacky sit he laugh all day.
White fella want to give it back to Jacky
No fear Jacky won't have it that way.
Cricketah boobelah will-de-mah
Billa na ja jingeree wah.

Jimmy Ah Foo

A real-life Chinese counterpart to Jacky Bindi-i was Jimmy Ah Foo, a publican in outback Queensland. His great skill was reputed to lie in making himself as agreeable as possible to his customers. In the process, he always seemed to benefit. During the shearers' strikes of the 1890s, there were serious outbreaks of anti-Chinese violence, since many shearers feared that Chinese workers would be used as strike breakers. A deputation of local shearers visited Jimmy's pub and told him to sack his Chinese cook. They would be returning the next day to see that he did so. Next day the shearers showed up again. 'I've done as you asked,' Jimmy said. 'I'm the cook now.'

Corny Kenna

An Anglo-Saxon version of the jokester is Victoria's Cornelius Kenna (pronounced Ken-*ah!*)

*C*orny, as he is generally called, is served an under-measure whisky in the pub one day. Seeing his frown, the barmaid defensively says the whisky is thirty years old. 'Very small for its age,' says Kenna.

Another time, Corny is taking a lady through the bush in a timber jinker. A storm closes in, and he whips up the horses. Rattling along, the cart hits a tree stump and overturns. Corny's infuriated passenger says, 'I knew this would happen!' Replies Corny: 'Well, why the devil didn't you tell me?'

Corny lends a horse to a man who vows to return it next day. Nearly two weeks later, the horse still unreturned, Corny meets the man at a local auction. 'Oh,' says the embarrassed horse borrower, 'I've meant to bring it back a dozen times.' 'Once will be enough,' says Corny.

～

On another occasion a city slicker asks Corny for directions to Yaapeet, calling him 'Jack' in the superior manner of many city dwellers when addressing someone from the country. Corny asks the city slicker how he knew that his name was 'Jack'. 'I guessed it,' says the slicker. 'Well guess how to get to Yaapeet, then,' replies Corny.

Three blokes at a pub

Many Australian yarns are not about anyone in particular—just 'a bloke' or 'a couple of blokes', or in this case, three of them.

*T*hree blokes walk into a busy pub. The first one orders a beer, but the barman is too busy to take his money and moves on to serve another customer. Later, he returns to the bloke and asks for the money. 'But I already paid yer,' says the bloke. 'You went and served someone else, came back for my money, took it, and put it in the till with the other money you had.'

The barman, thinking he must have forgotten, says 'OK.' The bloke finishes his drink and leaves.

Then the second orders a beer. The barman serves him without taking the money, serves another customer, then comes back and asks him to pay. 'I already did,' says the bloke. The barman concedes that he must have forgotten and the second bloke leaves.

The third bloke now comes up to the bar. The wary barman tells him, 'Look, two blokes have just ordered beers and I'm pretty sure they didn't pay. Next bloke who tries anything funny like that is going to get it.' And he reaches under the counter and pulls out an iron bar. 'Mate,' says the third bloke, 'I'm sorry for your troubles. All I want is me change, and I'll be out of here.'

The smarter soldier

'Working one's nut' was a World War I expression for manipulating the system. Pat, or P.F., of the 3rd Battalion AIF, was especially good at it, as this affectionate trench journal anecdote illustrates.

*T*here are still many old hands left in the Battalion who remember P.F. It is over three years since he went, but his memory is still green in my mind, and his ingenuity still haunts me.

Early on Anzac, he turned down Sergeant's stripes (this fact is not in official records!) and became a batman. As such we speak of him here.

At this time our rations were pure, unadulterated bully beef, hard biscuits, tea and rice; but we had P.F. and his wonderful brains.

The proximity of battleships and hospital ships riding outside Anzac Cove instantly fired his genius. On the former he knew there would be poultry pens; on the latter an ample supply of good provisions. The problem was how to procure them.

A sailor's costume and a few bandages solved the difficulty.

For the rest, he always had plenty of money. Where it came from one cannot say. Perhaps some digger who felt like floating a war loan, ten minutes after pay, can make a shrewd guess.

He has been seen on a lighter in sailor's clothes—hence eggs; and on two occasions live poultry arrived in the 3rd Battalion trenches.

He was probably evacuated through the Beach Clearing Station more than any other man on Anzac.

It is thought that he rather overdid it the day he was evacuated twice onto the same ship, and was, unfortunately, recognised by the M.O. on the gangway. However, he had the cunning of the Scarlet Pimpernel, and got away—his duty nobly done; hence fresh bread and milk in the mess that night.

He would see a fatigue party unloading flour—off with his coat and to work with them for an hour or so. One bag would, sooner or later, be over-carried, and find its way to our dug-out. One day, not content with the flour, he also 'lifted' a mule from a mule train, and arrived at the trenches, mule and flour in good order.

To wait in the queue for water was a waste of time to Pat's inventive mind. Woe betide the new chum he saw with two full tins of water. A conversation for five minutes or so and Pat had the full tins. 'So long mate, I had better get my water'—and he was out of sight. The new chum had the two empty tins and another two or three hours' wait in the queue to fill up again.

Goodness knows what would have become of him had not the General Staff decided Lone Pine. I saw him that day, as full of life as ever—I have not seen him since. Two days later after Lone Pine I saw a neat little bundle marked 'Killed in action'. Contents: one pay-book, one pocket-book, and photos, and one identity disc marked P.F., D. Coy., 3rd Bn. So poor Pat was dead! I believe I shed a genuine tear. The next I heard that he was inspecting one of the military hospitals as a Padre, and tipping the wink to a 3rd Battalion man who recognised him.

How he got away I never heard definitely, but I can imagine someone with a bloodstained bandage round one arm staggering into the clearing station and handing in the dead body on the way down—and P.F., alias Tom Jones was evacuated to the hospital ship. On arrival there I cannot imagine what he would do, but it is quite likely he became a steward or an A.M.C. orderly, or he even may have thrown the skipper of the boat overboard and taken charge.

If ever I want a 'tenner' and P.F. is about, I'll look him up. I know, even if he has not got it—which is not likely—he will know where it is to be got!

— ∾ —

Taken for a ride

An oft-told tale of the turf involves a city bookie taking his horse from the city to a country race meeting.

A bookie decides to get a jockey to run his horse 'dead', meaning that it will lose the race even though it is a good horse. He inflates the odds to 2–1.

A punter then approaches the bookie to make a bet on a three-horse race. Depending on which version of the story is being told, either the punter or the bookie pumps up the odds on the favourite to the point where the punter has laid out a lot of money. The race begins and the favourite, despite being held back by the jockey, still somehow wins against the unbelievably slow two local horses. At this point the bookie, facing a very large payout, snarls at the punter and says something like 'Hey, mate, you think you're pretty bloody clever, don't you? But you didn't know I owned the favourite.'

The punter laughs and says, 'I know, but I own the other two.'

10

Hard cases

How would I be? How would I bloody well be!
The world's greatest whinger

AUSTRALIANS NOTORIOUS FOR miserliness, bloody-mindedness or a generally contrary nature are often referred to as 'hard cases'. Quite a few of them—named and unnamed—are celebrated in folk stories.

The cocky

Cocky is slang for a small farmer, the kind who scraped a living from marginal land. Cockies' miserliness and dourness make them among the hardest of Australian hard cases, as the poem 'The Cockies of Bungaree' indicates.

> We used to go to bed, you know, a little bit after dark,
> The room we used to sleep in was just like Noah's Ark.
> There was mice and rats and dogs and cats and pigs and poulter-ee,
> I'll never forget the work we did down on Bungaree.

A cocky hires a labourer on the basis that work stops at sunset. When the sun goes down, the worker says, 'Time to call it a day.' 'Sun hasn't set yet,' says the cocky. 'You can still see it if you climb up on top of the fence.'

In another, the worker succeeds in getting the upper hand when the farmer wakes up his new labourer well before sunrise and says he needs a hand getting in the oats. 'Are they wild oats?' asks the sleepy labourer. 'No,' says the cocky, taken aback. 'Then why do we have to sneak up on 'em in the dark!'

Another cocky's new labourer asks when he will have a day off. 'Every fourth Sunday's free,' the cocky says. 'Much to do round here on me day off?' asks the worker. 'Plenty,' says the cocky. 'There's cutting the week's firewood, mending the harnesses, tending the vegetables and washing the horses. After that, you can do whatever you like.'

One night in the pub, a local bloke congratulates a cocky on the coming marriage of his daughter. 'That'll be the fourth wedding in your family in the last few years, won't it?'

'Yes,' replies the cocky. 'And the confetti is starting to get awful dirty.'

Other yarns are a little more forgiving of the cocky, stressing the hardships of his situation.

*T*he drought had lasted so long that when a raindrop fell on the local cocky, he fainted clean away. They had to throw two buckets-full of dust into his face to bring him back to consciousness.

Times were so hard that all the cocky had to eat was rabbits. He had them for every meal, week in, week out. He had them stewed, he had them fried, he had them boiled he had them braised. Feeling rather ill, he decided to give himself a dose of Epsom salts. When that didn't help, he went to the local doctor, who asked him what he'd been eating. 'I've had nothing but rabbits for months,' the cocky said. 'Taken anything for it?' the doctor asked. 'Epsom salts,' said the cocky. 'You don't need Epsom salts,' said the doctor with a laugh, 'you need ferrets.'

Three cocky farmers were chatting over a beer. The first, who came from the Riverina, said he could run three head to an acre all year long. The second cocky, from central New South Wales said that he could run two head to an acre. The third cocky was from out Bourke way. 'Well, we run ninety-five head to an acre,' he says. 'You're bloody kidding,' said the other two. 'It's true,' he insisted, 'I run one head of sheep and ninety-four rabbits.'

―

Hungry Tyson

James Tyson (1819–1898) was a highly successful pastoralist, or 'squatter', who made a fortune through acquiring rural land during the mid to late nineteenth century. Despite his wealth he lived simply, neither smoking, drinking nor swearing, probably something of a novelty for his time and geography. In folklore, Tyson was renowned for his stinginess and known universally as 'Hungry'Tyson. His Scrooge-like character was even memorialised in folk speech through the saying 'mean as Hungry Tyson'.

Sayings and yarns about Tyson echo his legendary meanness. He is rumoured to have once claimed that he hadn't got rich by 'striking matches when there was a fire to get a light by'.

Once, Hungry Tyson had to cross the Murrumbidgee River. The cost of being ferried across in the punt was one shilling. To save having to pay the money, the tight-fisted grazier swam over.

A rural newspaper of 1891 carried a selection of Tyson yarns in the context of his opposition to the bitter strike of the Queensland shearers:

*T*he name of Mr. James Tyson (or, as he is familiarly called, 'Old Jimmy'), the Queensland millionaire, is so well known throughout this and the other colonies, says the *Narrandera Ensign*, and as he is at present making a most determined stand against the Queensland Union shearers, perhaps the following few anecdotes about the old gentleman may be of some interest. That 'Jimmy' is a very eccentric fellow no one who has ever come in contact with him will deny, and he has made several attempts to perform big public business; attempts which would have brought a less reserved man into prominent notoriety.

The first of these was to offer to construct a line of railway from Rockhampton to the Gulf of Carpentaria, the farthest coastal point in Queensland. The recompense 'James' required from the Government was three miles depth of frontage along the whole route; but the representatives of the people in Bananaland thought the offer was a bit one-sided, and declined to negotiate.

We next find Mr. Tyson in New South Wales, at the recent financial crisis, offering to take up £4,000,000 worth of Government Treasury bills at a moderate rate of interest. As the public well know, this offer was also declined.

A few years back, when the large cathedral that adorns Brisbane was in course of construction, the collector for the building fund called upon a well-known mercantile firm for a subscription, but he was politely told that he should go to the rich people of Queensland, who may be in a better position to 'help the work along'.

'To whom shall I go?' queried the collector.

'Well, go to Jimmy Tyson,' was the answer. 'He has more than any of us.'(I might mention that up to that time 'Jimmy's' name was never seen on any list for more than £1).

'Well,' said the collector, 'as Tyson is a rich man I will go to him for a donation.'

'Do,' said the head of the firm, 'and whatever he gives you we will guarantee you the same amount.'

The collector, a few days after meeting Mr. Tyson, related to him what had taken place, and concluded by saying, 'So, Mr. Tyson, I do not know what amount the firm is going to give until I have your name on my list.' 'Well,' said Tyson in a gruff voice, 'give me yer pen and ink and I'll give yees a bob or two.'

'Jimmy' went into a private room and wrote out a cheque for £5000, and gave it to the astonished collector who in turn presented it to the more astonished merchant, who, however, could not 'ante up' more than a century.

On another occasion the subject of this sketch sent a lady a cheque for £300 towards a 'parsonage fund'. The lady, in a jocular manner, sent the cheque back, and asked Mr. Tyson if he bad not forgotten the other '0' at the end of the figures. It is needless to say Mr. Tyson felt aggrieved, and immediately burnt the cheque—and did not subscribe one shilling.

Meeting a friend on one occasion on the platform at the Orange railway station, the friend expressed surprise at seeing Mr. Tyson riding in a second-class carriage.

'Do you know why I do ride in a second-class compartment?' said Mr. Tyson.

'No, I do not know why,' said the acquaintance.

'Well,' said 'Jimmy', 'it is because there is no third-class', and with a broad smile he resumed his seat, and the friend looked crestfallen, and went and drowned his contempt for the 'old fellow' in a bottle of Bass' ale.

The writer of these lines was at one time engaged by Mr. Tyson for three days to do some clerical work, and when the work was completed, he (Mr. Tyson) reviewed the job, and asked me how much he had to pay me. 'Half-a-guinea a day,' was the reply.

'I wish to goodness I could use the pen as well as you do,' said Mr. Tyson. 'If I could I would be a rich man in a few years.' (He had banked the day before a total of £170,000.)

'You are now a very rich man, Mr. Tyson, are you not?' queried I.

'No, I am not,' said 'Jimmy'. 'No man is rich until he has as much as he wants, and I have not near that yet. However, as you have done your work to my satisfaction, kindly accept my cheque for £35.'

It is not necessary for me to state here that I accepted.

Many people are under the impression that Mr. Tyson is a man devoid of all sense of liberality, but they are, in my opinion, sadly mistaken, for although he has been known to refuse a swagman a match lest he was paid for it, he has, on the other hand, been known to help widows and orphans to the tune of thousands, and when he leaves the scene of his earthly struggles, and his life is recorded, I am sure that his liberality and generosity will overbalance the charge laid against him by a certain section of the community, viz.— parsimony.

'Banjo' Paterson wrote a poem about Tyson and he was said to have frequently dressed as a swagman on his own property, sleeping outside until the manager came back from his duties. In contrast to his miserly image, Tyson was also said to be an anonymous doer of good deeds, as Paterson suggests in his poem 'T.Y.S.O.N.'

Across the Queensland border line
The mobs of cattle go;
They travel down in sun and shine
On dusty stage, and slow.
The drovers, riding slowly on
To let the cattle spread,
Will say: 'Here's one old landmark gone,
For old man Tyson's dead'.
What tales there'll be in every camp
By men that Tyson knew;
The swagmen, meeting on the tramp,
Will yarn the long day through,
And tell of how he passed as 'Brown',
And fooled the local men:
'But not for me—I struck the town,
And passed the message further down;
That's T.Y.S.O.N.!'

There stands a little country town
Beyond the border line,
Where dusty roads go up and down,
And banks with pubs combine.
A stranger came to cash a cheque—
Few were the words he said—
A handkerchief about his neck,
An old hat on his head.

A long grey stranger, eagle-eyed—
'Know me? Of course you do?'
'It's not my work,' the boss replied,
'To know such tramps as you'.
'Well, look here, Mister, don't be flash,'
Replied the stranger then,
'I never care to make a splash,
I'm simple—but I've got the cash,
I'm T.Y.S.O.N.!'

But in that last great drafting-yard,
Where Peter keeps the gate,
And souls of sinners find it barred,
And go to meet their fate,
There's one who ought to enter in,
For good deeds done on earth;
Such deeds as merit ought to win,
Kind deeds of sterling worth.

Not by the strait and narrow gate,
Reserved for wealthy men,
But through the big gate, opened wide,
The grizzled figure, eagle-eyed,
Will travel through—and then

Old Peter'll say: 'We pass him through;
There's many a thing he used to do,
Good-hearted things that no one knew;
That's T.Y.S.O.N.!'

At his death, Tyson's estate was worth two million pounds, a fact that gave further force to an apparently existing outback folk belief that the money was cursed, as a literary-minded contemporary wrote shortly after the pastoralist died:

Tyson died alone in the night in his lonely bush station, with thousands of stock on it, but with no hand to give him even a drink of water, and no voice to soothe or to console him in his last struggle with death. He was hurriedly buried. No requiem was sung at his grave. He died, and was forgotten. Only his millions, which Bacon calls 'muck', and Shakespeare 'rascally counters', remained for his shoal of relatives to fight for through the law courts. Some of them were but struggling for an overdose of mortal poison, as the gold proved to be to some persons at least.

There is a strange legend regarding this man's money. The old hands out back will tell you that every coin of it is cursed, and if we follow the havoc some of the money has caused, there is much food for the superstitious mind.

Tyson's folktale image is similar to that of another wealthy pastoralist of a slightly later era, Sidney (later Sir) Kidman (1857–1935). Many of the tales of miserliness are told of both men.

Ninety the Glutton

Tasmania's face-stuffing folk hero is said to have got his name when he was set to look after a mob of sheep. After grazing them for three months, he brought them in for shearing, but he was ninety sheep short. What happened? their owner wanted to know. 'Well, I ate one a day for me rations,' said Ninety.

Ninety wandered all over Tasmania in search of work—and food. Smart farmers would give him one large feed and send him on his way. One, however, pointed to a crate of apples. 'You can have some of these,' he told Ninety. The apples were about to go bad, in any case. About an hour later, the owner came back to find Ninety sitting amid a pile of apple cores. 'What time's dinner, boss?' he said.

Queensland's Ninety is Tom the Glutton, who can polish off a crate of bananas, sometimes including the skins, in just ten minutes.

Galloping Jones

Galloping Jones is thought to have lived in northern Queensland and died in 1960. Jones was a bush fighter, a drinker, and a thief, who was not above stealing stock, selling it, and stealing it back again the very same night.

*O*nce, Galloping Jones was arrested by a policeman and an Aboriginal tracker for illegally slaughtering a cow. The evidence was the cow's hide, prominently marked with someone else's brand. On the way back to town, Jones's captors made camp for the night. Jones managed to get them both drunk, and when they fell asleep, he rode away. Instead of escaping, however, he returned a few hours later with a fresh cow hide, substituted it for the evidence, and went to sleep. The party continued to town, and Jones was duly tried. But when the evidence was pulled out, the hide bore his own brand: case dismissed.

Jones was again captured by a young policeman who he fooled into letting him go behind a bush to relieve himself. Of course, Jones escaped and the policeman had to return to town without his captive.

When he got to town to report his failure to the sergeant, who was in his usual 'office', the pub, there was Jones, washed and shaved and having a beer. The embarrassed policeman threatened to shoot Jones, but the trickster just said that he felt the need for a cleanup and a drink and that he would now be happy to stroll down to the lockup.

The Eulo Queen

Barmaids who may also be prostitutes are not the most likely of heroines, but such was the Eulo Queen or Eulo Belle. The original of the folk figure is thought to have been named Isabel Gray. She is variously said to have been born in England or Mauritius, probably in 1851, and to have been the illegitimate daughter of a British army captain. She apparently reached Australia in her late teens, when she married the first of three husbands. Some twenty years later, she turns up as the owner of the Eulo Hotel (among other establishments) in the small Queensland opal-mining town of that name, west of Cunnamulla. Eulo was on the legendary Paroo Track, a notoriously hot, dry and dusty way described in Henry Lawson's poem 'The Paroo':

> It's plagued with flies, and broiling hot,
> A curse is on it ever;
> I really think that God forgot.
> The country round that river.

She is said to have got her name when, ejecting a drunken patron, she yelled: 'I'm the Eulo queen—now get out!' She was apparently a noted beauty; in any case, there was little competition in that part of the country, and she attracted many admirers, growing wealthy from their gifts. These enabled her to lead a flamboyant lifestyle and acquire another couple of husbands. Estranged from her third, she—and Eulo town—fell on hard times. She died in a Toowoomba psychiatric hospital in 1929, reputedly in her nineties and with only £30 to her name.

Dopers

The racetrack has long been a stamping ground for hard cases of all types. This yarn involves the practice of doping a horse in hopes of making it run faster:

a trainer makes up some dope, soaks a sugar cube in it and slips it to his horse. Along comes the Chief Steward of the track, known as the stipe. 'What are you feeding that horse?' the stipe asks. 'Just a little treat to calm him down,' says the trainer. Seeing that the stipe is still suspicious, he picks up another cube and eats it. 'Give me one,' says the stipe. He apparently finds nothing wrong with it and continues on his way, leaving the trainer free to saddle his horse for the race. As the jockey mounts it, the trainer whispers to him to let the horse simply run the race: 'Give him his head and don't use the whip.'

'But what if someone starts closing on me in the straight?' asks the jockey.

'Don't worry,' replies the trainer. 'It will only be me or the bloody stipe.'

Wheelbarrow Jack

Also known as Russian Jack, Wheelbarrow Jack was a twenty-two-year-old Russian or Finn who arrived in Western Australia in the late 1880s and headed for the Kimberley gold rush. He was said to be tall, well built and extraordinarily strong. A popular mode of transport among the prospectors was the wooden wheelbarrow.

Jack built one to carry his goods overland to the diggings. It was unusually large, matching his strength, and said to be able to carry loads of 50 kilograms or more. Jack and his barrow soon became legends. When a fellow would-be digger fell ill along the way, Jack loaded his goods and eventually the man himself onto the barrow and wheeled them far along the track until his ailing passenger died.

The numerous stories about Jack focus on his generosity and unstinting mateship. Most are documented, but there are also less reliable tales; all, however, reflect the esteem in which Jack was held in the frontier country of the northwest.

*W*hen a mate breaks his leg, while they are out hunting, Jack loads him onto his barrow and wheels him into town. The townsfolk gather round, and Jack tells them how many miles of hard country he's covered. 'And you hit every rock along the way,' pipes up his invalid mate.

At the Mount Morgan gold mine, Jack falls down a shaft and lies there for three days before he's found. Badly injured, his first concern is that he's missed his work shift.

Once, while working for a station owner, he is sacked—a move that so angers him that he bends a crowbar with his bare hands. His only weakness is for grog. It's said that a coach driver stopped near his lodgings and offered him a swig of whisky. 'No, I'm off the grog,' Jack said. Prevailed upon to have a small drink, he swallowed the half remaining bottle of whisky in one gulp. 'If this is what you're like when you're not drinking,' said the driver, 'I'd hate to see you when you are.'

Another time, Jack's love of alcohol is almost the ruin of him. After a few beers too many, he loads up his barrow to make the trek back to his camp, a few miles out of town. On it he throws a box of firing caps for the dynamite he is also carrying. Seeing him weave down the street, the local policeman decides to escort Jack out of town—then spots the firing caps and decides to arrest him. Jack's intoxication and strength make this something of a challenge. The imaginative policeman manages to steer Jack, merrily singing, towards the police tents, where other policemen offered him a cup of tea and repacked his wheelbarrow to make it safe.

Jack dozes off, and the police handcuff him to a very large log. They then go off to attend to business. When they return, Jack has vanished—and so has the log. Tracks in the sand lead to the local pub, where the police find Jack drinking a beer with his unchained hand and the log propped up on the bar. Thirsty, he had simply thrown the log onto his shoulder and made for the pub. 'Have a drink with me and I'll go back to jail,' says Jack. Rather than drink on duty, the men follow Jack, still shouldering the giant log, back to the police tents, where they share a billy of tea.

☞

Jack also attracted the interest of many journalists, including Mary Durack and Ernestine Hill. After his death, in 1904, a local newspaper published this obituary:

*A*n old identity, John Fredericks—but a hundred times better known as 'Russian Jack'—died a few days ago. His death came as a surprise, for no one could imagine death in the prime of life to one of such Herculean strength. He was, so far as physical manhood is concerned, a picture, but he combined the strength of a lion with the tenderness of a woman. Though he had a loud-sounding sonorous voice that seemed to come out of his boots, there was no more harm in it than the chirp of a bird. Many instances are known of his uniform good nature, but his extraordinary kindness, some years ago, to a complete stranger—that he picked up on the track in the Kimberley gold rush—exemplified his mateship. The stranger had a wheelbarrow and some food, and the burly Russian picked the stranger up, placed him on his own large wheelbarrow, together with his meagre possessions, and wheeled him nearly 300 miles to a haven of refuge.

～

It was Ernestine Hill who first suggested that a statue be raised to commemorate Russian Jack. Eventually in 1979, one was erected at Halls Creek. The statue depicts Russian Jack in his Good Samaritan role, carrying a sick digger in his wooden wheelbarrow.

Russian Jack is a Western Australian version of a folktale type known as 'German Charlie' stories. While the heroes of such tales are not always called 'German Charlie', they are usually nicknamed that way because of their national or ethnic origins. These stories tell how some special, unusual or exaggerated skill or attribute is brought to an Australian community. Using that skill in helpful, often humorous, sometimes absurd ways, German Charlies become accepted members of their communities and feature in commonly told tales of their real and fancied exploits. Russian Jack's wheelbarrow, his assistance to the needy, his strength and his prodigious boozing all combine to make him another example of a type of hard case found all around Australia.

The jilted bride

Eliza Donnithorne is perhaps the most unusual hard case of all, not only because she is a woman, but also because of the rumour that she was the model for the disappointed bride Miss Havisham in Charles Dickens' *Great Expectations*. Miss Havisham spends the rest of her life wearing her wedding dress and sitting among the mouldering ruins of her planned wedding feast.

Eliza Donnithorne arrived in Sydney as a child in the mid-1830s. At the age of thirty, she accepted a proposal of marriage. On the appointed day the guests assembled in St Stephen's Church, Newtown, and the bride in her fine wedding dress awaited the arrival of the groom. He never came. Shattered, she returned to the family home, Camperdown Lodge, put up the shutters and lived ever after in candlelight, attended only by two faithful servants and her pets. She died in 1886, not having set foot outside for thirty years.

In some of the stories about Eliza, she is said to keep the front door permanently ajar on a chain in the hope that her groom would one day return. She orders that her wedding feast is to remain on the table, and refuses to take off her wedding dress. The various reasons given for the groom's failure to arrive at the church include that he was of relatively low status and that her family paid him to disappear, he fell from his horse as he galloped to the wedding, or that he was a military man and suddenly shipped out to India. Yet another variant holds that Eliza was pregnant but the baby was stillborn.

In the late 1880s the bookseller James Tyrrell wrote what may have been the first published account of the legend, recalling that in his boyhood he'd heard Camperdown Lodge was haunted, though it was not until some years later that he heard about its jilted inhabitant.

*I*n my day in Newtown the cemetery was still in use, but it was already a ghostly old graveyard . . . The visitor to the cemetery [today] may see the graves of Judge James Donnithorne and his last surviving daughter, Eliza Emily, who is shown as having died in 1886. In my day the Donnithorne residence, Cambridge Hall [as the house was subsequently renamed], in what is now King Street, came under the wide designation of 'haunted', and I was still young enough to keep to the other side of the road in passing it, especially at night. Still, I would glance fearfully over to its front door, which, by night or day, was always partly open, though fastened with a chain.

Eliza Donnithorne's will included a bequest to the Society for the Prevention of Cruelty to Animals and 'an annuity of £5 for each of my six animals and £5 for all my birds'. She was buried in St Stephen's churchyard and her grave is now a popular tourist destination, the story of her unhappy life and its literary associations, true or not, attracting many visitors.

It is likely that this story is a case of retrospective myth making and that Eliza Donnithorne was not the prototype for Dickens' Miss Havisham. Instead, his story enveloped the Australian tale and partly fused with it. Certainly, although he transported Magwitch to Australia, there is no evidence that Dickens kept up with everyday events in colonial Sydney while he was writing *Great Expectations*.

Long Jack

Another Jack came into legend on the Western Front in World War I. He was said to have been a member of the 3rd Battalion AIF and to have stood out because of a chronic stutter and the speed with which he responded to any perceived slight. Long Jack's exploits were recorded by an anonymous contributor to the *Third Battalion Magazine* some time around 1917:

*T*here are certain characters, which pass through our Battalion life, which are more than worth perpetuating. Such a one was long Jack Dean. In regard to his figure he was an outsider, as he was 6½ feet tall and as slender as a whippet. As a wit he stood alone. A man needed more than ordinary morale to meet him on this ground, and many who purposely or inadvertently engaged him have cause to be sorry for themselves, but glad that they were a party to adding another witty victory to Jack's account. The quickness and smartness of his retorts took the sting from them, and there was no more popular man in the unit than he. This sketch aims at reproducing some stories which came from him, and through which the man himself may be seen.

At the outbreak of war, or soon afterwards, he presented himself before the Recruiting Officers, but his physique was against him. His keenness, however, was proof against his setback, and he came again and again, only to meet with the same result. At last, he asked with his inimitable stutter; 'If you c-c-can't t-take me as a s-s-soldier—s-s-send me-me as a m-m-mascot!'

The Recruiting Officer had become used to his applications, and, recognising the keenness of the man he was dealing with, answered: 'I'll tell you what I shall do. Bring me twelve recruits, and I shall accept you.' 'Done!' said Jack. 'It's a bargain.' He turned up with seventeen fit men and was taken on strength. One can imagine him taking his place among the other recruits at the training depot. His 'length without breadth' immediately singled him out as a butt [of jokes] and one misguided youth was foolish enough to say as he passed him: 'Smell the gum-leaves.' 'Yes,' said Jack, 'feel the branches.' And his long, wiry right shot out with good effect.

He must have been the despair of all that tried to make a smart soldier out of him. Working on the coalface does not keep a long man supple; but in due time he arrived in France, and joined the Battalion—just in time to face the second time 'in' on the Somme. He quickly made himself at home, and in a very short time was known to everybody in the Battalion. It is said that Colonel Howell Price asked him if he had any brothers. 'Y-yes, sir,' he answered: 'one—he's t-t-taller than me, b-but n-not n-n-nearly so well developed.'

Being thin made him appear taller than he actually was, and his height was always the point in question to those who were not used to it. A Tommy saw him ambling along the road very much the worse for wear as a result of a tour in the line and in the mud. 'Reach me down a star, choom,' said the Tommy. 'Take your pick out of these, sonny,' was Jack's answer, together with a very forceful uppercut to the chin. Our late Brigadier never failed to talk to Jack when he met him.

'Good-day, Jack,' was his invariable greeting. 'G-g-g-good day, Brig.,' was always Jack's reply, and it never failed to amuse Brigadier Leslie.

There is one other story which illustrates J.D.' s democratic soul. The Brigadier stopped to have a word with him, and remarked that he wasn't getting any fatter. 'How the hell can a man get fat on 8 [men] to a loaf?' was the response.

Jack's feet were always his worst enemy, and they were the cause of him falling to the rear on one occasion, during a rather stiff route march. He was getting along as best he could when he came up with the Brigadier. 'What Jack! You out!' said the latter. 'Me blanky p-p-p-paddles h-have gone on me, Brig,' replied Jack.

It is only possible to write this sketch because the subject is no longer with us. We hope he is now on his way to Australia, as he has done his bit well, and had come to that stage when he could not effectively carry on. While waiting for the Board which was to examine and determine his future, one of the Sisters, like all who saw him for the first time, said; 'What a lot of disadvantages there must be for such a tall man.' 'Yes,' said Jack. 'The greatest trouble I have is with the rum issue; it dries up before it hits my stomach.'

Jack will remain in our memories and we are grateful to him for these and many other sayings of his which have amused us at all times when we needed the lift of genuine amusement.

~

The world's greatest whinger

Sometimes said to be as old as the Boer War, this elaborate anecdote probably dates only from World War II. This is one of many versions that have appeared in print:

I struck him first on a shearing station in outback Queensland. He was knocking the fleeces from a four-year-old wether when I asked him the innocent question: 'How are you?'

He didn't answer immediately, but waited till he had carved the last bit of wool from the sheep, allowing it to regain its feet, kicking it through the door, dropping the shears and spitting a stream of what looked like molten metal about three yards. Then he fixed me with a pair of malevolent eyes in which the fires of a deep hatred seemed to burn, and he pierced me with them as he said:

'How would I be? How would you bloody well expect me to be? Get a load of me, will you? Dags on every inch of me bloody hide; drinking me own bloody sweat; swallowing dirt with every breath I breathe; shearing sheep which should have been dogs' meat years ago; working for the lousiest bastard in Australia; and frightened to leave because the old woman has got some bloody hound looking for me with a bloody maintenance order.

'How would I be? I haven't tasted a beer for weeks, and the last glass I had was knocked over by some clumsy bastard before I'd finished it.'

The next time I saw him was in Sydney. He had just joined the A.I.F. He was trying to get into a set of webbing and almost ruptured himself in the process. I said to him: 'How would you be, Dig?'

He almost choked before replying. 'How would I be? How would I bloody well be? Take a gander at me, will you? Get a load of this bloody outfit—look at me bloody hat, size nine and a half and I take six and a half. Get a bloody eyeful of these strides! Why, you could hide a bloody brewery horse in the seat of them and still have room for me! Get on this shirt—just get on the bloody thing, will you? Get on these bloody boots; why, there's enough leather in the bastard to make a full set of harness. And some know-all bastard told me this was a men's outfit!

'How would I be? How would I bloody well be?'

I saw him next in Tobruk. He was seated on an upturned box, tin hat over one eye, cigarette butt hanging from his bottom lip, rifle leaning against one knee, and he was engaged in trying to clean his nails with the tip of his bayonet. I should have known better, but I asked him: 'How would you be, Dig?'

He swallowed the butt and fixed me with a really mad look. 'How would I be? How would I bloody well be! How would you expect me to be? Six months in this bloody place; being shot at by every Fritz in Africa; eating bloody sand with every meal; flies in me hair and eyes; frightened to sleep a bloody wink expecting to die in this bloody place; and copping the bloody crow whenever there's a handout by anybody.

'How would I be? How would I bloody well be?!'

The last time I saw him was in Paradise, and his answer to my question was: 'How would I be? How would I bloody well be! Get an eyeful of this bloody nightgown, will you? A man trips over the bloody thing fifty times a day, and it takes a man ten minutes to lift the bloody thing when he wants to scratch his shin! Get a gander at this bloody right wing—feathers missing everywhere. A man must be bloody well moulting! Get an eyeful of this bloody halo! Only me bloody ears keep the rotten thing on me skull—and look at the bloody dents on the bloody thing!

'How would I be? Cast your eyes on this bloody harp. Five bloody strings missing, and there's a band practice in five minutes!

'How would I be? you ask. How would you expect a bloody man to bloody well be?'

THE BULLOCKY.

11

Working people

Eventually we will cross the cats with snakes, and they will
skin themselves twice a year, thus saving the men's wages for
skinning and also getting two skins per cat per year . . .

Working on the Dimboola Cat Farm, c. 1920s

TALES ABOUT CO-WORKERS and work-related events are told in
most industries, trades and professions—though they seldom travel
far beyond them. In-group references and jargon can make such
stories all but incomprehensible to outsiders. But many contain
enough of the common stuff of working life to be told, or adapted
for telling, in practically any workplace—as in the yarn about the
boss who scolds an employee for failing to clean up. 'The dust on
that table is so thick I could write my name in it,' he says. 'Yes,'
says the worker, 'but then, you're an educated man.'

Most tales of working life are humorous, though they often have
a point to make about conditions, management or other aspects of
the working day. They provide a way to carp and laugh at the same
time—a release valve for tensions that might otherwise cause conflict.

Crooked Mick and the Speewah

Crooked Mick is the legendary occupational hero of Australian
shearers and other outback workers. He can shear more sheep,

fell more trees, and do anything better and faster than anyone else. Julian Stuart, one of the leaders of the 1891 shearers' strike in Queensland, made the earliest known printed reference to Crooked Mick in *The Australian Worker* during the 1920s:

I first heard of him on the Barcoo in 1889. We were shearing at Northampton Downs, and we musterers brought in a rosy-cheeked young English Johnny who, in riding from Jericho, the nearest railway station to Blackall, where he was going to edit the new paper, had got lost and found himself at the station, where we were busily engaged disrobing about 150,000 jumbucks.

He was treated with the hospitality of the sheds, which is traditional, and after tea we gathered in the hut—dining room and sleeping accommodation all in one in those days—and proceeded to entertain him.

Whistling Dick played 'The British Grenadiers' on his tin whistle; Bungeye Blake sang 'Little Dog Ben'; Piebald Moore and Cabbagetree Capstick told a common lie or two, but when Dusty Bob got the flute I sat up on my bunk and listened, for I knew him to be the most fluent liar that ever crossed the Darling.

His anecdotes about Crooked Mick began and ended nowhere, and made C.M. appear a superman—with feet so big that he had to go outside to turn around.

It took a large-sized bullock's hide to make him a pair of moccasins.

He was a heavy smoker. It took one 'loppy' (rouseabout) all his time cutting tobacco and filling his pipe.

He worked at such a clip that his shears ran hot, and sometimes he had a half a dozen pairs in the water pot to cool.

He had his fads, and would not shear in sheds that faced north. When at his top, it took three pressers to handle the wool from his blades, and they had to work overtime to keep the bins clear.

He ate two merino sheep each meal—that is, if they were small merinos—but only one and a half when the ration sheep were Leicester crossbred wethers.

His main tally was generally cut on the breakfast run. Anyone who tried to follow him usually spent the balance of the day in the hut.

Between sheds he did fencing. When cutting brigalow posts he used an axe in each hand to save time, and when digging post holes a crowbar in one hand and a shovel in the other.

⌖

This depiction gives a good idea of the context in which Crooked Mick tales were told and of the (equally legendary) ability of the liar Dusty Bob to string otherwise unconnected fictions into a crude but engaging narrative, a talent not uncommon among real-life bush yarn spinners.

How did Mick come to be called Crooked? As Mick tells it (and there are other versions, of course), he was ploughing one very hot day, and it got so hot that the fence-wire melted. When he took the horses to have a drink, he put one leg in the water bucket. The leg was nearly molten, and when he lifted his other leg, putting his weight on the one in the water, it buckled. It's been that way ever since, which is why Mick walks with a slight limp.

In later life, Mick's escapades included trying to stone the crows by throwing Ayers Rock (Uluru) at them, harnessing willy willies to improve the flow of a water windmill and becoming the ringer of the Speewah shed. Here he set an unbeaten record of 1,847 wethers and twelve lambs, all shorn in just one day using hand blades.

The Speewah is an outback never-never land where everything is gigantic: the pumpkins so big they can be used as houses, the trees so tall they have to be hinged to let in the sunlight, and the sheep so large they can't be shorn without climbing a ladder. Many wondrous sights can be witnessed on the Speewah, which is located where the crows fly backwards. The Speewah is so hot in summer that its freezing point is set at 99°F. It is so cold in the winter that the mirages freeze solid and the grasshoppers grow fur coats. Droughts are not over until the people of the Speewah are able to have water in their tea.

The creatures of the Speewah form a weird menagerie that includes the small ker-ker bird, so named from its habit of flying across the Speewah in summer crying 'ker-ker-kripes, it's hot!' Then there is the oozlum bird, which flies tail first in ever-decreasing circles until, moaning, it disappears inside itself head first. Hoop snakes and giant mosquitoes are commonplace on the Speewah, as are giant emus, wombats, crocodiles and boars. The roos are so big they make the emus look like canaries, and the rabbits so thick, large and cunning that Mick had to go off to the war to save himself.

Mick is only one of the Speewah's larger-than-life characters. These include Prickly Pear Pollie, so plain that a cocky farmer hires her as a scarecrow. She's so good at scaring the birds that they start returning the corn they stole two seasons ago. Another is Old Harry, the building worker with one wooden leg. One night he came home and his wife noticed that he only had one leg left. Harry looked down and was amazed to discover she was right. He had no idea how he'd lost it, hadn't even noticed it was gone. Irish Paddy is so good at digging post-holes that he wears his crowbar down to the size of a darning needle. There was Bungeye Bill, the gambler, and Greasy George, the third assistant shearer's cook, who is so greasy that people's eyes slide right off him as they look.

The Speewah shearing shed itself is so large it takes two men and a boy standing on each other's shoulders to see the whole of it, and the boss takes a day or more to ride its length on horseback. Traditions of outsize shearing sheds and stations featuring men of the stamp of Crooked Mick are also found under names like Big Burrawong and Big Burramugga (Western Australia), suggesting that the tales of Mick's doings and those of the mythic stations may have been independent.

Crooked Mick tales have been recounted to many folklorists, but collections of shearer anecdotes made in the past fifty years make no reference to them, suggesting that Crooked Mick may be having a tough time surviving change, despite his prowess.

Crooked Mick has an affinity with other folk heroes of labour. The American lumber worker folk hero, Paul Bunyan, is a superman who performs prodigious deeds of strength and occupational skill. Working conditions on the frontiers of the New World produced many such fabulous figures, including the American cowboy known as Pecos Bill. Seamen in the days of sail also had a similar unnaturally strong and bold figure known as 'Stormalong John', or just 'Old Stormy', who sailed giant ships blown so fiercely onto the Isthmus of Panama that it cleaved out the Panama Canal.

In some Speewah stories Crooked Mick is the cook and is said to have made pastry so light that it floated into the air when the wind blew. These skills link him with another stock character of bush and, later, digger lore.

Bush cooks were the subject of many humorous anecdotes and yarns especially the shearer's cook, also known as a 'babbling brook', or just a 'babbler', in rhyming slang. Many well-worn bush cook yarns have been collected from around the country. This is probably the most popular:

As the tale usually goes, the shearers or other station workers are fed a monotonous diet of something indigestible for a number of weeks. At first they bring the matter to the attention of the cook, who either refuses to change his menu or, as in the version given by Bill Wannan, claims he is unable to make the custard requested by the shearers because 'there ain't a pound of dripping in the place'. The shearers then begin to abuse the cook on a constant basis until he complains to the boss about the bad language. Fed up with all the irritation, the boss finally calls the shearers together and demands to know 'Who called the cook a bastard?' Quick as a flash came the gun shearer's reply: 'Who called the bastard a cook?'

This tradition of the execrable cook continued into the folklore of World War I diggers. Sometimes known as 'bait-layers' from the poisonous nature of their offerings, the army cook was basically the bush cook in uniform.

I came out of my dugout one morning attracted by a terrible outburst of Aussie slanguage in the trench. The company dag was standing in about three feet of mud, holding his mess tin in front of him and gazing contemptuously at a piece of badly cooked bacon, while he made a few heated remarks concerning one known as Bolo, the babbling brook. He concluded an earnest and powerful address thus:

'An' if the _____ that cooked this bacon ever gets hung for bein' a cook, the poor_____ will be innocent.'

A variant story piggy-backs on this one.

A digger is being questioned by the officer in charge of his court-martial: 'Did you call the cook a bastard?'

'No,' the digger answers, 'but I could kiss the bastard who did!'

Historian of the war C.E.W. Bean provided an insight into the dual roles of the cook in digger culture, roles that were also at the base of the cook's bush personality. 'This individual was both a provider of sustenance and the (mostly) willing butt of humour within the military group with which he was affiliated, bearing the "oaths and good-natured sarcasm" of those who had no option but to consume his offerings, with equanimity and humorous forbearance.'

Slow trains

Modern Australia's development was made possible by the railway. After Federation, the various states' railways were linked together via the Transcontinental Railway, or 'the Trans'. The railways' importance, and the armies of workers they employed, gave rise to a large fund of railway yarns, many of which are still told among railway folk. The slow train is a popular theme.

a man jumps off a train as it approaches the platform and rushes up to the station master. 'I need an ambulance!' he cries. 'My wife's about to have a baby.' The station master phones for the ambulance, then says, 'She shouldn't have been travelling in that condition, you know.' The man replies: 'She wasn't in that condition when she got on the train.'

On another slow trip a passenger looks out the window and sees the engine driver throwing seeds onto the sides of the track. All day, as the train crawls along, the driver keeps sowing. Eventually the passenger goes up to the engine and asks, 'Why are you throwing seeds onto the side of the line?'

The driver fixes the passenger with a doleful eye and drawls: 'The guard's picking tomatoes.'

✀

On another journey, a notoriously slow train pulls into the station right on time. An astonished passenger rushes up to the driver and congratulates him for being punctual for a change. 'No chance, mate,' came the laconic reply, 'this is yesterday's train.'

a Texan and an Australian are thrown into each other's company one day on a train. The Texan begins to brag to the Australian about the size of his home state.

'In my state, you can get on a train, travel all day and night but still be in Texas the next morning.'

'Yeah,' drawls the Australian, 'we have slow trains here too.'

Bushies

Anecdotes about real or imagined bush life are a staple of Australian folklore, and many revolve around the itinerant bush workers known as swagmen. In this one, the swaggy is a taciturn loner:

a swaggy is plodding along the dry and dusty track in blazing heat. A solitary car approaches and stops near him. The driver leans out the window and asks, 'Where ya goin', mate?'

'Bourke,' the swaggy says.

'Climb in, then, and I'll give you a lift.'

'No, thanks; you can open and shut your own bloody gates.'

The bullock driver, or bullocky, was an important part of the rural labour force in the era before cars and, in some places, for long after. The ability to control and work a team of sweating, bad-tempered and reluctant beasts was highly prized. A good bullocky could get work just about anywhere. It was a hard job, though, requiring not just strength but a loud voice and special calls, often given in extremely colourful language. A bullocky's ability to swear—creatively and to good effect—was a measure of his status.

Variants of this tale have been well honed over the decades. One was published in the 1940s in Lance Skuthorpe's 'The Champion Bullock Driver', and another, titled 'The Phantom Bullocky', in Bill Wannan's *The Australian* of 1954. The latter version goes like this:

*T*he boss is in need of a bullocky. His eight-yoke team of especially wild beasts has already sent fourteen drivers to their graves. A bushman shows up, looking for a job. 'Can you swear well enough to handle a team?' the boss asks. Assured that the bushman can, the boss decides to give the bloke a trial. He asks him to demonstrate his skills by imagining that eight panels of the wood-and-wire fence are eight bullocks. 'Here's a whip,' says the boss, giving him one eighteen feet long.

The bloke runs the whip through his fingers, then begins to work the fence, swearing, cheering and cracking the whip. Before long there is a blue flame running across the top fence wire. Suddenly, the graves of the fourteen dead bullockies open. They jump out, each with a whip, and, cheering and swearing and cracking their whips along the now fiery fence wire, hail the bloke as King of the Bullockies. Suddenly the fence posts began to move forward, just like a team of reluctant bullocks. The phantom bullockies and the bloke continue exhorting the fence, plying their whips all the while, until the fence strains so hard it rips out a stringybark tree and moves off at a flying pace over the hill with the bloke behind.

The fourteen phantom bullockies give another rousing cheer and disappear back into their graves. The bloke returns with the fence, and the amazed boss says, 'You're the best bullocky I've ever seen. You can have the job.'

The bloke laughs, gives another cheer and jumps into the air. He never comes down again.

~

Later versions of the tale drop the phantom fourteen and simply end with the bloke accepting the job. Another variant has him letting the fence disappear into the back blocks, then asking, 'Can I have the job?' 'Any man who starts up a team an' fergits to stop 'em is no bloody good to me!' says the boss.

Another bullock-driver tale has a bullocky in very trying circumstances cursing his beasts in fine style. The parson happens by. 'Do you know where that sort of language will lead?' asks the reverend. 'Yair,' the irate driver replies. 'To the bloody sawmill—or I'll cut every bastard bullock's bloody throat.'

The bullockies' facility with bad language forms the basis of an oral poem known as 'Holy Dan'.

One bullocky doesn't swear like the rest. When teams die of thirst in the Queensland drought, he tells his fellow drivers it is:

The Lord's all-wise decree,
And if they'd only watch and wait,
A change they'd quickly see.

Eventually even Holy Dan's twenty bullocks begin to die of thirst, and he entreats the Lord to send rain. No matter how hard he prays, the rain fails to fall. Finally there is only one bullock left:

Then Dan broke down—good Holy Dan—
The man who never swore.
He knelt beside the latest corpse,
And here's the prayer he prore:

'That's nineteen Thou hast taken, Lord,
And now you'll plainly see
You'd better take the bloody lot,
One's no damn good to me.'

The other riders laughed so much,
They shook the sky around,
The lightning flashed, the thunder roared,
And Holy Dan was drowned.

The wharfie's reply

Another much-yarned-about worker is the wharfie:

*A*t the end of each shift at the dockyard, the old wharfie would wheel his barrow out for the day. All the wharfies were searched as they left the docks in case they'd pilfered something. But no matter how carefully he frisked the wharfie, the dockyard guard never found any loot on the old bloke.

Eventually, the wharfie retired. A few months later the guard came across him in a waterside pub. 'Howya goin', mate?' said the guard, and bought the wharfie a beer for old time's sake. Conversation turned to working life. After a while, the guard said, 'You're well out of there now, mate, so why don't you tell me the truth? I knew yer were knockin' something off, but we never found anything on you. What were yer stealin'?'

The wharfie, smiling broadly, said: 'Wheelbarrows.'

The union dog

Trade unions' long influence, not only on the railways and docks but in manufacturing and mining, ensure that they feature in many work yarns.

*F*our union members are discussing how smart their dogs are. The first, a member of the Vehicle Workers' Union, says his dog can do maths calculations. Its name is T Square, and he tells it to go to the blackboard and draw a square, a circle and a triangle. This the dog does with consummate ease.

The Amalgamated Metalworkers' Union member says his dog, Slide Rule, is even smarter. He tells it to fetch a dozen biscuits and divide them into four piles, which Slide Rule duly does.

The Liquor Trades Union member concedes that both dogs are quite clever, but says his is even cleverer. His dog, named Measure, is told to go and fetch a stubby of beer and pour seven ounces into a ten-ounce glass. It does this perfectly.

The three men turn to the Waterside Workers' Union member and say, 'What can your mongrel do?' He turns to his dog and says, 'Tea Break, show these bastards what you can do, mate!'

Tea Break eats the biscuits, drinks the beer, pisses on the blackboard, screws the other three dogs, claims he's injured his back, fills out a Workers' Compensation form, and shoots through on sick leave.

The Dimboola Cat Farm

This tale began life at least as early as the 1920s, when it circulated in the form of a letter. Since then it has been updated in various ways in photocopied, facsimile and email forms.

Wild Cat Syndicate
Dimboola

Dear Sir,

Knowing that you are always interested and open for an investment in a good live proposition, I take the liberty of presenting to you what appears to be a most wonderful business, in which no doubt you will take a lively interest and subscribe towards the formation of the Company. The objects of the Company are to operate a large cat ranch near Dimboola, where land can be purchased cheap for the purpose.

To start with we want 1,000,000 cats. Each cat will average about 12 kittens per year; the skins from 1/6 [1 shilling, 6 pence] for the white one to 2/6 for the pure black ones. This will give us 12,000,000 skins a year to sell at an average of 2/- each, making our revenue about £2500 per day.

A man can skin about 100 cats a day, at 15/- per day wages, and it will take 100 men to operate the ranch; therefore the net profit per day will be £2425. We feed the cats on rats and will start a rat ranch; the rats multiply four times as fast as the cats.

We start with 1,000,000 rats and will have four rats per cat from which the skins have been taken, giving each rat one quarter of a cat. It will thus be seen that the whole business will be self-acting and automatic throughout. The cats will eat the rats and for the rats' tails we will get the government grant of 4d. [4 pence] per tail. Other by-products are guts for tennis racquets, whiskers for wireless sets, and cat's pyjamas for Glenelg flappers. Eventually we will cross the cats with snakes, and they will skin themselves twice a year, thus saving the men's wages for skinning and also getting two skins per cat per year.

Awaiting your prompt reply, and trusting that you will appreciate this most wonderful opportunity to get rich quick.
Yours faithfully
Babbling Brook,
Promoter

A half-century or so later, the story was still going the rounds in the form of a photocopied page but the 1920s good-time girls known as 'flappers' had disappeared and the figures were in decimal currency. There was also a more modern enticement to invest: 'The offer to participate in this investment opportunity of a lifetime has only been made to a limited number of individuals—so send your cheque now!!' Otherwise, it was the same bizarre tale.

A farmer's lament

The conversion from imperial to metric units that took place in Australia in the 1960s gave rise to this mild satire:

It all started back in 1966, when they changed to dollars and overnight my overdraft doubled.

I was just getting used to this when they brought in kilograms and my wool cheque dropped by half.

Then they started playing around with the weather and brought in Celsius and millimetres, and we haven't had a decent fall of rain since.

As if this wasn't enough, they had to change over to hectares and I end up with less than half the farm I had.

So one day I sat down and had a good think. I reckoned with daylight saving I was working eight days a week, so I decided to sell out.

Then, to cap it all, I had only got the place in the agent's hand when they changed to kilometres and I find I'm too flaming far out of town!

～

The little red hen

This is one of many tales that turn on tensions between the boss and the workers. Based on a folktale that has itself been around since at least the nineteenth century, this photocopied satire from the 1980s still resonates today with its down-to-earth simplification of industrial politics.

*O*nce upon a time there was a little red hen who scratched around and found some grains of wheat. She called on the other animals to help her plant the wheat.

'Too busy,' said the cow.

'Wrong union,' said the horse.

'Not me,' said the goose.

'Where's the environmental impact study?' asked the duck.

So the hen planted the grain, tended it and reaped the wheat. Then she called for assistance to bake some bread.

'I'll lose my unemployment relief,' said the duck.

'I'll get more from the RED [Royal Employment Development scheme],' said the sheep.

'Out of my classification, and I've already explained the union problem,' said the horse.

'At this hour?' queried the goose.

'I'm preparing a submission to the IAC [Industry Assistance Commission],' said the cow.

So the little red hen baked five lovely loaves of bread and held them up for everyone to see.

'I want some,' said the duck and sheep together.

'I demand my share,' said the horse.

'No,' said the little red hen. 'I have done all the work. I will keep the bread and rest awhile.'

'Excess profit,' snorted the cow.

'Capitalist pig,' screamed the duck.

'Foreign multi-national,' yelled the horse.

'Where's the workers' share?' demanded the pig.

So they hurriedly painted picket signs and paraded around the hen, yelling, 'We shall overcome.' And they did, for the farmer came to see what all the commotion was about.

'You must not be greedy, little red hen,' he admonished. 'Look at the disadvantaged goose, the underprivileged pig, the less fortunate horse, the out-of-work duck. You are guilty of making second-class citizens out of them. You must learn to share.'

'But I have worked to produce my own bread,' said the little red hen.

'Exactly,' said the farmer. 'That is what free enterprise is all about these days. You are free to work as hard as you like. If you were on a Communist farm you would have to give up all the bread. Here you can share it with your needy companions.'

So they lived happily ever after. But the university research team, having obtained a large government grant to study this odd happening, wondered why the little red hen never baked any more bread.

<hr />

The airline steward's revenge

This recent urban legend nicely encapsulates the workplace fantasy of getting one's own back on an especially difficult customer.

A steward was working in First Class on a plane from South Africa to Sydney. On the flight was a very wealthy and snooty elderly couple. A little way into the flight, the steward came along the aisle to where the pair were seated. 'What would you like to drink, Madam?' he asked.

There was no reply. Thinking that the woman might not have heard him, the steward asked again.

Once more she ignored him. But her husband leaned over and said, 'My wife doesn't speak to the help. She would like a bottle of red.'

So the steward went off to get the wine. As he walked away, the man called out 'Boy, boy!' The steward quickly returned to the couple. 'Yes, Sir, how can I help you?'

The man said, 'My wife was wondering about the situation with domestic help in Australia.'

'Oh, Sir,' the steward replied, 'I'm sure Madam will have no trouble at all finding a job.'

The boss

This item, still emailed around, is based on a fable at least as old as Aesop:

*W*hen the Lord made man, all the parts of the body argued over who would be the BOSS.

The BRAIN explained that since he controlled all the parts of the body, he should be the BOSS.

The LEGS argued that since they took the man wherever he wanted to go, they should be the BOSS.

The STOMACH countered that since he digested all the food, he should be the BOSS.

The EYES said that without them, man would be helpless, so they should be BOSS.

Then the ARSEHOLE applied for the job.

The other parts of the body laughed so hard that the ARSEHOLE got mad and closed up.

After a few days the BRAIN went foggy, the LEGS got wobbly, the STOMACH got ill and the EYES got crossed and unable to see.

They all conceded defeat and made the ARSEHOLE the BOSS.

This proves that you don't have to be a BRAIN to be BOSS . . . JUST AN ARSEHOLE.

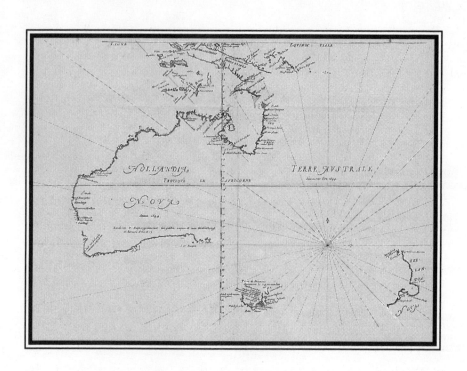

12

Wide, brown land

The wide, brown land for me!

Dorothea Mackellar, 'My Country' (1908)

AT THE BASE of the great, wide treasure trove of Australian stories lies the land: the natural features, the environment, the people and places upon it and the things that have been done in those places. Indigenous stories are all about the land and the links between it, the ancestral creators, its plants and animals and the human beings who lived here for 50,000 years, perhaps longer. When visitors from other places began to arrive seeking trade and, later, settlement, they too needed to create an understanding of the land and to express it in their stories. Different though these stories are, they also tell of ways of living on and relating to the environment we all share.

Dorothea Mackellar's famous poem 'My Country' first appeared in a slightly different form in the English *Spectator* magazine in 1908 and was not published in Australia until 1911. Dorothea was only 22 at the time of writing and homesick for her home country while travelling in Britain. Her patriotic creation is often criticised as overly sentimental and unconscious of the Indigenous connection to country. On the other hand, it pointedly breaks with the British connection in its first verse, the fields and coppices the 'ordered woods and lanes' that 'I know but cannot share'.

The next verse begins with the lines best known to generations of schoolchildren: 'I love a sunburnt country'. The remainder is a highly emotional testament of love for the harsh environment: 'Core of my heart, my country'.

Ever since its first Australian publication, the poem—or 'verse' as Mackellar might have called it, refusing to be called a 'poet'—has been a touchstone for popular ideas of national identity and relationship to the land. But long before then, Aboriginal Australians were expressing their unique connections to the wide, brown land.

Eaglehawk and Crow

The wedge-tailed eagle or eaglehawk lives across the continent in considerable numbers. Not surprisingly, this fierce hunter appears frequently in traditional Aboriginal mythology. In Tiwi tradition (Melville and Bathurst islands, Northern Territory), Jurumu is the name for the wedge-tailed eagle, which, with Mudati the fork-tailed kite, made fire when they accidentally rubbed some sticks together. For the Wonnarua people of the Hunter Valley, Kawal is the wedge-tailed eagle, created by the great spirit Baiame (Byamee) to watch over them. In Victoria, Bunjil is the wedge-tailed eagle, the creator of the Kulin nation.

The eagle may also be associated with totems of one kind or another, and with the complex human and spiritual relationships in Aboriginal culture.

There are many wedge-tailed eagle stories, some involving Crow, who often represents the complementary darkness to the eagle or eaglehawk's light. Crow may also be a trickster figure and is frequently associated with fire. In some stories, the characters end up as stars in the night sky, as in traditions recorded along the Murray River. Here it was said that the earth was inhabited by a race of very wise black birds long before humans came to be there. The eaglehawk was the leader of this group and Crow was his deputy. The eagle's son was killed by Crow. In some versions, Eagle trapped Crow and killed him but the wily black bird came back to life and then disappeared. In this telling of the story, the argument between Crow and Eagle explains how crows come to be black.

*O*ne day, a crow and a hawk hunted together in the bush. After travelling together for some time, they decided to hunt in opposite directions, and, at the close of the day, to share whatever game they had caught. The crow travelled against the sun, and at noonday arrived at a broad lagoon which was the haunt of the wild ducks. The crow hid in the tall green reeds fringing the lagoon, and prepared to trap the ducks. First, he got some white clay, and, having softened it with water, placed two pieces in his nostrils. He then took a long piece of hollow reed through which he could breathe under water, and finally tied a net bag around his waist in which to place the ducks.

On the still surface of the lagoon, the tall gum trees were reflected like a miniature forest. The ducks, with their bronze plumage glistening in the sun, were swimming among the clumps of reeds, and only paused to dive for a tasty morsel hidden deep in the water weeds. The crow placed the reed in his mouth, and, without making any sound, waded into the water. He quickly submerged himself, and the only indication of his presence in the lagoon was a piece of dry reed which projected above the surface of the water, and through which the crow was breathing. When he reached the centre of the water-hole he remained perfectly still. He did not have to wait long for the ducks to swim above his head. Then, without making any sound or movement, he seized one by the leg, quickly pulled it beneath the water, killed it, and placed it in the net bag. By doing this, he did not frighten the other ducks, and, in a short time he had trapped a number of them. He then left the lagoon and continued on his way until he came to a river.

The crow was so pleased with his success at the waterhole that he determined to spear some fish before he returned to his camp. He left the bag of ducks on the bank of the river, and, taking his fish spear, he waded into the river until the water reached his waist. Then he stood very still, with the spear poised for throwing. A short distance from the spot where he was standing, a slight ripple disturbed the calm surface of the water. With the keen eye of the hunter, he saw the presence of fish, and, with a swift movement of his arm, he hurled the spear, and his unerring aim was rewarded with a big fish. The water was soon agitated by many fish, and the crow took advantage of this to spear many more. With this heavy load of game, he turned his face towards home.

The hawk was very unfortunate in his hunting. He stalked a kangaroo many miles, and then lost sight of it in the thickly wooded hills. He then decided to try the river for some fish, but the crow had made the water muddy and frightened the fish, so again he was unsuccessful. At last the hawk decided to return to his *gunyah* [shelter] with the hope that the crow would secure some food, which they had previously agreed to share. When the hawk arrived, he found that the crow had been there before him and had prepared and eaten his evening meal. He at once noticed that the crow had failed to leave a share for him. This annoyed the hawk, so he approached the crow and said: 'I see you have had a good hunt to-day. I walked many miles but could not catch even a lizard. I am tired and would be glad to have my share of food, as we agreed this morning.'

'You are too lazy,' the crow replied. 'You must have slept in the sun instead of hunting for food. Anyhow, I've eaten mine and cannot give you any.'

This made the hawk very angry, and he attacked the crow. For a long time they struggled around the dying embers of the camp fire, until the hawk seized the crow and rolled him in the black ashes.

When the crow recovered from the fight, he found that he could not wash the ashes off, and, since that time, crows have always been black. The crow was also punished for hiding the food which he could not eat by being condemned to live on putrid flesh.

Great floods

Indigenous tradition contains many stories of great floods. From Arnhem Land to coastal Queensland, in South Australia, Gippsland and into Western Australia, legends of catastrophic floods have been widely collected. Many of these stories seek to provide explanations or rationales for the way in which the natural world is organised. This one from southeastern Australia also involves Eaglehawk and Crow, as well as many other animals. Its theme is timeless and universal and could well speak to some modern Australian issues.

*T*he animals, birds, and reptiles became overpopulated and held a conference to determine what to do. The kangaroo, eaglehawk, and goanna were the chiefs of the three respective groups, and their advisors were koala, crow, and tiger-snake. They met on Blue Mountain.

Tiger-snake spoke first and proposed that the animals and birds, who could travel more readily, should relocate to another country. Kangaroo rose to introduce platypus, whose family far outnumbered any others, but the meeting was then adjourned for the day.

On the second day, while the conference proceeded with crow taunting koala for his inability to find a solution, the frilled lizards decided to act on their own. They possessed the knowledge of rain-making, and they spread the word to all of their family to perform the rain ceremony during the week before the new moon. Thus would they destroy the over-numerous platypus family.

They did their ceremonies repeatedly, and a great storm came, flooding the land. The frilled lizards had made shelters on mountains, and some animals managed to make their way there, but nearly all life was destroyed in the great flood.

When the flood ended and the sun shone again, the kangaroo called the animals together to discover how the platypus family had fared. But they could not find a single living platypus. Three years later, the cormorant told emu that he had seen a platypus beak impression along a river, but never saw a platypus.

Because of the flood, the platypuses had decided that the animals, birds, and reptiles were their enemies and only moved about at night. The animals organized a search party, and carpet-snake eventually found a platypus home and reported its location back to the others. Kangaroo summoned all the tribes together, even the insect tribe. Fringed lizard was ejected for doing mischief; he has turned ugly because of the hate he dwells upon. The animals and birds found they were both related to the platypus family; even the reptiles found some relationship; and everyone agreed that the platypuses were an old race.

Carpet-snake went to the platypus home and invited them to the assembly. They came and were met with great respect. Kangaroo offered platypus his choice of the daughter of any of them. Platypus learned that emu had changed its totem so that the platypus and emu families could marry. This made platypus decide it didn't want to be part of any of their families. Emu got angry, and kangaroo suggested the platypuses leave silently that night, which they did.

They met bandicoot along the way, who invited the platypuses to live with them. The platypuses married the bandicoot daughters and lived happily. Water-rats got jealous and fought them but were defeated. Platypuses have tried to be separate from the animal and bird tribes ever since, but not entirely successfully.

Firestick farming

When Europeans came to Australia they were surprised to find that much of the country had a park-like appearance. Many observers described the regular patterns of land management in terms of English gardens and grand estates. They saw carefully defined demarcations between bush, grassland and watercourses and wondered how people they usually considered to be 'savages' could have evolved and maintained such an advanced and effective system for managing their harsh environment and for surviving, even prospering, in it.

Those who took the time and trouble to look into this unexpected feature of the unknown south land soon discovered the Aboriginal skill with fire. One of the most perceptive and knowledgeable of all the European explorers was Ludwig Leichhardt. He disappeared during an attempt to cross the continent from east to west in 1848 and his fate remains a mystery today, but in the journals of his previous expeditions he recorded what he saw of 'firestick farming', as this method of environmental resource stewardship has become known. On his journey from Moreton Bay to Port Essington in 1844–45, a distance of almost 5000 kilometres, Leichhardt documented his firsthand experience of management by flame.

*T*he natives seemed to have burned the grass systematically along every watercourse, and round every water-hole, in order to have them surrounded with young grass as soon as the rain sets in. These burnings were not connected with camping places, where the fire is liable to spread from the fire-places, and would clear the neighbouring ground. Long strips of lately burnt grass were frequently observed extending for many miles along the creeks. The banks of small isolated water-holes in the forest, were equally attended to, although water had not been in either for a considerable time. It is no doubt connected with a systematic management of their runs, to attract game to particular spots, in the same way that stockholders burn parts of theirs in proper seasons; at least those who are not influenced by the erroneous notion that burning the grass injures the richness and density of the natural turf. The natives, however, frequently burn the high and stiff grass, particularly along shady creeks, with the intention of driving the concealed game out of it; and we have frequently seen them watching anxiously, even for lizards, when other game was wanting.

Leichhardt was frustrated by those settlers who could not or would not see that this fire regime was the correct way to manage the country and wrote elsewhere: 'I longed to move those stupid enemies of fire onto such a plot of young grass to hear lectures alternately from horses, sheep, oxen and kangaroos about the advantages of burning the old grass.'

Leichhardt's concerns, as well as those of a few others, had little impact on the development of agriculture and land management. But the issue remains very much alive today as increasingly devastating bushfires roar across the land and we search for ways to minimise them.

'The landscape looked like a park'

In September 1853, squatter John G. Robertson of Wando Vale responded to an invitation from Governor La Trobe to detail his experiences on the new land. Robertson had arrived in Van Diemen's Land (VDL) in 1831 and 'like many of my countrymen, with a light purse—one half-crown and a sixpence was all my pocket contained'. By his own account he worked hard for three years and saved the considerable sum of 3000 pounds, which allowed him to set up as a farmer in Victoria. At the end of a very lengthy account, the tough squatter tells how his land has begun to change under the impact of agriculture.

*T*he few sheep at first made little impression on the face of the country for three or four years; the first great change was a severe frost, 11th November 1844, which killed nearly all the beautiful blackwood trees that studded the hills in every sheltered nook—some of them really noble, 20 or 30 years old; nearly all were killed in one night; the same night a beautiful shrub that was interspersed among the blackwoods (Sir Thomas Mitchell called it *acacia glutinosa*) was also killed. About three weeks after these trees and shrubs were all burnt, they now sought to recover as they would do after a fire.

This certainly was a sad chance; before this catastrophe all the landscape looked like a park with shade for sheep and cattle. Many of our herbaceous plants began to disappear from the pasture land; the silk-grass began to show itself in the edge of the bush track, and in patches here and there on the hill. The patches have grown larger every year; herbaceous plants and grasses give way for the silk-grass and the little annuals, beneath which are annual peas, and die in our deep clay soil with a few hot days in spring, and nothing returns to supply their place until later in the winter following. The consequence is that the long deep-rooted grasses that held our strong clay hill together have died out; the ground is now exposed to the sun, and it has cracked in all directions, and the clay hills are slipping in all directions; also the sides of precipitous creeks, long slips taking trees and all with them. When I first came here, I knew of but two landslips, both of which I went to see; now there are hundreds found within the last three years.

A rather strange thing is going on now. One day all the creeks and little watercourses were covered with a large tussocky grass, with other grasses and plants, to the middle of every watercourse but the Glenelg and Wannon, and in many places of these rivers, now that the only soil is getting trodden hard with stock, springs of salt water are bursting out in every hollow or watercourse, and as it trickles down the watercourse in summer, the strong tussocky grasses die before it, with nil others. The clay is left perfectly bare in summer.

The strong clay cracks; the winter rain washes out the clay; now mostly every little gully has a deep rut; when rain falls it runs off the hard ground, rushes down these ruts, runs into the larger creeks, and is carrying earth, trees, and all before it. Over Wannon country is now as difficult a ride as if it were fenced. Ruts, seven, eight, and ten feet deep, and as wide, are found for miles, where two years ago it was covered with tussocky grass like a land marsh.

I find from the rapid strides the silk-grass has made over my run, I will not be able to keep the number of sheep the run did three years ago, and as a cattle station it will be still worse; it requires no great prophetic knowledge to see that this part of the country will not carry the stock that is in it at present—I mean the open downs, and every year it will get worse, as it did in V.D.L.; and after all the experiments I worked with English grasses, I have never found any of them that will replace our native sward. The day the soil is turned up, that day the pasture is gone for ever as far as I know, for I had a paddock that was sown with English grasses, in squares each by itself, and mixed in every way. All was carried off by the grubs, and the paddock allowed to remain in native grass, which returned in eight years. Nothing but silk-grass grew year after year, and I suppose it would be so on to the end of time. Dutch clover will not grow on our clay soils; and for pastoral purposes the lands here are getting of less value every day, that is, with the kind of grass that is growing in them, and will carry less sheep and far less cattle. I now look forward to fencing my run in with wire, as the only chance of keeping up my stock on the land.

Captain Cook's Law

As well as the myths of creation and the ancestors, Aboriginal tradition includes more modern stories, or cycles of stories. One of these concerns Captain James Cook, still sometimes said to be the 'discoverer' of Australia. While Cook is a venerated figure in the history of navigation and maritime exploration, and rightly so, he has a much more negative image in Indigenous legend. In these stories, recorded from Aboriginal tellers around the country, Captain Cook arrives from the sea bringing disruption and violence.

In one version of the tale told in the Kimberley region, Cook uses gunpowder against Aboriginal people and then returns to his homeland claiming that the land is empty and can be settled. This is 'Cook's Law', by which the country is unfairly colonised and which is in direct contradiction to the traditional law and order of the original inhabitants.

In northern Queensland, Cook is depicted as a violent marauder who deceives the local people into showing him the place where they camp. This knowledge enables him to establish the cattle industry and also brings about massacres of Aboriginal people.

The Northern Territory story similarly revolves around Captain Cook stealing the land, violently oppressing the people and bringing a 'law' of dispossession. An Arnhem Land variation on this theme has two Captain Cooks arriving. The first is a good one who fights with an evil figure called Satan and wins. The victorious Cook returns to Sydney where he is rejected by his own people and dies. He is then followed by a whole lot more Captain Cooks who make war on the people.

The Indigenous people of the Bateman's Bay area in New South Wales tell simply of Cook coming with gifts of clothes and hard biscuits. He then sails away and the not so lucky receivers of his gifts cast them into the sea in disgust. Interestingly, this closely parallels the reactions of the Aborigines Cook did encounter during his voyage along the east coast: the newcomers' gifts were politely received but then discarded, as the Aboriginal people had no use for them.

Another Queensland tradition has it that Cook and his companions were seen not as intruders and murderers but as the returning spirits of the ancestors. These ghosts offered drugs, food and drink to the local people in the form of tobacco, beef, flour and tea. These were prepared in the European manner: the tobacco in a pipe, the beef salted and boiled, the flour baked and the tea in a kettle or billy. The Aboriginal people did not like the pipe, the tea or the bread. But the boiled beef was considered edible as long as the salt was washed away. Cook then took his men and sailed away to the north, leaving the Aboriginal people in dismay as the spirits of their ancestors disappeared.

The corners

There is a place where you can celebrate New Year three times. Called Poeppel or Poeppel's Corner, it is in the middle of nowhere, lying where the boundaries of Queensland, South Australia and the Northern Territory intersect—to be precise, at latitude 26 degrees S and longitude 138 degrees E.

In 1880, Augustus Poeppel identified this important point and drove a small tree trunk into the exact spot. Born in Germany, Poeppel had previously worked in a number of Australian colonies and in New Zealand. Later, his work in the outback led to him suffering from trachoma and the eventual loss of an eye. He was forced to retire and died in 1891 aged only 52. The original 'Poeppel's Peg' is now in the Migration Museum, South Australia, where it is known as 'Poeppel's Corner Post', a memento of the heroic feats of surveying undertaken in the colonial era and of their significance for the expansion of the Australian frontiers.

The vast expanse of land that lay beyond the western border of Queensland was almost totally unknown, an emptiness that swallowed the explorers Burke and Wills. When rescue parties went out to find them they stimulated interest in the region and settlement slowly began in the Barcoo, the Cooper, then Diamantina and the Channel country. By the 1870s it was necessary to draw some boundaries to prevent disputes between settlers, and the developing trade in the region also meant that customs barriers were needed, so the exact location of those borders had to be marked. Each colony set up its own customs departments to ensure collection of duties whenever their borders were crossed.

Poeppel and his team were in some of the continent's harshest land. They struggled across its hot, dry plains surviving on salt beef, damper and the kindness of Aboriginal people who showed them where to get water. They finally reached their goal late in 1880 and marked it with the timber post that came to be known as 'Poeppel's Peg'. It had to be moved later due to a slight measurement error and the original intention of establishing the corner between Queensland and South Australia failed, but Poeppel's accomplishment was hailed nevertheless as a great feat of surveying.

Poeppel's Corner has been the focus of an extended controversy, though. There has been a suggestion, based on evidence from the 1936 visitor Edmund Colson, that Poeppel tried to conceal his calculation error, committed because he was over-fond of the grog. The more or less official story goes that Poeppel's measuring tape somehow stretched, causing the error.

After the original survey party left, very few people went to Poeppel's Corner. There were visits in 1883, 1936 and again during the 1960s, but by then the post was rotten and termite-eaten and needed to be removed for conservation. In 1966, the Leyland brothers proved that the Simpson Desert could be accessed with four-wheel-drive vehicles and the area was subsequently opened up to tourism, and the corner is now quite frequently visited.

There are other 'corners' established by survey along many state borders. Surveyor-General's Corner lies on the intersection of the South Australian and Western Australian borders. Haddon's Corner is found where the northern boundary of South Australia turns south, and Cameron's Corner is on the same southerly line at the point where it joins the New South Wales and Queensland borders. These spots are also popular with four-wheel-drive tourists and are tangible memorials to the carving up of the continent.

13

Upon the fatal shore

The first day that we landed upon the fatal shore,
The planters came around us—there might be twenty score or more.
They ranked us up like horses and sold us out of hand,
They yoked us in a plough, brave boys, to plough Van Diemen's Land.

Street ballad

As SOON AS the news about founding a penal colony at Botany Bay broke in 1787, the British press went into action. Articles, pamphlets and street ballads appeared almost overnight. 'Botany Bay: A New Song' was a tongue-in-cheek roll call of the English underworld, the source of most of our first settlers. There were 'night-walking strumpets', 'lecherous whoremasters', 'proud dressy fops' and 'monopolisers who add to their store/By cruel oppression and squeezing the poor'. The second-last verse of this street ballad expressed the popular view of the time:

The hulks and the jails have some thousands in store,
But out of the jails are ten thousand times more,
Who live by fraud, cheating, vile tricks and foul play,
They should all be sent over to Botany Bay.

This song also raised the possibility that the transports and their keepers might 'become a new people at Botany Bay'. Of course it did, though there were many unhappy moments along the path to nationhood, especially in the convict days. But mostly, convictism was about the personal trials, tragedies and triumphs of the 160,000 or so men and women transported to Australia between 1788 and 1868.

Leaden hearts

Transportation to the far ends of the earth, even for a relatively short term of seven years, meant the end of lives and loves for many convicts. Even before the settlement of Port Jackson, a custom grew in which convicts departing to penal colonies had coins filed smooth and an affectionate message engraved on both sides. These often handmade tokens—or 'leaden hearts'—were left with wives, families or lovers in the hope that they would not forget, even if the sentence were for life. Brief though these messages had to be, they hint at many poignant stories from the Australian experience of transportation.

Seventeen-year-old Charles Wilkinson stole a handkerchief and was transported for life in 1824. The crude carvings on his token read:

Your lover lives for you
CL
Only.
Til death

The reverse of his token told the story in a few terse words:

C Wilkinson
Lag[ged] for Life
Aged 17
1824

'C.L.' probably never saw Charles again. Wilkinson reoffended in Australia and did not receive a free pardon for twenty years. Like most convicts he probably remained here, unable to afford a passage home and after such a long absence perhaps not seeing much reason to return.

A Michael Williams (alias Flinn) was sentenced to death for stealing tea from the wharves in London. His token read:

M Flinn
Aged 25
Cast for death
September 16
1825

On the back:

A token of true love
when this you se[e]
remember me

Fortunately, his sentence was commuted to transportation for life.

Sometimes tokens expressed a degree of remorse and moralising. Joseph Kelf, aged twenty, was 'cast for death' after burgling a Norfolk home in 1833. His sentence commuted, he had a token made with the homily:

Honesty is the best policy

Many of these keepsakes were in verse, some elaborately so. John Waldon was given a fourteen-year stretch in 1832. His token reads:

No Pen can Write
No Tongue can Tell
The Aching Heart
That Bids Farewell.

Thomas Alsop, a Staffordshire sheep stealer, was 21 when transported for life in 1833. He could not write but had two fine tokens made, one for his 'dear mother':

The rose soon dupes and dies
The brier fades away
But my fond heart for you I love
Shall never fade away.

Convicted of murder in 1832, William Kennedy was lucky to have his sentence cut to a lifetime of labour in the colonies. He had the engraver inscribe his coin with a defiant verse:

When this you see
Remember me
And bear me in your mind.
Let all the world
Say what they will
Speak of me as you find.

Another 'When this you see think on me' token was made for Thomas Burbury of Coventry, who was convicted of rioting and machine breaking in 1832. Machine breakers, or 'Luddites', destroyed factories and mechanical weaving devices in the accurate belief that these devices would rob them of their employment as skilled handloom weavers working from their cottages. Sentences for these acts were severe and Burbury was sentenced to hang. But the local community, not considering such actions to be crimes, exerted enough pressure to have his sentence commuted to transportation for life.

He landed in Tasmania in 1832. Only a few months later, his wife and child also arrived, having been provided with a passage through public donations. Reunited with his family, Burbury began to buy land in his wife's name and became a valued assigned servant, helping to hunt down bushrangers. By 1837, he had his ticket of leave and a full pardon two years later. He went on to become a local council employee and a member of Oatlands local council, and died a respected local pioneer, as did many transported convicts.

The Ring

Almost as old a settlement as Port Jackson, Norfolk Island became known as one of the worse convict hellholes. A penal station was established on the island only a few months after the arrival of the First Fleet but was abandoned in 1814, and in 1825 a second penal colony was founded. There was a need for somewhere to put 'the worst description of convicts'; Norfolk was intended to be a place of no hope, where hard cases would be imprisoned and worked in irons until they died.

The island rapidly gained a reputation for horrifying brutality and sadistic oppression by a succession of military commanders and their squads of willing brutalisers. There was an unsuccessful revolt or mutiny in 1834 and when the Vicar General of Sydney, the Very Reverend William Ullathorne, arrived to tell the offenders who would live and who would die, he reported, 'As I mentioned the names of those men who were to die, they one after another, as their names were pronounced, dropped on their knees and thanked God that they were to be delivered from that horrible place, whilst the others remained standing mute, weeping. It was the most horrible scene I have ever witnessed.'

Despite these disturbing images, historical research suggests that while Norfolk Island was not a pleasant place to be, the more extreme images of brutality and degradation may be based on a selection of unusually brutal incidents and the amplifying effect of folk tradition. However, there are persistent tales of the terrors experienced on the island between 1825 and the penal station's final closure in 1856, largely in response to a number of damning reports.

An especially intriguing story involves an alleged secret society known as 'the Ring'. In Marcus Clarke's famous novel *For the Term of His Natural Life*, we first hear of the Ring when Rufus Dawes is sent to Norfolk Island and becomes its leader. In another Ring story, three convicts agree to drawing lots to decide which one will kill another, leaving the third as a witness against the murderer, ensuring that he will be hanged. This is based on a claim made in a British Select Committee of Parliament in 1838 by Colonel George Arthur: '... Two or three men murdered their fellow-prisoners, with the certainty of being detected and executed, apparently without malice and with very little excitement, stating that they knew that they should be hanged, but it was better than being where they were.'

In the writings of Clarke and Price Warung (William Astley), this relatively rare horror is transformed into a Ring custom. In *For the Term of His Natural Life*, Clarke has one of his characters note in his diary:

May 16th.—A sub-overseer, a man named Hankey, has been talking to me. He says that there are some forty of the oldest and worst prisoners who form what he calls the 'Ring', and that the members of this 'Ring' are bound by oath to support each other, and to avenge the punishment of any of their number. In proof of his assertions he instanced two cases of English prisoners who had refused to join in some crime, and had informed the

Commandant of the proceedings of the Ring. They were found in the morning strangled in their hammocks. An inquiry was held, but not a man out of the ninety in the ward would speak a word. I dread the task that is before me. How can I attempt to preach piety and morality to these men? How can I attempt even to save the less villainous?

In Warung's later short stories, said to be based on interviews with ex-convicts, we also read about an elaborately structured clandestine order existing within the prison system and effectively running it. Led by the One, the Ring is said to have been a hierarchy of 25 members. The lowest order consisted of nine members and was known as the Nine; the next were the seven members of the Seven; then the Fives and Threes. Only the Threes knew the identity of the One. Only the worst of the worst were invited to join at the bottom level and could work themselves up to the higher orders by even more evildoing. The Ring's rationale was complete denial of all penal authority. Any member who had any dealings with the gaolers was to be killed, and only then could a new recruit fill the gap. While the members of each order were known to each other, those of the other orders did not know them. Nor did anyone outside the Ring, convict or gaoler, know the identity of its initiates. But no one was in any doubt of its existence.

When the Ring decided to meet, word went through the prison that no non-member, including guards, should enter the prison yard. The One entered the yard first and faced a corner of the wall. He was followed by the Threes, Fives, Sevens and Nines, each arrayed in a semi-circle behind him. All were masked. Satanic prayers were intoned:

Is God an officer of the establishment?
And the response came solemnly clear, thrice repeated:

No, God is not an officer of the establishment.

He passed to the next question:

Is the Devil an officer of the establishment?

And received the answer—thrice:

Yes, the Devil is an officer of the establishment.

He continued:

Then do we obey God?

With clear-cut resonance came the negative—

No, we do not obey God!

He propounded the problem framed by souls that are not necessarily corrupt:

Then whom do we obey?

And, thrice over, he received for reply the damning perjury which yet was so true an answer:

The Devil—we obey our Lord the Devil!

And the dreaded Convict Oath was taken. It had eight verses according to Warung:

Hand to hand,
On Earth, in Hell,
Sick or Well,
On Sea, on Land,
On the Square, ever.

It ended—the intervening verses dare not be quoted—

Stiff or in Breath,
Lag or Free,
You and Me,
In Life, in Death,
On the Cross, never.

They all then drank a cup of blood taken from the veins of each man.

After these rites were performed, the Ring would conduct their business, usually involving a trial and sentence of suspected collaborators among the convict population or of any of their gaolers who showed an inclination to be lenient to the prisoners.

At first look, the florid stories of the Ring seem more like a Masonic or occult order than a self-protection association of convicts on a remote Pacific island. Certainly Warung had a fertile imagination and colourful writing style. Historians have also pointed out that evidence for the existence of such an elaborate organisation depends on a single documented mention of Norfolk Island convicts defying their gaolers—not an uncommon event.

But despite the absence of historical evidence, the story of the Ring lives on, along with the darker suspicions about the depravity, degradation and despair of the Norfolk Island 'system'. While the secret order of the Ring and some of the more extreme events alleged to have occurred may be exaggerated, the remaining realities of Norfolk Island were horrifying enough to support the belief that an organisation like the Ring could have, and perhaps should have, existed.

The melancholy death of Captain Logan

Captain Patrick Logan was in charge of the Moreton Bay penal settlement on the Brisbane River from 1826. His tenure was notorious among convicts for its extreme cruelty, especially flog-gings while lashed to the 'triangle', a wooden structure designed to spreadeagle its victims to ensure maximum infliction of the lash across the back of the body.

In October 1830, Logan lost his life in an attack by 'natives', as Aborigines were invariably described in the nineteenth century. Captain Clunie of the 17th Regiment reported the details, as far as they could be ascertained, to the Colonial Secretary in Sydney on 6 November 1830. Logan was returning home from a mapping expedition near Mount Irwin when he became separated from his party. They went to find him a day or so later:

. . . we naturally concluded he had fallen into the hands of the natives, and hoped he might be a prisoner and alive, parties were sent out in every direction to endeavour to meet them; while, in the meantime, his servant and party found his saddle, with the stirrups cut off as if by a native's hatchet, about ten miles from the place where Captain Logan left them, in the direction of the Limestone station. Near to this place, also, were the marks of his horse having been tied to a tree, of his having himself slept upon some grass in a bark hut, and having apparently been roasting chestnuts, when he made some rapid strides towards his horse, as if surprised by natives. No further traces, however, could be discovered, and though the anxiety of his family and friends were most distressing, hopes were still entertained of his being alive till the 28th ultimo, when Mr Cowper, whose exertions on this occasion were very great, and for which I feel much indebted, discovered the dead horse sticking in a creek, and not far from it, at the top of the bank, the body of Captain Logan buried about a foot under ground. Near this also were found papers torn in pieces, his boots, and part of his waistcoat, stained with blood.

From all these circumstances it appears probable that while at this place, where he had stopped for the night, Captain Logan was suddenly surprised by natives; that he mounted his horse without saddle or bridle, and, being unable to manage him, the horse, pursued by the natives, got into the creek, where Captain Logan, endeavouring to extricate him, was overtaken and murdered.

Logan's pregnant widow had his body shipped to Sydney for burial, mourning the loss of her husband as the captain's colleagues regretted the loss of an efficient commander. But the convicts reacted very differently.

Some time after Logan's death a new ballad began to circulate, and has done ever since. The song told the story of an Irish convict transported to Moreton Bay, where he meets another prisoner who tells him:

I've been a prisoner at Port Macquarie,
At Norfolk Island, and Emu Plains;
At Castle Hill and cursed Toongabbee—
At all those places I've worked in chains:
But of all the places of condemnation,
In each penal station of New South Wales,
To Moreton Bay I found no equal,
For excessive tyranny each day prevails.

Early in the morning when day is dawning,
To trace from heaven the morning dew,
Up we are started at a moment's warning,
Our daily labour to renew.
Our overseers and superintendents—
These tyrants' orders we must obey,
Or else at the triangles our flesh is mangled—
Such are our wages at Moreton Bay!

For three long years I've been beastly treated;
Heavy irons each day I wore;
My back from flogging has been lacerated,
And oftimes painted with crimson gore.
Like the Egyptians and ancient Hebrews,
We were oppressed under Logan's yoke,
Till kind Providence came to our assistance,
And gave this tyrant his mortal stroke.

The song ends with an expression of gratitude in the lines:

My fellow-prisoners, be exhilarated,
That all such monsters such a death may find:
For it's when from bondage we are liberated,
Our former sufferings will fade from mind.

The death of Logan was such a great moment in convict culture that its impact continued for another 50 years or more. The event was still very much alive in Ned Kelly's mind when he composed the Jerilderie Letter in the late 1870s:

... more was transported to Van Diemand's Land to pine their young lives away in starvation and misery among tyrants worse than the promised hell itself all of true blood bone and beauty, that was not murdered on their own soil, or had fled to America or other countries to bloom again another day, were doomed to Port Mcquarie Toweringabbie norfolk island and Emu plains and in those places of tyrany and condemnation many a blooming Irishman rather than subdue to the Saxon yoke Were flogged to death and bravely died in servile chains but true to the shamrock and a credit to Paddys land.

Before that, a convict known as Francis MacNamara would get the credit for composing the ballad of Logan's death. Whether he did or not, his story is another memorable tale of the convict era.

A Convict's Tour to Hell

Francis MacNamara—better known to his convict peers by the moniker of 'Frank the Poet'—may have penned the original version of the powerful lament of 'Moreton Bay', although he did not arrive in Australia until twelve years after Logan's death.

Arriving in Sydney in 1832 for the crime of breaking a shop window and stealing a 'piece of worsted plaid', MacNamara was one of the convict period's greatest characters. Like many of his Irish fellow convicts, he had a passionate hatred of the English and the convict system. Unlike most, he also had the ability to express his antagonism in witty and satirical verse. MacNamara's work was often more ambitious than the usual doggerel of the street ballads and included a parody of the literary versions of the mythic descent into the underworld theme, notable in the work of Dante and Swift. *A Convict's Tour to Hell* is a small masterpiece in which Frank dreams that he has died and, like Dante, must journey through the underworld to find his true resting place for all eternity. He visits Purgatory, which he finds full of priests and popes 'weeping wailing gnashing' and suffering the 'torments of the newest fashion'. He journeys on to Hell:

And having found the gloomy gate
Frank rapped aloud to know his fate
He louder knocked and louder still
When the Devil came, pray what's your will?
Alas cried the Poet I've come to dwell
With you and share your fate in Hell
Says Satan that can't be, I'm sure
For I detest and hate the poor
And none shall in my kingdom stand
Except the grandees of the land.
But Frank I think you are going astray
For convicts never come this way
But soar to Heaven in droves and legions
A place so called in the upper regions . . .

In Hell, Frank finds the overseers, floggers and gaolers of the convict system writhing in perpetual torture for the crimes they committed against poor convicts while alive on earth. Captain Cook, 'who discovered New South Wales', is here, along with dukes, mayors and lawyers. They are not alone.

> Here I beheld legions of traitors
> Hangmen gaolers and flagellators
> Commandants, Constables and Spies
> Informers and Overseers likewise
> In flames of brimstone they were toiling
> And lakes of sulphur round them boiling
> Hell did resound with their fierce yelling
> Alas how dismal was their dwelling . . .

One unfortunate seems to be suffering special torments so Frank asks:

> Who is that Sir in yonder blaze
> Who on fire and brimstone seems to graze?

Satan tells him that it is 'Captain Logan of Moreton Bay'.

While he witnesses this dreadful scene there is suddenly a great commotion in Hell. Drums are beaten, flags waved:

> And all the inhabitants of Hell
> With one consent rang the great bell
> Which never was heard to sound or ring
> Since Judas sold our Heavenly King
> Drums were beating flags were hoisting
> There never before was such rejoicing
> Dancing singing joy or mirth
> In Heaven above or on the earth
> Straightway to Lucifer I went
> To know what these rejoicings meant . . .

Satan is senseless with joy as the chief tormentor of all the convicts in New South Wales—Governor Darling—enters Hell. Satan's assistants have already chained him and prepared the brimstone in which he will writhe forever. Satisfied to have witnessed this wonderful sight, Frank travels on to 'that happy place/Where all the woes of mortals cease'. He knocks at the pearly gate and is met by St Peter, who asks him who in heaven he might know. Frank answers by naming bushrangers:

> Well I know Brave Donohue
> Young Troy and Jenkins too
> And many others whom floggers mangled
> And lastly were by Jack Ketch strangled ...

Then,

> Peter, says Jesus, let Frank in
> For he is thoroughly purged from sin
> And although in convict's habit dressed
> Here he shall be a welcome guest ...

A great celebration is then had by all the hosts in Heaven, 'Since Frank the Poet has come at last'. The poem ends with the lines:

> Thro' Heaven's Concave their rejoicings range
> And hymns of praise to God they sang
> And as they praised his glorious name
> I woke and found 'twas but a dream.

'Make it hours instead of days'

With a story like this, it is no surprise that Frank the Poet was still remembered into the twentieth century. In 1902, a rural newspaper published a memoir of Frank's life and times. The historical details are often wrong (Frank never actually met Captain Logan) but the spirit of the story and the respect for Frank's abilities is clear.

*F*rancis MacNamara was a man who came out to Botany Bay in the early days for the benefit of his country and the good of himself. He was one of those mixed up in the political intrigues of the 'Young Ireland Party,' and for the part he took in such with Smith O'Brien and others he was 'transported beyond the seas.' He was well educated, and gifted with a quick perception and ready wit. His aptitude in rhyming gained for him the appellation of 'Frank the Poet,' and many stories used to be told by old hands of his smartness in getting out of a difficulty.

During a time that he was under Captain Logan at Moreton Bay he was frequently in trouble. On one occasion he was called to account for some misdeed, and asked why he should not be imprisoned for fourteen days. He answered promptly—

'Captain Logan, if you plaze,
Make it hours instead of days.'

And the Captain did.

On another occasion he was brought before Logan for inciting the other inmates of his hut to refuse a bullock's head that was being served to them as rations. Captain Logan, in a severe tone, asked him what he meant by generating a mutinous feeling among his fellows.

'Please, sir. I didn't,' said Frank 'I only advised my mates not to accept it as rations because there was no meat on it.' 'Well MacNamara,' said the Captain, 'I am determined to check this insubordinate tendency in a way that I hope will be effective. At the same time, I am willing to hear anything you may have to say in defence before passing sentence on you.'

'Sure, Captain,' said Frank, 'I know you are just, and merciful as well. Kindly let the head be brought in, and you will see yourself that it is nothing but skin and bone, and ain't got enough flesh on it to make a feed for one man. I only said we won't be satisfied with it for our ration.' The Captain ordered the head to be brought, and when it was placed on the table he turned to Frank and said, 'There's the head. Now what about it?'

Frank advanced to the table, picked up a paper-cutter, and said to the Captain and those with him, 'Listen, your honours, to the "honey" ring it has,' and, tapping it with the paper knife, recited in a loud tone the following lines : —

'Oh, bullock, oh, bullock, thou wast brought here,
After working in a team for many a year,
Subjected to the lash, foul language and abuse
And now portioned as food for poor convicts' use.'

'Get out of my sight, you scoundrel,' roared Logan, 'and if you come before me again I'll send you to the triangle.' It is needless to say that Frank was quickly out of the room, chuckling to himself at his good luck. Some time after he was assigned to a squatter in New South Wales, and as was his wont, always in hot water. He was at last given a letter to take to the chief constable in the adjoining town.

Frank suspected the purport of the letter to be a punishment for himself, so he raked his brain in devising a means of escape. Having writing materials, and being an efficient penman, he addressed a couple of envelopes, and, putting them with the one he had received to give the officer, he started. On the outskirts of the town he met a former acquaintance, who was on 'a ticket of leave,' and a stranger to the district. Frank had known him elsewhere, and remembered him as a flogger: and on one occasion he had dropped the lash on himself.

Here was what Frank styled a heaven-sent chance, and it would be a sort of revenge for a past infliction if he succeeded in getting this fellow to deliver the letter. So he sat down and chatted for a while, and pulling out the three envelopes, regretted that they could not have a drink together. If his business was finished, they could; but his master, he said was a Tartar, and it wouldn't be safe to neglect it. So he would have to deliver the letters first. 'Perhaps I might be able to help you,' said the other. 'Blest if I know,' answered Frank, 'it would be all right so long as the cove didn't find it out.' 'Oh, chance it,' said the other, 'and we can have another hour together.'

Frank thought for a while, turning the letters about in his hands, and at last made up his mind to let the other assist him, so handed him the letter addressed to 'Mr. Snapem, Concordium.' They went on into town, and Frank, directing the ex-flogger, turned into a shop. Sneaking on a few minutes after, he heard enough to satisfy him that his surmise was correct, and he left.

On his return to the station, he was asked by the squatter if he had received any reply to the letter. 'Oh, yes,' answered he: 'a feeling reply, that I am likely to remember.' While having tea he appeared in such excellent humour that one of his mates asked the cause. 'Oh, nothing much,' said Frank, 'only circumstances to-day enabled me to pay a debt that I have owed for some years: and I am glad about it.'

Captain of the push

The newspaper also published another recollection of Frank's doings, this time in Sydney town with the forerunners of the larrikin 'pushes' or gangs who often terrorised the streets later in the nineteenth century: Frank had a great down on a 'push' in Sydney known as the 'Cabbage-Tree Mob', their symbol being the wearing of a cabbage-tree hat. Well, on one occasion they bailed up poor Frank, and asked him what he had to say that they should not inflict condign punishment on him. 'Well, boys,' he said,

'Here's three cheers for the Cabbage-tree Mob—
Too lazy to work; too frightened to rob.'

They made for Frank, but just then came along a policeman known as the 'Native Dog'; so Frank escaped that time.

The street gangs of Sydney and Melbourne are almost as old as the cities themselves. In Sydney, the 'Cabbage-Tree Mob' was frequently mentioned in negative terms in the local press: 'There are to be found all round the doors of the Sydney Theatre a sort of loafer known as the Cabbage-Tree Mob. The Cabbage-Tree Mob are always up for a 'spree' and some of their pastimes are so rough an order as to deserve to be repaid with bloody coxcombs.'

Probably not a coherent gang or 'push' so much as an occasional assembly of young working-class men, the mob was distinguished by the kind of headgear they favoured, a hat made from cabbage-tree fronds. Whatever their exact nature, the Cabbage-Tree Mob hung around theatres, race grounds and markets and specialised in catcalling and otherwise harassing the respectable middle classes. Some of them were ex-convicts; some were descended from convict stock.

By the 1870s, groups of this sort were being called 'larrikins'. Their favoured pastimes were a development of the earlier troublemakers and included disrupting Salvation Army meetings with volleys of rotten vegetables, rocks and the odd dead cat. The larrikins were also noted for dancing with young women friends, events often portrayed by journalists as 'orgies'. By the 1880s, observers began to speak of larrikin 'pushes' or gangs, also sometimes referred to as the 'talent'. These were usually associated with particular suburbs or areas; in Sydney there were the 'Haymarket Bummers', the 'Rocks push', the 'Cow Lane push' and the 'Woolloomooloo push'. In Melbourne it was the 'Fitzroy forties', the 'Stephen Street push' and the surely ironic 'Flying Angels', among others. The pushes were mostly male, young and with a strong loyalty ethic, each supporting the others when needed.

The larrikins revelled in fighting with police and resisting arrest, and there were notable pitched battles between them and large groups of police in the last decades of the nineteenth century. Despite, or because of, their criminality and antisocial behaviour, the crudely colourful larrikins soon became the objects of literary interest. Henry Lawson's 'The Captain of the Push' was an early rendering of the larrikin culture.

Based loosely on real events, 'The Captain of the Push' (also unprintably parodied as 'The Bastard from the Bush') begins:

As the night was falling slowly down on city, town and bush,
From a slum in Jones's Alley sloped the Captain of the Push;
And he scowled towards the North, and he scowled towards the South,
As he hooked his little finger in the corners of his mouth.
Then his whistle, loud and shrill, woke the echoes of the 'Rocks',
And a dozen ghouls came sloping round the corners of the blocks.

The ghouls, called the 'Gory Bleeders', 'spoke the gutter language' of the slums and brothels and swore fearsomely and fulsomely with every breath. Their 'captain' was:

. . . bottle-shouldered, pale and thin,
For he was the beau-ideal of a Sydney larrikin;
E'en his hat was most suggestive of the city where we live,
With a gallows-tilt that no one, save a larrikin, can give . . .

He wears the larrikin outfit of wide-mouthed trousers, elaborate boots, uncollared shirt and necktie. The gang encounters a stranger in the street, who turns out to be a man from the bush who wants to join the gang. He has read of their exploits in the *Weekly Gasbag* and, sitting alone in his bush humpy, decides that he

'. . . longed to share the dangers and the pleasures of the push!
'Gosh! I hate the swells and good 'uns—I could burn 'em in their beds;
'I am with you, if you'll have me, and I'll break their blazing heads.'

The larrikins demand to know if the bushman would match them in perfidy and violence. Would he punish an informer who breaks the code of loyalty?

'Would you lay him out and kick him to a jelly on the ground?' Would he 'smash a bleedin' bobby', 'break a swell or Chinkie' and 'have a "moll" to keep yer'? To all of which the stranger answers, 'My kerlonial oath! I would!' They test him practically by asking him to smash a window. The stranger is sworn in and becomes an exemplary larrikin, if a little over-zealous even for the Gory Bleeders.

One morning the captain wakes and finds the stranger gone:

Quickly going through the pockets of his 'bloomin' bags,' he learned
That the stranger had been through him for the stuff his 'moll'
    had earned;
And the language that he muttered I should scarcely like to tell.
(Stars! and notes of exclamation!! blank and dash will do as well).

The rest of the bleeders soon forget the bloke who briefly joined them and robbed their leader. But the captain 'Still is laying round in ballast, for the nameless from the bush.'

Louis Stone's flawed masterpiece, *Jonah*, presented a more realistic picture of the Sydney slum lifestyle that produced and nourished the larrikins. Its eponymous hero makes his own fortune by hard work and astute business sense, though forfeits his working-class roots, loses in love and fails as a decent human being in the process.

Probably taking his lead from this approach, C.J. Dennis began writing the verse that would eventually become the much-loved classics *The Songs of a Sentimental Bloke* and *The Moods of Ginger Mick*. These were highly romanticised and bore almost no resemblance to the realities of the street, with soft Bill 'the Bloke', his love for Doreen and friendship with street rabbit-seller Ginger Mick, and other characters who hung around Melbourne's 'Little Lon'. These verse novellas sold in great numbers, making Dennis a wealthy man and establishing the 'rough diamond' with a soft centre stereotype of the larrikin, recycled for decades in stage shows and the early Australian cinema. The image lives on still.

The Prince of Pickpockets

It is difficult to sift fact from folklore in the life of George Barrington (1755–1804). The Irish-born rogue of uncertain parentage was a colourful man-about-town in early nineteenth-century London, though his early life began in obscurity and crime.

His story begins with him stabbing a schoolmate and robbing his teacher. The sixteen-year-old ran away and joined a travelling theatre troupe where he gave himself the name George Barrington and learned the pickpocketing business. He then went to London where he affected the wealth and style of a gentleman, his eloquence assuring him of acceptance into even the highest circles. It became something of a social honour to have had one's pocket picked by the great thief. He notoriously relieved the Russian Count Orlov of a diamond-encrusted silver snuffbox said to be worth 30,000 pounds, an unimaginable sum for most people at the time. Barrington was caught and made to return his booty. Orlov refused to prosecute.

But the incorrigible Barrington was later arrested on another charge and sentenced to three years' hard labour. He was described at the time as 'the genteelest thief ever remembered seen at the Old Bailey', despite the fact that he lived in Charing Cross, then one of London's less respectable districts.

The Prince of Pickpockets was out after serving barely a year of his sentence. After his release he returned to his nefarious trade and was soon arrested again, this time going down for five years. He was freed through the influence of friends in high places on condition that he left the country. He did so briefly, but soon returned and was caught thieving yet again.

During his last appearance at the Old Bailey, Barrington made a lengthy and elaborate speech in his defence and argued against his hanging. This was quite unnecessary, as his crime was not a capital offence. Without delay the jury pronounced him guilty. Always wanting to have the last word, the eloquent cutpurse replied:

My Lord,

I had a few words to say, why sentence of death should not be passed upon me; I had much to say, though I shall say but little on the occasion. Notwithstanding I have the best opinion of your lordship's candour, and have no wish or pleasure in casting a reflection on any person whatever; but I cannot help observing that it is the strange lot of some persons through life, that with the best wishes, the best endeavours, and the best intentions, they are not able to escape the envenomed tooth of calumny: whatever they say or do is so twisted and perverted from the reality, that they will meet with censures and misfortunes, where perhaps they were entitled to success and praise. The world, my lord, has given me credit for much more abilities than I am conscious of possessing; but the world should also consider that the greatest abilities may be obstructed by the mercenary nature of some unfeeling minds, as to render them entirely useless to the possessor. Where was the generous and powerful man that would come forward and say, 'You have some abilities which might be of service to yourself and to others, but you have much to struggle with, I feel for your situation, and will place you in a condition to try the sincerity of your intentions; and as long as you act with diligence and fidelity, you shall not want for countenance and protection?' But, my lord, the die is cast! I am prepared to meet the sentence of the court, with respectful resignation, and the painful lot assigned me, I hope, with becoming resolution.

This was Barrington being brief! He was given seven years' transportation. Even his silver tongue could not save him from this fate.

By now the artful Barrington had become a celebrity criminal. His gentleman thief image, his clever tongue and ability to wriggle out of prison sentences made him a sensation of the London gossips and the press. The papers embroidered and invented exploits as outrageously as they do today. Even before he was transported to Botany Bay the papers reported his alleged attempt to escape Newgate wearing his female accomplice's dress. He was also reported to be lamenting that the great Barrington was to be banished to a land where the natives had no pockets for him to pick.

Little more than a year after his arrival in New South Wales, the pickpocket's talents and abilities saw him quickly freed, soon to become a superintendent of the convicts he had once laboured among and, later, chief constable of Parramatta. Governor Hunter granted him land and he purchased more, prospering as a farmer and more or less reformed character. Pensioned off the government service in 1800, Barrington's behaviour became increasingly erratic. He was declared insane and died in 1804.

But his legend lived on. Like many folk heroes, he was said by some to have lived to a ripe old age. His faked memoirs were frequently reprinted and he featured in newspapers even a century and a half after his death. Barrington was also, inaccurately, credited with some often-quoted lines that have passed into the traditions of transportation and convictism. At the opening of the colony's first theatre in 1796 he is supposed to have delivered this verse:

From distant climes o'er widespread seas we come,
Though not with much eclat or beat of drum.
True patriots all; for be it understood,
We left our country for our country's good.

Many other stories were told about him, not only in the raffish memoirs he allegedly penned but in folk tradition as well. One yarn had it that there was a party at the home of a wealthy Sydney merchant during Barrington's time in the colony. The gossip-worthy pickpocket came up as a topic during conversation. The merchant's wife and hostess of the event firmly proclaimed that she did not believe the outlandish yarns about the smooth-talking Barrington and his thieving skills.

A couple of days after the party a gentleman called asking to speak with the hostess's husband. He was away, so the hostess showed off her array of expensive jewels while they waited. But the husband did not return as expected and the man said he would try again another day. As he left, the debonair visitor put his hand in his coat and drew out the hostess's gold earrings and necklace. He bowed, saying, 'I think these are yours, madam. Kindly tell your husband that Mr Barrington called.'

14

Plains of promise

Our hearts they were willing, our bodies they were young
Upon the Plains of Promise we were broken by the sun.

From Anon., 'Plains of Promise'

THE EUROPEAN SETTLEMENT of Australia was a series of voyages
from the old world to the new. It began with convicts and
their gaolers but was soon followed by ships of free migrants
searching for a better life, looking to make a fortune or even
just planning to spend a few years in the colonies. The vast
majority of those who came here before the 1950s were British,
bringing their customs and traditions with them. A few of these
thrived, many faded and others were adapted to form the basis
of a national identity.

Promising though Australia was for many settlers, their voyages
were often hard and tragic.

'I was not expected to survive'

Many were prepared to risk much, often all, in pursuit of the plains
of promise. Ellen Moger arrived in Adelaide in January 1840. She
wrote home to her parents after the voyage from England, 'four
months to a day on the Great Deep':

*P*oor little Alfred was the first that died on the 30th of Oct, and on the 8th of Nov, dear Fanny went and three days after, on the 11th, the dead babe was taken from me. I scarcely know how I sustained the shock, though I was certain they could not recover, yet when poor Fanny went it over-powered me and from the weakness of my frame, reduced me to such a low nervous state that, for many weeks, I was not expected to survive. It seems I gave much trouble but knew nothing about it and, though I was quite conscious that the dear baby and Fanny were thrown overboard, I would still persist that the water could not retain them and that they were with me in the berth. I took strange fancies into my head and thought that Mother had said I should have her nice easy chair to sit up in and, if they would only lift me into it, I would soon get well. I had that chair of Mother's in my 'mind's eye' for many weeks and was continually talking about it.

Later in the letter she discusses the health of her surviving daughter:

My dear Emily now seems more precious to us than ever, and I feel very thankful I did not leave her in England. Her health is not as good as formerly, having something Scurvy, the effects of Salt diet. She is also troubled with weak eyes, a complaint exceedingly common in this town, from the great degree of heat, light and dust.

⌀

Ellen Moger's tragedy was not unique. The poorer assisted-passage emigrants shipped in steerage class, herded together for many months in crowded and often unsanitary conditions, ideal for the incubation and spread of frequently fatal diseases including scarlet fever, measles, typhus and even cholera on some ships. Illness struck children and adults alike, but it was the infants who died in the greatest numbers, often from the less exotic but equally lethal cases of severe diarrhoea.

In 1839, Sarah Brunskill watched her infant son die of convulsions following acute diarrhoea. Twenty-four hours later, her two-year-old daughter died in an agonising fever so hot that her mother found it painful to touch her.

'She, like her brother, was thrown into the deep about the same time on the Thursday. The Union Jack was thrown over them, and the burial service Performed.' Sarah thought that they were like 'two little angels, they looked so beautiful in death'.

Multiple deaths from disease were not uncommon in the early decades of sailing ship migration. From the 1850s, sanitation and health care improved and mortality rates dropped considerably. Deaths aboard migrant ships fell to a level equal to, or even less than, those on land for adults and older children, though infants remained at great peril. Sarah Brunskill and her husband were among the better-off passengers, though this factor did not spare their children.

The shipboard experience of some migrants was sometimes as bad as the worst of the convict ships. In some ways it was even more despairing. At least the transports looked forward to little, while the migrants left home full of hope for a new and better life for themselves and their children.

The town that drowned

They called it the 'valley of hope'. The mainly German migrants who came to South Australia from the 1830s wanted land to grow their crops and a place to practise their religious beliefs unhindered. Early arrivals soon found the Barossa region and other suitable places and were followed by families and single men of Lutheran beliefs, establishing settlements and using the housing and agricultural styles that were familiar to them. Of course, they also built churches as the single most important structures in each settlement.

In 1847–48, the village of Hoffnungsthal was founded. Its settlers included Christian Menzel and Maria Richter with their ten children, the Huf family of six, the Beinkes and the Seelanders, among others. By 1848 they had nearly 400 acres under cultivation and began building a church and looking for a pastor.

Each year they celebrated the leaving of their homelands and their settling at Hoffnungsthal.

*T*hey were happy people, those dwellers in old Hoffnungsthal. To them this new country looked like the Land of Canaan, for it flowed with milk and honey. In the great old gums the bees had their hives and in very warm weather, the combs overflowed and the honey dropped to the ground. And if anyone was lucky enough to possess a cow or two, he also had milk. So abundant was the feed for the cows, that often, too, these could not retain their milk, and like the honey, it flowed to the ground. There were no fences in those days, the country was open in all directions and the cows were free to wander and seek for themselves the most succulent grasses. In the gullies of the Barossa Ranges, the pasture was sweet and the water in the creeks as clear as crystal.

For the farmers and tradesmen and their families, this was as close to paradise as they were likely to get this side of the grave. They took to their new country with enthusiasm and the same intensity as they brought to their religious values, growing wheat, barley, oats, peas, beans, lentils and potatoes from the seeds they had carefully brought with them. They brought their distinctive dress with them, too, including the black suits the men wore to church and perhaps other religious occasions. They made 'coffee' with rye and milk and their cottage gardens supplied many of their wants, along with the bounty of the countryside: wild ducks, white cockatoos and kangaroo. It was reported that the local Aboriginal people were greatly impressed with the efficiency of the German firearms in downing wildlife.

In other things they followed the ways of their homeland, apparently unaware that they had built on dangerous country. The Peramangk people of the area called the place Yertalla-ngga, meaning 'flooding land'. Their story is that one of their men, known as Jemmie, warned the newcomers against building in their valley of hope because it was prone to serious flooding. Biblically, they ignored this good advice and after a few years of this happy life:

*L*arge tracts of bush country had been cleared and the good people were beginning to feel settled and comfortable. But the happiest conditions of life may come to an end very suddenly. It was about the year 1853 in the month of October when the disaster came. It rained heavily and continuously. For a day and a night the rain came down like a deluge. One family had to leave its house during the night and seek refuge beneath a huge boulder on the side of the hill. In the morning a scene of desolation met the gaze of the people as they emerged from their cottages. All the farms and gardens were submerged. The water was already entering the homes and was rising rapidly. In great haste they had to open pens and yards for pigs and cattle to escape. Then was there much weeping among mothers and children and many were asking why the hand of the Lord had thus descended upon them. Had they done anything to offend God? With a little reflection they had to admit that they themselves were to blame for the disaster that had overwhelmed them. The old blacks had warned them that sometimes much water would flow together there where they had built their village, although possibly they had not understood the warning. They had not had much experience of the vagaries of the Australian climate. It was hardly to be expected that God would alter the laws of nature on their account. Their work of clearing the land of timber and brush had made the progress of the flood waters all the more rapid. Before the creeks and gullies had finished emptying out their waters Old Hoffnungsthal was submerged beneath some eight feet of water.

⌒

The valley of hope had become a lake of lapping waters, and there was no way to economically drain it. There was nothing else for the people of Hoffnungsthal to do but to leave their homes, hopes and memories behind and move on to start again. Some founded a new settlement, which they called Neu Hoffnungsthal. Some moved to Victoria, where they established Hochkirch (now Tarrington). Some were so disillusioned that they left Australia altogether and voyaged to America.

Although the town was no more, the area retained some settlers and gained new ones. Roads, bridges and other improvements still needed to be maintained and developed for the overall infrastructure of the area. In 1883 there were more floods, though with minimal damage. The town's name was changed to Karrawirra in World War I due to anti-German prejudice, but was restored in 1975.

Little now remains of old Hoffnungsthal: one or two buildings and the sturdy church, built high on a hill to be closer to God. Over the years, this gradually decayed and its stones were salvaged for other buildings around the region. Today there is not much to see but a few stone heaps.

Wine and witches

The sunny Barossa Valley winelands are an unlikely setting for dark mutterings from the age of witchcraft, but tales of occult beliefs and practices lingered there for a very long time. It all began with the migration of the early German settlers. Many of these people were Lutherans or members of other sects with a strong belief in good and evil, which could lead to superstitious behaviour. Locals used to guard against witchcraft by wearing red ribbons around their necks or putting their clothes on inside out, using magic to fight magic.

The story of the devil coming to the Barossa's largest hill, Kaiserstuhl, stems from an incident in the very early years of settlement. A group led by Pastor Kavel concluded that this would happen on a certain night. They had a blacksmith forge a mighty chain that would last for 1000 years, and took the chain to the hill with the intention of capturing the devil and locking him away from the world so he could do no more evil. As far as anyone knows, the devil did not make an appearance, but one night the same pastor took a group of his followers to a spot outside Tanunda, where they intended to wait out the end of the world, an event that would destroy what they saw as the debauchery of the settlement. While Tanunda burned, Kavel and his people would enter into paradise in a state of natural grace. Instead, it rained, and the end-of-days enthusiasts had to return home drenched to their beds.

It is also whispered in local tradition that the occult text known as the *Sixth and Seventh Books of Moses*, or known more popularly as *The Witches' Bible*, was circulating in the valley, perhaps as early as 1842. Although banned by the Lutheran Church, copies of this work were known to have been secreted by some and also handed on from generation to generation in the belief that anyone who owned this book would never be able to die unless it was given to another. If that were not possible, the book might be laid in the coffin along with its last owner. The coffin then had to be dropped to the ground three times in a ritual of farewell and finality.

This book is said to have contained spells for all manner of magical operations, including hexes. One story has it that a farmer and his wife had an argument one morning. He stamped out to plough and she went huffily off to market to sell the vegetables, hexing him as he went. When she returned at the end of the day, her husband was still standing at the plough, just as he had been when she had left in the morning. The story does not say whether his wife had calmed down enough to release the farmer from the plough.

Barossa legend is full of tales about wheels falling off or locking up on wagons passing particular houses, cows suddenly losing their milk or hens failing to lay eggs. There were reported incidents of witchcraft in the Barossa as late as 2007 and local landmarks such as The Sanctuary, a grassed rectangle of land with a group of stones at one end, are said to have occult associations.

Phantoms of the landfall light

Born in the wake of a maritime tragedy and said to be haunted by several ghosts, the Cape Otway Lighthouse has an intriguing history. The powerful beacon is known as a 'landfall light', meaning the first coastal light to be seen by ships at sea. After Bass Strait was opened up as a shorter passage to Victoria in the early nineteenth century, the lighthouse was the first sight that many migrants had of Australia after their long voyage away from home.

Only the second lighthouse to be built on the mainland, its light first flashed out in 1848. Although there had long been plans to build a light on the Cape, the difficulty of access and cost of construction held the project back until the *Cataraqui* was wrecked off King Island in September 1845, with the loss of more than 350 lives and a handful of survivors. This was not the first and far from the last tragedy in the hazardous Bass Strait. Public dismay and outrage stirred the government into finally tackling the challenging building project. Even with the help of local Aborigines and plenty of resources, it took the Port Phillip District Superintendent C.J. La Trobe three attempts and a whole year to reach the Cape by land. Then they had to map and build a road. Then they had to build a very large structure, together with buildings to house its keepers. After mammoth efforts by land and sea, the lighthouse was completed and equipped with the latest optical technology in 1848. Every 50 seconds the sperm oil-powered reflectors lit the night sky for three seconds, heralding the arrival of another ship of migrants and making the remainder of their journey as safe as possible.

The isolation of the Otway light meant that the keepers and their families could receive supplies by boat only twice a year. The little community needed to do everything themselves, including giving birth. Catherine Evans, wife of Assistant Light Keeper William Evans, lost two children at birth during their 22 years at the light. Born in 1867 and 1868, the children's graves are among the earliest still to be found in the local cemetery.

This is only one of many sad stories that provide the lighthouse with the right atmosphere for some supernatural traditions. According to another story, the wife of Assistant Light Keeper Richens was driven to mental instability by the isolation and harshness of the life and had to be institutionalised until her death in the 1930s. Her ghost is said to trouble the building in which she once lived, nowadays the café. Known as 'the Lady in Grey', she is said to simply appear and join groups of visitors. Some have heard her singing lullabies, together with other physical manifestations of a presence.

Another tradition concerns a four-year-old girl who died at the telegraph station adjacent to the lighthouse during the 1870s. The coolest place to keep the body until the medical examiner could make the long trek was a cupboard, so she was locked in there. No evidence for this happening has ever been found, but now some women entering the station experience unexplained sadness, cameras mysteriously fail and dogs refuse to enter the building. Mediums also claim to have been distressed at hearing a little girl's voice during their paranormal investigations.

After many upgrades, the Cape Otway light was decommissioned in 1994 and is now the focus of a busy local tourism industry, trading in part on its ghosts. There is certainly a folkloric basis for these stories, mostly unfounded in documentation. Now a guide at the light, Malcolm Brack, the son of a keeper, lived there for many years, and recalls that the keepers believed the signal station was haunted.

Ongoing inquiries by local historians and paranormal investigators may reveal further folklore and facts about the history of the lighthouse. Whether they do or not, the landfall light will always have the honour of having shown thousands of migrants the way to their new lives and to have saved the lives of uncounted mariners.

Tragedy on Lizard Island

Hard times forced the Oxnam family, like so many others, to leave the Cornish town of Truro in 1877. They sailed to Queensland, where their seventeen-year-old daughter Mary found work as a governess and also set up a private school in Cooktown. Mary was reportedly 'reserved, nervous and delicate', though her skills at the piano made her popular. She married Captain Robert Watson, part owner of the Lizard Island *bêche-de-mer* (sea cucumber) station, in 1880 and the following year gave birth to their son, whom they named Ferrier.

Towards the end of 1881, Captain Watson was away from the island on other business. Mary and Ferrier, accompanied only by Ah Leong, the gardener, and a houseboy named Ah Sam, were attacked by Aboriginal men from the mainland. Unwittingly, the factory and household had been set up on ground important to the local Aboriginal people, probably related to its being the home of the sand goanna, *manuya*. According to Mary's diary, Ah Sam noticed smoke from the Aborigines' camp on 27 September. Two days later Ah Leong was speared to death at the farm, not far from the cottage. At seven the following evening, Mary drove a group of Aborigines off the beach with her revolver. The next day Ah Sam was speared seven times, though he survived. There was nothing else to do but leave by sea with the wounded Ah Sam and baby Ferrier. Mary recorded their desperate voyage on a few pencilled pages:

*L*eft Lizard Island October 2nd 1881, (Sunday afternoon) in tank (or pot in which beche de mer is boiled). Got about three or four miles from the Lizards.

October 4 Made for the sand bank off the Lizards, but could not reach it. Got on a reef.

October 5 Remained on the reef all day on the look out for a boat, but saw none.

October 6 Very calm morning. Able to pull the tank up to an island with three small mountains on it. Ah Sam went ashore to try to get water as ours was done. There were natives camped there, so we were afraid to go far away. We had to wait return of tide. Anchored under the mangroves; got on the reef. Very calm.

October 7 Made for another island four or five miles from the one spoken of yesterday. Ashore, but could not find any water. Cooked some rice and clam-fish. Moderate S.E. breeze. Stayed here all night. Saw a steamer bound north. Hoisted Ferrier's pink and white wrap but did not answer us.

October 8 Changed anchorage of boat as the wind was freshening. Went down to a kind of little lake on the same island (this done last night). Remained here all day looking out for a boat; did not see any; very cold night; blowing very hard. No water.

October 9 Brought the tank ashore as far as possible with this morning's tide. Made camp all day under the trees. Blowing very hard. No water. Gave Ferrier a dip in the sea; he is showing symptoms of thirst, and I took a dip myself. Ah Sam and self very parched with thirst. Ferrier is showing symptoms.

October 10 Ferrier very bad with inflammation; very much alarmed. No fresh water, and no more milk, but condensed. Self very weak; really thought I would have died last night (Sunday).

October 11 Still all alive. Ferrier very much better this morning. Self feeling very weak. I think it will rain to-day; clouds very heavy; wind not quite so hard. No rain. Morning fine weather. Ah Sam preparing to die, have not seen him since 9th. Ferrier more cheerful. Self not feeling at all well. Have not seen any boat of any description. No water. Nearly dead with thirst.

That was the final entry in Mary's sea-stained journal. Searchers found it three months later, along with the remains of the three and Mary's Bible.

Outrage, fear and hatred gripped the settlers in the area, fanned by inaccurate newspaper reports relying on prejudice and fear rather than the facts. Retribution against the perpetrators, actual and assumed, came swiftly. Men, women and children of the local Aboriginal groups were slaughtered, many of those massacred seemingly not of the same group that had attacked Mary's household. And so one tragedy was made even greater.

The bodies of Mary, Ferrier and Ah Sam were buried in

Cooktown, and in 1886 the citizens raised an impressive memorial fountain. The Mary Watson fountain is inscribed:

In MEMORIAM
MRS WATSON The Heroine of Lizard Island, Cooktown,
North Queensland, A.D. 1881

Erected 1886 Edward D`Arcy, Mayor 1885.

Five fearful days beneath the scorching glare
Her babe she nursed God knows the pangs that woman
had to bear
Whose last sad entry showed a Mother's care
Then—'Near dead with thirst.'

Who was Billy Barlow?

With migrants arriving in more or less steady streams in the colonial period, 'new chums' became a popular stereotype. Colonial folksong and literature is full of disparaging references to newcomers who were not properly dressed or equipped, or emotionally prepared for the rigours of pioneer life. It was even suggested that they should be shipped back to where they came from when they failed to measure up:

When shearing comes lay down your drums
And step to the board, you brand new chums
With a row-dum, row-dum, rubba-dub-dub
We'll send 'em home in a limejuice tub

The song makes fun of the unskilled and unhardened British recruits to the backbreaking shearer's trade and profoundly masculine lifestyle. It ends by suggesting that the new chum would be better off going back home in a 'limejuice tub', a British sailing ship—than 'humping your drum in this country'. Eventually the new chums either went home with their tails between their legs or became 'old hands' themselves, adopting the attitudes of their detractors and subjecting newcomers to the same treatment in their turn. So prevalent was the new chum that he came to be represented by a mythical figure named 'Billy Barlow', ridiculed in song and on stages across the country.

The earliest reference to Billy Barlow popped up in the 1840s, though the earliest song seems to date from an American minstrel song of a decade or so earlier. The newspaper review of an amateur theatrical production one 1843 evening noted, 'Several songs were sung, and the following, which was written expressly for the occasion by a gentleman in Maitland, was received with unbounded applause.'

In this version of the story, poor Billy is left a thousand pounds by his old aunt and decides to further his fortunes in Australia. By the second verse he has already been taken down:

> When to Sydney I got, there a merchant I met,
> Who said he would teach me a fortune to get;
> He'd cattle and sheep past the colony's bounds,
> Which he sold with the station for my thousand pounds.
> Oh dear, lackaday, oh,
> He gammon'd the cash out of Billy Barlow.

Things go from bad to worse; as Billy goes 'up the country' he is bailed up by bushrangers and left for dead tied to a tree. Eventually freeing himself, he is arrested because his belongings have been stolen and so he cannot identify himself. Taken to Sydney, he is eventually identified and released but on returning to his station discovers Aborigines have speared his cattle. Even nature conspires against the hapless new chum:

And for nine months before no rain there had been,
So the devil a blade of grass could be seen;
And one-third of my wethers the scab they had got,
And the other two-thirds had just died of the rot.
Oh dear, lackaday, oh,
'I shall soon be a settler,' said Billy Barlow.

Deep in debt, Billy is reduced to poverty and hunger—'as thin as a lath got poor Billy Barlow'. He is arrested and imprisoned for debt back in Sydney again and listed as an insolvent, or bankrupt:

Then once more I got free, but in poverty's toil;
I've no 'cattle for salting,' no 'sheep for to boil';
I can't get a job—though to any I'd stoop,
If it was only the making of 'portable soup'.
Oh dear, lackaday, oh,
Pray give some employment to Billy Barlow.

Despite his tragi-comic trials, Billy Barlow is not totally ground down and still contemplates repairing his fortunes in the final verse:

But there's still a 'spec' left may set me on my stumps,
If a wife I could get with a few of the dumps;
So if any lass here has 'ten thousand' or so,
She can just drop a line addressed 'Mr. Barlow'.
Oh dear, lackaday, oh,
The dear angel shall be 'Mrs. William Barlow'.

So popular and pervasive was the contempt for the new chum that 'Billy Barlow' became a stock character of popular entertainment for decades. He assumed all sorts of guises, including rat catcher, London street clown, butcher, clerk and gold-digger, as well as the know-nothing tenderfoot of Australian tradition. Although now long forgotten, we still don't know who Billy Barlow was, or if he ever existed outside ballads and the popular theatre of Britain, Canada, America, South Africa and colonial Australia.

The temple of skulls

On 25 July 1836, Charles Morgan Lewis and his crew were razing the Torres Strait island of Aureed to smoking oblivion. Searching for any survivors of the *Charles Eaton* wrecked in those parts a few years earlier, they had found what they were looking for and they did not like what they saw.

Bound for Canton (now known as Guangzhou) under Captain Morley, the barque *Charles Eaton* was wrecked in the little-known Torres Strait in mid-August 1834. The passengers and crew were thrown into several groups in their desperate efforts to survive. Some escaped to the Netherlands East Indies on the ship's cutter, and one group of six managed to build a makeshift raft. Among the group were the first officer, Mr Clear; the second officer; a crewman; and three ship's boys, one named John Ireland. After drifting through the shallow waters for several days and nights they encountered a group of islanders in canoes. The islanders demonstrated that they were unarmed and signalled the Europeans to join them in their craft. After some discussion, the castaways got into the canoes. They were paddled to a cay where they searched for food accompanied by the islanders, but it was not long before the survivors of the *Charles Eaton* sank onto the ground in exhaustion. Their rescuers now began to laugh and gesture in an unfriendly way and the survivors realised they intended to kill them. The first officer, a minister's son, calmly led the little group in prayer and resignation to their fate. Completely fatigued and despite their peril, the survivors fell asleep.

Young John Ireland awoke to the sound and sight of his

companions having their brains beaten out with islander clubs. Only he and another boy named Sexton were spared. Both the boys fought back; although wounded, their resistance and their youth probably saved them. Nearby, the islanders celebrated their victory dancing around a large fire, and in the flickering light Ireland saw the decapitated heads of his companions and the remains of their bodies floating in the surf.

The islanders took the boys to Pullan Island in the Torres Strait, where they met the remnants of another group of *Charles Eaton* survivors who had suffered much the same fate. Their severed heads, still recognisable, were also on the island. After a few months, Ireland and an infant survivor of the second group named William D'Oyley were taken on a lengthy voyage by their captors. Eventually the two passed into the care of a Mer (Murray) Islander named Duppar, who purchased them for two bunches of bananas. Duppar treated Ireland kindly, effectively adopting him, while D'Oyley was entrusted to the care of another Mer Islander named Oby.

While these terrifying events were taking place at the northern extremity of Australia, efforts were being made in England to mount a search and, hopefully, a rescue mission. The crewmen who had escaped in the cutter were eventually rescued and gave their version of events, and there were rumours that others had also escaped. Although many of these accounts and speculations were contradictory and vague, there was some reason to hope that at least some passengers and crew of the *Charles Eaton* were still alive somewhere. Eventually there would be several expeditions, but it was one mounted from Sydney under Charles Lewis on the *Isabella* that finally solved the mystery.

On 19 June, *Isabella* anchored off Mer. Among a large group of islanders on the beach, Lewis saw a European man. Four large outrigger canoes came alongside the *Isabella*, indicating a desire to trade for axes and knives. After some difficult negotiations, the islanders accepted an array of these items in return for freeing their European captive. Although he could now barely speak English, Lewis soon confirmed that the boy was the missing John Ireland.

Further negotiations and a show of strength from the armed crew of the *Isabella* eventually produced William D'Oyley, but the youngster did not want to leave Oby and clung crying to his adoptive father. Lewis showered gifts on Duppar and Oby in recognition of their kindness to the boys and wisely followed this up with more gifts to the other Mer Islanders. The *Isabella* departed a few days later, the best of friends with the local people.

Lewis had achieved a part of his goal in rescuing the two boys. But what of the other survivors? As Ireland gradually regained his English, he was able to tell Lewis more of the gruesome story and direct him to where the other survivors might be. After conversations with Darnley Islanders, it was confirmed that the second group of survivors had been murdered and their heads were kept on Aureed Island, a ritual centre for local beliefs. The Darnley people also told Lewis that the killers had eaten the eyes and cheeks of the dead, forcing their children to do the same, in accordance with the belief that this would make them strong warriors.

Lewis made for Aureed. By the time he arrived the island was deserted, as word of his coming had travelled ahead. Following a red shell-lined avenue, in the islander village he entered a low thatched hut, where he found a grisly icon of tortoiseshell, feathers and shells, in the form of a mask about five feet long by two and a half feet high. Around the edges were many skulls, held to the mask with ships' rope. Many of the skulls were battered and cracked but in some cases could be identified as those of women and children. Lewis had found the remains of the murdered group.

Taking the ritual figure to his ship, the disgusted Lewis angrily gave orders for his men to torch the 'temple of skulls', as it would later be dubbed, along with any other structures. Soon the entire island was ablaze. While cutting down the remaining coconut trees, they found two more scorched skulls to add to those on the mask. Lewis renamed the place 'Skull Island'.

The *Isabella* returned to Sydney on 12 October, having been away for almost twenty weeks. There was a dispute over the reward for the rescue and Lewis was denied his money. Eventually he went mad and by 1845 was totally destitute. With support from his friends he was finally awarded a significant gratuity of 300 pounds.

In 1844, a British navy ship revisited Mer and inquired after Duppar. An elderly man with grey beard and swollen limbs identified himself as the boys' saviour. He was presented with a large ceremonial axe in gratitude for helping John Ireland and William D'Oyley.

And what of the skulls? Governor Bourke had them detached from the mask and buried beneath a large altar stone in the cemetery then at Devonshire Street. As for the mask, long thought to have been destroyed by fire, it has recently been suggested that it has lain hidden among artefacts gifted to the National Museum of Denmark in the 1860s, incorrectly labelled through a series of museum clerical errors.

In 2011, Britain's famous Natural History Museum announced that it would repatriate the remains of 138 Torres Strait Islanders souvenired, traded or otherwise acquired during the period of colonisation. Many of these items were skulls.

Chimney Sweeps' Day

Most traditional British customs failed to make the transition from one side of the world to the other, but one May Day custom that did persist for some time in Australia was known as Chimney Sweeps' Day. Adapted from earlier customs involving the soliciting of money on their annual holiday, chimney sweeps in larger towns and cities developed the custom of parading a roughly two-metre-high flower- and leaf-covered, bell-shaped 'Jack-in-the-Green'. This was originally a simple floral decoration traditional to May Day celebrations. Over many years the garland expanded to the point where it completely covered the wearer. The person carrying this device danced along the street, usually accompanied by an appropriately dressed 'Lord' and 'Lady', sometimes by a 'wife' known as Judy, and beribboned sweeps, crashing their brooms and shovels together to create 'rough music'. Sometimes there was more formal musical accompaniment of whistle, fiddle and tabor (a small drum). The group processed through the streets, soliciting donations from passers-by. In some cases, these activities would be kept up for some days after 1 May, or even begun a day or two earlier. No doubt there was a fair bit of drinking as well.

The custom appeared in Hobart in the early 1840s and seems to have been observed there, and in Launceston, until at least the 1870s. Chimney Sweeps' Day was also recorded in Sydney during the 1840s. However, the dramatic seasonal and other differences took a heavy toll on this British custom as the nineteenth century progressed. Newspaper descriptions of the Sweeps' Day in Tasmania from the 1840s to the 1870s reveal an almost annual shrinking of numbers, gaiety and enthusiasm, as the antipodean seasons, public opinion and, it seems, a declining need for chimney sweeping combined to render the celebration pointless.

But there may have been additional reasons for the demise of Jack-in-the-Green. May Day, later Labour Day, celebrations have long had a clear political–industrial agenda, deriving from the struggle for the eight-hour working day that occupied Australian industrial relations for decades through the nineteenth century. The earlier craft guild May Day observation of Jack-in-the-Green could also be associated with pointed political comment and activity. In 1857, a poem titled 'Reflections by a Chimney Sweep', or 'chummy' as they were known, was specifically critical of politicians and the political system. It began:

I'm glad I'm not an M.L.A.
Least ways in Hobart Town;
I'd rather much a chummy be,
And earn an honest crown.

The poem continued:

If we were sent to parliament
We wouldn't mop and mow,
Like apes and other animals
I've seen at Wombwell's show.

Later, it criticises the Tasmanian attorney-general by name. Two years before this poem was published, the 'King of the Hobart Sweeps', John Gordon, upset many citizens by taking part in the Jack-in-the-Green procession with his ribbons the colours of a candidate in the local elections.

Other imported customs also gradually faded with the century. The merrymaking Whitsuntide customs associated with the Christian feast of Pentecost, still featured throughout Britain today, seem to have ceased in Australia by the 1890s, while May Day was only rescued from oblivion and school dancing classes by its association with the trade union movement. In many cases, as in Britain and elsewhere in Europe, the spirit of the times was against the old customs, often considered backwards, silly and uncomfortably superstitious by the Victorian middle-class mind. After welcoming the Jack-in-the-Green custom in Hobart during the 1840s, by the 1860s the local newspapers were hoping that this 'foolish custom' was quickly dying out.

The dragon of Big Gold Mountain

They came in their thousands: Chinese gold-diggers drawn by the hope of striking it rich in the rushes that began in 1851. The Chinese called the Victorian diggings Dai Gum San, meaning Big Gold Mountain, and by the middle of the 1850s there were around 4000 on the Bendigo fields, many having walked overland from the port of Robe in South Australia, a distance of almost 500 kilometres.

Fearful of Chinese competition and also of the 'yellow peril', the Victorian government imposed a restrictive entry tax on Chinese hopefuls, although there were no such restrictions in the colony of South Australia. The Chinese were industrious and successful in their gold mining, attracting prejudice as well as economic jealousy from the predominantly European goldfields population. There was violence, discrimination and numerous attempts to stop or restrict Chinese gold-seekers.

But there was a brighter side. The riches of the gold rushes soon generated prosperous communities in Ballarat and Bendigo and in 1869 (some sources say 1870), a fair and procession were established as an Easter celebration and to raise funds for charity. The Chinese joined the parade a couple of years later and within ten years had become the major feature of the Bendigo Easter Fair, as it became known. Australia had seen nothing like it before. Traditional costumes, flags and decorations of all kinds were imported from China in large quantities and displayed during the parade. In 1892 the longest dragon in the world arrived, a fearsome five-clawed beast known as *loong*, the Chinese word for 'dragon'. *Loong* has continued to be the major feature of the fair, along with other Chinese customs, some of which no longer exist in China.

As well as the Chinese contribution, the early fairs were extravaganzas of wild animal shows, theatrical performances, magicians, singing, art displays, dancing booths, fairground rides and a sideshow alley, as well as the inevitable hucksters. Police had to remove a three-card-trick shyster at the 1874 fair. That year there were 20,000 paid admissions, with plenty to drink and plenty of legal gambling in the form of lotteries. The opening ceremony and grand procession were gala events, with orchestras, a Chinese band, representatives of various friendly societies and masonic lodges, a wild man, and 'lady' cricketers 'in their gay blue and pink uniforms, in three vehicles, forming a galaxy of beauty that attracted all eyes'. Following the fire brigade there was a presumably spoof 'His Celestial Majesty Jam Je Bu-ic-ker':

> . . . preceded by six retainers, all in gorgeous attire. His Majesty was dressed in loose trousers and Chinese jumper of rich blue satin magnificently worked with flowers and dragons in different colors. Around his neck was a yellow silk scarf beautifully worked with flowers, a black cap with rosette of peacocks' feathers adding to the effect. He carried an umbrella of novel pattern, there being one large oval of yellow silk, fringed with blue, while on the top of that was a small parasol of red silk fringed with yellow. The dress was a gorgeous one. A fine tail 4 feet long, completed the outfit. The dresses of his retainers were of richly flowered chintz robe with blue trousers, with black stripes, while on their backs and breasts were rosettes of peacocks' feathers.

At night, even more people seemed to crowd the scene. The grounds were lit up with multi-coloured Chinese lanterns strung between the trees, 'giving a most fairy-like and enchanting appearance to the scene'. The night finished with a fireworks display watched and applauded by thousands and, 'It was not until a late hour that the grounds were cleared.'

Sun Loong first appeared at the 1892 procession and was an immediate hit:

The Chinese made a magnificent display nearly a thousand of them marching, and their brilliant raiment, queer musical instruments, and quaint battle weapons created much interest. A novel feature of the procession was a huge dragon. This was 200ft long supported by 80 Chinamen, and consisted of [a] wire framework, covered with gorgeous silk. The dragon was made to sway about, whilst its rolling eyes, lolling tongue, and generally ferocious appearance were sources of great wonderment and consternation to the children. The dragon was preceded by copious discharges of fireworks and revolving balls, which were symbolical of stars that the dragon was seeking to devour.

Today, the celebration remains a major local, state and national event known as the Bendigo Easter Festival. Still organised by the descendants of the original Bendigo Easter Fair Society, it is the oldest continually running festival of its kind in the country.

15

A fair go

Do you call this a fair go?

Shearers' strike leaders being arrested by police, 1891

ONE OF AUSTRALIA's most powerful beliefs is the idea expressed in the phrase 'a fair go'. Convicts, swagmen and workers of all kinds, as well as Indigenous people, have felt compelled to express their discontent and ask for a fair go in stories that go to the heart of the Australian sense of national identity.

In 2006, a survey showed that 91 per cent of Australians put 'a fair go' at the top of their list of values. This is nothing new, of course. The idea that it is important for everyone in the country to have equal opportunity goes back to the earliest years of modern Australia, closely associated with the enforced levelling of convict society, with pioneering and with the creed of mateship.

Black Mary

Armed with a musket and a brace of pistols, she became known to history and legend as 'Black Mary'. But the name she went by in colonial Tasmania was Mary Cockerell. Like many Indigenous Tasmanian women of the time, Mary worked as a servant for a settler family named Cockerell, taking that name as her own. She became the lover of Michael Howe, joined his bushranging gang and became an effective accomplice until the gang was attacked by soldiers. During this attack, Howe allegedly wounded the heavily pregnant Mary in order to facilitate his own escape. An early Tasmanian settler recalled the events many years later when the layers of folklore had settled over the facts:

*H*owe and the girl, Mary, were traced and pursued near Jericho by a party of soldiers, and being hard pressed, Howe, to facilitate his own escape, fired at the poor black girl, who was wounded and captured. Her injuries proved but slight, and the treatment received from Howe led to her turning against her former associates, and she subsequently became of great assistance to the military as a female 'black tracker'.

Howe wrote to the Governor offering to give himself up and furnish important information about his former associates and their haunts, and the offer was accepted, Howe arriving in Hobart on 29th April, 1817. He underwent various examinations, but little information was obtained from him, and at length, on the plea that confinement was impairing his health, Howe was allowed to go about with a constable, an indulgence he repaid by escaping in July.

Watts, who had once been a companion of Howe, now determined to save his own neck by capturing Howe, and communicated with the authorities. With the assistance of Black Mary and a stockkeeper named Drewe, Howe was run down and taken while asleep. They bound him, and were marching him to Hobart, Watts being in front with a loaded gun, and Drewe, who was unarmed, following Howe, when Howe disengaged his hands, and drawing a concealed knife, with a sudden spring stabbed Watts in the back. As Watts fell Howe seized his gun and shot Drewe dead. Black Mary escaped into the bush, while Howe was swearing he would shoot Watts as soon as he loaded his gun. Watts managed to crawl into the bush, when Mary returned with assistance, and Howe made his escape. Watts was removed to Hobart, but died three days after his arrival.

Howe was not heard of for some time, but necessity compelled him to commit robberies on distant stockkeepers. After his daring exploit none dare venture it [sic] personal attack upon him, but Black Mary was continually on his heels, guiding the military.

↝

Howe had been transported for highway robbery in 1811, escaped two years later and quickly became a scourge of the settlers, attacking their properties, stealing their stock and mistreating many of those he took captive. It was also rumoured that many were in mutually beneficial relationships with the outlaw in order to protect their lives and property.

After his own lucky escape from the wrath of Black Mary, Howe disappeared for some time. He began styling himself 'lieutenant governor of the woods' in dark contrast to the official lieutenant governor of the colony. During this period he had a substantial 100-guinea reward placed on his head, later doubled, with any convict who caught him guaranteed a pardon and free passage home.

Howe was tracked by an Aboriginal convict from New South Wales known as Musquito, who had been captured in 1805 and took up the hunt to gain a passage back to his country. Then, towards the end of 1818:

A soldier named Pugh, of the 48th Regiment, and a stockkeeper named Worrall determined to capture Howe. They entered into a league with a kangaroo hunter named Warburton, who agreed to join them. Howe had to meet Warburton, who had agreed to let him have some ammunition if he would come to his (Warburton's) hut. Howe, after great hesitation, ventured into the hut, where Pugh and Worrall were concealed. As soon as Howe entered he cocked his gun, and Pugh fired at him, but missed. Howe retreated a few paces and then returned the fire, but also missed, and Worrall fired, but with no better effect. Howe then retired, loading his gun as he retreated backwards, and was followed by the other men. Howe fired at Warburton and fatally wounded him, and was then rushed by the two others, a desperate encounter taking place. Howe fought long and died hard, dangerously wounding Pugh, but was overpowered, his head being battered to pieces. They then cut off Howe's head, which was taken to Hobart, the body being buried near the scene . . .

On their way back to Hobart, the bounty hunters met the prominent settler Dr Ross and his travelling companions, who asked them what they had in the bloodstained blue bag they carried. The men 'good-naturedly opening the bag, showed them a human head'. Then:

*T*aking it by the hair, he held it up to our view, with the greatest exultation imaginable, and for a moment we thought we had indeed got amongst murderers, pondering between resistance and the chance of succour or escape, when we were agreeably relieved by the information that the bleeding head had belonged two days ago to the body of the notorious bushranger, Michael Howe, for whom, dead or alive, very large rewards had been offered. He had been caught at a remote solitary hut on the banks of the River Shannon, and in his attempt to break away from the soldiers who apprehended him, had been shot through the back, so that the painful disseverment of the head and trunk, the result of which we now witnessed, had been only a postmortem operation.

Howe's severed head was then displayed in Hobart town as proof of the rule of law. It was a popular display with the colonists.

While these events were playing out, Mary had been sent to Sydney to prevent her returning to Howe's side. Now that he was dead, she was allowed back to Hobart. While Worrall and Pugh were rewarded for the death of Howe, Mary's only reward for her service to the Crown was free victuals from the government stores. Nor did they have to hand these out for long. She died, probably of tuberculosis, the following winter. Musquito received no reward at all and went on to become a threat to colonial order in his own right, partly as a result of the failure of the government to honour the promise of repatriation. He was captured, tried and hanged on dubious legal grounds in 1825.

The Tambaroora line

When the goldfields towns of Hill End, Sofala and Tambaroora started growing from the early 1850s, they needed transport links with Bathurst and beyond. In those days it was only a coach and horse to transport people and goods from place to place, and there were carriers of all kinds, none more colourful than Bill Maloney.

Small operators like Maloney were threatened when Cobb & Co. began in the 1860s. Not only could the new competition boast better and faster coaches, but they were organised along corporate lines that gave them an extra edge. According to legend, Bill Maloney took this in his stride. The only way to hold his own against the rivals was to drive faster and along shorter but more dangerous routes. Bill was skilled at this, but whenever he did encounter or pass a Cobb & Co. coach on the road, he bawled out a special ditty he had composed to the tune of a popular bush song:

> Now look here, Cobb & Co.,
> A lesson take from me,
> If you meet me on the road
> Don't you make too free,
> For if you do you'll surely rue . . .
> You think you do it fine,

But I'm a tip-and-slasher
Of the Tambaroora line.

Then into the boastful chorus:

I can hold them, steer them
And drive them to and fro,
With ribbons well in hand, me boys,
I can make 'em go.
With me foot well on the brake, lads,
I'm bound to make them shine,
For I'm a tip-and-slasher
Of the Tambaroora line.

This went on for years. Cobb & Co. tried to buy Hill out but he would not budge. Although Cobb & Co. could offer a better service, most of Bill's customers admired his spirit and travelled with him whenever they could. And eventually, Bill won. Cobb & Co. decided to suspend its Bathurst operation. Shortly before closing down, the managing director of Cobb & Co., James Rutherford (see Chapter 11), invited his tenacious local rival to the factory where the company built its cutting-edge coaches. They walked through the works until they came to an especially well-built and -equipped coach painted out in the same colours that Bill used for his own coaches.

'What do you think of this one, then, Bill?' asked Rutherford.

Despite himself, Bill was impressed and said so, wishing that he could afford such a fine piece of equipment. Rutherford then handed Bill the reins and said he was gifting it to him for being such a worthy competitor.

Maloney received this magnanimous gift with gratitude and used it for many successful years on the Tambaroora line, later succeeded by his son.

Mates

Australia's tradition of mateship can be traced from the rough necessity of convict survival, through the tribulations of pioneering, the excitement of the gold rushes and the formation of trade unions from the 1890s, and finding its most evocative location on the ridges of Gallipoli and the trenches of the Western Front during World War I. Along the way, a number of outstanding examples of men's loyalty to each other include Ned Kelly returning to the fight at Glenrowan to help his mates and the story of Simpson and his donkey, among many others. C.E.W. Bean, a major influence on the Anzac legend, wrote that the typical Australian was rarely religious and:

> So far as he held a prevailing creed, it was a romantic one inherited from the gold-miner and the bushman, of which the chief article was that a man should at all times and at any cost stand by his mate. That was and is the one law, which the good Australian must never break. It is bred in the child and stays with him through life . . .

At the shining end of this spectrum, mateship is an admirable quality. At its darker extremes it can exhibit shades of misogyny. This is why the topic has always been controversial. Even mateship's greatest singer recognised its realities: many of Henry Lawson's stories and poems celebrate mateship, if with a jaundiced eye. In one titled *A Sketch of Mateship*, Lawson tells it like it probably was:

*B*ill and Jim, professional shearers, were coming into Bourke from the Queensland side. They were horsemen and had two packhorses. At the last camp before Bourke Jim's packhorse got disgusted and home-sick during the night and started back for the place where he was foaled. Jim was little more than a new-chum jackeroo; he was no bushman and generally got lost when he went down the next gully. Bill was a bushman, so it was decided that he should go back to look for the horse.

Now Bill was going to sell his packhorse, a well-bred mare, in Bourke, and he was anxious to get her into the yards before the horse sales were over; this was to be the last day of the sales. Jim was the best 'barracker' of the two; he had great imagination; he was a very entertaining story-teller and conversationalist in social life, and a glib and a most impressive liar in business, so it was decided that he should hurry on into Bourke with the mare and sell her for Bill. Seven pounds, reserve.

Next day Bill turned up with the missing horse and saw Jim standing against a veranda-post of the Carriers' Arms, with his hat down over his eyes, and thoughtfully spitting in the dust. Bill rode over to him.

'Ullo, Jim.'

'Ullo, Bill. I see you got him.'

'Yes, I got him.' Pause.

'Where'd yer find him?'

"Bout ten mile back. Near Ford's Bridge. He was just feedin' along.'

Pause. Jim shifted his feet and spat in the dust.

'Well,' said Bill at last. 'How did you get on, Jim?'

'Oh, all right,' said Jim. 'I sold the mare.'

'That's right,' said Bill. 'How much did she fetch?'

'Eight quid;' then, rousing himself a little and showing some emotion, 'An' I could 'a' got ten quid for her if I hadn't been a dam' fool.'

'Oh, that's good enough,' said Bill.

'I could 'a' got ten quid if I'd 'a' waited.'

'Well, it's no use cryin'. Eight quid is good enough. Did you get the stuff?'

'Oh, yes. They parted all right. If I hadn't been such a dam' fool an' rushed it, there was a feller that would 'a' given ten quid for that mare.'

'Well, don't break yer back about it,' said Bill. 'Eight is good enough.'

'Yes. But I could 'a' got ten,' said Jim, languidly, putting his hand in his pocket.

Pause. Bill sat waiting for him to hand over the money; but Jim withdrew his hand empty, stretched, and said: 'Ah, well, Bill, I done it in. Lend us a couple o' notes.'

Jim had been drinking and gambling all night and he'd lost the eight pounds as well as his own money.

Bill didn't explode. What was the use? He should have known that Jim wasn't to be trusted with money in town. It was he who had been the fool. He sighed and lent Jim a pound, and they went in to have a drink.

Now it strikes me that if this had happened in a civilized country (like England) Bill would have had Jim arrested and jailed for larceny as a bailee, or embezzlement, or whatever it was. And would Bill or Jim or the world have been any better for it?

Henry Lawson was realistic enough to recognise that mateship was often something that grew in the glow of a drink or three, once stating: 'The greatest pleasure I have ever known is when my eyes meet the eyes of a mate over the top of two foaming glasses of beer.'

Mateship is most frequently linked with another Australian characteristic, usually known as anti-authoritarianism, though more flowingly expressed in the phrase 'Jack's as good as his master', sometimes followed with 'if not better'. Again, the origins of this attitude can be traced to the convict era, through the relationships between bosses and workers in the bush, in factories, on building sites and wharves, as well as a dislike of uniformed authority in particular and regulation in general. Most famously we find it in the reluctance of Australian volunteer soldiers in World War I and after to salute their officers, the subject of endless digger yarns. Again like mateship, this idea is sometimes considered to be a myth.

A glorious spree

Australia's long love affair with the grog begins with the 'Rum Corps' in colonial New South Wales and extends to the present. Along the way have been told many beery tales of mammoth sprees and monumental hangovers. The balladry of the bush overflows with references to alcohol, much of it 'sly' or illegal. The 'hocussed' or adulterated shanty grog took down many a shearer's cheque. A famous example occurs in the traditional song 'On the Road to Gundagai', where a bloke named Bill and his mate make the mistake of camping at Lazy Harry's sly grog tent on their way to Sydney with the season's shearing wages.

> In a week the spree was over and our cheque was all knocked down
> So we shouldered our Matildas and we turned our backs on town.
> And the girls they stood a nobbler as we sadly said goodbye,
> And we tramped from Lazy Harry's on the road to Gundagai.

In vain did the forces of law and order try to police and control the sly grog trade. Colonists mostly insisted on their right to a drink and the grog quickly became an element of the 'fair go' ethos, as events at Pakenham demonstrated in 1879:

*A*n interesting raid was made by the revenue officers of the Shire of Berwick, on Wednesday last, on a number of unlicensed shanty-keepers, who for some time past have been carrying on an illicit traffic in liquor in the neighbourhood of a large quarry near the Gippsland railway, about seven miles from Berwick, from which metal has been obtained for the Oakleigh end of the line. At this place a large camp of quarry men and stonebreakers has been formed consisting of about 100 tents and shanties of all kinds and descriptions, and as there are no public houses in the locality sly grog-selling is carried on to a great extent.

It came to the knowledge of the Revenue officers a few days ago that a large quantity of spirituous liquor had been sent up to the camp and having determined to take some action to put a stop to this illicit traffic, the revenue inspector, Mr. Robinson, visited the place on Wednesday last, accompanied by the inspector of licensed premises, Mr A. Cartledge, and three mounted constables, and made a sudden descent on the camp before the casks and cases containing the liquor could be removed or secreted by their owners. At the first place which was visited, that of Mr. R. Stout's, about a dray load of stock was seized and placed in a dray which had been provided for the occasion.

In the meantime a large number of the navvies had assembled, and seeing the state of affairs commenced looting the shanties and grogshops in spite of the efforts of the police, who endeavoured to roll back the casks into the tents as the mob took them out, but of course were outnumbered, and the result was that casks of bottled beer and cases of brandy, whisky, &c. were smashed open and rifled. By this time the mob had increased to about 100 persons, and an assault was made on the police by a party armed with pickhandles, sticks and other weapons, and the police were rather severely handled—so much so that they had to produce their revolvers, and the revenue officer's party took advantage of the tranquilising effect which this manoeuvre produced to retire from the camp.

The scene that ensued baffles description; yelling and screaming the mob either stoved in the ends of the casks and opened the cases and removed their contents for immediate consumption, or took them away into the bush for a future occasion. It is estimated that about £30 of spirituous liquor was taken or destroyed by the mob, including the dray load, which the inspector had seized.

Not surprisingly, the police were planning to summon the known rioters to court.

The Greenhide Push waltzes Matilda

Our unofficial national anthem had humble origins as a ditty knocked up by 'Banjo' Paterson and Christina Macpherson at Dagwood Station near Winton in 1895. In those days, people entertained themselves and the opportunity to sing a new song around the piano was highly appreciated, especially when it was such a rousing lyric and tune as that of 'Waltzing Matilda'. Almost as soon as the song was composed it flew off into oral tradition around northeast Queensland. It was sung with gusto in that part of the country long before it was the popular piece it has since become.

Just how popular the song was—in at least one of its different versions—is conveyed in an account of events at Hughenden race time in April 1902. All the young bloods in town organised a procession along the main street. They called themselves 'the Greenhide Push' and they were armed with the then-new hit, assisted by the local newspaper, which had thoughtfully printed up the lyrics on flyers and had them posted around town. Old Queensland hand Fred Archer was there and recalled the scene over forty years later:

*T*hey got the Salvation Army's big drum, some cornets and tambourines and the black boys' gum leaves. The streets were crowded with people. The drum boomed, wild notes came from the cornets, tambourines clashed—all in the theme song, 'Waltzing Matilda'.

The crowds on the footpath took it up, horses started to buck and throw their riders, the black boys thumbed their mounts and beat them with their wide-brimmed hats. They yelled and so did everyone else. The drummer was down but couldn't care less, he still continued whacking the drum—boom-boom. Bucking horses were everywhere. Finally, the procession reached the Great Western-Hughenden Hotels and such horses as were under control were tied to hitching posts.

Tall, lean men in white Canton riding trousers, red shirts, riding boots and long-necked spurs were among the crowds that milled through the hotels, thumped the pianos, roared 'Waltzing Matilda' from beginning to end, over and over again, in parlour, bar and verandah, while excited horsemen rode into the middle of the singers and took up the chorus . . .

And so the party went on for hours. The following day the makeshift band was placed on a wagon and dragged around the town to play the song wherever they stopped. In the evening mounted men galloped through town firing guns in time with the music: 'This they kept up till they reached the police station, yelled out for troopers 1, 2, 3, then laid whips to their horses and bolted . . .' Not surprisingly, the local police were unimpressed with this larrikinism. Such roistering scenes are difficult to imagine today, especially with the inspiration being a song. It was an age when the sung and spoken word was still a powerful form of conviviality and communication, assisted in this case by high spirits, grog and the irresistible urge of the Greenhide Push to call out the police using the anti-authoritarian lines of the song.

The Bunuba resistance

On the morning of April Fool's Day 1897, the outlaw Jandamarra was shot dead outside his cave hideout at Tunnel Creek. The man who shot this feared scourge of the settlers was another Aborigine known as 'Micki', a police tracker. Jandamarra had led the remnants of his people in a prolonged resistance through the rugged region of Western Australia's northwest.

Australia's vast and mostly arid northwest had been largely ignored until the 1880s, when its almost infinite acres attracted sheep and cattle farming and its seas an embryonic pearling industry. As settlement increased, the newcomers increasingly encroached on the traditional lands of the many Indigenous groups in what would become known as the Kimberley region. Some of these groups resisted; others seemed to fade away as the frontier pushed relentlessly north and east. The Bunuba were not inclined to simply walk off their land and nurtured an ongoing resistance that eventually produced their hero.

Jandamarra was already approaching initiation age when his country became the object of commercial and political interest. At around eleven years of age he was taken into employment on a local station to be trained as a stockman. Jandamarra appeared to be the ideal type for such conversions, quickly excelling at the necessary skills and eventually also becoming a crack rifle shot. Although he was unusually short for a Bunuba man—they were typically six foot or more—he had great speed and agility, leading to the settlers nicknaming him 'Pigeon'. Working and living in the company of the settlers caused Jandamarra to grow up without being initiated into the spiritual secrets that would rightly have belonged to a Bunuba man, so although Jandamarra would come to know his country, its gullies, hills, trails and caves intimately, he was never fully a man in Bunuba society.

None of these matters worried Jandamarra, it seems. He was content to work for the settlers and even to become a blacktracker or adjunct member of the police force and take part in tracking down other Aboriginal men and women wanted by the law.

Meanwhile, resistance to settlement continued. Stock was speared, supplies stolen and whites attacked by one or usually small groups of Aborigines. The settlers reacted with violence based on fear as much as racism, and attack led to counterattack as Aborigines sought to stem the unstoppable advances of the settlers and the settlers sought to 'disperse' the Aborigines so their stock could graze the grassland and drink from the waterholes.

A noted Bunuba warrior of the time was a man named Ellemarra. Through the late 1880s he offered fierce and ongoing resistance to the settlers, often being arrested but usually escaping again. So dangerous did Ellemarra become that the settlers called for 'the whole tribe of natives inhabiting the Napier Range to be outlawed'. Ellemarra was among the most wanted of the resisters and Jandamarra, caught between the worlds of white and black, formed part of a police party sent out to bring him in, effectively going against his own people. Ellemarra was flogged and imprisoned. He eventually escaped again but was recaptured and chained with a group of other Aboriginal prisoners. But again, possibly with the help of Jandamarra, Ellemarra managed to break his chains and escape.

Now Jandamarra had to again take part in tracking down Ellemarra, under the command of a policeman named Richardson. Jandamarra led the policeman to his countrymen and they were captured in late October 1894, the largest haul of resisters the police had yet netted. Richardson delayed returning with them in order to gain a greater allowance for being on active duty. It was a fatal mistake. The Bunuba men naturally placed pressure on Jandamarra to let them go and acknowledge his true Bunuba identity. Eventually Jandamarra accepted their argument, released Ellemarra and shot Richardson dead while he slept. The two men then released their comrades, took the guns and ammunition and disappeared into the bush. They soon raised a large group of Bunuba and engaged in a large-scale battle with police sent to track them down for the murders of a number of settlers in November. Ellemarra and a number of Bunuba women were killed in the shooting and Jandamarra seriously wounded. He managed to escape, evading the pursuit through his unparalleled knowledge of the country. An undeclared war was in progress, which would make Jandamarra a great hero to his people and their struggle.

While Jandamarra was in hiding, recovering from his wounds, the government sent police reinforcements to the Kimberley as quickly as was possible at the time.

The police had almost convinced themselves that the Bunuba resistance was broken when rumours of Jandamarra's survival were confirmed in May 1895. Jandamarra and the Bunuba now conducted a guerrilla war; police continually came across the outlaws' tracks, only to lose them in the rocks and ravines.

The Bunuba people also employed the characteristic tactic of using outlaw sympathisers. Misleading the police with false information was effective and had the advantage of making the police look like fools, further demoralising them in their futile hunt for Jandamarra and his now small, mobile band.

In October 1895, Jandamarra became over-confident and failed to post a guard around his camp, and the police surprised him and his band. Employing his legendary agility, Jandamarra disappeared into a convenient cave, but most of his band was captured.

Over the following months Jandamarra concentrated on harassing and demoralising police and settlers by demonstrating his mastery of the country and of stealth. He robbed storehouses, visited police camps at night and shadowed police patrols, always ensuring they knew he had been among them. Jandamarra, the uninitiated man, now came to be seen by his own people as a lawman, an individual with great spiritual authority and great magical powers. He was said to be able to turn himself into a bird and fly away from the police. He was also said to be invulnerable because his real spirit was hidden at his hideout, and it was only his animated body that crossed his country to taunt the police and the settlers.

This went on for many months, including the besieging of the police outpost at Lillimooroola station, immediately below the limestone cliffs that marked the easily defended edge of Bunuba country. Towards the end of 1896 the settlers began forcing their cattle deep into Bunuba land, effectively going behind Jandamarra's front line. The Bunuba resistance went back into action with psychological warfare and attacks on settlers. The police cranked up their attempts to end the conflict, committing more atrocities against the Bunuba, but had no more success than in their previous attempts.

But within the police ranks was a secret weapon. An Aboriginal member of the force named Micki was from far outside Bunuba country and had no loyalty towards Jandamarra's fight. The Aborigines also considered him to have magical powers. On 23 March 1897, Micki was solely responsible for capturing five of Jandamarra's band. Jandamarra attempted to free his comrades but was badly wounded. He was pursued through the ranges as he struggled towards his hideout cave at Tunnel Creek, 30 miles east. He made it back inside the cave through one of its many secret entrances, but Micki was waiting for him outside the cave's main entrance. The two lawmen faced each other with Winchester rifles. Jandamarra missed and Micki's shot sent him hurtling down a 100-foot cliff. The police reached the scene, confirmed the body was that of their feared foe and then chopped the head from the torso with a tomahawk. It was reportedly despatched to adorn the trophy wall of a British arms manufacturer.

The Bunuba resistance was finally broken with Jandamarra's death, but his legend lived on, becoming a powerful oral tradition in the Kimberley. It has also been the subject of several books and is being turned into a feature film.

The bagman's gazette

The 'bagman's gazette' was a term for the efficient word-of-mouth network on the track. News, rumour and gossip were carried along this unofficial route with amazing speed. Under the title 'Bagman's Gazette', 'The Organiser' began his column for the *Darwin Northern Standard* in the Depression year of 1931 with a quotation from Lewis Carroll's famous nonsense poem 'The Walrus and The Carpenter'. The article was about wages and politics, suggesting that not much had changed since the strikes of forty years before:

'The time has come,' the Walrus said,
'To talk of many things;
Of shoes—and ships—and sealing wax—
Of cabbages—and kings—'

*B*agmen discussing politics at a recent session around the Camp fire touched on the so-called necessity for equal sacrifice taking it for granted that all sections would be required by this to dub up in proportion so as to save the country from financial chaos. After disposing of the theory that lower wages would increase employment and quoting their experiences in search of employment in the pastoral industry in Queensland, where wages are as low as 15/- a week, one bagman quoted the proposed British Budget as a sample of equal sacrifice. It is proposed to save Britain by reducing the unemployment dole by £66,500,000 and education grants, and teachers' salaries by £13,000,000. This makes a total of £79,500,000 out of £96,500,000 it is proposed to save. The workers even contribute a big part of the remaining £17,000,000.

Now if this equal sacrifice were a real thing and if those who have no income can contribute £66,500,000 to the national income, how much can those who do not work, never have worked, never will work, and have huge incomes, contribute in this 'equal sacrifice' humbug? Then again in Australia if a worker on five quid a week can sacrifice 20 per cent of that for the national good, a judge or a politician or a bondholder should be able to sacrifice all the income he or she gets above five quid. They would then still be 20 per cent above the poor plugger that works for his bit and it is more questionable whether they are worth 20 per cent more.

The bagmen were unanimous that the only patriot expected (in war time or peace) to sacrifice everything for his Country is the toiler and they furthermore thought that it is time the Workers of Australia put up a fight against this 'equal sacrifice' humbug and wage reduction campaign of the super patriots, but they are only bagmen.

Homes of hope

As the Great Depression rolled over the lives and hopes of millions, an Anglican minister came up with a plan to house some of the families evicted from their homes, often with no means of financial support. Robert Hammond was archdeacon at St Barnabas' Anglican church in Sydney's Broadway. Wondering what he could do to alleviate the suffering he saw all around, he invited married men to a meeting in February 1932. His idea was what he called a 'consolidated settlement', a residential development on new land where the families of unemployed would help themselves and each other to build, rent and eventually purchase their own homes. Each would use their skills to help others and after around seven years would have paid sufficient rent to own their houses outright.

To qualify for the scheme a married couple needed to be unemployed, have at least three children and possess a skill useful to the community. They had to show that they had been recently evicted and make a commitment to joining the community in growing its own food. Rents were very reasonable and did not need to be paid by those who continued to be unemployed.

The 'Pioneer Homes' scheme, as it was originally known, received 800 applications and began with 13 acres near Liverpool. Although the initiative received little official support, donations from the public enabled it to expand and by the end of the next year 26 homes were completed. Another 40 homes were built the following year, and another 150 acres were purchased with a generous individual donation. By 1937, 110 homes were housing families. Hammondville, as it came to be called after its visionary founder, had a church, post office, general store and school by 1940. A senior citizens' facility was developed in later years and Hammondville continued to thrive.

The community grew further during the war, and many of the men served in the armed forces. By the end of the war in 1945, most families had already paid off their properties and now owned them along with the acre of land on which they stood.

Hammondville tradition is full of stories about individuals who made great contributions to a unique community. They include Constance Jewell and her 'Depression recipe' cakes, so popular at dances and fundraisers. Shopkeeper Alf Morley was known as the 'Mayor of Hammondville' because of his popularity. Alf opened the town's first shop with a 100-pound loan from the founder and provided generous terms of payment as well as free ice-creams for the kids.

Other notable people from the community include property developer Jim Masterson and politician John Hatton. Reverend Bernard Judd and his wife, Ida, had a long connection with Hammondville and were prime movers in establishing various local institutions, including the Girl Guides and the Senior Citizens' Home.

Robert Hammond's vision and energy were recognised in 1937 when he was awarded an OBE. He died in 1946, almost 76 years of age.

16

How we travel the land

With a ragged old swag on their shoulder,
And a billy quart-pot in their hands,
I tell you they'll 'stonish the new chums,
When they see how we travel the land.

'The Springtime it Brings on the Shearing'

MOVEMENT ACROSS THE vast distances of the continent is one of
the deepest and most persistent themes of Australian tradition.
Aboriginal creation myths speak of ancestral beings travelling
far across the country to make the rivers, mountains and plains.
Aboriginal peoples moved constantly around their countries,
following the seasons and acknowledging the sacred sites that
lay along their 'songlines', preserving this ancient knowledge in
a rich culture of song, dance, art and story.

When Europeans arrived, they explored and opened up new
lands for agriculture and the pastoral industries that largely made
the nation in the nineteenth century. The lore of the bush is full
of overlanders, bullockies and swagmen who rode or walked across
the country. Even that enigmatic figure, the bushranger, 'ranges'
the country in search of sustenance and plunder, trying to keep
a few steps ahead of the mounted troopers close behind, often
assisted by deadly efficient blacktrackers.

When horses began to give way to motor vehicles, it was still a common sight to see swagmen 'humping their bluey' along isolated bush tracks. Many had to take up this itinerant way of life during the Depression of the 1930s. Sometimes the railways might assist them, if they were clever enough to 'hook a rattler' and get off it again without being caught by the police. Spending a night or two in the cells for vagrancy—sometimes after a beating—was a topic sung about in the country ballads of that era.

Today, the familiar sight of 'grey nomads' on a campervan or caravan pilgrimage around the country is perhaps an updated expression of this ancient Australian need to travel the land.

Rangers and rouseabouts

The ballads of the bush began to describe and celebrate the roaming necessities from early times. The famous chorus of 'The Wild Colonial Boy' is all about movement and freedom:

> So come along my hearties, we'll roam the mountains high,
> Together we will plunder, together we will die.
> We'll gallop across the mountains and scour across the plains
> And scorn to live in slavery, bound down in iron chains.

The development of sheep and cattle production created new groups of travellers. This time they were either working or in search of work, rather than plunder. The 'overlanders' were a flamboyant group of men who carried out some legendary feats of droving across usually harsh terrain, celebrated in many ballads and in the popular literature of the time.

> There's a trade you all know well, it's bringing cattle over
> On every track to the Gulf and back, men know the Queensland
>   drover.

So, pass the billy 'round, boys, don't let the pint-pot stand there
For tonight we'll drink the health of every overlander.

And so it went on, bragging about the deeds of the Queensland drovers. Another ballad on the same themes, 'Brisbane Ladies', told of their exploits.

We'll rant and we'll roar, like true Queensland drovers,
We'll rant and we'll roar as onward we push
Until we return to the Augathella station,
For it's bloody dry going in the old Queensland bush.

The wool industry produced another swag of now-iconic songs about shearers and rouseabouts, all spreading out across the land to clip the fleeces that, for a long time, provided the backbone of the Australian economy. One of many was 'The Springtime it Brings on the Shearing':

Oh, the springtime it brings on the shearing,
And then you will see them in droves,
To the west country stations all steering,
Seeking a job off the coves.

With a ragged old swag on their shoulder,
And a billy quart-pot in their hands,
I tell you they'll 'stonish the new chums,
When they see how we travel the land.

The 'coves' mentioned in 'The Springtime it Brings on the Shearing' were the bosses, the owners or managers of the sheep stations. There was strong tension between the shearers and their employers, a troubled relationship that was an important element in the formation of the trade union movement in the late nineteenth century. The tension was reflected in 'Banjo' Paterson's poem 'A Bushman's Song'. The continual movement of the song's main character to 'the stations further out' captures the necessity for, but also the freedom to be had from, the travelling life.

'A Bushman's Song', usually known in its bush ballad form as 'Travelling Down the Castlereagh' or 'The Old Jig-Jog', hymns the freedom of the wandering life and tells the story of a station hand travelling down the Castlereagh River 'handy with a roping pole and handy with a brand'. He is always moving further away from the settled regions further out:

So it was shift, boys, shift, there wasn't the slightest doubt
I had to make a shift for the stations further out
Saddle up my horses and whistle up my dog
And it's off across the country at the old jig-jog.

He gets a job with his brother on the Illawarra but finds that he has to 'ask the landlord's leave before he lifts his arm', which doesn't suit him at all. He then takes a job at shearing 'along the Marthaguy' but finds they shear non-union—'I call it scab, says I'. Finally, the station hand decides to go 'where they drink artesian water from a thousand foot below'. Here he meets the overlanders and their mobs, where they 'work a while and make a pile, then have a spree in town'.

'A Bushman's Song' captures the independence and dream of freedom that pioneering life promised for many men at that time. The hero of the song is fortunate enough to travel the land on horseback; many others went on foot, often called 'swagmen'.

The swagman's union

Folklore has it that there was such a thing as a 'swagman's union', and according to this account there was such an organisation.

Formed in the 1870s, this association had some interesting rules by which its members were allegedly regulated.

*T*he old-time swagman is fast disappearing, but to-day my thoughts go back to some of the real old-time 'whalers' of the Murrumbidgee and other Southern watercourses (writes 'Bill Bowyang'). The genuine 'whaler' in the halcyon days of yore was a feature of the Murrumbidgee tracks and along the routes fringing some of the Western Queensland rivers.

Those who carried the swag on the Lachlan were known as the 'Lachlan Cruisers' but there were also the 'Darling Whisperers', the 'Murray Sundowners' and the 'Bogan Bummers'. Each member cherished an unbounding pride in his clan, and there were at times fierce fights under the big river gums when some favored fishing hole was usurped by an interloper from an alien band.

Scanning an old scrap book recently I came across an interesting record of an occurrence that at the time created a great stir in swag-men circles throughout the West. It tells of a meeting that was held to bring about a combination of the scattered units of swaggydom in a society known as the 'Amalgamated Swagmen of Australia'. This first union was formed in a bend of the Lachlan, near Forbes, in 1877, and a conference of delegates from far and wide gathered for the occasion. They were a motley crew, frowsy dead beats, loony-hatters, and aggressive cadgers.

By the fitful flames of yarran and myall fires, officers were elected, branches formed, and rules drawn up. Sir William Wallaby was the first President, and Sir John Bluey, secretary; T. Billy Esq., is named as treasurer, and Dr. Johnny Cake medical adviser. The well-known firm of Walker and Tucker were solicitors. The rules were as follows:

1. No member to be over 100 years old.
2. Each member to pay one pannikin of flour entrance fee. Members who don't care about paying will be admitted free.

3. No member to carry swags weighing over ten pounds.

4. Each member to possess three complete sets of tucker bags, each set to consist of nine bags.

5. No member to pass any station, farm, boundary rider's hut, camp, or private house without 'tapping' and obtaining rations or hand-outs.

6. Each member to allow himself to be bitten by a sheep. If a sheep bites a member he must immediately turn it into mutton.

7. Members who defame a 'good' cook, or pay a fine when run in, shall not be allowed to enter the Kingdom of Heaven. Amen.

8. No members allowed to hum baking powder, tea, flour, sugar, or tobacco from a fellow unionist.

9. Non-smoking members must 'whisper' for tobacco on every possible occasion, the same as smokers.

10. At general or branch meetings non-smoking hums must give up their whispered tobacco to be distributed amongst the officers of the society.

11. Any member found without at least two sets of bags filled with tucker will be fined.

12. No member to own more than one creek, river, or billabong bend. To sell bends for old boots or sinkers is prohibited.

13. No member to look for or accept work of any description. Members found willing will be at once expelled.

14. No member to walk more than five miles per day if rations can be hummed.

15. No member to tramp on Sundays at any price.

This union is many years defunct and its original members as widely scattered as the ashes of their long-dimmed camp-fires, yet the spirit and the rules are adhered to sacredly, even in these days, by those who hump the swag. Par chance these rules extend to Paradise, and the sturdy beggars still tramp through eternity with Matilda up.

Amongst the old time 'whalers' Scotty the Wrinkler was perhaps the most famous. A garrulous Scotch man of scholarly attainments, he had, perhaps, less need to cadge than any other. Scotty I always recognised as somewhat of a poseur. His habits were so settled that he dwelt most of the year in a huge hollow log on the banks of the Murrumbidgee, near Narrandera, and he even acquired his name from the original holder, who was a Darling River Whisperer.

The oozlum bird

The oozlum bird is an Australian version of a mythical creature also found in British and American traditions. 'Ouzel' is a name given to a variety of bird species in the British Isles, most commonly, it seems, the blackbird. In Ireland the water ouzel is associated with the danger of malignant disease, while the blackbird is the carrier of numerous superstitions, as in English folklore. The ouzel also appears in Welsh mythology and in that of the Ainu, the aboriginal inhabitants of what is now Japan. Intriguingly, in this belief system, the ouzel is associated with improved sight, perhaps echoed in the Australian version's capabilities, or lack of them.

Our oozlum bird flies backwards, either because it wishes to gaze admiringly at its own tail feathers or to keep the dust out of its eyes. Or it could be because it likes to know where it has been because it does not know where it is going. It can be large enough for a human to ride upon. If startled, the oozlum bird may fly in smaller and smaller circles until it eventually disappears into its own fundamental orifice—sometimes in a puff of blue smoke.

Around 1897, the journalist and poet W.T. Goodge penned a few verses featuring the oozlum bird, also helpfully explaining how the town of Birdsville got its name. The poem begins by introducing 'Ginger Joe' of the Diamantina:

He was old and he was ugly,
He was dirty, he was low.

Joe was also a noted teller of tall tales, and the best anyone ever heard him tell was about Jock McPherson's trip to Sydney on the famously speedy oozlum bird. According to Joe, this is just how it happened:

You can talk about yer racehorse
And the pace as he can go,
But it just amounts to crawlin',
'Nothink else!' said Ginger Joe.
And these cycle blokes with pacers,
You can take my bloomin' word,
They're a funeral procession
To the blinded Oozlum Bird!

Do yez know Marengo station?
It's away beyond the Peak,
Over sixty miles from Birdsville
As you go to Cooper's Creek,
Which the blacks call Kallokoopah,
And they tell you that Lake Eyre
Was one time an inland ocean.
Well, the Oozlum Bird is there!

Bet yer boots it ain't no chicken,
It's as big and wide across
As the bird what beats the steamships,
What's it called? The albatross!
That's the bird! And old King Mulga
Used to tell the boys and me
They were there when Central 'Stralia
Was a roarin' inland sea!

I was cook at old Marengo
When McTavish had the run,

And his missus died and left him
With a boy—the only one.
Jock McPherson was his nephew,
Lately came from Scotland, too,
Been sent out to get 'experience'
As a kind of Jackeroo!

Well, this kid of old McTavish
Was a daisy. Strike me blue!
There was nothing, that was mischief,
That the kiddy wouldn't do!
But he was a kindly kinchen
And a reg'lar little brick,
And we all felt mighty sorry
When we heard that he was sick!

But, McTavish! Well, I reckon
I am something on the swear,
But I never heard sich language
As McTavish uttered there;
For he cursed the blessed country,
And the cattle and the sheep,
And the station-hands and shearers
Till yer blinded flesh would creep.

It was something like a fever
That the little bloke had got,
And McTavish he remembered
(When he'd cursed and swore a lot),
That a chemist down in Sydney
Had a special kind of stuff
Which would cure the kiddy's fever
In a jiffy, right enough!

So he sends me into Birdsville
On the fastest horse we had,
And I has to wire to Sydney
For the medsin for the lad.
They would send it by the railway,
And by special pack from Bourke;
It would take a week to do it
And be mighty slippery work.

Well, I gallops into Birdsville
And I sends the wire all right;
And I looks around the township,
Meanin' stopping for the night.
I was waitin' in the bar-room—
This same bar-room—for a drink
When a wire comes from McPherson,
And from Sydney! Strike me pink!

I had left him at Marengo
On the morning of that day!
He was talking to McTavish
At the time I came away!
And yet here's a wire from Sydney!
And it says: 'Got here all right.
Got the medsin. Am just leaving.
Will be home again to-night!'

Well, I thought I had the jim-jams,
Yes, I did; for, spare me days!
How in thunder had McPherson
Got to Sydney, anyways?
But he'd got there, that was certain,
For the wire was plain and clear.

I could never guess conundrums,
So I had another beer.

In the morning, bright and early,
I was out and saddled up,
And away to break the record
Of old Carbine for the Cup.
And I made that cuddy gallop
As he'd never done before;
And, so-help-me-bob, McPherson
Was there waiting at the door!

And the kid was right as ninepence,
Sleepin' peaceful in his bunk,
And McTavish that delighted
He'd made everybody drunk!
And McPherson says: 'Well, Ginger,
You did pretty well, I heard;
But you must admit you're beaten,
Joe—I rode the Oozlum Bird!'

Said he'd often studied science
Long before he'd came out here,
And he'd struck a sort of notion,
Which you'll think is mighty queer—
That the earth rolls round to eastward
And that birds, by rising high,
Might just stop and travel westward,
While the earth was rolling by!

So he saddled up the Oozlum,
Rose some miles above the plain,
Let the Earth turn underneath him
Till he spotted the Domain!

Then came down, and walked up George-street,
Got the stuff and wired to me;
Rose again and reached Marengo
Just as easy as could be!

'But,' says I, 'if you went westward
Just as simple as you say,
How did you get back?' He answered:
'Oh, I came the other way!'
So in six-and-twenty hours,
Take the yarn for what it's worth,
Jock McPherson and the Oozlum
Had been all around the earth!

It's a curious bird, the Oozlum,
And a bird that's mighty wise,
For it always flies tail-first to
Keep the dust out of its eyes!
And I heard that since McPherson
Did that famous record ride,
They won't let a man get near 'em,
Couldn't catch one if you tried!

If you don't believe the story,
And some people don't, yer know;
Why the blinded map'll prove it,
'Strike me fat!' said Ginger Joe.
'Look along the Queensland border,
On the South Australian side,
There's this township! christened Birdsville,
'Cause of Jock McPherson's ride!'

Another variation exists in the United States military, where an 'Oozlefinch' has been the official mascot of the Air Defense Artillery since the early twentieth century. As befits an air force mascot, the featherless Oozlefinch flies at the incredibly fast pace that sped Jock McPherson to Sydney and back, but has the additional military advantage of tearing enemy aircraft from the skies. Like our own species, the Oozlefinch flies backwards, but is not thought to perform the same unique vanishing act when alarmed.

The Tea and Sugar Train

The world's longest stretch of straight railway line runs for 478 kilometres along the track that tethers Port Augusta to Kalgoorlie, forming part of the Trans-Australian Railway. It was a condition of Federation that the 'Trans' be built across the Nullarbor Plain to link up the east and west coasts. When the rails were finally connected in 1917 it was possible to travel across the continent by rail for the first time—as long as passengers did not mind frequent stops and transfers to the different rail gauges that were then a feature of the railway system. As the visiting American humourist Mark Twain remarked after experiencing this irritation in the 1890s—'Now comes a singular thing, the oddest thing, the strangest thing, the unaccountable marvel that Australia can show, namely the break of gauge at Albury. Think of the paralysis of intellect that gave that idea birth.'

During the gruelling seven years of surveying and building the nearly 1700 kilometres of the Trans, workers had to be supplied by trains coming from the South Australian and the Western Australian ends of the line. At an indeterminate time during and after the construction of the line, the regular service that came to be known as the 'Tea and Sugar Train' appeared. No one knows just when it started running, but the 'Tea and Sugar', as it was affectionately known, was well established by 1917. At this stage, the train consisted of a fruit and vegetable carriage, a butcher's shop and a general supply van. Because there was no refrigeration at that time, the butcher's van had to carry live sheep, slaughtering them as they went. The train was gradually improved, though it was still lacking a stove in 1919. Staff had to jump off the train when it stopped, light a fire and boil their billy beside the line. It was not unusual for the train to leave before they could brew a cup of tea.

Because the line was so long and crossed some very tough terrain, maintenance was—and is—a big issue. A number of settlements of railway workers and their families grew up along the track, including a number named after prime ministers and other notable Australians, as well as Boonderoo, 913 Mile, Rawlinna and Ooldea. Somehow, these tiny settlements had to be supplied with the necessities of life—including water—and the Tea and Sugar was the only way to do it. The needs of these communities were stored in a vast warehouse in Port Augusta, from where the Tea and Sugar would roll out for the four-day trip to a few miles outside Kalgoorlie. The journey took 57 hours, though the train travelled only by day, stopping at night to take orders for the next trip.

In 1925, life was still a frontier experience for the people living along the Trans:

Sometimes the scene is picturesque. Bush men mounted on horses, mules or camels may rub shoulders with uniformed railway employees and their women folk and children and it is not unusual for scantily clad aboriginals to patronise the moving stores. The train-shopkeepers are smartly clad in the regulation garb of their particular trade. Mr. K.A. Richardson, who for many years prior to the coming of the East-West train, carried mails from Port Augusta to Tarcoola, has seen wild natives hovering

about the train. That was in the early days of the line, and most
of the natives are now semi-civilised.

Conditions for those living and working on the line were
extreme, as an observer related in 1928:

> Here and there along the railway line are little settlements
> mostly composed of railway workers. The huts that these workers
> live in are of the two-compartment shanty type or one room.
> At least, you can hardly call them rooms. In the hot summer
> sun (the temperature is 116 degrees in the shade) the workers
> and their wives suffer and stew, and the little children cry for
> a cool drink. Meanwhile, in the trans train, the toff-class enjoy
> themselves to the limit.

The highlight of the year for the children of the Trans was
Christmas. The anxiously awaited Tea and Sugar would arrive
with a special load of seasonal treats, otherwise impossible to
come by in the emptiness of the Nullarbor Plain.

The importance of this lifeline was highlighted during World
War II, when shortages prevented the Tea and Sugar running.
After two to three weeks without bread, meat and other supplies,
the workers along the line threatened to stop work. The Australian
Workers Union had to step in to get the train running once again.

By 1955, the pioneering efforts of Dr Eleanor (or Rita, as
she was known) Stang (1894–1978) saw an infant health and
mother-care 'oasis' attached to the Tea and Sugar, bringing much-
needed medical care and advice to the isolated mothers along the
line. In the 1970s, general medical services were also sometimes
available through the train.

The Tea and Sugar Train continued to bring food and comforts
to the families along the line until 1996. By then it boasted air
conditioning and a conversion to a rolling supermarket through

which buyers walked and selected their needs from rows of shelving. The Tea and Sugar is still fondly remembered by many.

The black stump

Where is it? How did it originate? What does it mean? That iconic Australian expression 'beyond the black stump' or 'not this side of the black stump' refers to any location considered to be far away from the speaker, usually well beyond the rural urban fringe, in the bush or in the outback. No one is quite sure where the outback begins and ends, but we all know that it's a long way away and very big. So important is the black stump that it has evolved its own considerable body of lore and legend to explain its existence.

Some stories rely on what the dictionary makers call etymology, the history of a word from its origins—at least as far as these can be determined—and its appearance in books, newspapers and other documentary sources. There are various tantalising allusions to the black stump in nineteenth-century sources of this kind, but nothing very conclusive; we have to wait until the twentieth century to find references. Before that, so the story goes, the term originated among rural carriers who used fire-blackened tree stumps as way finders; for example, 'Turn left at the third black stump after the river.' Needless to say, there is absolutely no evidence for this belief, which, of course, does not mean it is wrong, just unsubstantiated.

A number of bush towns claim the honour of being the location of the original black stump. As in all good folklore, each has an elaborate tale to justify its claim. In Coolah, New South Wales, it is said that one of the early 'limits of location' involved the boundary of a property known as the 'Black Stump Run'. Later, in the 1860s, an inn was built in the area and named The Black Stump Inn. This establishment was an important stop for travellers and so 'beyond the black stump' came into use as a reference to going beyond the boundaries of settlement. Variations on this theme include the suggestion that blackened stumps functioned as unofficial markers for property boundaries.

A colourful legend underlies the Riverina village of Merriwagga's claim to be the location of the original blackened stump. In 1886, the wife of a passing carrier, Barbara Blain, was burned to death when her dress caught alight in the flames of the camp fire. It is said that in describing the body, her husband said it resembled a black stump. A local waterhole is named Black Stump Tank.

Not to be outdone by New South Wales, the Queensland town of Blackall has a scientific legend to bolster its claim. A surveying party visited the area in the late 1880s and established a site for observing longitude and latitude. Theodolites mounted on tree stumps were used for this work, a number of which were fire-blackened. The remote country beyond this site was considered to be 'beyond the black stump'.

Just how remote and isolated the black stump and beyond could be is highlighted in at least one traditional yarn.

Some time in the 1930s a boundary rider is well out beyond the black stump. He comes across an old prospector who asks him how the war is going. Taken aback, the boundary rider tells him that the 1914–18 war has been over for years.

'Really!' exclaims the prospector. 'Can you tell me who won it?'

'Our mob won, of course.'

The prospector cackled. 'I expect Queen Vic is happy then, she never liked the bloody Boers.'

It has also been said that the term originated in an Aboriginal story. A giant Aboriginal man once threw an enormous spear high into the sky. When it eventually returned to earth most of the wooden spear had been burned away, leaving only the blackened stump in the ground where it fell. Apparently, the legend does not say exactly where the spear fell, which is the whole point (ouch!) of the story.

There are also outrageous assertions that New Zealand actually originated the phrase. The Kiwis might use it, but of course they got it from us!

Whatever we might think of these passionately held claims to the first black stump, they do not explain those other essentials of bush geography like Oodnagallabie, Woop Woop, Bullamakanka or simply 'out to buggery'. Where are these places?

The rise and fall of Cobb & Co.

The legendary coaching line known as Cobb & Co. has a special place in Australian history. The company, in one or another of its various forms, was an integral element of everyday life from the 1850s to the early twentieth century (for more on Cobb & Co., see Chapter 4).

The company saw off its many rivals over that time, basing its success on its ability to provide a faster and, sometimes, more comfortable means of getting from place to place. Then, as now, time was money, and the men who established and ran Cobb & Co. profited handsomely from their ability to exploit this reality.

Cobb & Co. was established during the Victorian gold rush era by expatriate Americans Freeman Cobb and three others. The company imported 'Concord coaches' from the United States, a sturdy design well suited to the difficulties and distances of Australian roads and tracks. One of its features was a suspension system of leather straps supposed to make the ride a more comfortable experience for the passengers, which gave Cobb & Co. a competitive edge over their many rivals.

Freeman Cobb sold out after a few years and returned to America, leaving the company in the hands of a consortium, the main figure in which turned out to be another American. James Rutherford was a chronic over-worker, almost continually on the roads, railways and coaching routes from before dawn until after dark. He kept up a punishing schedule of surprise visits on the company's employees, deal making and generally powering the enterprise that would make a modern CEO wilt.

A secret of Cobb & Co.'s success was its ability to win government mail contracts. And when they could not win them, there were always competitor companies holding such contracts to be bought out and closed down. Almost continual expansion and agglomeration were key features of the business model.

As the enterprise expanded into different colonies, it split into different businesses, though all retained the valuable asset of the Cobb & Co. name. It is arguable that Cobb & Co. was Australia's first iconic brand name, so widespread, influential and recognised did it become.

From the mid-1860s, the success of the business allowed its owners to branch into other areas of opportunity, including extensive pastoral properties and minerals development. Success also allowed the continual improvement of the vehicles and their horses, though coach travel always remained the ordeal it had been in 1860 when a visiting Englishwoman described her experience of travelling 'up the country':

> But oh! The crushing misery. The suffocation of these public conveyances . . . These vehicles are licensed to carry far too many passengers—from forty or fifty, including those outside. Inside they hold twelve to fifteen. I do not know how many inches are allotted to each passenger; I fancied that only about fifteen fell to my share . . . I know that I was condensed to a smaller compass than I could have imagined possible.

She went on to describe the closeness of those beside her and those opposite her 'keeping from us the pure air'. Just as she felt that she would faint, the woman sitting beside her did so.

Despite these discomforts, by the mid-1860s it was possible to travel on the Cobb & Co. brand from Cape York, down the eastern seaboard and into South Australia. The coaching company's mileage was probably the world's most extensive, larger even than that of the American Wells Fargo.

The main threat to Cobb & Co. was the railways. Rather than try to compete head-on, the coaching men worked with the railways to provide transport to and from railheads and important stations. This strategy served the company well until they were tempted to have a try at railway-line building. While this might otherwise have been a smart move, the company's inexperience in building transport routes as opposed to developing and running them was an expensive financial disaster.

It is likely that this experience contributed to the decline of the company in later years. But so complex and diverse were the incomes and expenditures of Cobb & Co.'s interlocking business interests that it is impossible to tell. Perhaps it was just the passing of time.

As the business aged, so did its operators. Although Rutherford lived well into his eighties, his mental health deteriorated along with his grasp of the business. The company failed to perceive the value of the motor vehicle, resisting motorisation until it was already providing smaller competitors with the essential edge, and was in receivership by 1911. The last horse-drawn coach ran in 1924.

A vintage British and Australian television series called *Whiplash* was loosely based on the Cobb & Co. story, filmed during 1959–60 and first reaching Australian screens in 1961. The 'Australian western' series starred the American actor Peter Graves in the lead role of Freeman Cobb, though the rest of the cast were locals, including Leonard Teale, Chips Rafferty, Lionel Long and Robert Tudawali. Although a rather painful, sometimes jarring representation of colonial life, the series did help the developing Australian industry move towards more realistic depictions of its history in shows like *Rush*, *Cash and Company* and *Against the Wind*.

The Long Paddock

The Long Paddock is the unofficial name for Travelling Stock Routes, or TSRs. Mostly originating in the nineteenth century, these are official routes for droving livestock from place to distant place, with wide strips of grass at each side to allow the passing sheep or cattle to graze. Water points are available at regular intervals, although these can easily fail in times of drought. Many Long Paddocks are famous in Australian tradition, including the Canning Stock Route (established 1906–10) between Wiluna and Halls Creek; the Birdsville Track (1880s), 520 kilometres from Birdsville in Queensland to Maree in South Australia; and the Tanami Track, between Halls Creek and the MacDonnell Ranges in the Northern Territory. Many of these TSRs have colourful tales to tell.

The Strzelecki Track runs through South Australia and was established by the bushranger Harry Redford, or 'Starlight', who drove 1000 stolen cattle from Queensland to Blanchewater (South Australia) in 1870, selling them for a large amount of money but later apprehended for the crime. He was tried but found not guilty by a jury impressed with his outstanding journey and unintended contribution to rural infrastructure.

One of the deadliest tracks is known as the 'Ghost Road of the Drovers'. It's only 230 kilometres long, but the Murranji Track runs through dense scrub from Newcastle Waters to Old Top Springs and is a shortcut between the Kimberley and markets in

Queensland. Formed in 1885 and taking its last mob in 1967, the track was notorious for its difficulty of access and the frequent failure of its water supply. At least eleven bodies are said to lie at Murranji Bore and Waterhole, which is also a sacred site to the Mudburra people. In 1942, Billy Miller passed on his recollections of the track in its early days.

*I*n 1886 . . . Nat Buchanan first crossed what is now the Murranji Track, going through from Newcastle Waters to Victoria River. Beginning at Newcastle Waters, the Track follows the Four Mile Creek for twenty-five miles until it reaches a waterhole, called by the drovers The Bucket. Here the Track leaves the creek and goes west, crossing a plain for about fifteen miles, after which it enters thick scrub of hedgewood and lance-wood. Thirty-five miles further on it reaches the Murranji Waterhole, which is surrounded by old box trees. This is the loneliest place I have seen in all 'the Outback' of the north.

Thirty-five miles west from here the Track reaches an aboriginal 'mickeree' (native well). The aborigines dug these wells so that they could walk down to the water. They had a crude but effective way of timbering them. The earth dug out in making or deepening them is not piled up at the edges, but scattered about the surrounding land; the idea being not to make the wells conspicuous. Aborigines never make camp close to the water—always over a mile away in some thick patch of scrub. In walking to the water to fill their coolamons, they avoid going the same way twice, thus making no pad that would lead strangers to the mickerees.

A further fifteen miles brings the Track to the Yellow Waterholes (native, 'Bin-kook-wee-charra'). Nine miles west from here it reaches the Jump Up. On the 109 miles from The Bucket Waterhole to the Jump Up there were only two surface waters—that is, in the old days—which explains the aborigines' need to guard their mickerees. To-day there is a cut line through the dense scrub, and there are bores with large tanks and pumping plants also. It is no trouble now to cross the Murranji Track.

In 1894, when I was stockkeeping on Newcastle Waters cattle station, the blacks about the Yellow Waterholes were very hostile. Some packers from the Cook Town country were going out to Halls Creek, I recall, and, at night, when they were camped, blacks threw spears into their mosquito nets, but luckily did not kill anyone.

In 1900, 'Mulga Jim' McDonald and Hardcastle were camped at the Yellow Waterholes, and, in the night the blacks attacked their camp also. A spear struck Hardcastle in the chest, but, as it was a cold night, he had two rugs and a camp sheet over him, and these stopped the point from penetrating deeply. However, the spear wound caused his death two years later.

On Armstrong's Creek about twenty miles west of the Yellow Waterholes, Jim Campbell and I were camped one night, when the natives let go a shower of spears at our mosquito net. The spears hit our packsaddles, but missed us! They missed because, having learned from experience, we anticipated the raid and, rigging our nets as usual, slept a little way off in the grass. That tricked them!

Thirty-eight years ago I was working on a newly-formed station called Illawarra. The leased country held by the owners was from Top Springs to the Yellow Waterholes, so that cattle travelling the Murranji Track would traverse the station for 40 miles.

When Ben Martin, Jim Campbell and Mick Fleming took the country up, cleanskin cattle were plentiful and very wild. We were moonlighting and running them in to 'coachers' and throwing and tying. Eventually we pulled a fair-sized herd together.

Wave Hill Station was sending bullocks away, some to Queensland and some to Oodnadatta. Victoria River was also sending two mobs of cows to Kidman's Annandale Station on the Lower Georgina. I had to pick up each mob at Top Springs and go with them through the Illawarra country to the Yellow Waterholes, a distance of 40 miles. And I had to keep our station cattle from boxing with the travelling mobs!

With me were two blacks about 17 years of age, who, only three years previously, had been living a stone-age life and had never seen a white man. Now they were top-notch riders. They could take their place 'moonlighting' and could throw and tie up a beast as well as the best of us.

The first mob I picked up was with Blake Miller, a contract drover. He had 1,000 head of cows from Victoria River Downs. After seeing him through to the Yellow Waterholes I returned to Top Springs and picked up Steve and Harry Lewis, who had 1,000 head of Wave Hill bullocks for Oodnadatta.

Bringing down the next mob I was with 'Jumbo' Smith ('Brown of the Bulls' in 'We of the Never Never'). Suddenly, in the darkness, the cattle rushed off the night camp. I heard the stampede, jumped out of bed, and picked up my bridle and whip. My horse was close at hand. I jumped on bare-back and raced for the lead. I put the stockwhip into the leaders and had them blocked, when one of my black boys came up. Then 'Jumbo' Smith (he weighed 18 stone) arrived on the scene. We put the cattle back onto camp, and at day-light 'Jumbo' counted them. He found that we were only two short!

The next lot to be pushed through was a mob of 1,500 head of Wave Hill bullocks, with Jack Dick Skuethorp contract drover. Following him was Oswald Skuethorp, who had 1,250 head of Wave Hill bullocks.

On the second day Oswald asked me to take charge of his bullocks as he wanted to stay with his waggonette to help the cook, who was also the driver. The road was rough limestone in places and very difficult for a vehicle. A wheel of the waggonette broke, as Oswald feared it might, and, worse still, as they were fixing it up the horses strayed away. They did not get them together until late. Putting some cooked tucker on the horses, Oswald started on in the night, hoping to pick up the cattle. However, he did not turn up. In the darkness he had mistaken a cattle pad for the road and 'gone bush'.

The food for the cattlemen was with the waggonette. I had my horses and packs with me, so I knocked up some johnny cakes, boiled some corned beef, and fed the men. I put two of my horses and my two black boys to help with the night watch. The next day we went on but by nightfall there was still no sign of the waggonette, the boss, or the cook. The following day we went up the Jump Up and on to the Yellow Waterholes. We had watered the bullocks and they were feeding on the small plain close to the water when we saw Oswald Skuethorp coming up with the horses and waggonette. We were right glad to see them, as the food supply was exhausted.

It used to be assumed that pioneers developed these vital transport corridors from scratch, but recent research suggests that while this was so in some cases, many follow traditional pathways. While the TSRs are little used for droving these days, there are calls to preserve them as important elements of the environment as well as for their heritage value.

A final surprising fact about the Long Paddock: the Bradfield Highway that crosses Sydney Harbour Bridge is officially designated as a Travelling Stock Route.

The real Red Dog

The earliest European visitors to the continent often commented on the many dogs they saw accompanying Aboriginal groups. When the new settlers came they soon realised the value of canine companions, and dogs became as much a part of the working stock of the land as horses, bullocks, sheep and cows. They accompanied drovers overland, keeping mobs of cattle and flocks of sheep in order. They hunted, retrieved, protected and became an inseparable part of many families. Dogs also featured in songs, stories, art and even in early silent movies, where they often appeared in the chase scenes, well beyond directorial control and simply enjoying the thrill of it all.

Lawson wrote of the dog loaded with a stick of explosive. The famous song about whatever the dog did on—or in—the tucker box at Gundagai entered folklore, as did the wild native dog, the dingo. Dogs were often mascots in military units, the best known being Horrie, the war dog of the 1939–45 conflict, though he was only one of many fighting hounds. Dogs were an indispensible element of Australian life and are still with us as family pets, sporting beasts and the cargo in the back of country utes.

One of the most famous dogs of recent times was known simply as 'Red Dog'. Red Dog was a crossed Kelpie–cattle dog born in Paraburdoo in 1971, known as 'Tally' or 'Blue' in some areas of the vast distances he is said to have covered in his travels. Red Dog became a well-known, if smelly, wanderer throughout the Pilbara region. Many tales were and are told of his amazingly long and arduous journeys and gargantuan appetite, not only for food but for lady dogs as well. He was a generally loved character in the region, frequently being given lifts by passing vehicles as he made his way from one favourite feeding place to another. He even made a trip as far south as Perth.

Not everyone liked Red Dog, though. He took, and was probably given, a strychnine bait in Karratha on 10 November 1979 and died ten days later. Red Dog was buried between Roebourne and Cossack and commemorated in a statue at Dampier, in verse, as well as in a number of books and especially in Pilbara folklore.

In 1998, the writer Louis de Bernières travelled to the Pilbara and saw the locally famous statue. He became fascinated by the story and returned a few months later to collect Red Dog yarns still being told by the locals, turning these anecdotes into a bestselling book published in 2001. Being a writer, de Bernières naturally made an even better tale out of the legends and it is now even more difficult to tell where truth ends and fiction begins. Not that it matters. Assisted by the hit movie based on the book in 2011, Red Dog is now a household name throughout Australia, having made the leap from local legend to national hero.

What a hound! Perhaps Red Dog could only have become such a figure in Australia with its long and strong canine tradition. The movie was a great hit here, but did not do so well overseas. But those with a commercial interest in this venture are not too worried. To date, *Red Dog* is the eighth-highest grossing Australian film and plans are said to be well in hand for *Red Dog the Musical*.

17

Doing it tough

'The banks are all broken,' they said,
'Times will be hard and rough.
There's relief for the poor
At the dole-office door
But you'll have to keep doing it tough.'

Anonymous

ALTHOUGH AUSTRALIA HAS often proved a bountiful place for many, it also has a long history of hard times. The image of the battler is a well-known one and a term that is still often heard today in relation to people who, for whatever reason, are forced to do it tough just to scrape by.

The free selectors of the post-gold rush years lived notoriously basic lives, often subsisting on 'pumpkin and bear' and little else. People had to fend for themselves as far as their health was concerned and in just about every other aspect of life, work and leisure. When the Great Depression hit Australia in the 1930s, very many people who had previously held decent jobs and rented or were purchasing homes were thrown out of work and often onto the street. They coped by adopting some of the strategies of earlier generations who knew what doing it tough meant.

Depending on the harvest

In April 1880, a journalist for the *Argus* newspaper travelled through northeast Victoria interviewing hard-pressed selectors 'where hopefulness was coupled with rough living and plenty of work'. This is what he found.

*T*he husband was out ploughing, behind a pair of horses, and the wife was occupied in 'burning off' which meant hauling small logs and boughs to the heaps of dead timber, and keeping several fires in a state of activity. The children, too small to be of any use, were amusing themselves picking up sticks, and following their mother about. They were very poorly clad all of them and had evidently not worn new clothes for several seasons. The husband was very glad to leave off ploughing to have a consultation with his friend and adviser the bailiff. He took up 320 acres in February, 1877, beginning with a capital of £200. He had fenced all the land in, and was now getting 70 acres ready for sowing. Last season the crop was good, but the season before he did not gather in a single bushel.

Nothing looked better in the summer of 1878–9 than the standing corn but owing to the rust the grain never formed in the ear. He was depending on the harvest of 1879 for the means of clearing off liabilities and did not realise a penny. In this instance the selector had bought a stripper, on bills, in anticipation of the harvest. Having no means of meeting the bills he had to make arrangements with his storekeeper for an advance. In 1878 the account against him stood at £64 and though he sent £154 worth of corn to his storekeeper in January last, there was still a heavy balance against him in the books. The storekeeper was dealing very fairly with him, charging 12 per cent on the bills, which were renewed from time to time and threatening no pressure. The lease was due, but the selector could not take it up until he paid £96 in rent—ie £64 arrears under the licence, £16 under the lease, and £16 more coming due. Should the harvest of 1881 turn out a good one, he would be able to clear off his debts and raise enough money on the lease to carry him on for the future. Just now he was in doubt how to act. Having only paid £32 (one year's rent), ought he to forfeit the amount, as some advised, and start afresh under the Act of 1878 paying only £16 a year instead of £32?

So long as he was without the lease, no one except the Crown could dislodge him; but he saw no hopes of being able to pay rent, or any of his other obligations, before next February. The horses and plant were covered by bill of sale, and there was nothing on which he could just now raise any money. He bought 100 sheep on credit for £44 some time ago, but they got out through the fences, and 80 had been lost. It was likely when a muster took place at the station that most of them would be recovered. The man he bought the sheep off would take them back, and if they fetched within £10 of what was due on them probably he would be satisfied. Sheep had fallen in price since the purchase of this flock. He had two horses before beginning to plough but one took ill and he was obliged to borrow £5 to buy another.

This was the case of a man absolutely destitute of ready cash, with 10 borrowed months before him, no means of raising any funds, and carrying on only by the forbearance of the storekeeper, whose long bill was produced for our inspection. The first half of the account was contained in one line—'account rendered', and the remainder filled two pages of foolscap. No item in it looked unreasonable, and the goods supplied consisted chiefly of requisites for earning on farming. The family lived in a bark hut, divided into two apartments by a partition. The inner room, where all the family slept, was not lighted by any window. Indeed, but for two doors the whole place would have been dark. A mud floor worn into holes and dusty walls with a few paper decorations, some sacks of wheat kept for seed, a wide fireplace, a kettle swinging over the fire, a table, and a piece of dried meat hanging in a smoky place—these were the only noticeable features of the interior. In the old gold-digging times rough men would have been contented with similar lodging but it could not be said that the place was a suitable one for bringing up three children, shortly to be increased to four.

The children, being under six, were too young for school but in a year or two it would be safe to let them walk by themselves across the bush to the schoolhouse. It cannot be said that selectors in distress have failed for want of industry. Here was this one, out first thing every morning with his horses ploughing, preparing the ground for a harvest 10 months distant, and his wife (who would not be equal to field work long) helping him in the afternoons at 'burning off'. Everything in this instance was depending on the results of the harvest of 1881, and favourable weather in the meantime—on a fall of rain at proper intervals, dry days at ripening time, a good yield, assistance in money from the storekeeper at reaping and threading (for the harvest labourers must be paid in cash) and a good market when the grain is ready for sale—a good market depending on the state of affairs in Europe as well as on the condition of things here. And when the corn is being threshed out, the storekeeper will be standing by to make sure of the bags of grain. Until his account is squared up there will be nothing available for the payment of arrears of rent or for the purposes of another season's preparations. If anything, the facts of this case have been understated.

'Women of the West'

George Essex Evans was an English-born Australian balladist and writer whose work was very popular during his short life. He died in 1909 at the age of 46 after a varied life as a failed settler, journalist and public servant. The work he is best remembered for is 'The Women of the West'. Although the poem speaks of the collective story, it sums up the experience of many women along the 'frontiers of the Nation' and 'the camps of man's unrest'. Many people at the time and since have found this poem well captures the often forgotten experiences of the wives, mothers, daughters and sisters of the 'men who made Australia', celebrated by Henry Lawson in his poem of that name, written a few years earlier.

> They left the vine-wreathed cottage and the mansion on the hill,
> The houses in the busy streets where life is never still,
> The pleasures of the city, and the friends they cherished best:
> For love they faced the wilderness—the Women of the West.
>
> The roar, and rush, and fever of the city died away,
> And the old-time joys and faces—they were gone for many a day;
> In their place the lurching coach-wheel, or the creaking bullock chains,
> O'er the everlasting sameness of the never-ending plains.
>
> In the slab-built, zinc-roofed homestead of some lately-taken run,
> In the tent beside the bankment of a railway just begun,
> In the huts on new selections, in the camps of man's unrest,
> On the frontiers of the Nation, live the Women of the West.
>
> The red sun robs their beauty, and, in weariness and pain,
> The slow years steal the nameless grace that never comes again;
> And there are hours men cannot soothe, and words men cannot say—
> The nearest woman's face may be a hundred miles away.
>
> The wide Bush holds the secrets of their longings and desires,
> When the white stars in reverence light their holy altar-fires,
> And silence, like the touch of God, sinks deep into the breast—
> Perchance He hears and understands the Women of the West.
>
> For them no trumpet sounds the call, no poet plies his arts—
> They only hear the beating of their gallant, loving hearts.

But they have sung with silent lives the song all songs above—
The holiness of sacrifice, the dignity of love.

Well have we held our fathers' creed. No call has passed us by.
We faced and fought the wilderness, we sent our sons to die.
And we have hearts to do and dare, and yet, o'er all the rest,
The hearts that made the Nation were the Women of the West.

Cures!

Hard times seem to bring out the make-do spirit in Australians.
Clearing land on the frontier, surviving in war, or coping with
the hardships of the Great Depression were experiences that have
inspired inventions of all kinds. As well as inventing new things,
Australians have continually recycled and repurposed sugar bags,
furniture, clothing, bedding and anything else deemed useful for
an application other than its original purpose. This inventiveness
and resilience is a feature of Australian identity and can be seen
in some of our favourite character types, including the digger, the
bushman and especially the battler.

Making do also involves looking after the health of families far
from professional—or even unprofessional—medical assistance.
Usually by necessity, medicine was often homemade as well.

Constipation, colds, hiccups, head lice and the panoply of
family ailments were treated with medicines sometimes efficacious,
sometimes calamitous! Favourites were molasses, perhaps a herbal
poultice or brew of some kind, cod liver oil and castor oil, applied
in liberal quantities to cure everything from constipation to skin
irritations. Kerosene was good for cuts, as was tar if you could
get it. Spider webs were also used to treat wounds. Piles could be
treated with a preparation of copper sulphate known as 'Bluestone',
which was added to a bucket of boiling water over which the
luckless sufferer squatted.

Ginger was good for arthritis, while tennis balls sewn into pyjamas would reduce snoring. Honey helped hay fever and dandelion helped kidney stones. Colds might yield to garlic and rum or six drops of kero on a teaspoon of sugar. Sore throats were treated with iodine, painted on the throat with a chook feather, or by tea leaves wrapped in a tea towel and wrapped around the neck—especially good for tonsillitis.

In German tradition, potato water was good for frostbite. So was urinating on your hands in the unlikely event that you suffered that problem in most parts of Australia. Upset tums were said to surrender to flat lemonade, Coca-Cola, plain toast or, more enjoyably, port wine and brandy. Boils were susceptible to a dose of shotgun cartridge powder or a poultice of sulphur and molasses. And of course that old standby for insect bites and stings, a bag of Blue, once a common detergent.

The notion that chicken soup and hot lemon juice are good for colds is old and pervasive, and folk wisdom even provided helpful medical advice, such as 'feed a cold, starve a fever'. These cures and nostrums could even extend into the realms of magic, with wearing red flannel scarves to supposedly protect against a sore throat and removing warts by rubbing them with meat, burying the meat and waiting for it to rot. The wart would allegedly decay in magical sympathy with the meat.

Around Condobolin the Kooris swear by the bush medicine known as 'old man's weed'. It will cure anything.

Aboriginal bush medicine could perform some remarkable cures, according to many bush observers. Retired prospector Jock Dingwall recalled seeing a fight between some Aboriginal men, somewhere at the back of Kuranda. The fight ended with one man speared in the stomach, one with a broken arm and a third with a battered skull. The wounds were treated with a mysterious white substance, not unlike chewing gum, found growing in a seam across the river. The broken head was coated in the white substance and bound up with vines. After returning the broken arm bones to their proper location, the jagged wounds were plastered with the bush medicine. The man with the spear wound had his stomach covered in swamp weed and the magical white salve. All three recovered in a month or so.

Jock's experience of Aboriginal bush medicine was recorded in 1972, by which time he'd tried many times to locate the site of the fight and of the magical natural medicine. He reckoned it would be valuable, although he could never find it.

As well as making home remedies essential, the lack of doctors left a wide field for the purveyors of commercial cures and potions. These were advertised widely, often through verse. Even Henry Lawson, always in need of a bob, knocked out one of these for the cough medicine known as 'Heenzo'. Henry called it 'The Tragedy—A Dirge'.

> Oh, I never felt so wretched, and things never looked so blue,
> Since the days I gulped the physic that my Granny used to brew;
> For a friend in whom I trusted, entering my room last night,
> Stole a bottleful of Heenzo from the desk whereon I write.
>
> I am certain sure he did it (though he never would let on),
> For he had a cold all last week, and to-day his cough is gone:
> Now I'm sick and sore and sorry, and I'm sad for friendship's sake
> (It was better than the cough-cure that our Granny used to make).
>
> Oh, he might have pinched my whisky, and he might have pinched
>   my beer;
> Or all the fame or money that I make while writing here—
> Oh, he might have shook the blankets and I'd not have made a row,
> If he'd only left my Heenzo till the morning, anyhow.
>
> So I've lost my faith in Mateship, which was all I had to lose
> Since I lost my faith in Russia and myself and got the blues;

And so trust turns to suspicion, and so friendship turns to hate,
Even Kaiser Bill would never pinch his Heenzo from a mate.

A seasonal guide to weather and wives

Do-it-yourself weather forecasting has long been a favourite activity, especially among farmers. Before the era of scientific weather forecasting, farmers and anyone else needing to know if it would rain or not used traditional methods to decide when to plant or when to take an umbrella. In practice, this meant knowing a great many seemingly trivial pieces of information about the relationship between plants, animals and the seasons.

In springtime, if you saw a rainbow round the moon it would rain in two days. Black cockatoos calling meant that rain was on the way. If ants built their nests high, a lot of rain was on the way. If the currawongs called to each other, a southerly change was coming. If the sky was yellow at sunset, there would be wind tomorrow. The other seasons had their traditional forecasts, all equally reliable.

SUMMER

If it rains on a full moon, it's going to be a wet month.
Herringbone sky, neither too wet nor too dry.
When the kookaburras call, the rain will fall.
Spider webs in the grass in the morning mean it will not rain that day.
If there is heavy dew, it will not rain.
When flies are hanging around the doors and windows, it is a sign of rain.
Cows lying down are good indication of rain.
A ring of clouds around the moon means it will rain within a day.
When the ants build nests in summer, rain is one week away.
If flying ants are about, rain is only six hours away.

AUTUMN

If the moon is tilted sideways or upside down, it will rain.

Mackerel sky, mackerel sky—never long wet, never long dry.

If flies land on you and bite, it is going to rain.

Croaking frogs mean rain is coming.

If it rains on the new moon, it will either rain again a week later,
  or rain for a full week, or the month will be generally wet.

Moss dry, sunny sky, moss wet, rain we will get.

WINTER

A ring around the moon means rain in five days.

Rain before seven, clear by eleven.

Winter is not over until you see new buds on a pecan tree.

When the fog goes up the hill it takes the water from the mill.

When the fog comes down the hill, it brings the water to the mill.

Herringbone sky, won't keep the earth 24 hours dry.

If anthills are high in July, winter will be snowy.

If ants build in winter, rain is one day away.

A lot of this information was handed down through the generations and a lot of it also turned up in almanacs and farmers' guides. These were full of useful information about planting times, dates, seasons and all manner of things necessary for agriculture. They also carried other items that could just turn out to be useful for the man on the land. If he needed to determine the nature of a potential wife, he could turn to folklore for an indication of what married life might be like. All he needed to know was the birth month of his wife-to-be:

A January bride will be a prudent housewife and sweet of temper.

A February bride will be an affectionate wife and a loving mother.

A March bride will be a frivolous chattermag, given to quarrelling.

An April bride is inconsistent, not over wise, and only fairly good looking.

A May bride is fair of face, sweet tempered and contented.

A June bride is impetuous and open-handed.

A July bride is handsome but quick of temper.

An August bride is sweet-tempered and active.

A September bride is discreet and forthcoming, beloved of all.

An October bride is fair of face, affectionate but jealous.

A November bride is open-handed, kind-hearted, but inclined to be lawless.

A December bride is graceful in person, fond of novelty, fascinating, but a spendthrift.

Backyard brainwaves

The great urge to invent things has long been an Australian characteristic. The need to adapt to a strange and usually harsh environment inspired some earlier inventions such as the stump-jump plough. Long before then, Indigenous Australians had been creating new tools such as the boomerang and the woomera, or spear thrower. A characteristic of these devices was that they were often multipurpose. Not only was a boomerang efficient in bringing down game, but it could also be used as a musical instrument to beat out a rhythm. Similarly, the woomera could be used as a digging tool. Aboriginal people were also quick to adopt items they found useful from Europeans. The first known Europeans to set foot on Australia came with Willem Jansz in 1606. Because they were seeking exploitable riches, the Dutch brought various trade items with them, including glass and metal objects, and the Aborigines they met quickly saw the cutting value of a glass shard and the hardness of metal.

Famous agricultural inventions from the time of European settlement include the grain stripper devised by John Bull and

John Ridley in 1843, followed by the stump-jump plough in 1876, which, as the name suggests, did exactly that, allowing for faster and more efficient clearing of land for agriculture. Another agricultural invention was the Sunshine header harvester, an improvement on an 1880s invention of the stripper harvester by Hugh McKay. While this was a useful device, it could not cope with crops laid flat by wind or rain. Headlie Taylor taught himself the essentials of mechanics and built his first header harvester in 1914, which solved the flattened crop problem and caused less damage to the harvested heads of wheat.

The need to preserve food was especially important in the bush, particularly where there was a little water and a lot of heat. In the 1890s, the goldfields town of Coolgardie saw Arthur McCormick, an amateur handyman, use his observation and wits to construct the first fridge, the Coolgardie Safe. He made a wooden box covered with a hessian bag draped with strips of flannel, put a metal tray on top, and filled it with water twice daily. The water flowed slowly down the strips, keeping the bag wet and the contents inside the 'meat safe', as these devices were often later known, nice and cool. (The famous bushman's hessian water bag works on the same principle.) While this ingenious arrangement of evaporation largely solved the problem of keeping food cool, it didn't stop the ants crawling into the food. A homemade remedy for this was to place a tin can full of kerosene at the bottom of each leg of the safe, which the ants would not cross.

McCormick was a keen gardener and noted amateur athlete who later became mayor of the goldfields town of Narrogin from 1927 to 1930. He does not seem to have made any money from his useful invention.

The sea has been another important focus of Australian inventiveness. The familiar reels used by surf lifesavers to control their safety lines were thought up by Lester Ormsby and first used in 1906 at Bondi. Speedo swimming costumes, 'togs', 'bathers' or 'budgie-smugglers' first appeared in the late 1920s.

At Gallipoli, Australian soldiers invented the periscope rifle, an ingenious device that allowed a sniper to fire at a target observed through a series of lenses mounted in a wooden box with complete safety, as the device could be fired by pulling on a string attached to the trigger and ending well below the top of the trench. It was especially handy for use at short range, the minimal distance between the Turkish and Anzac trenches being sometimes less than 50 metres. Credit for this idea is due to Lance Corporal William Beach, who came up with it in May 1915. A makeshift assembly line was set up on the beach to satisfy the demand for periscope rifles throughout the campaign.

Another innovation was the jam tin bomb. Not unique to Gallipoli, but a characteristically spontaneous element of the fighting, this simply involved filling empty jam tins with spent cartridge cases, bits of Turkish barbed wire and explosive. They were used like an old-fashioned grenade, with a fuse protruding from the top. This had to be lit before throwing, so timing was crucial: if the bomb were thrown too early, the enemy had time to pick it up and lob it back. If it was held too long there was a danger of it exploding in the thrower's hand. A citation for Lance Corporal Leonard Keysor's VC won at Lone Pine gives a graphic insight into the use of grenades in hand-to-hand combat:

On the morning of 7 August, as the Turks developed their counter-attacks, a great bombing duel developed at the positions held by the 1st and 2nd Battalions. As pressure mounted on the forward posts, the Colonel of the 2nd Battalion was killed and junior officers badly wounded.

It was now that Keysor's bravery and skill was fully demonstrated. Using little cover, he flung dozens of bombs, returned some Turkish ones and smothered others with sandbags. At times, much to the amazement of his comrades, he was seen to catch incoming bombs in flight and throw them straight back. In all, he was an inspiration to the weary defenders.

Despite the efforts of Keysor and others they were forced gradually back and positions had to be given up. Rallying behind new barricades, Keysor continued his bomb throwing despite being twice wounded. Indeed, he kept up his efforts for over 50 hours until the 1st Battalion was relieved by the 7th on the afternoon of 8 August, so ending what was described as 'one of the most spectacular individual feats of the war'.

This make-do approach was also in evidence when the Anzacs departed Gallipoli in December 1915. Normal rifles were often set up with water-dripping or candle-burning arrangements so that they would fire automatically, giving the Turks the impression that the Anzacs were still in their positions.

Another fertile ground for spontaneous wizardry has been the backyard. Various forms of clothes line were developed to dry the washing of Australia's families, ranging from a handy tree limb or bush to lengths of twine held up by forked poles or similar supports. A rotary clothes hoist was first developed in the 1920s but it was the Hills Hoist that became the iconic backyard feature. In 1945, returned digger Lance Hill's wife was unhappy about the way the traditional pole and rope line interfered with the garden plan. Lance went off and improvised the first of his hoists out of some metal tubing and bits of wire, then invented a cast aluminium winding mechanism to wind the hoist up and down. Adopted enthusiastically, the Hills Hoist was known as the 'gut buster' because of the tendency of its early versions to suddenly wind down without warning, giving the luckless clothes hanger an unwelcome thump in the stomach.

That other essential of the backyard, the Victa lawnmower, also attained a folk name early on: developed in the 1950s by Mervin Victor Richardson, it was known as the 'toe-cutter', for obviously painful reasons. Later models greatly improved the safety of the machine. It was not the first rotary blade mower, but it was lighter and more powerful than its predecessors, and ideal for the tough backyards of the fibro frontier springing up across the country as the post-World War II baby boom encouraged people to throw up suburban houses in the hundreds of thousands. Mervyn knocked out the early models in his garage and sold them locally; people soon heard about them, and the rest is history.

Sugar bag nation

The sugar bag or chaff bag was used for carrying all sorts of loose dry goods in colonial Australia, and for long after. Made of hessian or burlap, they were cheap and could simply be thrown away after use, then becoming handy carrying bags for those who could not afford better, such as swagmen and battlers. During the Great Depression the sugar bag could be seen all over the country as people did it tough and made do to get by as best they could. The humble sugar bag was used for carrying feed for livestock, as mats, as blankets often in the form of the 'Wagga rug', as curtains, beds, hammocks and whatever else human need could contrive for them.

The Great Depression is usually said to have started with the Wall Street stock market crash of 1929. British and American bankers called in the loans they had made to the rest of the world, including Australia, and began the long, grinding process of unemployment and despair that, for many, lasted throughout the 1930s. For many working Australians and their families, life became a constant struggle to survive, as Isy Wyner recalled in 1999:

... you'd line up there and walk past these cubicles with your sugar bag, and they'd throw a hunk of meat at you and stick it in the bag—and a couple of loaves of bread and a pound of tea, and you'd figure, well, you'd then have to hump that home.

Many Australians felt that the Depression did not really end for them until the outbreak of World War II in 1939. By then the nation had endured a decade of misery, deprivation and social dislocation so profound that the folk memory of the time was transmitted down the generations.

In New South Wales, the Labor government of Premier Jack Lang repudiated the state's debts to the British banks and defied Canberra's economic strictures derived from the prescriptions of a visiting banker, Sir Otto Niemeyer. Niemeyer insisted that the Australian government cut spending, exactly the wrong response to the drying up of money and credit and one that made the Depression harder and longer than it needed to be. In the streets, they sang to the tune of 'Titwillow':

What Rot-o
Sir Otto
Niemeyer

In the crisis that followed, the Governor, Sir Phillip Game, dissolved the New South Wales Parliament, effectively ending Lang's government. While these events played out in the maelstrom of political and financial power, many lost their livelihoods, their homes and their families.

The Great Depression polarised political points of view and strong parties emerged at both ends of the political spectrum, the proto-fascist New Guard on the right, and various socialist and workers' groups on the left, most notably the Australian Communist Party. In 1999, the 90-year-old Jock Burns, still an active member of the Communist Party, rendered a Depression ditty to the tune of a popular song of the era, 'I'm Forever Blowing Bubbles':

> I'm forever striking trouble,
> Striking trouble everywhere,
> The landlord came, the landlord went,
> I said I've no work, no rent,
> The butcher wants his money,
> Baker, grocer too,
> I sent all the bills to Jack Lang,
> 'Cause he said he'd pull us through.

Jock added: 'Which he never!'

Jack Lang, demonised as a dangerous radical, attracted both support and censure. To the tune of 'Advance Australia Fair' his supporters sang:

> Now Premier Lang for us will fight
> We've got to see it through
> His motto clear is 'Lang is right'
> We've got to see it through
> He's blotting out our enemies
> His courage never fails
> So give three cheers for Premier Lang and good old New South Wales
> So sing and let your voices ring for Lang and New South Wales.

His opponents had their own song to the tune of an Irish song known as 'The Stone Outside Dan Murphy's Door', an indication of the ethnic background of many working-class people of the time:

> The songs that we sang were about old Jack Lang
> On the steps of the dole-office door

He closed up the banks, it was one of his pranks
And he sent us to the dole-office door

We molested the police, 'till they gave us relief
On the steps of the dole-office door
Yes, the songs that we sang were about old Jack Lang
On the steps of the dole-office door

Many returned soldiers from World War I could not get work during the 1920s, a period when Australian society and politics were fragmented and conflicted. It was not uncommon to see men dressed in the remains of their uniforms, sometimes maimed, begging in the street or selling self-penned and -published collections of verse and yarns door to door. For such people, and for many in the country, the onset of the Depression in the 1930s was hardly noticed, so impoverished had their lives become. As a bush worker remembered:

Depression! There's always been a depression in Australia as far back as I can remember. I was walking the country looking for work from the end of the First World War until the start of the Second, till 1939!

On a similar theme, but with more direct bitterness at the way in which returned soldiers had been treated, was 'Soup', to the tune of 'My Bonnie Lies Over the Ocean':

We're spending our nights in the doss-house
We're spending our days on the streets
We're looking for work but we find none
Won't someone give us something to eat?

Soup, soup, soup, soup,
They gave us a big plate of loop-the-loop.

Soup, soup, soup, soup,
They gave us a big plate of soup.

We went and we fought for our country
We went out to bleed and to die
We thought that our country would help us
But this was our country's reply:

Soup, soup, soup, soup . . .

While governments—state and federal as well as local—were considering what to do, people simply had to get on with living as best they could. They coped, as always, by laughing at their circumstances. They parodied popular songs to make light of their lot:

When your hair has turned to silver we will still be on the dole
We'll live in Happy Valley where the Reds have got control
We'll draw the weekly ration and the child endowment too
And when we get the old age pension I will leave the rest to you.

As unemployment increased, those affected found it difficult to keep up with mortgage or rent payments. Many landlords decided to evict families who could no longer pay, an action that caused a number of violent eviction riots. Among the most notorious were those in Newtown and Bankstown in 1931:

For we met them at the door,
And we knocked them on the floor,
At Bankstown and Newtown,
We made the cops feel sore,
They outnumbered us ten to one,
And were armed with stick and gun,

But we fought well, we gave them hell,
When we met them at the door.

The Great Depression didn't so much end as fade into World War II. After a decade of hard times things had started to improve and with the need for soldiers, industry and other war supplies, the unemployed were soaked up. Soon there would not be enough people to do the work and even women would have to be drafted as factory workers, transport drivers and food producers.

Happy Valley

One of the darkest years of the Depression was 1933. It had been going for years and for many, poverty had become a way of life. All over the country shantytowns known as 'Happy Valley' grew up on wasteland. Those in Sydney were typical of hundreds more 'unemployed camps' in other states.

*O*n the left of the tramline at La Perouse two of these colonies can be seen. They are easily distinguishable. Made for the most part of scraps, usually galvanised iron, they are not a pleasant sight. The roofs are all of iron, old and rusty. A few lengths of stove or some other piping may serve for a chimney. Doors may be real or a piece of sacking hung from the frame. Stones may keep the roof on. There may be an open square for a window, or it may have glass. The hut may be of one room, or it may consist of three or four. It may be ugly and have canvas walls. Still, home—home for somebody.

A few have a show of making an 'appearance'—really comfortable little homes built in house style, but small. One or two are weatherboard; perhaps there is a tiny verandah. Fences of odd sticks, bits of wire, brushwood, and other materials are around the garden plots, and the vegetable growth in the sand is astonishing. Occasionally one comes on a bed of bright, cheerful flowers. Apparently a man erects a hut at a place which suits his ideas, puts some plants or seeds in the ground, and fences the plots. They are in no way regularised allotments. The settlements are on a haphazard plan, facing every and any way. But from the outside the general appearance is one of dilapidation and squat ugliness, the low roofs and the rusty iron dominating the landscape. Water at the settlement at Long Bay is obtained from 'soaks'—spots to which the moisture seeps down the hillsides, filtering through the white sand. There are about 50 or 60 camp dwellings in the settlement near Long Bay on the Commonwealth ground, on which are the rifle ranges.

Near the tram terminus at La Perouse the line skirts a gully in the sandhills lying to the left. The verdure is profuse, and the huts are scattered in it, about the hillsides, and along the ravine towards the ocean. Several of them have taken on the air of permanent dwellings, with an occasional coat of paint. There are glass windows with curtains, and some brick chimneys. Most have their tiny gardens. Children are everywhere. Dogs abound—happy dogs and happy children, un-touched by the cares of a distressing economic situation. There are no hard paths, no lighted roadways, no electric supply. There is no rent to pay, no municipal rates, no income returns to bother about. Clothes do not matter. Nobody wears boots. The beaches are close. Down the gully is the ocean. Over the hill is the bay. Trams pass every quarter of an hour. A water pipe runs through the settlement, with taps at intervals. This is what has been dubbed Happy Valley, and it looks as though life might be happy enough if it was not for the curse of idleness.

'I've been here three years,' said a young man with a snug-looking shanty behind a small garden. 'Three wasted years of life!' The bachelor abode can be distinguished from the one sheltering a family. It needs only one room. The real stringency of circumstances is to be detected in the ragged tent, or the hessian-sided hut, where the late-comers are establishing themselves.

'How do you like living this way?' a reporter asked a woman with three lusty, bare-footed youngsters playing about. She said it was 'Good-o'. The children probably never think it anything else. Even the dogs—well fed, somehow or other—seemed to find it the same. There is work now and again. The relief work gives a little cash, and child endowment will also provide some income. About 150 dwellings are in the gully and on the hillsides.

Over on the other side of the neck of land, which ends at Bare Island, and between La Perouse and the Bunnerong Powerhouse, are probably some hundreds of huts on the sandhills. They have in general the rusty scrap iron appearance, but a few have an air of substantiality. There is more space available and no crowding. In several a wireless mast and lead-in wire indicate some degree of comfort, and generally there is evidence that one must not altogether judge by exteriors, as quite good furniture is in some of the dwellings. At Yarra Bay, which is in Botany Bay, the hills on which they stand slope gently, and the windows or open doors look out over the shimmering blue water. Rockdale has about 150 scattered along the foreshores at Brighton-le-sands, all of the same character as the others. An occasional business sign is to be seen where an artisan is ready for customers. After the manner of human proclivities in the gathering together of people with a common interest, there is an 'Unemployed Campers Association'. At Clontarf, in the Manly Municipality, there are about 40 or 60 camps on a pleasant area close to the silvery sands and the crystal clear water of Middle Harbour.

The municipalities are perturbed about the growth of a new class of citizenry—these new suburbanites, who pay no rent, ask for no leases, and put up my kind of a habitation. The hitherto inviolate rules that have pressed a little hardly in requirements on the residents are broken. Ejection seems impossible, for if deprived of their shelter the campers must be provided for in some way. They are treated sympathetically. Rockdale sends them fruit, vegetables, firewood, and other things, attends to the sanitary necessities, and provides water.

A tram guard on the La Perouse line deposits daily a can of milk by the wayside. It is given by a company. And so on. It is the cheapest way of living for those who would otherwise be thrown on the hands of the authorities. They are on Crown lands, and not encroaching on private property, but the householders in the vicinity, who have undergone considerable expenditure and pay heavily towards the peace, order, and good government systems under which they live, look perplexedly at the deteriorative effects of the invasion of shanties, and wonder what is to be the end of it.

The Rockdale Council gave notice to a number of campers some time ago that they would have to move to make way for a relief work, about 20 being affected. The Manly Council, alarmed at the growth of the claim to permanence on the Clontarf reserve, gave notice that the camps would have to be vacated and demolished by the end of December, but representations were made, and delay has been granted until a further investigation is made.

The matter of these camps having become so important, it was put before the Government some time ago, and consideration is being given to it.

Sergeant Small

A notorious figure during the Great Depression was a burly Queensland policeman known to every bagman as 'Sergeant Small'. The sergeant seemingly took it upon himself to make the lives of those hopping freight trains in search of usually non-existent work even more desperate than they needed to be. His favourite trick was to disguise himself as a swaggie and clamber aboard a rail truck carrying an illegal fare. When he was close enough to collar his prey, the sergeant dropped his fake swag and arrested the unfortunate. The victim would suffer a pummelling from the Sergeant's fists, then spend the night or even longer in the local gaol on a vagrancy charge. Sergeant Small was, not surprisingly, a deeply unpopular man whose name became a byword for ill-treatment of this kind.

Country singer Tex Morton, himself no stranger to the travelling life and the odd brush with the law, wrote a song about the Sergeant. The song told the story of a bagman or 'hobo', as Morton sang, riding on a timber train and being hoodwinked by the Sergeant who 'dropped his billy and his roll and socked me on the chin'. The prisoner was taken to the police station where five policemen beat him up. Morton wished he was 'fourteen stone and I was six feet six feet tall' so he could take the train back north again just 'to beat up Sergeant Small'.

Morton recorded the song in 1938 but it was allegedly banned from the airwaves of the then fledgling Australian radio because it was considered to be potentially subversive with its strong anti-police theme. This did not stop it being a popular item in Morton's famous travelling shows and, in a reworked version, the song remains popular today, having been recorded by numerous folk and country artists.

What of the sergeant? Well, despite research by a number of people, there does not seem to have been a Sergeant Small working for the Queensland Police at the relevant time and place. He may well be a figure of folklore—the surname 'Small' for such a big bloke is perhaps a hint. But even if he is a myth, the uniformed authority figure wielding power in an excessive way is a common feature of Australian tradition. In this case, the story and characters are set in the Great Depression and represent an unpleasant experience suffered by many travellers searching for work during what were, for many, if not all, 'the hungry years'.

The farmer's will

Life on the land has always been tough, but dying on it can be even harder, as the maker of this will suggests:

I've left my soul to me banker—he's got the mortgage on it anyway.

I've left my conversion calculator to the Metrification Board. Maybe they'll be able to make sense of it.

I have a couple of last requests. The first one is to the weatherman: I want rain, hail and sleet for the funeral. No sense in finally giving me good weather just because I'm dead.

And last, but not least, don't bother to bury me—the hole I'm in now is big enough. Just cremate me and send me ashes to the Taxation Office with this note: 'Here you are, you bastards, now you've got the lot.'

A Farmer

18

Home of the weird

And the sun sank again on the grand Australian bush—the
nurse and tutor of eccentric minds, the home of the weird,
and of much that is different from things in other lands.

Henry Lawson, 'The Bush Undertaker'

FOR ALL THE gritty realities of colonial life, Australia has its fair
share of unexplained discoveries, odd events and mysteries of
all kinds. The continent had existed in myth for so long before
its actual discovery, charting and eventual European settlement,
that peculiarities appeared very early on. By the time Lawson
wrote his conclusion to his short story 'The Bush Undertaker',
the bush—meaning anywhere outside a city, quite an area—was
well known as a place of mystery as well as hardship.

Curious discoveries

In January 1838, an ambitious soldier named George Grey led
an exploration party into the completely unknown northwest of
Australia. Grey would go on to an astounding career in politics
and government in two Australian colonies, in New Zealand and
South Africa, and eventually would be knighted for his sometimes
controversial actions and approaches. But now he was still in his
mid-twenties and keen to make his name as an explorer. He was

totally inexperienced in Australian conditions, as were most of the others in his party. Nevertheless, Grey's military background and iron will kept the expedition going through unexplored terrain, battles with the local inhabitants and many other hardships recounted in his journals.

Grey and his men were the first Europeans known to have seen the Wandjina paintings and other ancient rock art of the Kimberley region. But they also made some even more enigmatic discoveries that continue to puzzle us today. In his journal, Grey describes his discovery of the cave containing the carved, or 'intaglio' head:

*A*fter proceeding some distance we found a cave larger than the one seen this morning; of its actual size however I have no idea, for being pressed for time I did not attempt to explore it, having merely ascertained that it contained no paintings . . .

I was moving on when we observed the profile of a human face and head cut out in a sandstone rock which fronted the cave; this rock was so hard that to have removed such a large portion of it with no better tool than a knife and hatchet made of stone, such as the Australian natives generally possess, would have been a work of very great labour. The head was two feet in length, and sixteen inches in breadth in the broadest part; the depth of the profile increased gradually from the edges where it was nothing, to the centre where it was an inch and a half; the ear was rather badly placed, but otherwise the whole of the work was good, and far superior to what a savage race could be supposed capable of executing. The only proof of antiquity that it bore about it was that all the edges of the cutting were rounded and perfectly smooth, much more so than they could have been from any other cause than long exposure to atmospheric influences.

One of the few people known to actually visit the area since Grey is Les Hiddins, the famous 'Bush Tucker Man'. He found the cave but was unable to find the carving until he used Google Earth, which revealed a passage Hiddins had missed on his previous visits. He intended to return in 2012 for another look but so far has not reported further.

Grey's outback adventure also turned up some other puzzling sights. He came across 'a native hut which differed from any before seen, in having a sloping roof'. Shortly after, on 7 April 1838, he found 'curious native mounds or tombs of stone'.

*T*his morning I started off before dawn and opened the most southern of the two mounds of stones which presented the following curious facts:

1. They were both placed due east and west and, as will be seen by the annexed plates, with great regularity.
2. They were both exactly of the same length but differed in breadth and height.
3. They were not formed altogether of small stones from the rock on which they stood, but many were portions of very distant rocks, which must have been brought by human labour, for their angles were as sharp as the day they were broken off; there were also the remains of many and different kinds of seashells in the heap we opened.

My own opinion concerning these heaps of stones had been that they were tombs; and this opinion remains unaltered, though we found no bones in the mound, only a great deal of fine mould having a damp dank smell. The antiquity of the central part of the one we opened appeared to be very great, I should say two or three hundred years; but the stones above were much more modern, the outer ones having been very recently placed; this was also the case with the other heap: can this be regarded by the natives as a holy spot?

We explored the heap by making an opening in the side, working on to the centre, and thence downwards to the middle, filling up the former opening as the men went on; yet five men provided with tools were occupied two hours in completing this opening and closing it again, for I left everything precisely as I had found it. The stones were of all sizes, from one as weighty as a strong man could lift, to the smallest pebble. The base of each heap was covered with a rank vegetation, but the top was clear, from the stones there having been recently deposited.

Grey also reported other perplexing discoveries he referred to as 'an alien white race'. He found among the Aborigines he encountered 'the presence amongst them of a race, to appearance, totally different, and almost white, who seem to exercise no small influence over the rest'. Grey thought that these people were the main leaders of attacks on his party and speculated that they were of Malay descent.

At Roebuck Bay, an officer aboard the *Beagle*, the ship that carried Grey's expedition to Australia and picked them up at the end of the expedition, also described fair-skinned Aborigines in the area:

*A*t this time I had a good opportunity of examining them. They were about the middle age, about five feet six inches to five feet nine in height, broad shoulders, with large heads and overhanging brows; but it was not remarked that any of their teeth were wanting (as we afterwards observed in others); their legs were long and very slight, and their only covering a bit of grass suspended round the loins. There was an exception in the youngest, who appeared of an entirely different race: his skin was a copper colour, whilst the others were black; his head was not so large, and more rounded; the overhanging brow was lost; the shoulders more of a European turn, and the body and legs much better proportioned; in fact he might be considered a well-made man at our standard of figure. They were each armed with one, and some with two, spears, and pieces of stick about eight feet long and pointed at both ends. It was used after the manner of the Pacific Islanders, and the throwing-stick so much in use by the natives of the south did not appear known to them.

After talking loud, and using very extravagant gestures, without any of our party replying, the youngest threw a stone, which fell close to the boat.

These accounts have led many to since speculate about the origins of the hut, the carving, so unlike Aboriginal art and building, as well as the 'individuals of an alien white race'. An early suggestion was that these discoveries were linked to a mythical French sojourn in the unknown southland as early as 1503. Others have tried to link the finds with survivors of Dutch shipwrecks in the seventeenth and eighteenth centuries. But the carved head, the stone tombs, if that is what they were, and the fair-skinned Aborigines remain some of the many mysteries of Australia's past.

The marble man

In mid-1889 a curious object was discovered in a marble quarry near Orange.

It is the body of a man about 5ft. 10in. in height, well formed, and evidently from the shape of the head and the contour of the features a European. To geologists and scientific men generally, an examination of this strange discovery should prove interesting.

The marble in which the body was found is of various colours, but the body itself is petrified in white marble. With the exception of the arms, which are broken off at the shoulders, the limbs and features are intact, the left side of the body, however, being slightly flattened, due no doubt to the fact that it was found lying on this side.

The object was taken to Sydney where the discoverers placed it on display to the public. The body, if it was one, excited immense interest. Speculation ran wild. It was an Aboriginal. It was an escaped convict. It was a hoax. Doctors, geologists, government officials and just about everyone else examined it, to judge by the number of opinions and suggestions published in the press. Not all of these were very serious: one correspondent pointed out that the body took a size 12 hat.

Another correspondent claimed to have found a similar figure near Mt Gambier in 1854—'a petrified blackfellow had been found in a cave on Hungry M'Konnor's station at Mosquito Plains, between Jatteara and a place called Limestone, and now known as Penoli. The blackfellow was in a standing posture.' The governor was said to have visited the object, which was protected beneath an iron grating.

A Bathurst district local, probably tongue in cheek, claimed to know the true origins of the man:

deer mr. Headhitter—This here putrified man are a stature, mr. jones, the Bathurst stonemasing, sais he were sculpted at a old public at cowflat. the wurk tooke ten weaks, and arterwards the stature were berried in the ground, then dug up, and hexibetted as a putrified man.

The police were called and investigated the matter, their report being discussed in the Legislative Assembly. The mystery only deepened though. The police believed that the mummy had never been in the quarry but had been fabricated by a certain Mr Sala for nefarious commercial purposes.

Then the plot took another twist. Two, in fact. Sala claimed that he had found not only the marble man in the quarry, but also a marble woman and a marble child. People were now expressing their incredulity about 'the Sydney Fossil', as an Adelaide newspaper called the object, but despite this, the 'two shilling show' exhibition was a commercial success.

This did not stop a court case from which Sala emerged unsentenced and with costs awarded, the magistrates considering that the matter should never have been brought before them. Rumour, speculation and commerce careened on and the newspapers of the land milked the story for all it was worth, which seems to have been quite a lot. Officials partially dissected the body, claiming the results proved that it was once human. The geologists analysed some chippings with inconclusive results. The wags did not miss an opportunity:

> 'Don't you think,' said the lunatic, 'it'ud be a good idea to run that petrified man from N.S.W. for a seat in the Legislature of Queensland?'
>
> 'No,' said the practical one, 'I don't; there are too many darned old fossils there already.'

The marble man even appeared in a spoof advertisement for Milk Arrowroot biscuits—'Now with added bone ash!' He was featured on stage by the Watson's Bay Minstrels in 'a very laughable farce'.

By this time the story had rolled on for months, boosted by the marble man's travels as he was exhibited around the country. During that time, ownership of the marble man seems to have changed hands. Who actually owned the object and was therefore responsible for its debts became the subject of legal action, which, like everything else about the marble man, simply raised further questions without answers.

Then, in August 1889, Sala produced the marble woman he had earlier claimed to have found beside the man:

> The body is apparently that of a young woman of spare build, 5ft. high, with the facial features flattened. The body appears to be solid marble. The legs are raised at the knees; the arms, hands, nails, and fingers appear very natural. The head and an arm have been broken and re-joined roughly with plaster.

She was shipped straight off to Sydney for exhibition and caused a similar flurry of interest and disagreement. One newspaper wondered if further searching in the Orange area might reveal a whole family—'seven children, a cat, a dog, a frying-pan, and a broom handle—all petrified or all marble'. The article concluded with a reference to the great American showman and shyster, P.T. Barnum: '... as Barnum used to say, "the public like to be gulled".'

By the end of September, Sala was in the bankruptcy court where more accusations of fakery were levelled against him. Others felt it necessary to air their opinions in the press, and further farcical depictions appeared on stage. The same year, Harry Stockdale, one of the first marble man's early owners, published a book titled *The Legend of the Petrified or Marble Man*, adding further fuel to the furore and, of course, to the publicity blaze.

The following May, Sala's son was displaying yet another marble man in Orange, at a shilling a time. The reporter was so impressed he went out to the marble quarry and, under the supervision of Sala junior, managed to unearth a few items of his own, including a woman's skull, a hand and a breast. The place was also littered with fossil remains of fish, horses and other animals. By June a marble horse taken from the quarry was on show. The next October the marble man had graduated to the Great Hall at Sydney University and was said to be soon off to even greater things in Chicago.

From then the marble man, woman, child and horse seem to fade from the newspaper columns. Was the marble man really a petrified human being, of whatever kind? Or just a showground hoax? And what about the other fossils, allegedly human and otherwise, discovered in the area near the quarry? Opinions remained divided at the time and no one seems to have come up with any answers since.

Was Breaker Morant the Gatton murderer?

In 1898, Gatton was a small Queensland town with fewer than 500 souls, located on a busy route to and from Brisbane, and travellers passed through on a regular basis. The Murphy family were local farmers around 13 kilometres outside the town. On the evening of Boxing Day 1898, Michael Murphy, aged 29, with his sisters Ellen, eighteen, and Norah, 27, left home in a borrowed sulky bound for a local dance. When they arrived, the dance had been cancelled and they headed back sometime around 9 p.m. They did not return home and the following morning their mother asked her son-in-law, William M'Neill, to look for them.

M'Neill had loaned his sulky to the three and soon found its tracks. He followed them through scrub for over a kilometre from the main road, coming to a field where he found their bound and beaten bodies carefully laid out with their feet pointing westwards. Norah's body was lying on a rug; Michael and Ellen were found lying back to back, a few feet apart. The horse drawing the sulky had been shot dead. It was later established that Michael had been shot in the head as well as bludgeoned. His sisters had both had their skulls fractured. Norah was probably strangled with the harness strap found around her neck. Both women had been raped. The murders were thought to have taken place between 10 p.m. and 4 a.m. the following morning.

Investigation of the dreadful crime was botched from the very beginning, with crowds of gawkers destroying much forensic evidence at the scene. The police were slow to arrive and conducted their inquiries in an oddly slapdash way. The post-mortem was careless too, and resulted in the bodies having to be exhumed for further examination. The Royal Commission eventually held to examine the whole affair confirmed all this, but despite this level of official investigation and activity, the murders remained a mystery. Who had committed such a savage act? And why? The victims were three locals with no links to criminal activity, simply driving home from a dance that never happened.

Suspects included a newcomer to the area named Thomas Day, various itinerants and even family members. There were suggestions of a failed abortion attempt on Norah and also of incest. There was no sign of the victims having been forced into the paddock, strongly suggesting their acquiescence and the presence of someone they knew. None of these possibilities were ever substantiated and the Gatton murders remained unsolved, but ever since, there have been frequent revelations of the killer's identity, all impossible to prove.

One of the most intriguing, if apparently left-of-centre, possibilities is that the famed horseman, womaniser and poet Henry 'the Breaker' Morant was the murderer. This theory was put forward by the folklorist John Meredith, who conceived it while researching a book on the poet Will Ogilvie, a mate of the Breaker's. The theory depends on aspects of Morant's personality and personal history and on some suggestive chronology.

The man who was executed for murdering a prisoner of war during the Boer War was an enigmatic and sometimes disturbing character. The Breaker's early life is as clouded in myth as his later years, a situation made worse by his romancing of his past.

He was born Edwin Henry Murrant in Somerset, England, into very ordinary circumstances, though he often intimated that his ancestry was considerably more exalted. He arrived in Australia at age eighteen in 1883 like many other young Britishers of the time looking to make a fortune, a name or even just a living, under a false identity. Over the next fifteen or so years he made a rip-roaring reputation as a flamboyant bush character and outstanding horseman, earning his nickname 'the Breaker'. His feats of horsemanship, particularly riding a buck jumper few others could master, are still legend among horse fanciers. His amorous adventures included marriage to Daisy May O'Dwyer, later to become famous as anthropologist and journalist Daisy Bates. According to the story, Daisy gave the Breaker his marching orders when he—characteristically—refused to pay for the wedding. He took off on a stolen horse, also characteristically, and that was the end of the relationship (though not the marriage, as they never divorced). The Breaker continued his roistering lifestyle. He worked at whatever was available and developed a literary reputation as a bush poet, becoming friendly with other poets like 'Banjo' Paterson, Henry Lawson and Will Ogilvie.

The Meredith theory revolves around the Breaker's relationship with Ogilvie and correspondence between them, as well as with several other bush nomads of the period. Like Morant and many others, the Scots Ogilvie was drifting around the backblocks doing whatever work there was and writing verse and journalism whenever possible. They were all wild boys—womanisers, drinkers, gamblers and mostly exceptional horsemen. Some, especially the Breaker, were already bush legends. Meredith argues that despite his skills and image, Morant was effectively a kind of split personality. When sober he was charming, witty and even urbane. But after one too many he could turn into a very ugly and intimidating animal. Men who were not generally frightened by very much at all were known to fear and hate Morant.

The Breaker also lived a dissolute life, habitually out of funds, scrounging on his mates and not being too fussy where he obtained his mount. Despite all this, Ogilvie maintained contact with Morant until a few months before the Gatton murders. Morant simply disappeared and was not seen again by those who knew him until around February 1899, when he appeared at the Paringa Station on the South Australian section of the Murray.

Where had he been?

According to Meredith, the Thomas Day initially suspected at Gatton was Breaker Morant. Day turned up in Gatton at the same time Morant vanished from his mates further south. He took a job with a local butcher, an occupation in which he was skilled, and in just a few days developed a local reputation as a taciturn loner. He frightened his workmate so much that he asked their boss to get rid of Morant, and he was often seen loitering near the spot where the murders were committed.

The locals had Day—only in town ten days—pegged as the murderer, though the detectives from Brisbane concentrated their investigations on another suspect. Meanwhile, Day became increasingly abusive to his employer and family and he was paid off in lieu of notice. The police cleared Day to leave town, and he took the train to Toowomba, then travelled to Brisbane via Gatton a few days later. Then he disappeared.

According to Meredith, he joined the militia under another name but deserted a few weeks later and was never heard of again. This was around five or six weeks after the murders. About a month later Morant turned up at Paringa Station while a mob of cattle was being swum across the Murray. He did not stay for long. On the outbreak of the South African war he left to enlist, probably in hope of returning eventually to England.

While Breaker Morant's story had some years to run until his ignominious end, there is more to tell of Thomas Day. Before Day had arrived in Gatton, fifteen-year-old Alfred Hill and the pony he rode were lured into the bush and shot dead. The bullet was a .380 calibre. Police arrested and charged a man on suspicion but he was later released. No further action took place but in the course of the Royal Commission into the Gatton murders, it was established that the man charged with Hill's murder was Thomas Day. Morant was known to carry a pistol, and the bullet found in the brain of Michael Murphy was .380 calibre.

The evidence is circumstantial, but no more so than the many other theories put forward over the years. The Gatton tragedy remains one of Australia's most gruesome and enigmatic murders.

Vanishing vessels

Australia's history of maritime exploration and disaster has produced many legends of lost ships and vanishing wrecks. The well-known story of the Mahogany Ship, said to lie somewhere beneath the sands of Armstrong Bay near Warrnambool, goes back to at least the earliest newspaper account in 1847. However, the area was barely settled at that time, though it was visited by whalers and sealers. It also lay on an overland droving route, so Europeans were in at least some contact with the place. It has also been suggested that the story of the Mahogany Ship derived originally from earlier wrecks—probably of whalers or sealers—in the Hopkins River area.

In 1876, a local man, John Mason, wrote a letter to the Melbourne *Argus* detailing what he saw while riding along the beach from Port Fairy to Warrnambool during the summer of 1846:

My attention was attracted to the hull of a vessel embedded high and dry in the Hummocks, far above the reach of any tide. It appeared to have been that of a vessel about 100 tons burden, and from its bleached and weather-beaten appearance, must have remained there many years. The spars and deck were gone, and the hull was full of drift sand. The timber of which she was built had the appearance of cedar or mahogany. The fact of the vessel being in that position was well known to the whalers in 1846, when the first whaling station was formed in that neighbourhood, and the oldest natives, when questioned, stated their knowledge of it extended from their earliest recollection. My attention was again directed to this wreck during a conversation with Mr M'Gowan, the superintendent of the Post-office, in 1869, who, on making inquiries as to the exact locality, informed me that it was supposed to be one of a fleet of Portuguese or Spanish discovery ships, one of them having parted from the others during a storm, and was never again heard of. He referred me to a notice of a wreck having appeared in the novel *Geoffrey Hamlyn*, written by Henry Kingsley, in which it is set down as a Dutch or Spanish vessel, and forms the subject of a remark from one of the characters, a doctor, who said that the English should never sneer at those two nations—they were before you everywhere. The wreck lies about midway between Belfast and Warrnambool, and is probably by this time entirely covered with drift sand, as during a search made for it within the last few months it was not to be seen.

⌒

Whatever the origins of the tale, it has attracted extensive investigation by historians, archaeologists, treasure hunters and history enthusiasts. One of the consistent, if controversial, themes in the story has it that the ship is a Portuguese—sometimes Spanish—caravelle wrecked in the area some considerable time before documented European occupation. It has also been claimed that the Mahogany Ship is of Chinese origin and that there is a local Aboriginal legend of 'yellow men' coming ashore. The few relatively reliable eyewitness accounts of the wreck before it disappeared beneath the shifting sand dunes suggest that the ship was of an unusual design. This could mean many things but has led to a suggestion that it might have been a roughly made craft from a documented Tasmanian convict escape attempt. Until the Mahogany Ship is rediscovered, or an authenticated document indicating contact found, speculation will continue.

A similar tradition exists on Queensland's Stradbroke Island, where the remains of a Spanish galleon are said to be disintegrating in coastal swamplands. The first documented sighting of the high-prowed timber ship dates from the 1860s. A local pilot and light keeper found the wreck at the southern end of the island and removed its anchor to use as an ornament in his home. His Aboriginal wife then told him of the local Indigenous knowledge of the wreck. There were further sightings in the 1880s, when the supposition that the mysterious vessel was of Spanish origin began to gain traction. This rapidly became a lost treasure tale and serious searches for the galleon began; one group in 1894 claimed to have found the wreck and removed a substantial load of copper fittings from it. When they tried to find the wreck again, the intriguing structure had disappeared.

Subsequent sightings have been either due to Aboriginal people taking settlers to the site, or after bushfires have revealed the smoking timbers through burnt-out vegetation. No sightings have been reported since the 1970s, though there are persistent suggestions that the locals hold secret knowledge of the galleon's treasure, fuelling continued searches for the site. A 2007 expedition unearthed a rusting coin that is said to date between the late 1590s and the 1690s.

Yet another intriguing mystery concerns the 'Deadwater Wreck'. In 1846, the surveyor and explorer Frank Gregory reported the 'remains of a vessel of considerable tonnage . . . in a shallow estuary near the Vasse Inlet . . . which, from its appearance I should judge to have been wrecked two hundred years ago . . .' The next recorded sighting of the wreck in the section of the

Wonnerup Inlet known as 'the Deadwater' was in 1856, though the account stated that it had been visible 'for years past'. There is a credible line of documentation back to the earliest years of European occupation in this area in the 1840s, and there is also the usual folklore surrounding this mystery. Unverified local tradition claims that early settlers massacred local Aboriginal people to obtain the gold ornaments that they possessed from some unknown source.

The decomposing ship was plundered in the 1860s, though almost certainly not by Aborigines, but there have been no credible sightings of it since. That has not quashed speculation and investigation about the ship's identity. Serious research and fieldwork into the wreck has been carried out, and based on estimates of the length of the Deadwater Wreck, it is suggested that the ship is a VOC *hoeker* named the *Zeelt*. This class of ship was around 30 metres in length and built in the high-stern style of many early East Indiamen, in accordance with some descriptions of the wreck before its disappearance beneath the sand and mud. The small 90-ton *Zeelt* went missing as early as 1672 on only her second voyage. This work may yet reveal the remains of the Deadwater Wreck, but there is also research suggesting *Zeelt* actually went down in southern Madagascar.

Yearning for yowies

What are we going to do about all these yowies? They're turning up everywhere around the nation in almost plague proportions. At least that is the impression given by the various websites dedicated to hunting the wild yowie.

Great Australian Stories included a solid section on yowies, as well as other mythical creatures of the bush, including the yarama, the bunyip and several other mysterious and usually unpleasant beings. Since then, the big, hairy creatures, reported from the time of the early colonial period, have been regularly sighted in the bush, and even in the suburbs: in 2010 a Canberra bloke met a hairy, apelike creature in his garage. Apparently, it wanted to communicate—but who knows what?

Canberra, Queanbeyan and surrounding areas have long been yowie hotspots. They became such a nuisance in the 1970s that a $200,000 reward was offered by the Queanbeyan Festival Board to anyone who could capture one of the elusive creatures. The money has never been claimed but that has had no effect on yowie sightings.

In 1903, Graham Webb of Uriarra recalled an encounter with 'some strange animal' that had taken place many years earlier:

*W*e were out in Pearce's Creek (a small stream between the Tidbinbilla Mountains and the Cotter River) in search of cattle. In the early part of the day we came upon the remains of a cow of ours. We recognised this beast by the head, as the blacks would only take the tongues out. That the blacks had speared and roasted it was evidenced by their stone oven which was close by. We searched the creek during the day, and having seen no indications of cattle being there, we decided to return to where the cow had been killed, and camp there for the night, as it was a good place for the safe keeping of our horses. The weather was very hot and dry; it was in the month of March, there was no moon, none of us had a match. We had supper as usual, and lay down.

Some time during the night, I think it must have been late, I awoke (the others were asleep) and I heard a noise similar to what an entire horse makes. I heard it again and awoke the others. We heard it some four or five times, and the noise ceased, but we could hear it walking along on the opposite side of the range, and when in a line with our camp, we could hear it coming down in our direction. As it came along we could hear its heavy breathing. About this time the dogs became terrified and crouched against us for protection. On account of a fallen tree being on the side the thing was coming, it had to come on one side or the other to get to where we were. My brother Joseph was on the lower side of this tree, I was on the upper side and my brother William in the centre. Not many seconds passed before Joseph sang out, 'Here the thing is,' and fired a small pistol he carried at it. Neither William nor myself, coming to the scrub got a sight of it. Joe says it was like a blackfellow with a blanket on him.

We did not hear it going away. We then tried to set our dogs after it, thinking they might find out where the thing went, but we could not get them to move. Had this thing been a little later in coming we could have seen what it was, as the day began to dawn in less than a quarter of an hour after Joe fired at it.

Webb also mentioned another incident in which Aboriginal people had killed a creature like the one that had terrified him and his brothers:

*T*he locality where the blacks killed it was below the junction of the Yass River with the Murrumbidgee. The animal got into some cliffs of rocks, and the blacks got torches to find out where it was hidden and then killed it with their nullah nullahs. There was a great many blacks at the killing, and he saw two dragging it down the hill by its legs. It was like a black man, but covered with grey hair.

Many consider the yowie to be related to the yeti or 'abominable snowman' of the Himalayas. In 2013, an Oxford University geneticist claimed to have matched DNA from alleged yeti hair samples showing that they matched those of a polar bear. This claim raised enormous interest around the world, though it has been challenged on the basis that polar bears are not likely to have ever existed in Nepal. Probably not in Australia, either.

Other speculations about the yowie include the possibility that the creature is a remnant of an earlier species. Aboriginal legends are often put forward as evidence for this.

Meanwhile, the hunt for our very own long-armed and hairy monster goes on. Sightings are regularly reported, especially from hotspots in Queensland but also in many other places. In the Queensland farming town of Kilcoy, they are so enthusiastic about their venerable yowie legends that they have erected a yowie statue in the local park, now called Yowie Park. In another sighting hotspot, the town of Mulgowie, the locals speak enthusiastically of sightings and speculations on the nature of their mysterious monster, the poetic Mulgowie Yowie. They have yowies in Woodenbong, New South Wales; they're in the Blue Mountains, near Taree, throughout Queensland, as well as the ACT infestations. We love a good yowie yarn almost as much as newspapers, radio and television do, in which even the sniff of a yowie is elevated to a major event. It seems that we really don't want to let our yowies go. If only someone could actually produce one. Perhaps we could grasp it by the leg?

19

Romancing the swag

North, west, and south—south, west, and north—
They lead and follow Fate—
The stoutest hearts that venture forth—
The swagman and his mate.

Henry Lawson, 'The Swagman and his Mate'

THE SWAGMAN—ALSO KNOWN as a 'bagman'—is one of Australia's most colourful characters. We first hear the word around the mid-nineteenth century, but the itinerant way of life was established long before. The need to travel long distances between settlements and properties meant that the ability to live on the road was vital for many people, and as the frontier expanded it became even more important for those without horses to 'go on the wallaby'. The essential equipment included something to sleep on, a billy for cooking and whatever other personal items were needed to survive what were usually long, hot and dusty journeys, mostly in search of work but sometimes avoiding it.

As early as the 1860s, landowners were complaining about men 'on the tramp' and the

...reckless system of life assumed by the generality of the men who back [*sic*] their beds, and shift from one part of the colony to another, during the intervals between sheep shearing and harvest, harvest and sheep shearing. Six months' work, six months' idleness—such is the year's programme of this gaberlunzie fraternity.

(A 'gaberlunzie' is an old Scots term for a beggar.) The writer went on to complain about the swaggies who 'knock down their entire earnings in the two great drinking bouts with which the two periods of industry are wound up.'

And there were plenty of others with the same view. Despite this, the nomadic labourer and bush worker was so necessary to the survival of the agricultural economy, especially the wool industry, that the swagman's way of life was followed by many.

Lore of the track

An extensive body of folklore grew up around the 'swaggie' who 'humped his drum' along the 'tucker track'. One of the many classic yarns highlights the legendary reluctance of swagmen to indulge in more conversation than was necessary.

A couple of swaggies are tramping along together in the usual silence. Around mid-afternoon they come across the bloated carcass of a large animal on the side of the road. That night as they settle down in their camp one says to the other, 'Did you notice that dead horse we saw this afternoon?'

It wasn't until lunchtime the following day that the other swaggie answered: 'It wasn't a horse, it was a bullock.' The next morning he woke up but his mate was nowhere to be seen. But he'd left a note. It read: 'I'm off, there's too much bloody argument for me.'

The swaggie's dry sense of humour features in more than a few yarns:

*O*ne day out on the track out the back of Bourke, a swaggie runs out of food. Somewhere along the Darling River he comes across a ramshackle selection. He knocks on the door of the tumbledown shack and asks the farmer's wife for some food for his dog, thinking perhaps that this would encourage her sympathy. But the wife refuses, saying she can't be handing out food to lazy tramps and flea-bitten mongrels.

'Alright then, Missus', say the swaggie, 'but can yer lend me a bucket?'

'What do you want that for?', she ask suspiciously.

'To cook me dog in.'

On another occasion, the same dry sense of humour was displayed by a one-time swaggie:

*B*illy Seymour was another well-known swagman of the 'Outback' tracks, but he has since turned cane-farmer, and the bush roads know him no more. Travelling somewhere over Muttaburra way one time Billy called at a roadside humpy, and appealed to the woman who presented herself at the door, to fill his ration bags. The woman was sympathetic but said that she had very little food in the house. Her husband had been away droving for three months, and she had received no money from him during his absence. If he didn't write soon she couldn't imagine what she was going to do.

Billy pulled his old battered tobacco-box from his pocket and opening it, drew from its interior a crinkled and worn one-pound note. 'Here, Missus' he said, 'take this; I was saving it until I got to town, but spare me days I reckon you need it more than I do.'

In this nugget from the 1930s, the swaggie is called a 'tramp' but his sense of humour and irreverence towards the archdeacon and his four white ponies is pure bush.

*A*rchdeacon Stretch, of Victoria, had been transferred to a big parish in New South Wales, where a kindly-disposed squatter, evidently somewhat partial to archdeacons, presented him with four handsome creamy ponies and a fine Abbott buggy. One day this Archdeacon was spinning along behind his creamies at a merry pace when he espied a tramp at the roadside whom he at once took aboard. Whether actuated by a purely generous impulse, or a wish to obtain the services of a gate-opener along the pastoral route, this article is little concerned. After a while, the tramp said: 'My word, that is a fine team of creamies, sir; when's the rest of the circus coming along?'

Sniffling Jimmy

Another colourful swagman ended up in the first AIF, where the skills of living off the land and often on one's wits stood them in good stead.

*n*omads of the long and dusty track!! Yes, I've met them and studied their habits and characteristics, and many of them have been strange folk indeed. Most of them belonged to the past generation of 'matilda-waltsers' [sic] who have since disappeared from the roads, and their place has been taken by others who will never possess the rare humor or suffer the hardships of the men I am now going to tell about. Throw a log on the fire, draw closer to the cheering blaze and listen:

Just before I left North Queensland in 1914 to enlist in the A.I.F. I met a well-known track character who was better known as 'Sniffling Jimmy'. He was a short nuggety-built fellow with a freckled face and a mop of fiery red hair that would have turned a Papuan green with envy. i.e., if the natives of our vast Northern island have a liking for red hair. He was about 35 years of age and said that in his time he had walked through nearly every city and township between Melbourne and Townsville. He rarely did any work, and with a merry twinkle in his eye he said that when a boy his mother was much concerned about his constitution, so he promised her that he would never do a day's work if he could help it.

Jimmy was one of the very few teetotal swagmen I have met, and when he refused my offer to come in and have 'one' he said that he never touched anything stronger than water in his life. However, his specialty was soliciting free rations at some wayside squatters' homestead or farmer's home. Rarely has a swagman ever uttered such a pathetic oration. If his appeal to have his bag filled met with an abrupt refusal he would rattle off something like the following: 'Oh, have a heart, lady. If it wasn't for me weak constitution I wouldn't be compelled to beg for food. You see, I was reared in poverty and besides me mother and an invalid father, there were 13 other children in our family. There wasn't enough money coming into the house to provide sufficient nourishment for all of us, and as a result I did not get much to eat.'

'But you appear healthy enough,' said a Proserpine woman one day.

'Ah yes, lady,' replied Jimmy, 'but you know that outside appearances are often deceptive; me constitution is injured in me interior.'

One day in 1915 I was carrying a bag of bombs from Monash Gully to Courtney's Post at Anzac, and about half way I came upon four men digging an eight-foot trench, through shaly ground, under snipers' fire. I instantly recognised one of the men as 'Sniffling Jimmy'.

'Hullo! You are working at last,' I said.

'Oh yes,' he replied, 'army rations agree with me constitution.'

Just then a sniper's bullet lifted the dirt a few inches away from where he was working and he began to dig the pick frantically into the ground. I passed on and did not meet him again, but I hope he returned to Australia without loss of health or limb.

The poetic swaggie

Others less literary and more unknown also caught the swaggie's lifestyle and ethos from another angle:

Kind friends, pray give attention
To this, my little song.
Some rum things I will mention,
And I'll not detain you long.
I'm a swagman on the wallaby,
Oh! don't you pity me.

At first I started shearing,
And I bought a pair of shears.
On my first sheep appearing,
Why, I cut off both its ears.
Then I nearly skinned the brute,
As clean as clean could be.
So I was kicked out of the shed,
Oh! don't you pity me, &c.

I started station loafing,
Short stages and took my ease;
So all day long till sundown
I'd camp beneath the trees.
Then I'd walk up to the station,
The manager to see.
'Boss, I'm hard up and I want a job,
Oh! don't you pity me,' &c.

Says the overseer: 'Go to the hut.
In the morning I'll tell you
If I've any work about
I can find for you to do.'
But at breakfast I cuts off enough
For dinner, don't you see.
And then my name is Walker.
Oh! don't you pity me, &c.

And now, my friends, I'll say good-bye,
For I must go and camp.
For if the Sergeant sees me
He may take me for a tramp;
But if there's any covey here
What's got a cheque, d'ye see,
I'll stop and help him smash it.
Oh! don't you pity me.
I'm a swagman on the wallaby,
Oh! don't you pity me.

Shopkeepers would often provide passing swaggies with the means to take them through to the next stage of their journey. Henry Lawson noted this during his trek to Hungerford in 1892:

We saw one of the storekeepers give a dead-beat swagman five shillings' worth of rations to take him on into Queensland. The storekeepers often do this, and put it down on the loss side of their books. I hope the recording angel listens, and puts it down on the right side of his book.

This was not because Hungerford was a prosperous place: 'Hungerford consists of two houses and a humpy in New South Wales, and five houses in Queensland. Characteristically enough, both the pubs are in Queensland.' It was one of the unspoken obligations of bush life in which it was customary to provide assistance to travellers down on their luck. One day you might be one too.

Swagmen were not necessarily poorly educated, and in some cases not even poor. There are many examples of swagmen who knew the classics, literature, art and philosophy, as well as some who were professors. Sometimes these were men who had fallen on hard times, frequently due to the grog, perhaps gambling or other problems. Some had the means to live a settled life but chose to carry their drums along the tracks of Australia. A well-known case is that of Joseph Jenkins (1818–98). After an early life as a successful farmer in Wales, Jenkins apparently suffered a breakdown of some sort aggravated by drinking and took passage to the colony of Victoria. Here he took to the road, taking whatever work he could get and writing award-winning poetry and campaigning in local newspapers to better the lot of bush workers. He kept a journal of his wanderings, later published as *Diary of a Welsh Swagman* (1975), in which he wrote about politics, social conditions and Aboriginal people, among many other topics.

Many men spent parts of their lives as swaggies, sometimes as a necessity, sometimes as a way of seeking their fortunes as in the classic fairy tales about ne'er-do-wells eventually doing well. Well-known examples include the bush entrepreneur R.M. Williams and the novelist Donald Stuart. Even aristocrats were known to shoulder their swags from time to time.

'There you have the Australian swag'

So, what was a swag? Obligingly, Henry Lawson has left us a detailed description of the typical swag of the late nineteenth century. He also gives an insight into the actual carrying of the swag.

*T*he swag is usually composed of a tent 'fly' or strip of calico (a cover for the swag and a shelter in bad weather—in New Zealand it is oilcloth or waterproof twill), a couple of blankets, blue by custom and preference, as that colour shows the dirt less than any other (hence the name 'bluey' for swag), and the core is composed of spare clothing and small personal effects.

To make or 'roll up' your swag: lay the fly or strip of calico on the ground, blueys on top of it; across one end, with eighteen inches or so to spare, lay your spare trousers and shirt, folded, light boots tied together by the laces toe to heel, books, bundle of old letters, portraits, or whatever little knick-knacks you have or care to carry, bag of needles, thread, pen and ink, spare patches for your pants, and bootlaces. Lay or arrange the pile so that it will roll evenly with the swag (some pack the lot in an old pillowslip or canvas bag), take a fold over of blanket and calico the whole length on each side, so as to reduce the width of the swag to, say, three feet, throw the spare end, with an inward fold, over the little pile of belongings, and then roll the whole to the other end, using your knees and judgment to make the swag tight, compact and artistic; when within eighteen inches of the loose end take an inward fold in that, and bring it up against the body of the swag.

There is a strong suggestion of a roley-poley in a rag about the business, only the ends of the swag are folded in, in rings, and not tied. Fasten the swag with three or four straps, according to judgment and the supply of straps. To the top strap, for the swag is carried (and eased down in shanty bars and against walls or veranda-posts when not on the track) in a more or less vertical position—to the top strap, and lowest, or lowest but one, fasten the ends of the shoulder strap (usually a towel is preferred as being softer to the shoulder), your coat being carried outside the swag at the back, under the straps. To the top strap fasten the string of the nose-bag, a calico bag about the size of a pillowslip, containing the tea, sugar and flour bags, bread, meat, baking-powder and salt, and brought, when the swag is carried from the left shoulder, over the right on to the chest, and so balancing the swag behind. But a swagman can throw a heavy swag in a nearly vertical position against his spine, slung from one shoulder only and without any balance, and carry it as easily as you might wear your overcoat.

Some bushmen arrange their belongings so neatly and conveniently, with swag straps in a sort of harness, that they can roll up the swag in about a minute, and unbuckle it and throw it out as easily as a roll of wall-paper, and there's the bed ready on the ground with the wardrobe for a pillow. The swag is always used for a seat on the track; it is a soft seat, so trousers last a long time. And, the dust being mostly soft and silky on the long tracks out back, boots last marvellously.

Fifteen miles a day is the average with the swag, but you must travel according to the water: if the next bore or tank is five miles on, and the next twenty beyond, you camp at the five-mile water to-night and do the twenty next day. But if it's thirty miles you have to do it. Travelling with the swag in Australia is variously and picturesquely described as 'humping bluey,' 'walking Matilda,' 'humping Matilda,' 'humping your drum,' 'being on the wallaby,' 'jabbing trotters,' and 'tea and sugar burglaring,' but most travelling shearers now call themselves trav'lers, and say simply 'on the track,' or 'carrying swag.'

Swags are still carried today, though they have been updated and redesigned for modern comfort and convenience. An exception is the swag of Cameron the Swaggie; Cameron lives the life of the traditional swagman, humping his blanket and billy from town to town and reciting bush poetry from his extensive repertoire to anyone who will listen. Billed by the occasional press article as 'the last swaggie', Cameron is but one of quite a few who still follow the Wallaby Track.

A swagman's death

One of the tensions between the swagman population and the people they worked for involved authority. The 'bloke' or 'cove' was the boss of the woolshed or station where those swaggies who were in work laboured for their wages. When times were good, which was often, relations were reasonably agreeable. But in hard times conflict was bound to arise. In the early 1890s much of the eastern Australian workforce was gripped by strikes and lockouts as depression strangled the economy. In the pastoral industries there was serious violence brought on by the graziers' refusal to pay the rate the shearers demanded due to the rapid fall in the market price of wool.

It was during this period that rural workers, most of whom were swagmen by necessity, established the labour movement in the form of organised trade unionism and the origins of the Australian Labor Party. Eventually, in early 1891, there was a serious possibility of insurrection as armed shearers gathered at Barcaldine and elsewhere in Queensland. There were riots, destruction of property including telegraph wires, and arson attacks. Armed troops were deployed and in May, thousands of striking shearers raised the Southern Cross flag and assembled beneath the famed ghost gum known as 'The Tree of Knowledge' at Barcaldine, giving birth to the Australian Labor Party. Significant as these events were, they are the subject of extensive romanticisation. The strike was called off in June in favour of direct political action through the ballot box, although fourteen shearers had been found guilty of conspiracy and imprisoned. The pastoralists had employed 'scab' labour from New South Wales but as tensions eased began to hire back the rebel shearers.

But all was not yet calm. In 1894, there were more strikes over an attempt to reduce wages. One of the most violent confrontations in this period had an influence on the creation of the best-known swaggie of all, the 'jolly swagman' of the famous song. On the night of 2 September 1894, a group of armed shearers attacked Dagworth Station, northwest of Winton on the Upper Diamantina River. The police magistrate at Winton wired the Colonial Secretary.

*D*agworth woolshed was burned down by sixteen armed men. The wire stated that at about half-past twelve on Sunday morning the constable and a station hand named Tomlin were on duty/guarding the shed. The first intimation they had of any attack was the firing of about a dozen shots through the shed. This woke the Messrs. Macpherson, and the others. The firing was continued, both sides engaging in it, for about twenty minutes. While this was going on, one of the unionists was seen to sneak up under cover of the fire of his comrades and set fire to the shed. The constables and the station hands kept firing at the party, and when this ceased it was not known whether anyone was wounded. About forty shots were exchanged. Three bullets were fired through the cottage where the Macphersons were sleeping. The unionists had taken up position in the bed of the creek, at the rear of the shed, where they were almost wholly protected from the fire of the defending party. Rain fell shortly after the men left. There is hardly any doubt but that this is the same gang that has been burning all the sheds.

A number of bullet-wounded unionists were later arrested in the shearers' strike camp and:

. . . a man named Haffmeister [sic], a prominent unionist, was found dead about two miles from Kynuna. The local impression is that he was one of the attacking mob at Dagworth, and was wounded there. There were seven unionists with Hoffmeister when he died, and these assert that he committed suicide. In consequence of the seriousness of this last event the Government are taking active steps to deal with persons who are found to be armed.

The story of swaggie 'Frenchy' Hoffmeister's death was the inspiration for Paterson to pen the verses that became 'Waltzing Matilda'. He was visiting the area the following year when the events were still on everyone's minds and tongues. Apparently hoping to impress Christina Macpherson, sister of the station manager, he wrote the poem for a tune she played on her autoharp. The rest is history, if of a kind complicated by folklore.

Where the angel tarboys fly

In 1908, a swaggie calling himself 'Vagrant' gave a blow-by-blow account of the great tallies of some legendary blade men. He managed to include a little verse, a yarn or two and a wonderful story made up of many stories about the competitive and boastful life of the shearer.

The shearing figures quoted in the 'Western Champion' of the 12th of September as to shearing tallies, are not quite correct. Andy Brown did not shear at Evesham in 1886. In 1887 Jimmy Fisher shore fifty lambs in one run before breakfast there. I do not know the time; but they used to ring the bell mighty early those days. I have seen spectral-like forms creeping across the silent space between the galley and the shed long before the kookaburra woke the bush with his laughing song, and he is a pretty early bird.

The same year Black Tom Johnson got bushed in the gloom of that space, and lost half a run before breakfast. Fisher shore 288 at Kynuna the following year: he was a wonderful man for his 8 stone of humanity. The same year Alf Bligh shore 254 at Isis Downs; he and Charlie Byers were the first two men to cut 200 sheep on the Barcoo. The same year Bill Hamilton, now M.L.A., shore 200 sheep at Manfred Downs, and to him belongs the credit of shearing the first 200 on the Flinders.

The next year Bill died at Cambridge Gulf; but as he is alive and all right now, the account was exaggerated. Bill says: 'That 200 at Manfred Downs was no "cake walk".' He used twelve gallons of water cooling down. Alick Miller shore 4163 sheep in three weeks and three days at Charlotte Plains, in 1885, and Sid ('Combo') Ross shore nine lambs in nine minutes at Belalie, on the Warrego, the year before.

In the early eighties there were a good number of 200 a-day men in New South Wales; but none of those celebrated personages ventured a pilgrimage northwards until 1887, when quite a number of fast men stormed the west, and their advent started a new era in the shearing world, improved tools and methods entirely superseding the old Ward and Payne, and Serby school, and the old rum drinking ringers of the roaring days were gradually relegated to the 'snagger brigade.' Paddy M'Can, Jack Bird, Tom Green ('the Burdekin ringer'), Ned Hyles, Jack Ellis (Bendigo), Mick Hoffman ('the Peak Downs ringer'), Billy Cardham, Jim Sloane, Jack Collins, and George Taylor ('the Native') had to give way to the younger brigade with improved Burgon and Ball tools, and new ideas, and, with the advent of Jack Howe, Christy Gratz, 'Chinee' Sullivan, Billy Mantim, George Butler, Jimmy Power, Alick Miller, Jack Reid, Allan M'Callum, and others, 180 and 200 were common enough.

Later, when machinery was introduced, tallies took a further jump. Jimmy Power shore 323 at Barenya in 1892 by machines. The same year Jack Howe shore 321 by hand at Alice Downs, his tallies for the week previous being 249, 257, 259, 263, 267, 144, a total of 1439 for the week. I doubt if this record has ever been beaten. I will say right here that Jack Howe was the best shearer I have ever seen at work. The only one approaching him was Lynch, of the Darling River, New South Wales.

No doubt figures get enlarged in circulation, and tall tallies in the bar-room mount up with the fumes of bottled beer—there is a lot of sheep shorn there. Shearers do not lie, as a rule: they boast and make mistakes casually. Jack Howe once told me the biggest mistake he ever made was in trying to shake hands with himself in a panel mirror in an hotel in Maoriland. He had just landed, and made for the first hotel. You see, he had grown a beard on the trip over, and looked like a chap he used to know on the Barcoo. The mistake was considerably intensified by the barmaid's smile, as she watched Jack's good-natured recognition of an old shearing mate from Queensland.

At Kensington Downs in 1885, a big Chinaman named Ah Fat rang the shed. He could shear all right, too. The men used to take day about to run him; but the Chow had too much pace. A shearer named George Mason made great preparations to 'wipe him out' one day, and, after nearly bursting himself up to dinner-time, discovered that Ah Fat was not on the board: he was doing a lounge in the hut that day. I think that Chinaman must have died; everyone loved him, and, like Moore's 'Young Gazelle,' with its gladsome eye, he was sure to go—

To that shed beyond the sky,
Where the angel tarboys fly,
And the 'cut' will last for ever, and
the sheep are always dry.

These records may be of interest to the survivors of the old school, and may, perhaps, stir up the dormant memories of the younger ones. They have been culled from past records, written on the backs of stolen telegram forms from almost every post office between Burketown and Barringun, and are given for what they merit.

Bowyang Bill and the cocky farmer

'Bowyang Bill' recalled an experience of his younger days, just around the turn of the twentieth century. If Bill is to be believed, on this occasion at least, he worked very hard for one of the notoriously tight-fisted and hard-handed cocky farmers. (A 'bowyang' was a length of string tied around trousers just below the knee to keep them up. They were commonly worn by working men in the nineteenth century and many illustrations of swaggies feature them.)

Bowyang Bill begins his story with a short verse that could be a memorial for the swaggies' way of life and death:

For they tramp and go as the world rolls back,
They drink and gamble, and die;
But their spirits shall live on the outback track.
As long as the years go by.

*R*emember those cockles who used to wake a fellow at 2 a.m. in the morning to start the day's work? They are not so plentiful as they were 30 odd years back, but there's still a few of them milking cows or growing spuds in this State.

All this takes me back to the time when I tied my first knot in the swag and started out along the dusty tracks to make my fortune. After many weeks I came to Dawson's place. He was a long, lean hungry sort of codger, and his bleary eyes sparkled when I agreed to work for five bob a week and tucker. I didn't know Dawson or I would have wasted no time in re-hoisting Matilda and proceeding on my way. I worked 16 hours a day on that place, and lived mostly on damper and flybog. I used to get up so early in the morning that I was ashamed to look at the sleeping fowls when I passed their camping place. I never saw those fowls moving about their yard. They were sleeping on their roosts when I went to work, and they were snoozing on the same roosts when I returned to the house at night.

Things went on like this until another young cove came along with a swag. It was also his first experience 'carrying the bundle,' and no doubt that was why he also agreed to work for Dawson. He said his name was Mullery. We had tea at 11 p.m. the day he arrived, and it was midnight when we turned into our bunks in the harness-room.

Before I went to sleep I told Mullery what sort of a place it was, but he said he would stick it—until he earned a few bob to carry him along the track. In the next breath he told me he was greatly interested in astronomy. I didn't know what that was until he explained he was interested in the stars. 'Well, by cripes,' I said, 'you'll get plenty of opportunities to examine them here.'

That cove was over the odds. I'm just dozing off when he leans over and says, 'Do you know how far it is from here to Mars?' Pulling the old potato bag wagga from my face I told him I hadn't the faintest idea, as I had never travelled along the road to the blanky place. He mentioned the millions of miles it was from here to there. 'Did you measure the distance with a foot-rule?' I asked as I again drew the wagga over my face.

When old Dawson pushed his head through the door at 2 a.m. I was awake but the new chap was dead to the world. Dawson went across and yanked the blanket off him. 'Here, hurry up,' he growled, 'and get those cows milked before they get sun-stroke.' 'What's going to give them sunstroke?' asked Muller, as innocent as you like. 'Why, the blanky sun, of course,' roared Dawson. The new chap made himself more comfortable in his bunk, then he drawled, 'There's no danger of that, sir, and allow me to inform you that at this time of the year the sun is 93 million miles from the earth.'

'You're a liar,' yelled Dawson, shaking the hurricane lamp in Mullery's face, 'and if you come outside I'll prove it to you. Why, the darned sun is just peeping over the tops of the gum trees half-a-mile from here, and by the time it's well above them you'll be on the track again. Yes, you're sacked, so get out of here quick and lively.'

The Mad Eight

So far into legend have the Mad Eight faded that no one can agree on the year of their amazing feat. Depending on the sources, it occurred in 1923, 1924 or 1925. Whichever of these dates is correct, the events took place in the Gascoyne region one shearing season. In those days shearers often formed 'teams', work groups who travelled together from station to station hiring out as a work unit.

In whichever year it was, the gun shearers Nugget Williams, Bob Sawallish, Vol Day, George Bence, Tiny Lehmann, Len Saltmarsh, Charlie Fleming and Hughie Munro got together and blazed their way across the country. In nine months they shore record-breaking tallies in eleven large sheds. But it was at Williambury Station where they propelled themselves into the colourful history of shearing; between them they shore nearly 18,000 sheep in two weeks—using hand shears. This was enough for the shearing team to enter shearing history. But when it was discovered that the average weight of a fleece that year was a solid 11 pounds, they moved from history into legend, where they remain firmly today.

In 1927, the fame of the Mad Eight even reached the federal Arbitration Court. During a hearing of a pastoral industry award claim, someone brought up the feat of the 'Mad Eight'. The Chief Judge, unaware of the intricacies of shearing culture, asked for an explanation and was told by the counsel representing the employers that 'the appellation was earned by the team because of the large number of sheep they shore in a day'. What the judge made of this was apparently not recorded.

The following year, the man who actually employed the Mad Eight published his account of the event and, incidentally, provides the most reliable date for their achievement. He began by pointing out that 1927 was not a good year for high tallies:

*T*herefore it is not likely that many teams this season will cut tallies such as were cut by the 'mad eight' which I had employed at Williambury in 1923. This was the team which came so much into prominence, and was commented on by advocates of the union.

They were known as the 'mad eight' on account of their pace, and the team consisted of A. Williams, R. Sawallish, Vol Day, F. Lehmann, L. Saltmarsh, George Bence, C. Fleming and H. Munro.

The tallies given for the Mad Eight were impressive by any measure and fully confirmed their claim to legendary status:

*T*he sheep shorn averaged 11 lb. wool, and therefore the following; figures showing the daily tallies of the eight shearers for two weeks are interesting. Commencing on September 3, the team shore 1509, 1708, 1577, 1748, 1698, 927 (Saturday, half day). Total for week, 9167.

Resuming on the second week the same team clipped 1189 on September 10, losing one hour through engine trouble, 1432, 1740, 2800, 1806, 803 (Saturday, half day). Total for week, 8770. The highest individual tally was 250, and two men obtained this figure. The shearers' highest daily averages were:- A. Williams, 213; R. Sawallish, 242; Vol Day, 242; F. Lehmann, 234; L. Saltmarsh, 216; George Bence, 222; C. Fleming, 226; and H. Munro, 205. Total, 1800, and average 225.

Eye-glazing though such statistics are for most city types today, they were lovingly collated and preserved by shearers and those in the wool industry back in the roaring days when the world was wide and the country rode on the sheep's back.

NED KELLY

(Sketched as he was Leaving Benalla).

20

After the Kellys

'I look upon him as invulnerable,
you can do nothing with him.'

Aaron Sherritt on Ned Kelly

THE NED KELLY story remains an important part of Australian history and folklore. Beginning as a fairly run-of-the-mill local conflict between free selectors, squatters and police, the murders at Stringybark Creek escalated the outbreak to the country's most serious episode of outlawry. The consequences of the Kelly saga continue to haunt us and the events, real and imagined, are continually recycled in books, films and the media. But there are many untold stories about what happened after the ironclad bushranger's execution. All have their origins in the events of 1878 to 1880.

The saga

Edward, the first-born son of Ellen and James ('Red') Kelly, grew up in the hothouse atmosphere of a combination of clan-like Irish-Australian families, the Kellys, Quinns and Lloyds. Each of these families had their own extensive histories of trouble with the Victorian and other police forces, surviving as they did by a combination of legal pastoral activities and stock stealing, or 'duffing'. The Kellys and their relations were by no means the only ones involved in this business. In fact, this was the normal means of existence for most free selectors at that time, the distinction between stock that had 'strayed' and that which had been stolen being a difficult one to make.

By 1871, at the age of sixteen, Ned Kelly already had numerous experiences with the law behind him, and had served one gaol sentence. In that year he was convicted of receiving a stolen horse and given three years in Melbourne's tough Pentridge gaol. He entered prison a high-spirited, 'flash' youth and came out a hard, bitter man in February 1874.

Ned went straight for a while, working as a timber-getter in the Wombat Ranges and keeping out of trouble—until September 1877. He was arrested for drunkenness and on the way to the courthouse attempted to escape. The ensuing brawl with four policemen and a local shoemaker is notable only for the fact that two of those policemen, constables Fitzpatrick and Lonigan, were to play small but significant roles in the coming Kelly drama.

Fitzpatrick was the first to make an entrance. Seven months after the fight with Ned, the constable, probably drunk, rode up to the Kelly homestead near Greta, alone and against orders, to arrest Ned's younger brother, Dan, on a charge of horse stealing. The truth of what occurred then will never be known, but Fitzpatrick later claimed to have been assaulted and shot by the Kellys, including Ned and Mrs Kelly. The family claimed that Fitzpatrick had tried to molest one of the daughters, probably Kate, and that their actions had been justified. Six months later, Judge Redmond Barry did not agree and sent Mrs Kelly to gaol for three years, saying that he would have given Ned and Dan fifteen years apiece, if they could have been found.

Of course, they could not be found; they were safely hidden in the rugged Wombat Ranges, accompanied by two other young friends, Joe Byrne and Steve Hart. In October 1878, a party of four policemen went into the ranges to hunt the Kellys down. In charge was Sergeant Kennedy, a good bushman and a crack shot. He was aided by constables Scanlon, McIntyre and Lonigan, the same Lonigan who had fought with Ned the year before. All these men had been hand-picked for their bush craft and general police aptitude, and they made it known that they intended to get the Kellys.

On the night of 25 October they camped along the edge of a creek known as Stringybark. The following evening the four-strong Kelly gang bailed up Lonigan and McIntyre, who were minding the camp while Kennedy and Scanlon patrolled the bush in search of the outlaws. McIntyre surrendered immediately, saving his life, but Lonigan was brave and foolish enough to clutch at his revolver. Ned Kelly shot him dead. On their return to the camp, Kennedy and Scanlon were called upon to surrender, but they resisted too, and Ned killed them both in the ensuing gunfight. During the fighting McIntyre managed to clamber onto a stray horse and ride for his life.

The Melbourne and provincial newspapers reacted to the shocking news, enabling the Victorian parliament to rush through an 'Outlawry Act' that rendered those persons pronounced outlaws totally outside the law. All rights and property were forfeit and the outlaw was liable to be killed on sight by any citizen. In addition, harbourers and sympathisers were liable to fifteen years' imprisonment with hard labour and the loss of all their goods.

Less than six weeks after Stringybark Creek, the Kellys struck again. This time they robbed the bank at Euroa, a busy town about 100 miles north of Melbourne, the state capital. The bushrangers escaped with around 2000 pounds in gold and cash. Ned also stole deeds and mortgages held in the bank safe, an action that endeared him to the struggling selectors of northeastern Victoria, most of whom saw the banks as 'poor mancrushers', as Ned himself was to describe them in his 'Jerilderie Letter'.

Acting on false information intentionally supplied by one of the Kellys' 'bush telegraphs', or informants, the police went looking for the gang across the border in New South Wales. Meanwhile, back in the 'Kelly country', the bushrangers divided up the Euroa loot between themselves, relatives and sympathisers. Over the next few months, many previously impoverished selectors managed to pay off their debts, usually with crisp, new banknotes.

Frustrated in their futile attempts to capture the outlaws, the police revenged themselves on the sympathisers. A score—including Isaiah 'Wild' Wright—were arrested and confined in Beechworth gaol for periods of up to three months without trial and without evidence against them. This misguided manoeuvre made the police even more unpopular in the district as many of the prisoners missed that year's harvest, causing severe hardship for their families.

The reward for the Kellys was increased from 2000 pounds to a total of 4000, a very large sum at that time. But this had no effect upon the loyalty of the sympathisers either. After the Kellys' next escapade the reward sum would be doubled again.

On 5 February 1879, the gang appeared at Jerilderie, 46 miles across the New South Wales border, where they locked the two astounded local policemen in their own cells. The Kellys spent that night and most of the next day in the town, masquerading as police officers in their stolen police uniforms. That afternoon they occupied the bar of the Royal Mail Hotel, handily adjacent to the bank, which they then robbed. Another 2000-pound haul was made and mortgages were burned to the accompaniment of cheers from the crowd held hostage in the hotel. Everyone was treated to drinks and a speech from Ned about the injustices he had suffered at the hands of the police, the government and the squatters. More importantly, he left with one of the bank tellers a 10,000-word statement that came to be known as 'the Jerilderie Letter'.

This fascinating document catalogues Ned Kelly's and his friends' complaints and grievances, and also gives an insight into the motives and attitudes behind their actions. Among other things, the letter complains of discrimination against free selectors and small farmers, like the Kellys, by the administration, which, it is claimed, was working hand in glove with the wealthy squatters against the poor. According to Ned, the police were:

> . . . a parcel of big ugly fat-necked wombat headed big bellied magpie legged narrow hipped splay footed sons of Irish Bailiffs or English landlords . . .

The letter ends with a stern warning for the rich to be generous to the poor and not to oppress them:

I give fair warning to all those who has reason to fear me to sell out and give £10 out of every hundred towards the widow and orphan fund and do not attempt to reside in Victoria but as short a time as possible after reading this notice, neglect this and abide by the consequences, which shall be worse than the rust in the wheat in Victoria or the druth of a dry season to the grasshoppers in New South Wales. I do not wish to give the order full force without giving timely warning, but I am a widows son outlawed and my orders must be obeyed.

In an earlier letter, written just before the raid on Euroa, Ned had cautioned his readers to 'remember your railroads'. The full implications of this mysterious warning became apparent on Sunday 27 June 1880. Glenrowan, a cluster of buildings and tents surrounding a railway station, fell to the bushrangers as easily as Euroa and Jerilderie. But this time they had not come to rob a bank; they had something more ambitious in mind.

The night before, Dan Kelly and Joe Byrne had 'executed' a

one-time companion named Aaron Sherritt. Sherritt had apparently been playing the dangerous role of double agent, playing the police off against the outlaws. But his murder also had another motive, to lure the bulk of the special district police force onto a train that would have to pass through Glenrowan on its way to the scene of the murder in the Kelly country. The bushrangers planned to wreck this train and pick off the survivors, particularly the Aboriginal blacktrackers who had several times brought the police a little too close to the Kellys for comfort. Exactly what the gang intended to do after this massacre remains controversial. It has been said that they merely aimed to rob as many unprotected banks as possible; others believe that their plans were far more enterprising, involving an insurrection to establish a 'Republic of North-eastern Victoria'. Whatever the bushrangers had in mind, they were well prepared for a hard fight.

During the months before the attack on Glenrowan, plough-shares and quantities of cast iron had been disappearing throughout the Kelly country. The reason for these unusual thefts became plain when the bushrangers herded most of Glenrowan's small population into Jones's Hotel that Sunday. In the back room were four rough suits of armour, consisting of back-plates and breastplates and an adjustable metal apron to protect the groin of the wearer. Each suit weighed about 80 pounds—almost 40 kilos—and there was one metal helmet, with eye slits and a visor, weighing about 16 pounds. Ned Kelly was the only member of the gang strong enough to wear both armour and helmet and still manage to handle a gun.

About ten o'clock that night, after a round of singing, dancing and drinking with the crowd in the hotel, Ned allowed a few prisoners to go home because the police train had not arrived as early as expected. This blunder ensured the failure of the bushrangers' plot. One of the freed prisoners, the Glenrowan schoolmaster Thomas Curnow, walked along the railway track and warned the police train just outside Glenrowan.

Hearing the train stop outside the town, the bushrangers realised what had happened, buckled on their armour and stood in front of the hotel to meet the police charge that very soon came. After a lengthy exchange of shots, Ned Kelly and Joe Byrne were wounded, and the clumsiness of their armour, together with the intensely painful bruises caused whenever a bullet smashed into the metal, had become apparent. Ned lumbered into the bush to reload his revolver and fainted from loss of blood. At about the same time, Joe Byrne was killed by a stray bullet that splintered through the wooden hotel wall.

The hotel was still full of prisoners, but the police raked the building with gunfire. A young boy and an old man were both wounded, and a woman with a baby in her arms and her family in tow was frustrated three times in her attempts to escape by the police's refusal to cease firing. She was finally helped to safety by the gallantry of a bystander who braved the gunfire to rescue her, though one of her children was wounded.

Shortly after this, Ned Kelly recovered consciousness and came crashing out of the bush, firing at the police from the safety of his armour. He was finally brought down by a shotgun blast to the upper legs fired by Sergeant Steele and taken into custody.

The police then sent to Melbourne for a field-gun to demolish the weatherboard hotel along with the two bushrangers left inside, Dan Kelly and Steve Hart. Long before the gun arrived, the prisoners were all released and the police set the hotel alight. A Catholic priest among the 500 sightseers who had gathered at the railway station rushed into the burning building. He found the bodies of Dan Kelly and Steve Hart, and rescued a badly wounded old man who had been forgotten by the prisoners in their rush to escape.

It was all over; the sightseers had nothing to do but wait for the blaze to subside and then hunt for souvenirs. The relatives of the dead bushrangers waited to claim the charred bodies for burial. Ned Kelly was taken to Melbourne, where he rapidly recovered from his 30 wounds and stood trial in front of the same judge who had sentenced his mother two years before.

Not surprisingly, the verdict was 'guilty' and Edward Kelly was sentenced to hang. Strong campaigning and a petition to have the sentence commuted were unsuccessful, and at ten o'clock on the morning of Thursday 11 November 1880, Ned Kelly dropped through the gallows' trapdoor and into legend. But that was not the end of it.

A Glenrowan letter

Young bank clerk Donald Sutherland wrote to his parents about what he saw in the immediate aftermath of the siege at Glenrowan.

My Dear Parents

I have your letter by the last mail all in good time. I am sorry to learn that Maggie Ben Hill had such a narrow shave in the neighbourhood of Spittal. By Jove she must have felt the cold pretty much I guess. The weather here just now is bitter cold. I was in Beechworth the other day and the snow was coming down in great flakes. Snow-balling being indulged in all the afternoon—the ground was literally covered. The mountains are all covered some time ago and the winter garments will continue being worn by them for about 6 months yet. We have hard frost every night and in the mornings the grass is quite brittle. The ice is not strong enough for skating though—in the shade in front of the Bank here and where the sun does not shine. We have frost all day—I sleep at night with three double blankets and a greatcoat and then feel the cold.

Fresh since I last wrote you we have had great doings here—the Kellys are annihilated. The gang is completely destroyed—you will see a long and full account of all that has been done in one of *The Australasians* which I send to you along with this letter. They had a long run but were captured at last. Glenrowan is only 8 miles from Oxley and 12 from Wangaratta being the next station on the line from the latter township to Melbourne. I always thought the Kellys were in the ranges about here although some people maintained that on account of their long silence they had got away from Australia altogether. On hearing of the affray, I at once proceeded to Glenrowan to have a look at the desperados who caused me so many dreams and sleepless nights. I saw the lot of them. Ned, the leader of the gang, being the only one taken alive. He was lying on a stretcher quite calm and collected notwithstanding the great pain he must have been suffering from his wounds. He was wounded in 5 or 6 places, only in the arms and legs—his body and head being encased in armour made from the moule boards of a lot of ploughs. Now the farmers about here have been getting their moule boards taken off their ploughs at night for a long time but who ever dreamed it was the Kellys and that they would be used for such a purpose. Ned's armour alone weighed 97 pounds. The police thought he was a fiend seeing their rifle bullets mere sliding off him like hail. They were firing into him at about 10 yards in the grim light of the morning without the slightest effect. The force of the rifle bullets made him stagger when hit but it was only when they got him in the legs and arms that he reluctantly fell exclaiming as he did so 'I am done I am done'. Steele was the man who dropped him and Kelly always boasted that he would burn Steele alive before he was captured. Steele is the sergeant in charge of the police at Wangaratta and a very nice fellow. The

Kellys this time had lifted the rails to upset the train and kill and shoot everyone on it. They were then going to make the engine driver run them down the line to Benalla where they would stick up all the banks, blow up the police barracks—in fact commit wholesale slaughter and then fly to their mountain fortresses.

Ned does not at all look like a murderer and bushranger—he is a very powerful man aged about 27, black hair and beard with a soft mild looking face and eyes—his mouth being the only wicked portion of the face. After his capture he became very tame and conversed freely with those who knew him. Not having the pleasure of his acquaintance I did not speak to him although I should have liked very much to ask why he never stuck up the Bank of Victoria at Oxley. Well he had it down on his programme at one time but a schoolmaster named Wallace and one who banks with us put him off it—at least Wallace got the news conveyed through Byrne, one of the gang that he had some deeds and papers here which he did not wish destroyed as it would ruin him. Ned had said I wont do it and he didn't do it and we were consequently saved from the presence of the gang. Poor Ned I was really sorry for him to see him lying pierced by bullets and still showing no signs of pain. His 3 sisters were there also, Mrs Skillion, Kate Kelly and a younger one. Kate was sitting at his head with her arms round his neck while the others were crying in a mournful strain at the state of one who, but the night before, was the terror of the whole Colony. The night that Byrne and Dan Kelly shot Sherritt at The Woolshed they rode through Oxley on their way to Glenrowan. Some of the people in the township heard the horses go by but I didn't being sound asleep. Byrne was shot in the groin early in the morning as he was drinking a glass of whisky at the bar. Then there remained only Dan Kelly and Steve Hart—whether they shot themselves or whether they were shot by the police will ever remain a mystery. At about 2pm a policeman named Johnstone whom I knew well at Murchison fired the house and it was only when no signs of life appeared that they rushed the place to find the charred remains of Dan and Steve Hart. They presented a horrible appearance being roasted to a skeleton, black and grim reminding me of old Knick himself.

Thousands of people thronged to Glenrowan on receipt of the news and not one of the crowd there had the courage to lift the white sheet off the charred remains until I came up and struck a match—it being dark—pulling down the sheet and exposed all that remained of the 2 daring murderous bushrangers. Dan and Steve are buried in the Greta Cemetery, Byrne is buried at Benalla and Ned is now in the hospital of the Melbourne gaol treated with every care until he is strong and well enough to be hanged. Such then is bushranging in Victoria so far. I may tell you however that it is not all over yet and my belief is that another gang will be out ere long to avenge the death of the present. I could tell you much more but time and space will not permit. You can read a full and correct account from *The Australasian*. I am quite well, hoping you are all ditto.

faithfully
D G Sutherland

PS The hair enclosed is from the tail of Ned Kelly the famous murderer and bushranger's mare. His favourite mare who followed him all round the trees during the firing. He said he wouldn't care for himself if he thought his mare safe.

'I thought it was a circus'

On Saturday 14 May 1881, less than a year after Dan's death and six months since Ned's hanging, the members of the Royal Commission investigating the causes of the Kelly outbreak rode up unannounced to the family home in Greta. They were met by Ned's mother, Ellen.

*H*er residence, a four-roomed slab hut, with a bark roof, stands in the middle of a paddock comprising about 10 acres. It is within a short distance from a mountain, called Quarry-hill, whence a good view of the surrounding country can be obtained. Within the paddock there were two or three horses and as many cows, and there were a few fowls and a tame kangaroo about the house. But the place presented a gloomy, desolate appearance. There was a very small kitchen garden, but there was no other land under cultivation. Some of the panes of glass in the windows were broken, and, excepting that some creepers had very recently been planted at the foot of the verandah posts, no attempt had been made to beautify the house, or make this home look homely.

When the commission pulled up on the road opposite the front-door that door was closed, there was no sign of any human being about. Presently, however, a child was observed peeping round the back of the house at the strangers. After a short consultation it was decided that it would be better for the commission, as they were near the house, to ask Mrs Kelly if she had any statement to make on the subjects that they have been appointed to inquire into. Accordingly, Messrs Graves and Anderson were told-off to go to the house and open up communication with Mrs Kelly. She came round from the back of the house to meet them, and intimated, when she was told of the object of the visit, that she had no objection to see the commission.

The remaining members were then called up, and introduced by Mr Graves to Mrs Kelly. She was dressed in black, and seemed to be between 40 and 45 years of age. In her younger days she was probably comely, and her hair is still abundant, and black as a raven's wing. Although looking careworn, she has evidently a large stock of vitality. Her eyes and mouth are the worst features in her face, the former having a restless and furtive, and the latter a rather cruel look. When Mr Graves introduced the other commissioners, Mrs Kelly said with a smile, 'I didn't know who you could all be; I thought it was a circus.'

. . . after a short and rather uncomfortable pause, Mr Longmore undeceived Mrs Kelly by informing her that they were the Police Commission and would be glad to listen to anything she had to say. She did not invite the commissioners into her house or open the front door, and two or three very young children—her offspring—could be seen inside the house, peering through a window. One of these children was a pretty little girl about four or five years old and her face reminded one very forcibly of Ned Kelly, whose hair and eyes were of a different colour from his mother's.

Ellen Kelly made the same charges she had made many times before and would make many times again:

*T*he police have treated my children very badly. I have three very young ones, and had one only a fortnight old when I got into trouble [referring to her recent imprisonment in connexion with the assault on Constable Fitzpatrick at Greta]. That child I took to Melbourne with me, but I left Kate and Grace and the younger children behind. The police used to treat them very ill. They used to take them out of bed at night, and make them walk before them. The police made the children go first when examining a house, so as to prevent the out-laws if in the house, from suddenly shooting them.

Kate is now only about 16 years old, and is still a mere child. She is older than Grace. Mrs Skillian is married, and of course, knew more than the others, who are mere children. She is not in the house now. Mr Brook Smith was the worst behaved of the force, and had less sense than any of them. He used to throw things out of the house, and he came in once to the lock-up staggering drunk. I did not like his conduct. That was at Benalla. I wonder they allowed a man to behave as he did to an unfortunate woman. He wanted me to say things that were not true.

My holding comprises 88 acres, but it is not all fenced in. The Crown will not give me a title. If they did I could sell at once and leave this locality. I was entitled to a lease a long time ago, but they are keeping it back. Perhaps, if I had a lease, I might stay for a while, if they would let me alone. I want to live quietly. The police keep coming backwards and forwards, and saying there are 'reports, reports.' As to the papers, there was nothing but lies in them from the beginning. I would sooner be closer to a school, on account of my children. If I had anything forward I would soon go away from here.

Mrs Kelly was then asked if her children had any complaints:

Mrs. Kelly knocked at the front door, and called out to her daughter Grace to open it. Grace did so, and after much persuasion on the part of her mother, came to the open door, but speedily retreated behind it. She seems about 14 or 15 years old, and bears a much greater resemblance to her brother Ned than either Mrs. Skillian or Miss Kate Kelly do. Most of the party, seeing that the girl was bashful, withdrew from the house, and then Grace made a statement to Mr. Longmore and one or two others to the effect that one of her brother Ned's last requests was that his sisters should make full statements as to how the police had treated them.

She then continued as follows:—'On one occasion Detective Ward threatened to shoot me if I did not tell him where my brothers were, and he pulled out his revolver. The police used to come here and pull the things about. Mr. Brook Smith was one of them. He used to chuck our milk, flour, and honey, on the floor. Once they pulled us in our night clothes out of bed. Sergeant Steele was one of that party.'

Mrs. Kelly further stated that when she 'came out' her children's clothes were rotten, because of their having been thrown out of doors by the police. The police, also, had destroyed a clock and a lot of pictures, and threatened to pull down the house over their heads. She was understood to make a statement to the effect that the police had made improper overtures to some of her daughters, but she afterwards said that she had no such charge to make.

Mr. Longmore and one or two others went into the sitting room, which was very poorly furnished, and the ceiling of which was in a very dilapidated condition. All the inside doors leading into this room were shut, and it seemed tolerably certain that the commission did not see all who were in the house.

A death in Forbes

On 18 October 1898, the Forbes newspaper carried a report of an inquest held at the pub. A 36-year-old local woman known as Ada Foster was dead. A young police constable gave his evidence:

I received information that the deceased had left her infant, five weeks old, without any person to care for it. I made diligent search to try and ascertain her whereabouts, but failed to find any trace; the infant and other three small children were taken care of by a neighbour; I communicated with her husband, and saw him on Saturday evening; I continued making search to find her whereabouts till yesterday about 12.30 when I was informed that the body was floating in the lagoon; in company with Constable Kennedy I proceeded town [*sic*] the lagoon down the Condobolin road, and at the rear of Ah Toy's residence, I there saw the body floating face downwards, about ten feet from the bank against a log; the lower portion of the back was bare, the clothes having fallen over the head; we removed the body from the lagoon and conveyed it to the Carlton Hotel . . .

The medical officer deposed:

*Y*esterday afternoon I made an examination of the body of the deceased; owing to the advanced stage of decomposition it was impossible to form any definite opinion as to the cause of death, or to recognise the presence of marks of violence; if the body was in the water seven or eight days it would present the appearance it did; I should think the body by its appearance had been laying in the water from four to eight days.

A neighbour gave evidence that Mrs Foster was 'slightly under the influence of drink' and asked her to look after her five-week-old infant 'as she wanted to go away for a couple of days to get straight'.

William Henry Foster, estranged husband of the deceased, had been in the marital home the day before his wife's disappearance. She 'was under the influence of drink', he said. He had 'frequently heard my wife threaten to commit suicide when under the influence of drink, especially since her sister did so'.

The verdict surprised nobody: 'found drowned in the lagoon on the Condobolin Road, on the 14th instant, but there was no evidence to show how deceased got into the water'.

A week or so later, a stranger drove into town in a dray to collect the three Foster children. His name was Jim, surviving brother of Ned. The woman who had come to such a miserable end in the Forbes lagoon was the famous Kate Kelly.

Known to the magazines of the day as 'the girl who helped Ned Kelly', Kate had been one of Australia's first teen celebrities. The momentous events of 1878–80 had thrust her into the local, colonial and national limelight. The press and the police had her down as one of the gang's main accomplices, secretly taking them food, clothes and ammunition and eliding the traps on wild goose chases miles from where the Kellys were hiding. Most of it was fiction; elder sister Maggie had done most of the aiding and abetting. But Kate was young, good looking and, like all the Kellys, feisty. They followed her movements, quoted her statements and made the ill-educated young girl a star.

Her notorious brother was hanged at 10 a.m. on 11 November 1880. That night, Kate and brother Jim, together with Ettie, Steve Hart's sister and reputed sweetheart of Ned, appeared on stage at the Apollo Theatre:

> A disgraceful scene took place last night at the Apollo hall, where Kate Kelly and her brother James Kelly were exhibited by some speculators. They occupied arm-chairs upon the stage, and conversed with those present. The charge for admission was one shilling and several hundreds of persons paid for admission.

The show was reported in Sydney a couple of weeks later. The police, worried about the impact on the local larrikins, closed it down. Subsequently, Kate was reportedly giving displays of her riding skills and working in an Adelaide hotel as a kind of celebrity barmaid. The press tracked Kate for a while but then she disappeared.

We now know that she went to live and work in the Forbes district. She married local man 'Brickie' Foster in 1888 and became Mrs Ada Foster to the world. She is buried in the Forbes cemetery under her married name, though 'nee Kelly' appears in brackets immediately below on her gravestone.

Living legends

One of the many Kelly legends had it that Dan Kelly and Steve Hart did not burn to cinders in the Glenrowan Hotel, but instead escaped to South Africa. In Pretoria, during the Boer War, the correspondent to the *London Daily Express* met them.

*O*ne night, when Pretorians, under martial law regulations, had long retired to rest, I was aroused by a knock at the door. On opening it my acquaintance, now nervous and excited, walked in. 'I have brought them,' he whispered mysteriously. 'What's that?' I asked. 'The boys.' 'What boys?' 'Dan and Steve.' 'Oh! you mean the Kellys? Show them in,' I said, flippantly.

He scowled reprovingly. He went out, and quickly returned with a deputation of two men of middle age, athletic, keen-eyed, sunburnt, firm-featured, typical Australian bushmen, who evidently knew what roughing it meant. There was no necessity for introductions. It was quite true I had met or nodded to them a score of times before that night. I did not know them, however, as 'Dan Kelly' and 'Steve Hart.' They sat down, and made themselves at home.

'Now, which is Dan Kelly?' I asked. 'Here,' said the darker-complexioned of the two, 'but you must not say that name again.' And don't say mine, either,' said Steve Hart. 'What! Are you afraid?' 'Well, we don't want it known,' said Kelly. Then he added earnestly, 'You promise never to mention this?' 'But why did you come to me?' 'Well, he,' pointing to the acquaintance, 'persuaded us. Now you promise that, or by—' His voice was husky, and I interrupted, 'You needn't fear, for, in the first place, I have only your word for it and, in the second place, I have no ambition to court the anger of the Kellys.' 'Well, that's all right.'

A bottle was opened, pipes were filled, and long after midnight Dan Kelly, who had listened enthusiastically to stories of Ben Hall, Frank Gardiner, Gilbert, Burke, Vane, O'Meally, and other earlier Australian bushrangers, combed his bushy hair with his fingers, and said:—'I don't mind you using this if it's worth while, but not before, say, three weeks, and we're safe away. Steve and me and Ned and Joe Byrne was in that hotel all right. Ned got away, and we wus to follow him; but Joe was drunk, and we couldn't pull him together.

'When we wusn't watching, Joe walked outside and wus shot. After that two drunken coves was shot dead through the window.

They wanted to have a go at the police, so we gave them rifles, revolvers, and powder and shot. The firing where they fell wus too hot for Steve and me to reach them, so our rifles and revolvers wus found by their remains. This wus why they thought we wus dead. I'm sorry these coves didn't take my tip, and go out with a flag, but they had the drink and the devil in them. I think Joe's recklessness maddened them.

'Well, me and Steve planned an escape. We wus in a trap and had to get out of it. We had with us, as we often had, traps' [police] uniforms and troopers' caps, and we put them on. We looked policemen in disguise all right, I tell you. The next question was how to leave the pub quietly. A few trees, bushes, and logs at the back decided us. We crawled a few yards and then blazed away at the shanty just like the traps. We retreated slow from tree to tree and bush to bush, pretending to take cover. Yes, cover from Steve and me!

'Soon we wus among the scattered traps, who, no doubt, reckoned we wus cowards. But we banged away at the blooming pub, more than any of them. The traps came from 100 miles around, and only some know'd each other. So how could they tell us from themselves? We worked back into the timber, and got away. Soon afterwards we saw the pub blazing. Then we thanked our stars we wus not burnt alive. Well, we got to a shepherd's hut, and we stayed there days.

'The shepherd brought us the Melbourne papers, with pages about our terrible end—burnt-up bodies and all that sort of stuff. We heard of Ned's capture, and we wus both for taking to the bush again; but the shepherd made us promise to leave Australia. He found us clothes and money. We got to Sydney and shipped to the Argentine. We've had a fairly good time since, and ain't been interfered with. We don't want to interfere with anybody either.

'A few days ago we crossed to South Africa. The war broke out, and, not having work, we went to the front. We had some narrer escapes, but nothing like the narrer escape from that pub. We're off in an hour or so, but we don't want the world to know where. You can say what I told you, but wait three weeks or a month. Now, listen! If you give Steve and me away, this little thing in the hands of a friend of mine will blow you out'—and he put the point of his revolver almost into my eye. I looked at him sharply, and the awful glare in his eyes convinced me he meant it.

Six weeks later I was surprised to encounter Dan Kelly and Steve Hart in Adderley-street, Cape Town. Dan Kelly said: 'Well, you kept y'r promise. We haven't heard nothing. You may write what you like after to-morrow.'

I did not inquire their destination, and they did not volunteer the information.

The stranger

Over six foot tall and weighing thirteen and a half stone, Isaiah 'Wild'Wright was one of the most colourful of the Kelly country's many brawlers. A relative of the Kellys by marriage, he had a fine eye for a horse and had done time for stealing some. He was a prominent sympathiser; after the shootings at Stringybark Creek, Wright and his brother were locked up for publicly goading the police.

On Monday, two friends of the Kellys came into the township from Benalla, viz, Isaiah (or Wild) Wright and his brother, a deaf and dumb man. Isaiah Wright underwent imprisonment about a year ago for horse-stealing. He stated in the hotel bars that he meant to go out and join Kelly, and somewhat in bravo style warned one or two persons to stay in the township to-day unless they wanted to get shot. He said he believed Kelly would torture Kennedy, and he was only sorry for Scanlan. Though a good many of Wright's remarks only amounted to his customary bluster, yet the police thought it prudent to lock both brothers up. They were about the streets when the party started, and had their horses ready, so it was not improbable that one of them meant to ride straight off with news to Kelly. The arrest of 'Wild' Wright was made so hurriedly that he had no time to resist.

Imprisonment had no effect on Wright. He continued to intimidate and insult the police at every opportunity:

There was considerable excitement in Mansfield last night, just as the people were going to church, occasioned by the freaks and threats of Wild Wright, a relative of the Kellys. A body of police, numbering about 13, including a black tracker, had just arrived, and some of them were standing at the corner of the street. Wright called them dogs, curs, and many other opprobrious names. He told them to follow him, and he would lead them to the Kellys, as he was going to join the gang. He was mounted on a good horse, and just keeping a short distance between himself and the police, he then asked the police to come out in the bush with him a little way and he would pot them. Four of the police made towards Wright, but he rode away out of their reach, and still threatened them if they would come a little distance out of the town. He said, 'All the f***ing police in Mansfield can't take me.'

Sub-Inspector Pewtress then ordered two troopers to mount and arrest him. They pursued him for about two miles, but Wright was too well mounted, and gave the troopers the slip on the Benalla road. This morning Mr. Pewtress has sent a constable with a summons to Wright's house for him to appear for using threatening language. It is to be hoped he will not be let off as easy as he was last time.

Later the same month, Wright was again reported in the Mansfield pub:

In the bar parlour of the principal hotel in Mansfield, this evening, Wild Wright said he had heard that Donnelly had turned policeman, and gone out with the traps after Kelly adding, if he had, he was a b***dy dog, and deserved shooting for so turning round; thus in the most open manner avowing his sympathy with the Kelly mob.

Wright was among the first fourteen sympathisers to be arrested in January 1879. Although there was no evidence to hold them, under the provisions of the *Felon's Apprehension Act*, they were continually remanded every seven days and would not be released for over three months. During the proceedings, Wild Wright addressed Superintendent Hare in court:

*n*o wonder you blush; you ought to be ashamed of your self'; and then turning to the Bench, 'Your Worship said you give me fair play, but you are not giving me fair play now. I don't know how some of these men stand it.'

Mr Wyatt said that he had been misunderstood and misrepresented on the previous Saturday. What he had meant was that he would give Wright fair play, and thought it best to be remanded.

Wright remained defiant, threatening the magistrate with violence when he was remanded yet again. He was not released until April, and was the last to be freed:

*W*hen the Kelly sympathisers were brought up yesterday, and Superintendent Furnell asked for a further remand, Mr Foster said it was his duty to act independently, and to do that which to his conscience seemed just and legal, and he did not feel justified in granting a further remand; he should there-fore discharge the accused. The whole of the men were then formally discharged. Isaiah Wright was brought up last, when Mr Foster said:— 'Isaiah Wright, your fellow prisoners have been discharged, and I propose to discharge you also. Several weeks since you, when in that dock, were foolish enough and cowardly enough to threaten me—foolish, because what you said could but prejudice your position; a coward, because you attempted to intimidate me when simply doing my duty, and that a very unpleasant one. My acts were official ones, and done in the interest of society, and it was a cowardly thing to make them the subject of personal enmity. It has been a subject of serious reflection with me whether I ought not to place you under substantial bonds to keep the peace, but this would probably cause your return to gaol, where you have so long been; and, trusting that the words were uttered in the heat of the moment, and that there is no ulterior intention of wrong, I discharge you.' Wright said 'Thank you,' and left the court.

Wild Wright missed no further opportunity to harass the police, even across the border into New South Wales after the Kellys robbed the Jerilderie bank.

*W*ild Wright has been in Jerilderie since Monday and is still here. He has been locked up and fined 5s [5 shillings] for being drunk and disorderly. To-day he was behaving in a most disgraceful manner, calling out in the street, when there was no police within hearing, 'Hurrah for the Kellys.' He is accompanied by another man.

Wright was one of the most important of Kelly's people, assisting with the preparations for Glenrowan and narrowly avoiding being arrested in the aftermath as he passed 'hot words' with the police taking the wounded Ned away. He tried to convince the police to give up the charred remains of Dan Kelly and Steve Hart and helped out at their funerals. After becoming involved with the petition to save Kelly from execution, he returned to his horse-stealing ways for a while, serving a seven-year sentence for one such crime.

He turned up again at Hartwood during the shearers' strikes of the early 1890s, where according to the memories of Hugh Eastman, Wright approached him for a job of shearing. Eastman asked the well-mounted bushman a few questions:

'Shearing anywhere this year?'

'Shure, I never shore a sheep last year.'

'Where were you shearing last year? You say you are a shearer.'

'Shure, I never shore a sheep last year.'

'What have you been doing in your spare time?'

'I've been doing a lot of jail, I'm just after doing seven years for stealing a horse along with Jim Kelly.'* (Wild now provided some helpful advice. 'If you are ever short of a horse, shake it on your own, don't go with another man or you are sure to be lagged.')

'What is your name anyhow?'

'You know my name right enough.'

'No, you are a stranger to me.'

'Well, I'm not woild at 'art, but they call me Woild Wright.'

'The devil you are. I wish I'd known that before giving you the pen.'

'Ah sure, you will not find me woild at arl.'

(* Not the brother of Ned, another Jim Kelly)

Wild Wright won the job and turned out to be 'one of the best blade men' Eastman had come across in a lifetime of sheep farming. He was still a prodigious drinker and still a show-off. Once while working for Eastman, Wright leapt onto the bare back of his horse, galloped straight at the shearer's dining area then vaulted over the animal's head to land on his feet inside. He sat down calmly to take his meal. Still 'flash'.

Wright then went to the Riverina, continuing his wild ways.

He turned up at the home of another old Kelly country mate, 'Bricky' Williamson, in Coolamon (New South Wales) around 1901, then disappeared. He died, probably in the Northern Territory in 1911. Or perhaps, as Eastman records:

*Y*ears afterwards, in the back country, a derelict, all broken up, was buried by the police on the roadside where he fell—the end of a queer misfit.

21

The child in the bush

Captain Cook
Broke his hook
Fishing for Australia,
Captain Cook wrote a book
All about Australia.

Colonial children's rhyme

THE LIVES OF colonial children were sometimes as hard as those of their parents. Often left to themselves, children developed their own ways to entertain themselves based on the venerable traditions of playing improvised games of chasing, hiding and running. Where there were any toys, they were few in number and so storytelling and, for younger children, nursery rhymes were important ways to learn and be entertained. Sadly, children were also vulnerable to the dangers of pioneering the bush.

The beanstalk in the bush

In the era before film, radio and television, people needed to entertain themselves. Much of this took place within the family and usually involved playing parlour games like charades, singing together and telling stories. So-called 'fairy tales' were popular, both with adults and children, to whom they were often told at bedtime. This very early version of the classic story about the naïve boy and his magic bean was told to a child in Sydney around 1860. Like many 'fairy' tales, there are no fairies in it.

*T*here was once upon a time a poor widow who had an only son named Jack, and a cow named Milky-white. And all they had to live on was the milk the cow gave every morning, which they carried to the market and sold. But one morning Milky-white gave no milk, and they didn't know what to do.

'What shall we do, what shall we do?' said the widow, wringing her hands.

'Cheer up, mother, I'll go and get work somewhere,' said Jack.

'We've tried that before, and nobody would take you,' said his mother; 'we must sell Milky-white and with the money start a shop, or something.'

'All right, mother,' says Jack; 'it's market-day today, and I'll soon sell Milky-white, and then we'll see what we can do.'

So he took the cow's halter in his hand, and off he started. He hadn't gone far when he met a funny-looking old man, who said to him: 'Good morning, Jack.'

'Good morning to you,' said Jack, and wondered how he knew his name.

'Well, Jack, and where are you off to?' said the man.

'I'm going to market to sell our cow here.'

'Oh, you look the proper sort of chap to sell cows,' said the man; 'I wonder if you know how many beans make five.'

'Two in each hand and one in your mouth,' says Jack, as sharp as a needle.

'Right you are,' says the man, 'and here they are, the very beans themselves,' he went on, pulling out of his pocket a number of strange-looking beans. 'As you are so sharp,' says he, 'I don't mind doing a swop with you—your cow for these beans.'

'Go along,' says Jack; 'wouldn't you like it?'

'Ah! you don't know what these beans are,' said the man; 'if you plant them overnight, by morning they grow right up to the sky.'

'Really?' said Jack; 'you don't say so.'

'Yes, that is so, and if it doesn't turn out to be true you can have your cow back.'

'Right,' says Jack, and hands him over Milky-white's halter and pockets the beans.

Back goes Jack home, and as he hadn't gone very far it wasn't dusk by the time he got to his door.

'Back already, Jack?' said his mother; 'I see you haven't got Milky-white, so you've sold her. How much did you get for her?'

'You'll never guess, mother,' says Jack.

'No, you don't say so. Good boy! Five pounds, ten, fifteen, no, it can't be twenty.'

'I told you you couldn't guess. What do you say to these beans; they're magical, plant them overnight and—'

'What!' says Jack's mother, 'have you been such a fool, such a dolt, such an idiot, as to give away my Milky-white, the best milker in the parish, and prime beef to boot, for a set of paltry beans? Take that! Take that! Take that! And as for your precious beans here they go out of the window. And now off with you to bed. Not a sup shall you drink, and not a bite shall you swallow this very night.'

So Jack went upstairs to his little room in the attic, and sad and sorry he was, to be sure, as much for his mother's sake, as for the loss of his supper. At last he dropped off to sleep.

When he woke up, the room looked so funny. The sun was shining into part of it, and yet all the rest was quite dark and shady. So Jack jumped up and dressed himself and went to the window. And what do you think he saw? Why, the beans his mother had thrown out of the window into the garden had sprung up into a big beanstalk which went up and up and up till it reached the sky. So the man spoke truth after all.

The beanstalk grew up quite close past Jack's window, so all he had to do was to open it and give a jump on to the beanstalk which ran up just like a big ladder. So Jack climbed, and he climbed and he climbed and he climbed and he climbed and he climbed and he climbed till at last he reached the sky. And when he got there he found a long broad road going as straight as a dart. So he walked along and he walked along and he walked along till he came to a great big tall house, and on the doorstep there was a great big tall woman.

'Good morning, mum,' says Jack, quite polite-like. 'Could you be so kind as to give me some breakfast?' For he hadn't had anything to eat, you know, the night before and was as hungry as a hunter.

'It's breakfast you want, is it?' says the great big tall woman, 'it's breakfast you'll be if you don't move off from here. My man is an ogre and there's nothing he likes better than boys broiled on toast. You'd better be moving on or he'll soon be coming.'

'Oh! please, mum, do give me something to eat, mum. I've had nothing to eat since yesterday morning, really and truly, mum,' says Jack. 'I may as well be broiled as die of hunger.'

Well, the ogre's wife was not half so bad after all. So she took Jack into the kitchen, and gave him a hunk of bread and cheese and a jug of milk. But Jack hadn't half finished these when thump! thump! thump! the whole house began to tremble with the noise of someone coming.

'Goodness gracious me! It's my old man,' said the ogre's wife, 'what on earth shall I do? Come along quick and jump in here.' And she bundled Jack into the oven just as the ogre came in.

He was a big one, to be sure. At his belt he had three calves strung up by the heels, and he unhooked them and threw them down on the table and said:

'Here, wife, broil me a couple of these for breakfast. Ah! What's this I smell?

Fee-fi-fo-fum,
I smell the blood of an Englishman.

Be he alive, or be he dead,
I'll have his bones to grind my bread.'

'Nonsense, dear,' said his wife, 'you're dreaming. Or perhaps you smell the scraps of that little boy you liked so much for yesterday's dinner. Here, you go and have a wash and tidy up, and by the time you come back your breakfast'll be ready for you.'

So off the ogre went, and Jack was just going to jump out of the oven and run away when the woman told him not. 'Wait till he's asleep,' says she; 'he always has a doze after breakfast.'

Well, the ogre had his breakfast, and after that he goes to a big chest and takes out of it a couple of bags of gold, and down he sits and counts till at last his head began to nod and he began to snore till the whole house shook again.

Then Jack crept out on tiptoe from his oven, and as he was passing the ogre he took one of the bags of gold under his arm, and off he pelters till he came to the beanstalk, and then he threw down the bag of gold, which of course fell into his mother's garden, and then he climbed down and climbed down till at last he got home and told his mother and showed her the gold and said: 'Well, mother, wasn't I right about the beans? They are really magical, you see.'

So they lived on the bag of gold for some time, but at last they came to the end of it, and Jack made up his mind to try his luck once more up at the top of the beanstalk. So one fine morning he rose up early, and got on to the beanstalk, and he climbed and he climbed and he climbed and he climbed and he climbed and he climbed till at last he came out on to the road again and up to the great big tall house he had been to before.

There, sure enough, was the great big tall woman a-standing on the doorstep.

'Good morning, mum,' says Jack, as bold as brass, 'could you be so good as to give me something to eat?'

'Go away, my boy,' said the big tall woman, 'or else my man will eat you up for breakfast. But aren't you the youngster who came here once before? Do you know, that very day, my man missed one of his bags of gold.'

'That's strange, mum,' said Jack, 'I dare say I could tell you something about that, but I'm so hungry I can't speak till I've had something to eat.'

Well, the big tall woman was so curious that she took him in and gave him something to eat. But he had scarcely begun munching it as slowly as he could when thump! thump! thump! they heard the giant's footstep, and his wife hid Jack away in the oven.

All happened as it did before. In came the ogre as he did before, said: 'Fee-fi-fo-fum,' and had his breakfast of three broiled oxen. Then he said: 'Wife, bring me the hen that lays the golden eggs.' So she brought it, and the ogre said: 'Lay,' and it laid an egg all of gold. And then the ogre began to nod his head, and to snore till the house shook.

Then Jack crept out of the oven on tiptoe and caught hold of the golden hen, and was off before you could say 'Jack Robinson'. But this time the hen gave a cackle which woke the ogre, and just as Jack got out of the house he heard him calling:

'Wife, wife, what have you done with my golden hen?'

And the wife said: 'Why, my dear?'

But that was all Jack heard, for he rushed off to the beanstalk and climbed down like a house on fire. And when he got home he showed his mother the wonderful hen, and said 'Lay' to it; and it laid a golden egg every time he said 'Lay.'

Well, Jack was not content, and it wasn't very long before he determined to have another try at his luck up there at the top of the beanstalk. So one fine morning, he rose up early, and got on to the beanstalk, and he climbed and he climbed and he climbed and he climbed till he got to the top. But this time he knew better than to go straight to the ogre's house. And when he got near it, he waited behind a bush till he saw the ogre's wife come out with a pail to get some water, and then he crept into the house and got into the copper. He hadn't been there long when he heard thump! thump! thump! as before, and in come the ogre and his wife.

'Fee-fi-fo-fum, I smell the blood of an Englishman,' cried out the ogre. 'I smell him, wife; I smell him.'

'Do you, my dearie?' says the ogre's wife. 'Then, if it's that little rogue that stole your gold and the hen that laid the golden eggs he's sure to have got into the oven.' And they both rushed to the oven. But Jack wasn't there, luckily, and the ogre's wife said: 'There you are again with your fee-fi-fo-fum. Why of course it's the boy you caught last night that I've just broiled for your breakfast. How forgetful I am, and how careless you are not to know the difference between live and dead after all these years.'

So the ogre sat down to the breakfast and ate it, but every now and then he would mutter: 'Well, I could have sworn—' and he'd get up and search the larder and the cupboards and everything, only, luckily, he didn't think of the copper.

After breakfast was over, the ogre called out, 'Wife, wife, bring me my golden harp.' So she brought it and put it on the table before him. Then he said: 'Sing!' and the golden harp sang most beautifully. And it went on singing till the ogre fell asleep, and commenced to snore like thunder.

Then Jack lifted up the copper-lid very quietly and got down like a mouse and crept on hands and knees till he came to the table, when up he crawled, caught hold of the golden harp and dashed with it towards the door. But the harp called out quite loud: 'Master! Master!' and the ogre woke up just in time to see Jack running off with his harp.

Jack ran as fast as he could, and the ogre came rushing after, and would soon have caught him only Jack had a start and dodged him a bit and knew where he was going. When he got to the beanstalk the ogre was not more than twenty yards away when suddenly he saw Jack disappear like, and when he came to the end of the road he saw Jack underneath climbing down for dear life. Well, the ogre didn't like trusting himself to such a ladder, and he stood and waited, so Jack got another start.

But just then the harp cried out: 'Master! Master!' and the ogre swung himself down on to the beanstalk, which shook with his weight. Down climbs Jack, and after him climbed the ogre. By this time Jack had climbed down and climbed down and climbed down till he was very nearly home. So he called out: 'Mother! Mother! bring me an axe, bring me an axe.' And his mother came rushing out with the axe in her hand, but when she came to the beanstalk she stood stock still with fright for there she saw the ogre with his legs just through the clouds.

But Jack jumped down and got hold of the axe and gave a chop at the beanstalk which cut it half in two. The ogre felt the beanstalk shake and quiver so he stopped to see what was the matter. Then Jack gave another chop with the axe, and the beanstalk was cut in two and began to topple over. Then the ogre fell down and broke his crown, and the beanstalk came toppling after.

Then Jack showed his mother his golden harp, and what with showing that and selling the golden eggs, Jack and his mother became very rich, and he married a great princess; and they lived happy ever after.

Forgotten nursery rhymes

Most of us associate nursery rhymes with faraway times and other countries. But in the nineteenth century and well into the twentieth, they continued to be an important part of growing up in Australia. There was a surge of interest in creating distinctively Australian rhymes and many writers as well as interested amateurs contributed their efforts to magazines and newspapers. Ethel Turner, author of the famed *Seven Little Australians*, came up with a number, including this one:

Have you seen the cat of Dorothy Lee?
The one she calls her Catty-Puss?
If she's proud of her pet, then what should I be?
I've got a duck-billed Platypus.

Some were dreadful, but many provide an insight into the times in which they were written.

A couple of efforts relate to the gold rushes:

Little Brown Betty lived under a pan,
And brewed good ale for digger-men.
Digger-men came every day,
And little Brown Betty went hopping away.

And:

Little Tommy Drew
Went to Wallaroo
To search for a mine.
He walked by the road
And found a big load,
And said, 'What a rich man am I.'

Not surprisingly for a country that owed much of its wealth to wool, many nationalistic nursery rhymes involved sheep:

The man from Mungundi was counting sheep;
He counted so many he went to sleep.
He counted by threes and he counted by twos,
The rams and the lambs and the wethers and ewes;
He counted a thousand, a hundred and ten—
And when he woke up he'd to count them again.

These simple rhymes could even be made to serve a political purpose, as in the 'Nursery rhyme for young squatters':

Baa baa squatter's sheep
Where is all the wool?
Lost by the floods and drought,
Save three bags full.
One for the mortgagee
And one for debts to meet;
And one for the greedy boys
Who rule Macquarie Street.

Sydney also featured in one or two ditties:

Johnny and Jane and Jack and Lou;
Butler's Stairs through Woolloomooloo;
Woolloomooloo, and 'cross the Domain,
Round the Block, and home again!
Heigh, ho! Tipsy toe,
Give us a kiss and away we go.

A more ambitious treatment of children's rhymes came from William Anderson Cawthorne, who provided an Australianised version of the classic 'Who Killed Cock Robin?'

Who killed Cockatoo?
I, said the Mawpawk,
With my tomahawk:
I killed Cockatoo.

Who saw him die?
I, said the Opossum,

From the gum-blossom:
I saw him die.

Who caught his blood?
I, said the Lark,
With this piece of bark:
I caught his blood.

Who'll make his shroud?
I, said the Eagle,
With my thread and needle:
I'll make his shroud.

Who'll be chief mourner?
I, said the Plover,
For I was his lover:
I'll be chief mourner.

Who'll dig his grave?
I, said the Wombat,
My nails for my spade:
I'll dig his grave.

Who'll say a prayer?
I, said the Magpie,
My best I will try:
I'll say a prayer.

Who'll bear him to his tomb?
I, said the Platypus,
On my back, gently, thus:
I'll bear him to his tomb.

Who'll be the parson?
I, said the Crow,
Solemn and slow:
I'll be the parson.

Who'll carry the link?
I, said the Macaw,
With my little paw:
I'll carry the link.

Who'll chant a psalm?
I, said the Black Swan,
I'll sing his death song:
I'll chant a psalm.

Who'll watch in the night?
I, said the Wild Dog,
As he crept from a log:
I'll watch in the night.

Who'll toll the bell?
I, said the Pelican,
Again and again:
I'll toll the bell.

Then droop'd every head,
And ceas'd every song,
As onward they sped,
All mournful along.

All join in a ring,
With wing linking wing,
And trilling and twittering,

Around the grave sing:

Alas! Cockatoo,
How low cost thou lie;
A long, sad adieu!
A fond parting sigh!

Not satisfied with one attempt, Cawthorne went on to pen a second instalment to the story:

Then came the Wild Cat,
And the bushy-tail Rat,
With a squeak and a mew;
While, in a hop,
Up came, with a pop,
The big Kangaroo.

The Quail, and the Rail,
Were there without fail;
And the pretty Blue Wren,
With master Emu,
And screeching Curlew,
From a beautiful glen.

And the bird of the Mound,
In Murray-scrub found,
With its eggs in a row;
And the Parrot with crest,
In a green and blue vest,
As grand as a beau.

And the Lyre Bird, grand,
That ne'er still will stand,

Came in on tip-toe.
And straw-colored Ibis,
Once worshipped with Isis,
Was present also.

And the Bronze-winged Pigeon,
And the roly fat Widgeon,
From hill and from dell;
And he that doth build
A bower well filled
With spangle and shell.

Then flying very fast,
Came Laughing Jackass,
Hoo hoo hoo! ha ha ha!
While he gobbled a snail,
And wagged his big tail!
Hoo hoo boo! ha ha ha!

And the Snake, sneaking sly
With his sharp glittering eye,
As he searches and pries;
And the Lizard with frill,
Like a soldier at drill,
That fights till he dies.

And the saucy Tom Tit,
With his pretty 'twit twit,'
And his tail in the air;
And the wary quick Snipe,
With a bill like a pipe,
Hopping hither and there.

O wicked Mawpawk!
We'll have you caught,
For the deed you have done;
We'll slyly creep
When you're fast asleep,
And break your bones ev'ry one.

'Yes, Yes,' said the Hawk,
And the bird that can talk,
'We'll strike off his head.'
'Ah, Ah,' said the Owl,
'By fish, flesh and fowl,
'We'll bang! shoot him dead.'

So they all flew away,
And still fly to this day,
O'er hill and o'er plain;
But he dives in the rushes,
And hides under bushes,
And they search but in vain.

Written in 1870, Cawthorne's verses reflect the Victorian fascination with death, though it reads rather morbidly today. By contrast, most of the forgotten nursery rhymes of Australia were just for fun:

Billy had a gum-boil
Which made poor Billy grumboil.
The doctor said: 'That's some boil!
And does your tummy rumboil?
It seems to me abnormoil;

You'd better try some warm oil.'
So Billy got some hot oil,
And boiled it in a bottoil,
And on his gum did rub oil—
Which ended Billy's trouboil!

And, perhaps an authentic children's ditty:

Captain Cook
Broke his hook
Fishing for Australia,
Captain Cook wrote a book
All about Australia.

The lost boys of Daylesford

One of Frederick McCubbin's many admired paintings is simply titled 'Lost'. Completed in 1907, it shows a young boy crying and alone in the bush. Lost children were one of settlers' great fears, which were frequently realised as children wandered off into unknown and near-impenetrable terrain, especially in wooded country. A sombre gravestone in Daylesford cemetery commemorates the sad tale of William Graham, aged six, his brother Thomas, aged four, and their friend, five-year-old Alfred Burman.

The three were out looking for lost goats along the Wombat Creek on 30 June 1867. When they did not come home, a search was mounted but had to be abandoned at darkness. The worst frost of the year fell overnight. The search resumed the next morning, and over the next two days, more than 100 searchers found nothing but two small footprints. Word spread and soon there were more than 100 mounted searchers and over 500 on foot. Next day all shops were closed and a public meeting raised over 70 pounds for a reward. The police officer in charge was Inspector Smith.

. . . he had telegraphed to every place where there were black trackers to have them sent on; and Mr. Joseph Parker said that he, so soon as the meeting was over, would start for [home] and bring with him in the morning two young men who in following up a trail were equal to any black trackers. These statements were received with much applause, as was one made by Captain O'Connell, that the Volunteer Fire Brigade had, prior to the public meeting, resolved on turning out on the morrow to a man and making a search.

Mr. Inspector Smith suggested that all who intended to join in the search should meet at the Specimen Hill works, the manager of which had, in case anyone might lose his way, offered to keep the engine whistle, which could be heard two miles, continually sounding for their guidance after nightfall. He also impressed on every volunteer the necessity of taking a little bread and wine with him, in case of discovering the lost ones, and cautioned those who found them against bringing them too suddenly into a heated room, and gave instructions for their treatment.

By 4 July the numbers hunting for the children swelled further, including 200 dogs. But heavy winter rain set in and made it impossible to find any trace of the boys. The local paper published a letter of thanks to the local community from the fathers of the boys.

*N*ow that the public excitement has partially subsided with regard to the 'Three Lost Boys', we beg to return our sincere and heartfelt thanks to the inhabitants of Daylesford and surrounding districts, for the great and praiseworthy search they have made for the recovery of the children.

None have been more astonished than we have been at the mighty phalanx of human aid, aye, and brute aid too, that have been engaged in this search, and although all efforts have been unsuccessful, the public sympathy evinced has been a source of great consolation to ourselves and the distressed mothers.

When we have returned home night after night to tell the same sad tale of our want of success; when we have recounted to them the deeds of endurance and energy, and the great sacrifice of time and money, this community have suffered, their tears have been dried, and we have all been satisfied with the assurance that all that human aid can do, has been done on this occasion.

We still trust and hope that with Divine aid the bodies of the children may yet be found ere long, not forgetting 'There is a Divinity that shapes our ends, rough hew then how we will'.

In conclusion, we beg again to tender our heartfelt thanks to the public for the zeal and energy evinced to restore us our lost children. Our prayer is that, no parents will ever have to mourn for the loss and death of their children in the wild bush of Australia.

Later in the month an inquest was held, finding that the children probably died of exposure on the first night. Almost two months later a settler's dog came home carrying a child's boot still clinging to the remains of a foot. The dog later found a human skull. They found the bodies next day. The younger children were inside a tree cavity and the older boy nearby.

The party named then formed themselves into a search party, going abreast at a certain distance from each other. Proceeding in this way for a short distance, David Bryan, in jumping a log forming part of a fence, discovered some bones and clothes lying about, and exclaimed, 'Here they are!' His brother Ninian was next to him, but on the opposite side of the log. Starting to join his brother, he went round a large tree standing and forming a corner to two fences. On rounding it he found it hollow, and a glance disclosed to him the bodies of two of the children. He started back, and said to his brother, 'Oh, Mike, here they are.' The others were speedily attracted to the spot, and watch kept over the remains till the police, who were sent for, arrived, and took them in charge. The remains too surely evidenced that they had been gnawed by dogs.

A witness favoured the local newspaper with a description of the scene with the kind of grisly details beloved of the era:

*T*he locality where the remains of the children who were lost from Table-hill on Sunday, the 30th June last, were found, in situate about a mile and a half from Wheeler's sawmills on the Musk Creek. The bodies of the two children which were found in the hollow tree were when discovered in a state of fair preservation, considering the length of time which had elapsed since they were lost; but the remains of the third consisted only of a few bones and the skull. The two bodies in the hollow tree when found were lying closely cuddled together, as if the children had by the warmth afforded by each other endeavoured to ward off the bitter wintry cold. The younger child had been placed inside, and the elder and stronger one had lain down beside him on the outer side. The backs of both were turned to the entrance of the cavity.

Here they must have lain and perished of cold and starvation. The elder boy had his legs completely under the body of the younger, and his cap lay on the floor of the cavity; the younger boy had his cap placed before his face. It is probable that the body of the third boy was also in the tree, but had been dragged thence by dogs. There are marks of hair outside on the roots of the tree. The elder boy had boots on, the younger had none, but a laceup boot broken at the heel was lying in the interstice of the tree just over his head. In the cavity were two sticks which they had evidently used in their wanderings. When the body of the elder boy was placed in the coffin, as the corpse sank into the narrow shell, his right arm was pushed forward, and his hand fell over upon his breast, and his face became uppermost. This hand was white, plump, and apparently undecomposed, but the whole of his features were gone, and nothing remained but a ghastly skeleton outline, with the lower jaw detached and fallen. The face of the younger child was, however, in a state of preservation, but perfectly black. The members of both bodies were much attenuated.

As so often happened in these cases, the lost children were within reach of help. But the density of the bush and difficulty of the terrain meant that even 200 yards was too far:

The position of the tree is at the corner of an old cultivation paddock in which potatoes are now planted. It is melancholy to reflect that these unfortunate children should have reached so near help and succour and failed to find it. Had they proceeded 200 yards farther up the fence, they would have come upon the hut of M'Kay. It would seem they had reached this place at night, and finding their passage impeded by the brush fence, turned into the hollow tree, not wishing to lose sight of it, thinking that the dawn of morning would set them right. Thus they must have lain down to sleep their last sleep.

Daylesford closed for the funeral. The streets were lined with mourners paying their last respects to the children and their families. Over 800 people attended the burial. The three boys were laid in their grave as they had been found, with the elder boy lying over the two younger ones in a forlorn attempt to keep them warm.

The town raised a fine monument above the graves of William and Thomas Graham and their friend Alfred Burman. The families founded a scholarship at the Daylesford Primary School as a mark of appreciation for the help they had received from the local people; known as the Graham Dux, it has been awarded every year since 1889. In 2013 the Daylesford and District Historical Society had the monument refurbished, including regilding the more than 400 characters that tell one of Australia's saddest lost child tragedies.

Fairies in the paddock

The flower fairy of European literary tradition is not a natural fit with the strongly realistic traditions of the Australian bush. Nevertheless, from around the middle of the nineteenth century writers began to adapt the fragile flower fairy to the local environment. Some also borrowed stories and ideas from Aboriginal tradition, a practice that eventually produced some of the darker elements of Australian children's stories in the form of the 'Banksia Men' in the *Snugglepot and Cuddlepie* stories by May Gibbs.

Most writers of local fairy tales were women, one of them just sixteen when she published her *Fairytales from the Land of Wattle* in 1904. Olga Ernst (Waller) presented 'What the Jackass Said' (i.e. the Kookaburra), 'The Opossum's Jealousy', 'The Bunyip and the Wizard' and 'The Origin of the Wattle' as tales told by herself as an older child to younger children.

> They are offered here as tales told by a child to younger children in the hope they will not only amuse the young, but will also win the approval of those to whom a loving study of tree and flower, bird and insect, and the association of familiar elements of old-world fairy love with Australian surroundings, commend themselves.

Olga Ernst provided a heady mix of European river sprites, goblins, little red elves, ugly gnomes and mermaids swimming near the mouth of the Yarra, together with bunyips and giants thundering across mountain ranges. There are magic runes, charms and magic elixirs aplenty, along with the 'Wizard of the Roper River' and the 'Mermaid of the Gulf of Carpentaria'. At the end of this story the mermaid is married to the Bunyip by a beautiful fairy and a witch turns the dust elves into the willy-willies or small dust storms.

In later life, Olga turned to writing mainly philosophical fantasy works and nursery rhymes. *Songs from the Dandenongs* was published in 1939 under her married name of Waller. It brought together Aboriginal names for natural features with the rhythms of British nursery rhymes, with music by Jean M. Fraser. The notes accompanying the verses included Olga's regret that many of the Aboriginal names had been lost or changed to banal English versions. In effect, this modest self-published collection was a pioneering attempt to familiarise children with Indigenous languages and appreciation of the landscape. 'A Mountain Jingle' began with the verse in the familiar rhythm of 'London Bridge is Falling Down':

We stand on top of Mt Dandenong,
Dandenong, Dandenong,
We stand on top of Mt Dandenong
And this is what we see:
Old Beenak has his cloud-cap on,
Cloud-cap on, cloud-cap on,
Old Beenak has his cloud-cap on
With a rainbow for a feather!

And so the book continued with information about local Aboriginal legends and practices, animals, birds, geology, weather and so on. Olga even had a rhyme for the recently completed dam, which she referred to as 'the Silvan Lake', 'only called a "dam" by the grossly unpoetic'.

It seems unlikely that many parents would have taken up any of the heartfelt recreations to sing to their children in those days. Olga died in 1972 and is remembered today only by her descendants and a few literary scholars.

Surviving Black Jack

In August 1835, two emaciated English youths staggered into the tiny settlement at King George Sound. They were little more than skeletons and had almost lost the power of speech. But they were alive. When their health began to return they told their strange tale of shipwreck, piracy and bare survival.

James Newell and James Manning sailed from Sydney aboard the schooner *Defiance* in August 1833. She was loaded with supplies destined to feed the ragtag bands of sealers, escaped convicts and deserters who haunted the islands around the southwest, near modern-day Albany. According to their own account they were cast away the next month when the *Defiance* was wrecked on Cape Howe Island. With the captain, another man and 'a native woman', they escaped aboard a whaleboat, eventually landing on Kangaroo Island. Here they built a house for the captain and his Aboriginal wife and planted a garden. The remainder of the schooner's crew, another six men, sailed for Sydney in another of the wrecked schooner's boats but were never heard of again.

In September, two black men arrived at the island, one of them a man named Anderson, a notorious local ruffian who would come to be known as the pirate 'Black Jack'. The young men took passage with Anderson to his stronghold on Long Island where they were compelled to work for their keep. A couple of months later, the captain of *Defiance* arrived and accused James Manning of stealing money from him. The captain, enthusiastically assisted by Anderson, took over 41 shillings from Manning at gunpoint.

While the two James were being held captive and robbed

on Long Island, another group of desperates resident on the island kidnapped five Aboriginal women, murdering two of their husbands in the process. Another Aboriginal man tried to swim to the island to rescue his wife but was drowned.

Not surprisingly, the two youths continually asked Anderson to put them ashore on the mainland, but he always refused. In January 1834 another small boat arrived under the command of a man named Evanson Janson. James Manning, apparently still with means, paid Janson for a passage on his boat to King George Sound. Instead, he was landed on Middle Island where Anderson again stole money from him, 50 shillings in English coins and Spanish dollars.

Eventually, in June, Manning and Newell convinced Anderson to land them. He did so but provided them with no gunpowder for hunting their food. They started walking, living on shellfish and grass roots. More than two months later they arrived at King George Sound, where they were cared for by local Aborigines of the White Cockatoo, Murray and Willmen groups who:

> . . . nursed, fed, and almost carried them at times, when, from weakness, they were sinking under their sufferings. This is a return which could scarcely have been expected from savages, who have no doubt been exposed to repeated atrocities, such as we have related in a previous narrative. Indeed, to the acts of these white barbarians, we may now trace the loss of some valuable lives among the Europeans, and more especially that of Captain Barker, which took place within a short distance of the scene of these atrocities.

The Aboriginal people were rewarded with gifts of rice and flour, and the sway of law and order in that wild part of the coast was lamented by the journalist who wrote up the story:

The habits of the men left on the islands to the southward, by whaling, or sealing vessels, have long borne the character given them by Manning and Newell; it appears, therefore, deserving of some consideration by what means their practices can be checked, as future settlers in the neighbourhood of Port Lincoln will be made to expiate the crimes and outrages of these lawless assassins.

It would be quite a few years before the law did rule the waves in this part of the country. But, as elsewhere, settlement eventually tamed the vast plains, mountain ranges and savage coasts.

PLAYGOERS PICTURES, INC.
presents
J. P. McGOWAN
in
"DISCONTENTED WIVES"

"WE'LL KEEP IT A SECRET FROM RUTH UNTIL IT'S ASSAYED."

22

Larger than life

They're a weird mob.

Nino Culotta (John O'Grady), 1957

FOR A COUNTRY that tends to pull down tall poppies, we seem to have an awful lot of them. The varied and often surprising stories of these lives are colourful cameos of the past. While some of the lives mentioned here have been mostly forgotten, in some cases the things they did have lived on in everyday Australian life.

The famous book *They're a Weird Mob*, later a film, picked up humorously on this aspect of the national character and is recognised as a classic. Tossed off, it is said, as the result of a ten-pound bet, John O'Grady was himself something of a character. He died in 1981, but his casual classic has become part of the national biographical tradition that includes all sorts and all comers.

The fate of Captain Cadell

Francis Cadell was one of those colourful, slightly larger-than-life characters who populate our colonial history and folklore. Along with such identities as the scoundrel 'Bully' Hayes (who also features in Cadell's life story), the fabulist Louis de Rougemont and the amazing Calvert, the sea- and river-going Captain Cadell

481

made a lasting impact on many parts of the continent, including Western Australia.

Born in Scotland in 1822, Cadell went to sea on an East Indiaman at the age of fourteen. By the time he was seventeen he had taken part in the so-called Opium Wars between Britain and China. He followed this early adventuring with a swashbuckling life that took in piracy, ship design, commanding naval engagements during the Maori Wars, exploring what is now the Northern Territory, gun running, pearling and the trade in human flesh known as 'blackbirding'.

His main claim to fame, though, was his almost single-handed creation of the Murray River paddle-steamer trade from the early 1850s. As with many other periods in Cadell's fortunate life, this one left him with a number of high-level allies who supported him in some of his less glorious subsequent careers.

Largely forgotten to the history books, Cadell's adventures regularly filled the pages of the newspapers during his tumultuous life. He was one of those aspirational, adventuring types often encountered in the Australian colonies, described by his biographer as one of 'those over-achieving British Empire-builders who litter the Victorian world like soldier ants on a forest floor—so competent, so dependable, so energetic and yet so relaxed about it all. They never seemed to doubt what they were doing as they walked into other people's countries and—outnumbered thousands to one—imposed British law and order, built railways and ports, made fortunes and went to church on Sundays.'

While Cadell may have broken more laws than he imposed and rarely seems to have stepped inside a church, he was one of these driven pioneers, if a decidedly ambivalent one.

One of the many dubious periods of Cadell's life involved him in the early days of the Western Australian pearling trade. He was another of the variously optimistic, crazed or desperate band of entrepreneurs who created that industry and, it seems, contributed to its unhappy record of human misery. As well as apparently mistreating his indentured labourers, Cadell was rumoured to be running barracoons, or slave markets, on islands off the Western Australian coast.

Cadell had the knack of allying himself with unsavoury partners while managing to remain more or less respectable. Certainly the fame he earned from his pioneering of the Murray paddle-steam trade—which materially assisted the development of South Australia, Victoria and New South Wales—convinced many to give him the benefit of the doubt throughout his numerous escapades.

During his Western Australian troubles, Sir Dominic Daly, the ex-governor of South Australia, fortuitously turned up in Perth. His friendship with the mariner apparently provided sufficient establishment influence to defuse the very strong interest the authorities were showing in Cadell's pearling activities.

But despite his friends in high places, his lovable rogue personality and his acumen, Cadell met an untimely and mysterious fate in what are now Indonesian waters. Ever the entrepreneur, he was pursuing another of his business schemes and pushed his crew just a little too hard. The boat returned without its captain and Francis Cadell was never seen again.

The Fenian

On 10 January 1868, an Irish political prisoner and Fenian named John Boyle O'Reilly was marched into Fremantle Prison. O'Reilly had been guilty of little active subversion, though he had plotted much. Following a brief career as a journalist, in 1863 he enlisted as a trooper in the 10th Hussars, then headquartered in Dublin. He was recruited to the clandestine Irish Republican Brotherhood (IRB, also known as the Fenians), a forerunner of the modern Irish Republican Army (IRA), in 1865. Participating in the preparations for a planned rising that never took place, O'Reilly was arrested along with most of his co-conspirators in February 1866. After a trial he was sentenced to death by firing squad, but had this sentence commuted to twenty years' penal servitude. With 61 other Fenians, O'Reilly was transported to Western Australia aboard the *Hougoumont* in October 1867.

Sixteen of these men, plus O'Reilly himself, had been members of the British army and were segregated from the civilian Fenians and the common convicts. When advance news of this Irish 'weight of woe' reached the colony, segments of the Swan River community went into panic, fearing that the dreaded Irish, especially those with military training, would murder them in their beds. The fear was especially high in Fremantle, where the Fenians would be held. So great was the consternation, heightened by threats from some quarters to prevent the Fenians disembarking, that the disciplinarian Governor Hampton had his residence moved from distant Perth to Fremantle in an effort to calm the more excitable colonists.

When they did arrive, the entire complement of convicts and Fenians was disembarked at dawn, and marched in chains through Fremantle's forbidding limestone prison. They then underwent the same initiation into servitude as all other prison inmates: each was bathed, cropped, barbered and examined by a doctor, and their physical and personal details were recorded. They were then issued with the regulation summer clothing: cap, grey jacket, vest, two cotton shirts, one flannel shirt, two handkerchiefs, two pairs of trousers, two pairs of socks and a pair of boots.

O'Reilly and his companions were now 'probationary convicts'. If they behaved themselves for the remaining half of their sentence, they could be granted a ticket of leave, a dispensation allowing them to live and work much as any free colonist as long as they reported regularly to the magistrate.

Like most other transports, John Boyle O'Reilly the revolutionary was soon sent to work on the road-making around Bunbury from March 1868. There were over 3220 convicts in the colony at this time, though only a hundred or so on the road gangs in the Bunbury area. Later in his life O'Reilly would publish a classic novel, *Moondyne*, based on his experiences in this part of Western Australia. He dedicated this work to 'the interests of humanity, to the prisoner, whoever and wherever he may be'.

In the novel itself, O'Reilly provides some evocative details of the conditions. He begins by describing the bush and the work of the free sawyers:

> During the midday heat not a bird stirred among the mahogany and gum trees. On the flat tops of the low banksia the round heads of the white cockatoos could be seen in thousands, motionless as the trees themselves. Not a parrot had the vim to scream. The chirping insects were silent. Not a snake had courage to rustle his hard skin against the hot and dead bush-grass. The bright-eyed iguanas were in their holes. The mahogany sawyers had left their logs and were sleeping in the cool sand of their pits. Even the travelling ants had halted on their wonderful roads, and sought the shade of a bramble.

He then goes on to contrast this with the lot of himself and the other convict toilers:

> All free things were at rest; but the penetrating click of the axe, heard far through the bush, and now and again a harsh word of command, told that it was a land of bondmen.
>
> From daylight to dark, through the hot noon as steadily as in the cool evening, the convicts were at work on the roads—the weary work that has no wages, no promotion, no incitement, no variation for good or bad, except stripes for the laggard.

Moondyne was written in the light of freedom, but it echoed some of the verse in which the unhappy O'Reilly cried out his fears and those of all transported to the Swan River colony:

Have I no future left me?
Is there no struggling ray
From the sun of my life outshining
Down on my darksome way?

Will there no gleam of sunshine
Cast o'er my path its light?
Will there no star of hope rise
Out of this gloom of night?

The light did shine for O'Reilly. The politics surrounding his fate and that of his rebellious companions was a cause célèbre of the time, resonating with the more romanticised aspects of the Irish struggle against English oppression. The correspondence files of the Colonial Office during this period are full of letters from respectable members of the British middle classes urging the release or pardoning of the Fenians, and there was also a considerable amount of correspondence relating particularly to O'Reilly's case. As well as these official representations, there were more clandestine plots in effect.

In early March 1869, the Fenian transportee was whisked away to freedom in the not-so-United States of America by a Yankee whaler. His rescue—an early example of globalisation—had been carefully plotted by the free Irish community in Western Australia, in league with elements of the Catholic Church, the American Irish community and its sympathisers. O'Reilly celebrated his 25th birthday in the middle of the Indian Ocean on his secret voyage back to England from where, under the noses of those authorities who badly wanted to capture him, he made his way to America, freedom and a promising future. In America he was influential in plans to free the Fenians remaining in Western Australia five years later. At Easter 1874, O'Reilly's six Fenian companions were rescued from bondage by an American whaler, the *Catalpa*, and taken to safety in the United States.

O'Reilly went on to a glittering journalistic and political career in America. He remained deeply involved in Irish patriotic activities and is remembered in that country, in Australia and in the country of his birth as an outstanding patriot.

The last bushranger

Jack Bradshaw, self-styled 'last of the bushrangers', was a spieler, or con man, who led a colourful life of crime, repentance and self-publicising that would not shame a modern marketing executive. He arrived in Australia from Ireland at the age of fourteen in 1860 and found work in the bush. He also worked as a petty trickster with a crook known as 'Professor Bruce', whose specialisation was reading people's heads and telling them amazing but true things about their character. This scam involved Jack arriving in town and finding out about the locals then slipping back to Bruce after a couple of days with the information. Bruce then entered the town in a flamboyant manner promising to reveal all—for a reasonable consideration.

Jack moved on to horse stealing with an accomplice endearingly named 'Lovely Riley'. But his real ambition was to rob a bank. He and Riley attacked the Coolah bank in 1876; they got the manager to open the safe but just as they began to rifle through its contents, the manager's pregnant wife came in. She gave the desperadoes a piece of her mind and they turned tail and fled, empty-handed.

Finally, at Quirindi in 1880, Jack realised his ambition and, once more in company with 'Lovely Riley', successfully robbed the bank of 2000 pounds. Escaping to New England, Riley's loose lips gave the game away and Jack decamped hurriedly to Armidale. Here, under a false name, he met, wooed and married the daughter of a wealthy squatter but was soon after unmasked and arrested. Fortunately, there was no bloodshed and he received a twelve-year sentence but was out again by 1888 and returned to his surprisingly amenable wife. Then, caught stealing mail, Jack went back to prison until 1901.

Inside, Jack saw the light and used the time to educate himself. When he got out he took up writing and lecturing about his highly glorified exploits. His first book, *Highway Robbery Under Arms*, told the story of the Quirindi robbery and was followed with several more, often overlapping titles that purported to tell the true stories of his relationships with many infamous bushrangers. Jack had made good use of his experience with Professor Bruce through all his years in prison, picking up inside knowledge of other criminals and their doings, real or not. He spun these into yarns that gave him a basic, if unreliable, living.

In 1928, the now ageing bushranger became a boarder in Phillipine Humphrey's grandmother's home. Phillipine recalled, 'He was the gentlest old man you could ever meet by then. He told lots of interesting stories and taught me many Irish songs.' Four years later, Jack moved to St Joseph's Little Sisters of the Poor Home in Randwick, New South Wales; Phillipine and her grandmother often visited Jack here, and he often said that the younger woman reminded him of his own daughter.

Jack died in 1937 at the age of 90 and was buried at Rookwood Cemetery in an unmarked grave, which has since been graced with a tombstone.

Lawson's people

People loved Henry Lawson not in spite of his failings and afflictions, but because of them. He was an extreme version of themselves, always struggling to make ends meet, battling the creature, looking for work, supporting—or not—a family. Forever striving and usually failing, just as they were, Henry Lawson's life was larger than their own but still essentially the same. His writing was infused with his life, and with theirs. 'My people', he called them.

The rugged contours of Henry Lawson's life began in 1867. Born to Peter and Louisa in Grenfell, New South Wales, he grew up in goldfields camps and bush huts, receiving an indifferent education, and from a young age was seen as an outsider. He did not mix well, was not good at physical activities, and was partly deaf. His schoolmates called him 'barmy Henry' and shunned him, as he ignored them in return.

Peter and Louisa's troubled marriage faded away in the late 1870s and Louisa moved to Sydney, where she eventually established a career as a writer and pioneer feminist. After working with his father on Blue Mountains building contracts, Henry joined his mother and siblings in 1883. He was apprenticed for some years as a coach painter. Aware of his educational failings, he studied at night school and twice attempted to matriculate, unsuccessfully, to Sydney University. Encouraged, if distantly, by his forbidding mother, Henry became interested in writing and slowly began to achieve some success. In 1887 he had his first piece, 'A Song of the Republic', accepted by the literary magazine *The Bulletin*. In the next few years some of his most popular verses appeared, including 'Faces in the Street' and 'Andy's Gone With Cattle'.

His fame grew and he published more and more verse, articles and later, short stories, the form in which he truly excelled. But his need to earn a living and to pay for his worsening addiction to alcohol meant that he needed to devote time and energy to finding work, time that took away from writing. In 1892, *The Bulletin* subsidised a trip to the drought-stricken regions of western New South Wales. He carried his swag for months, returning with the material that he would mine for the rest of his creative life. In the short term, the trip produced the classic stories 'The Bush Undertaker' and 'The Union Buries its Dead', among others. Four years later, his first important collection of stories, *While the Billy Boils*, was published, as was his verse collection, *In the Days When the World Was Wide*.

That same year he married Bertha Bredt. Family life began romantically, with a trip to Western Australia to dig for gold, but they only made it to Perth. Henry did some writing, house painting and other work but they were unable to make a go of it. Fed up with living in a tent, Bertha and Henry returned to Sydney where he soon took up again with his old mates and his old ways. Next year there was a futile trip to New Zealand where the family lived in deep isolation, teaching at a bush school. Once again, there was no alternative but to go home again. Through all this, Henry wrote, often drank and always struggled to make ends meet, particularly as children began being born. By 1898 his drinking had become so serious that he had to be institutionally 'dried out'. The treatment was successful and Henry remained sober for some years.

To say that Henry Lawson went to Britain would be inaccurate; he did take his family to London, but spent several years there without leaving the city. He succeeded in having a number of books published or re-published in Britain, but the event was a literary dead end. It also marked the effective end of his marriage. The return of his manic drinking, mood swings and frequent destitution were beyond even Bertha's toleration. She had her own serious mental problems requiring extended hospitalisation, and Henry's health also declined. In 1902, the family returned to Australia via Fremantle, where Bertha left Henry drinking and took the children home to Sydney. From that point Henry and his family were effectively estranged and he pursued his personal journey to hell, accompanied by the grog, madness, poverty, imprisonment and never-ending sponging off friends and colleagues.

With his marriage disintegrating, Henry tried to kill himself in December 1902. His drinking and inability to pay family support landed him in Darlinghurst Gaol on several occasions, accompanied by stints at the attached asylum, and there were a number of unsuccessful attempts to settle him in the country. Habitually drunk, impoverished and depressed, Lawson became a familiar pathetic figure on the streets of Sydney, cared for mainly by his long-suffering housekeeper Mrs Byers.

By 1916 Henry's loyal mates had become desperate and tried once again to save his life and the precious gift he had squandered so casually. A group of them gathered in the office of Labor Premier Holman. Led by F.J. Archibald, editor of *The Bulletin* and one of Henry's most loyal supporters and patrons, they discussed the need to save Lawson from himself, preferably by getting him away from the soaks of the city. There was the possibility of a pension, though this was difficult in an era before governments were expected to support the sick and elderly. Someone suggested that a better approach would be to give the writer a paid job of some kind. Why not post him to the recently initiated Murrumbidgee Irrigation Areas? He could have a regular wage and a cottage to live in, and in return would write verse and stories promoting the great experimental water dream. Best of all, the MIA was officially a 'dry' region in which alcohol was prohibited.

Henry Lawson's friends agreed and so the once passionate firebrand poet became a salaried bureaucrat of the New South Wales government service. Being Henry Lawson, though, it was not likely his career would proceed like that of any other public servant.

The Murrumbidgee Irrigation Areas scheme was the culmination of decades of water dreaming. As the early settlers and explorers confirmed the aridity of the vast continent they had colonised, the need for reliable water became a vital concern. In New South Wales, various ideas had been proposed and a Royal Commission recommended large-scale irrigation drawing on the Darling and Murrumbidgee rivers. It was the beginning of the troubles with the Murray-Darling basin waters that beset us still, but at the time it was a revolution given further urgency by the devastating 'Federation drought' from the mid-1890s. Construction of the Burrinjuck Dam began in 1906 and five years later the canals began to go in. The new towns of Leeton and Griffith were established and an official 'Turning on the Water' ceremony opened the scheme in 1912. The 'Area', as it was then known, was only a few years old when Henry's mates organised him into a cosy sinecure at Yanco, near Leeton.

Henry generally worked hard during his Leeton period. He and Mrs Byers shared a cottage provided by the Commission, probably the only dwelling he could even briefly call 'home' since childhood. He caught up with a few old mates from his swag days, all now settlers in the Area, and improved his health by working in the garden of his cottage. As well as his government post, he was receiving income from his other writing, from a successful stage adaptation of *In the Days When the World Was Wide*, and from several other occasional sources. But being Henry, he soon managed to establish a local supply of the supposedly unobtainable grog and returned to the bad old habits.

Between bouts of inebriation, depression and incapacity—together with many dashes by train back to Sydney for 'business'—Henry nevertheless managed to carry out a great deal of literary work, including rewriting and editing upcoming publications and composing new material. Some of this material was obedient to his brief of promoting the attractions of irrigation areas to sorely needed new settlers; some was of a more general nature or his response to the usually grim news of the war taking tens of thousands of Australian lives at the other end of the world. His plan was to first publish the poems and yarns in *The Bulletin* and anywhere else he could and then to write a great book, probably to be called *By the Banks of the Murrumbidgee*.

But life and the grog got in the way. Soon after his Yanco appointment came to an end his physical and mental condition began to deteriorate. He spent more time in asylums and hospitals and no more was heard of the Yanco book during these last grim years. His literary output drained away with his life force. He was hospitalised with a cerebral haemorrhage and although he recovered, it was to be only a few months before the inevitable.

On 4 September 1922, they sent Henry off in style with a state funeral, one of the largest in Sydney's history. The streets were so thronged with mourners that many of his old mates were unable to make it to the cemetery and were forced to stop at various pubs along the way to raise a glass or two to his memory. Henry would have been greatly amused by this and might even have spun it into a good yarn.

The Coo-ee Lady

One of the first words early settlers learned from Aboriginal people was 'cow-wee'. It was used in the Dharuk language around the Port Jackson area as a call to bring the community together. Later, other Aboriginal groups were heard using similar cries for the same purpose. Before very long, the drawn-out 'coo', followed by a high leap of the voice register to 'ee', rapidly became a widespread way to navigate the bush, find lost settlers and generally let anyone know you were around. By the 1840s it was said that visiting Australians would 'cooee' each other along the streets of London, hoping to find their way through the bustle and the fog, much to the bewilderment of the British.

So closely associated with Australia did the call become that it began to be used in popular literature. Even Arthur Conan Doyle had Sherlock Holmes solve a case through the great detective's knowledge of the call. In Australia, writers and poets featured 'cooee' and it became a popular subject for songs in the latter part of the nineteenth century. There was even a book titled *Coo-ee: Tales of Australian Life by Australian Ladies*. As national consciousness grew around the time of Federation, products of all kinds began to be branded with characteristically Australian names. It was possible to buy 'Coo-ee' wine, bacon and galvanised iron, among other items. Visiting or returning dignitaries such as Dame Nellie Melba were often greeted by cooeeing crowds. By the early twentieth century, the cooee was well established as a unique and characteristically Australian sound.

In 1907, an unhappy housewife in the dry dustiness of Kalgoorlie had a light-bulb moment. Maude Wordsworth James was in her early fifties when inspiration struck.

Most of Maude's childhood had been spent in Victoria with her English parents, Thomas and Alicia Crabbe. She married Charles James, a civil engineer, in 1875 and began a family. Charles took a job in Kalgoorlie in 1896 and the following year Maude and the children joined him but, used to the greener regions of Victoria, Maude was not happy in the west. She describes the country she experienced on her way to the golden city: 'After leaving Coolgardie, we continued on our journey over the same sort of country, through which we had come—only the farther we went, the redder the dust, and the drearier it all seemed.' She did come to appreciate the wildflowers and sunsets of the golden west but remained uneasy with her life in the dry and dusty land. Like most housewives of the time, though, she accepted her lot and busied herself with her home, garden and community life.

One night in 1907, her husband Charles, now the town surveyor, came home from work depressed about money. Maude lay awake wondering how she could make a lot of money very quickly. She wrote in her journal: 'Just as the dawn was breaking, an idea came to me that immediately arrested my attention.' Her idea—'entirely my own'—was that 'Australia has no Souvenir'. She was familiar with Tasmania's souvenir brooches in the form of gold maps of the state and the various other items produced by other states, all featuring native animals or plants. But Maude wanted a souvenir that would symbolise the whole country, and came up with the intention of 'making a fortune out of my favourite Australian word, "coo-ee"'.

From that day, Maude became the Coo-ee Lady, single-mindedly pursuing her idea of an all-Australian souvenir. She began designing, manufacturing and distributing a line of jewellery featuring distinctively Australian motifs, including the Aboriginal rainbow serpent, fashioned only from Australian gold, Kangaroo Island tourmaline, Broome pearls and Queensland opals. Her 'Coo-ee jewellery' began with brooches, cuff links, tie pins, bracelets and spoons, but Maude didn't stop there. She registered 'Coo-ee' as a trademark and patented her designs not only in Australia but also in New Zealand and in Britain. The *Australian Official Journal of Trade Marks* for 1907 shows there was little that Maude could not coo-ee-fy. It includes registrations for pendants, hat and scarf pins, earrings, photograph frames, hair combs, trinkets, pen handles, serviette rings, buttons, sleeve links, boxes, paper knives, scent bottles, blotters, bells, knockers, bangles, rings, parasol handles and even 'wishbones'. She began writing Coo-ee songs, ran Coo-ee competitions and expanded her wares to include chinaware and pottery. There was even a 'Coo-ee Calendar'.

Maude became completely obsessed with her empire and made a good deal of money, just as she had planned. Her most peculiar enterprise was the 'Coo-ee Corner'. Every Australian home would have one. It would be crammed with Maude's creations and would have a specially designed 'Coo-ee clock', an Australian version of the cuckoo clock. Every half-hour and hour the figure of an Aboriginal man waving a boomerang would pop out and call—you guessed it.

Maude came to think of the word as her private property. When a Heidelberg soldiers' welfare group made commemorative cooee medallions in 1916 she tried to claim royalties. But while it was possible to register designs using the word 'coo-ee', as Maude had astutely done, it was not legally possible to privately own the word itself because it was considered part of the national language: if you 'can't get/come within cooee' of something, then you're nowhere near or simply cannot hear it. They use the term in much the same way in New Zealand.

Maude left Kalgoorlie behind and moved to South Australia in 1908. During World War I she continued her 'Coo-ee' campaigns and even turned out a patriotic song on the theme. She lived in England for two years during the 1920s, then at Mosman in Sydney until 1931. That year she returned to South Australia and her son, Lieutenant Colonel Tristram James, came to live with her. Maude Wordsworth James died a widow at North Adelaide in 1936.

Australia's first Hollywood star

While most of us probably think of Errol Flynn as our first Hollywood export, he arrived there many years after a number of Australians who went to Hollywood in its very early years, including Louise Lovely (Louise Carbasse), Clyde Cook (The Kangaroo Boy) and the athletic stuntman Snowy Baker. American performers and crew also worked in Australia during the early years of our own industry.

But it was a South Australian railway worker's son who got there first. John Paterson McGowan (1880–1952) was Australia's first Hollywood star. In this country he is unknown rather than forgotten, but he is remembered in America as one of the pioneers of the movie industry.

Born in the South Australian railway town of Terowie in 1880, J.P. McGowan, or Jack as he liked to be known, had an average working-class childhood in Adelaide and Sydney. His father worked on the railways, a background that served McGowan so well that he became known in Hollywood as 'The Railroad Man'.

Before reaching the infant Hollywood of 1913, McGowan had many adventures that made him well suited for the various roles he would play in the cinema. He went to sea at seventeen and later worked as a stockman, becoming an expert horseman and sharpshooter. He won medals in the Boer War and then left Australia for the 1904 World's Fair in St Louis as part of a spectacular recreation of the South African conflict. For the next few years he acted in travelling theatrical troupes until employed by the Hollywood film studio Kalem Company, a buzzing whirl of enthusiastic amateurs keen to see what the developing technology of the silent screen could do. There was no union, no safety standards and no industry organisations; people just went there and made films.

McGowan was over six foot tall and strongly built, was handy with horses and guns, and could act at least as well as anyone else in those early years. His versatility as actor, director, writer, producer and occasional stunt man would result in over 600 productions in which he had one or several hands.

He began, as did just about everyone else in the business, with westerns. At that time the trend was for serials, which were churned out much like modern TV soaps. Some of McGowan's early titles were *The Railroad Raiders of '62*, *A Prisoner of Mexico* and *Captain Rivera's Reward*. As his career progressed he was involved in *The Bandit's Child*, *Whispering Smith* and *Medicine Bend*, among a slew of other stories about Ireland, ancient Egypt, pirates and espionage.

But it was in films about railroads, as the Americans call them, where he made his most celebrated contributions. He created many films on this theme, including *Fast Freight* and *The Express Car Mystery*. He also directed a 25-year-old John Wayne in *Hurricane Express*, an early role in which Wayne learned the skills that later propelled him to stardom.

Between 1914 and 1915 McGowan was strongly involved in many of the 119 episodes of *The Hazards of Helen* series, starring Helen Holmes, then McGowan's wife. Together they have a place in Hollywood history as the creators of the iconic scene in which the wicked villain ties the damsel to the train track; the episode was, of course, titled *The Death Train*.

The Australian continued his multi-skilled involvement in movie-making as actor, director, producer or writer—frequently more than one of these at a time. He also continued to be strong on westerns, with occasional productions of South Seas adventures, spy flicks and even a dog story. Later he developed a role in Hollywood industrial relations and eventually became Executive Secretary of the Hollywood Screen Directors Guild. The Guild recognised his service to the motion picture industry in 1950 with an Honorary Life Membership, together with such eminent Hollywood pioneers as D.W. Griffith, Walt Disney and Charlie Chaplin. No other Australian has attained this film industry acclaim.

A vision splendid

Kingsley Fairbridge was born in South Africa in 1885 and from the age of eleven was brought up in Rhodesia (now Zimbabwe). During a visit to England in 1903, he was deeply disturbed by the extent and depth of poverty in the industrial cities and especially horrified at the wasted human resources of children born into such poverty. He returned to Rhodesia a year later determined to do something to help these children, developing a vision that would initiate the Child Emigration Society, later the Fairbridge

Society, and lead to the establishment of settlements for orphaned and unwanted children in Rhodesia, New Zealand, Canada and Australia. The scheme that Fairbridge and his collaborators constructed was based on what he called his 'Vision Splendid':

I saw great Colleges of Agriculture (not workhouses) springing up in every man-hungry corner of the Empire. I saw children shedding the bondage of bitter circumstances and stretching their legs and minds amid the thousand interests of the farm. I saw waste turned to providence, the waste of un-needed humanity converted to the husbandry of unpeopled acres.

To realise this vision, Fairbridge determined that he needed to become a Rhodes Scholar to provide himself with the education and contacts he correctly believed necessary to achieving his aims. After four attempts (his primary and secondary education had been sporadic) he became the first South African to be successful in winning this demanding scholarship and returned to England to study at Oxford University.

On 19 October 1909, Rhodes Scholar Kingsley Fairbridge addressed a meeting of 49 fellow undergraduates at the Colonial Club, Oxford, on the subject of child emigration. The government of Western Australia made an offer of land and in 1912 Kingsley and his wife established the first Farm School (now Fairbridge Village) at a site south of Pinjarra, receiving the first thirteen orphans from Britain in January 1913. In 1920, the school was relocated to its current site north of Pinjarra.

Although Kingsley Fairbridge died in 1924 at the age of 39, his 'Vision Splendid' lived on in England, Rhodesia, New Zealand, Canada, elsewhere in Australia and, most persistently, in Western Australia. In 1937, a farm school was founded at Molong, New South Wales, and another at Bacchus Marsh, Victoria. Two smaller schools were also established at Draper's Hall, Adelaide and Tresca,

Tasmania in the 1950s. Canadian schools were established in 1935 and 1938. Today Fairbridge Village in Pinjarra is the last surviving intact Fairbridge operation with an important historical role in regional, state, national and international affairs in relation to migration, welfare and community development.

The schools were generally modelled on similar lines, with a number of cottages or cabins grouped into small settlements within a working farm, catering for children between six and fifteen. Each dwelling had a 'cottage mother' and the boys were trained in agricultural work skills while the girls were trained in domestic skills, their labour also producing most of their food. Food, worship, education and health care were communally provided. The scheme also provided preschool care for those under six, who were looked after in England until old enough to emigrate. After children left the schools there was also an after-care operation catering for individuals up to the age of 21.

This arrangement lasted until after World War II when, in response to changing circumstances in the Dominions and in Britain, ongoing administrative and managerial changes were made. Throughout these changes, Fairbridge farm schools continued to send considerable numbers of boys and girls to their various operations. From the 1960s, changing attitudes to welfare and immigration, new arrangements for child welfare and a decreasing demand for agricultural skills increasingly rendered Kingsley Fairbridge's basic scheme unviable.

At this time the 'One-Parent' and 'Two-Parent' schemes were introduced to cater for the increasing numbers of children still in a parental relationship of some kind. These were effectively family reunion operations in which the Village would take the child or children into care and the single parent, in the case of the One-Parent scheme, would be found employment and accommodation in the same state. The Two-Parent version operated for families of five or more children where both parents were still in the family relationship. In this case the Village looked after the children but took no responsibility for finding employment and accommodation for the parents. The desired result of these arrangements was that families under threat of splitting could be assisted long enough for the parents to establish a home, at which time the child or children could be returned to them.

Despite these innovations, the era of child migration had long ended and the Fairbridge farm schools gradually closed down or were repurposed. In 1981, the last of the operations, Fairbridge Village at Pinjarra, ceased to operate as a farm school. In 1983, the current Fairbridge Western Australia Inc. was established, achieving charitable status in 1996. The Village is now a non-profit charitable youth organisation and location for the popular Fairbridge music festival, among other activities.

The extensive folklore of Fairbridge farm schools includes parodic ditties made up by the children who resided there over the years. To the tune of the hymn 'There is a Golden Land', they sang:

> There is a mouldy dump, down Fairbridge way.
> Where we get bread and jam, three times a day.
> Eggs and bacon we don't see, we get sawdust in our tea.
> That's why we're gradually fading away.
> Fade away, fade away. Fade away, fade away.
> That's why we're gradually fading away.

Whimsical ditties like this seem at odds with revelations of widespread abuse within the Fairbridge system and other institutions for lone children. But, like many oral traditions of the disempowered, they satirise poor conditions in such places and are a form of protest veiled in humour.

The illywacker

Australia once had an unenviable reputation in the world of crime as the home of numberless confidence tricksters. 'Illywackers', 'ripperty men' or 'spielers', among other names given by those who had been conned, were a real danger in the late nineteenth and early twentieth centuries. Journalist and author Ambrose Pratt was apparently well acquainted with some of these characters and wrote a lengthy exposé of their tricks for the English newspapers.

Pratt began by pointing out that the spieler was 'a swindler and a black-guard' who preyed on 'simple-minded country folk, unsuspicious foreign visitors, and fools at large', either with one or two accomplices or in a large gang. The police at that time reckoned there were at least 100 spielers in Sydney alone. In 1902, Pratt described the typical shyster:

*I*n person the spieler is a man of respectable appearance and affable demeanour. A skilful impersonator, his shape is protean; he is by turns a squatter, a lawyer, a millionaire, a lucky digger, a Supreme Court judge, a gentleman of private fortune, an English 'Johnnie,' fresh from 'Home'—sporting a lisp and the conventional 'Haw! Haw! Doncher know, deah boy!'—a parson, an eccentric retired merchant, a capitalist looking for investments for his money, or a bookmaker. He is always a man of gentlemanly presence, sometimes he is a gentleman by birth.

The spieler was always well dressed, adorned with plenty of jewellery.

*H*e puts up invariably at the best hotels, for at such places he meets the majority of his victims. He is a bird of passage, flitting quickly from State to State, and he never appears twice in the same character in the same town or at the same hotel. Finally, he is a man of brains, a keen student of human nature, and an exquisite comedian.

⌒

The article went on to describe some of the cons of the spieler and his many guises.

*H*is favorite character is that of the wealthy do-nothing, a blase man of the world. In this guise he attaches himself to young men whom he meets at his hotel, fast or giddy young men whose tastes incline to gambling. Singling out a particular victim, the wealthiest, or, at least, the most foolish, he feigns a fancy and flatters the pigeon to the top of his bent. When the time is ripe, he hires two rooms in the same office building in the city, which he furnishes lavishly on the time payment system. Choosing a particular evening, he has his luggage taken to the railway station (without his victim's knowledge), and then, after dinner, off-handedly invites his 'dear young friend' to stroll round with him to his club. The victim consents, and they repair to the aforesaid two rooms, the 'club' forsooth. A confederate, in livery, admits them. Other confederates are lounging in both rooms, who, however, affect to take no notice of the newcomers. The spieler calls for drinks. The victim unsuspiciously imbibes a drugged whisky and soda.

Presently the spieler introduces his protege to his confederates. A game of cards is suggested. The victim sleepily agrees. He plays and loses. When he has lost all his ready cash he signs blank cheques, which are presented to him for that purpose by the spieler. The spieler later on takes him back in a cab to the hotel, his 'dear young friend' apparently reeling drunk, and cashes his cheques over the bar, feeing the obliging barman liberally for the service. An hour later the spieler is comfortably seated in a railway carriage—on his way to another town—often hundreds of pounds richer for his trouble.

Then there was the parson collecting funds for the poor of his parish or feigning to lend money to a mug with a mortgaged property. Another was a special Australian favourite, selling shares in non-existent mines. In the 'lucky digger' con, the spieler:

. . . exhibits marvellous specimens of gold quartz from his 'mine!' He lavishes money about and shouts 'champagne' for anyone who will listen to his 'lucky digger' stories. One evening, when apparently 'half seas over', he offers in a well-stimulated burst of good nature, to give any of those present (he takes care to have a tipsy crowd about him) a half share in his mine for a mere song, say £250. Astounding as it may seem, his offer is invariably rushed, and some would-be rogue (for no honest man would traffic with a drunken man) presses the money into his hand, and induces him to sign a scribbled document.

I once saw two rascally young idiots fight in a crowded bar for the privilege of buying a half share in such an imaginary mine. They compromised by each handing the spieler £200, and agreeing between themselves to halve the share they had bought. Next morning, to their surprise, and, I confess, mine (for I thought the lucky digger genuine), the spieler had vanished, leaving no address.

The crook who pulled this one off turned out to be an especially notorious character who had carried out a number of 'long firm' frauds.

Pratt concluded with a warning:

His tricks are innumerable, the repertory of his characters unlimited. He is, indeed, an interesting and instructive body, but young Englishmen would do well to beware of them—those, I mean, who contemplate a visit to Australia, for their class furnishes him with an unceasing supply of victims, and from long experience he knows them well, their faults, their follies, and their frailties.

Although the term 'spieler' is no longer with us, the practice certainly persists and a mug is still born every minute, if not more frequently.

"For gorsake, stop laughing:
this is serious!"

23

Working for a laugh

We, the willing, led by the unknowing,
Are doing the impossible for the ungrateful.
We have done so much, for so long, with so little,
We are now qualified to do anything with nothing.

Anonymous

ONCE DESCRIBED AS 'the curse of the drinking class', work is
the lot of most people. To be endured, work needs to be laughed
at as well as laughed about. Australians have a fertile supply of
workplace humour, past and present. From outback yarns to
modern office jokes, from stump speeches to secret occupational
lingo, we have been working for a laugh since we began to work.

Droving in a bar

They were boasting in the bar about the biggest mob of cattle
they'd ever driven, here, there and every-bloody-where. One had
driven a mob of 6000 from Perth to Wave Hill. At least, he had
6000 when he started but when he finished over two years later,
he had 10,000. And so it went on.

An old bloke sat quietly in the corner, taking it all in. When
there was a cool moment in the hot air, he piped up. 'You blokes
talk about droving! Let me tell you about a real drive with a really

507

big mob. Me and a mate broke the Australian droving record. We picked up a big mob at Barkly. Took us two days to ride right round 'em, it was that big. Anyway, we started with this mob and drove them clear down to Hobart.'

The bar fell into a stunned silence before one of the young blokes piped up. 'Ow'd ya get 'em across the Bass Strait?' he asked sarcastically.

The old drover looked closely at him and said, 'Don't be stupid, son, we went the other way.'

A fine team of bullocks

They've been telling this yarn since Coopers Creek was first named, and probably long before. The story goes that a bullock driver had a crack team of beasts and on one particular trip was forced to get across a heavily flooded Coopers Creek. Usually this is an impossible task, but on this occasion the floodwaters didn't look too deep, so the bullock driver decided to give it a try.

He drew his team and wagon of wool up on the northern bank and spoke lovingly to them in the tender way that bullockies have, telling them that they now had a big challenge to get across the torrent. The bullocky then walked into the water and found that it was just up around his knees, showing his animals that it was not too dangerous.

He then went back and spoke lovingly to each and every one of the 22 beasts in the team. He told them what fine beasts they were and how he wanted them to pull together across the stream. Off they went, the lead bullock bravely forging ahead and the bullock shouting encouragement to the team.

After a titanic effort, the bullocks, the wool wagon and the bullock made it onto dry land at the other side. 'Whoa,' cried the bullocky, 'time for a rest.' As they settled down the bullocky looked back and saw with amazement that his champion team of bullocks had pulled the river 200 metres out of its course.

Without a word of a lie.

A stump speech

The 'stump speech' is a form of polished gibberish about nothing at all. Stump speeches featured in the United States during nineteenth-century political campaigns and were also used as entertainment and as forms of 'spruiking' a product, often of the snake-oil variety. Australia has a similar tradition of these absurd but entertaining rants. This one is thought to date from the early Federation period with its reference to George Reid, leader of the first Federal opposition, free trade advocate and eventually prime minister in 1904–05.

*L*adies and gentlemen—kindly turn your optics towards me for a few weeks and I will endeavour to enlighten you on the subject of duxology, theology, botanology, zoology or any other ology you like. I wish to make an apology, yes my sorefooted, black-eyed rascals, look here and answer me a question I am about to put to your notice. I want to be very lenient with you, but what shall it be, mark you, what shall the subject of my divorce (excuse me), discourse, this evening be? What shall I talk about? Shall it be about the earth, sun, sea, stars, moon, Camp Grove or jail? Now I wish to put before your notice the labour question. It is simply deloructious—isn't that alright? Yes, allow me to state the labour question is not what it should be.

Now look here, when I was quite a young man I worked very hard indeed, so hard, in fact, that I have seen the drops of perspiration dropping from my manly brow onto the pavement with a thud. Excuse me—yes, I say we shall not work at all! Then again, my wooden, brainless youths, answer me this: should men work between meals? No, no certainly not; it is boisterous!

Other questions I would put before your notice tonight are—why does Georgie Reid wear an eyeglass? Ha, ha my friends we don't know where we are; therefore where we are we do not know. Yes my noble-faced, flat-feeted, cockeyed, rank-headed asses, I will put before your notice other questions but no longer will I linger on these tantalising subjects. As time wags on and as I have to leave you; certainly I will not take you with me, therefore I leave you. Now the best of fools must part and as I see a policeman coming along I will go. Goodnight!

Working on the railway

The Australian railways have provided a living and even a way of life for very many people. Railway tradition is rich with poems, songs and yarns about the joys and irritations of keeping the trains running; old-time railmen will tell you about boiling the billy and frying eggs on their coal shovels as they stoked the boilers of steam trains. Or regale you with yarns about having to burn the sleepers lying beside the track when the coal ran out, just to keep the 'loco' going and get passengers to their destinations on time. Despite this level of commitment and effort, the slow train is a common feature of railway lore, with countless yarns on the same topic being lovingly retold across the decades and across the country.

On many rural and regional lines, trains were once so regularly and reliably late that passengers had long been resigned to very long waits. But one day on an isolated platform that shall remain nameless, the train arrived smack on time. A delighted and astounded passenger was so overcome by the experience that he ran up to the engine driver and thanked him profusely for arriving on time this once. The driver smiled faintly and replied, 'No chance, mate, this is yesterday's train.'

An anonymous poet expressed the desolate feeling of waiting for a train that may possibly never come:

All around the water tank
Waitin' for a train.
I'm a thousand miles away from home
Just a'standin' in the rain.
I'm sittin'
Drinkin'
Waitin'
Thinkin'
Hopin' for a train.

Service!

In this yarn, a passenger receives impeccable service.

A passenger boarded the train in Melbourne intending to get off at Albury. But when the conductor checked his ticket he had to tell him that the train didn't stop at Albury. The passenger went into a panic. 'I have to get off at Albury, it's a matter of life and death.' And pleaded with the conductor to stop the train for him.

The conductor said, 'Sorry, Sir, we can't stop the train at an unscheduled station but I do have a suggestion. I will ask the driver to slow down at Albury and I'll help you to alight from the train. It will be tricky and dangerous, but if I hold you outside the door by the collar and you start running we should be able to get you down without injury when your legs reach the right speed.'

The passenger was so desperate to get to Albury that he immediately agreed to this hazardous suggestion. 'Just one thing though,' said the conductor, 'after you're down be sure to stop running before you reach the end of the platform.' The plucky passenger nodded his agreement.

As the train approached Albury, the engine driver duly slowed down as much as he could. As soon as the platform came in sight, the conductor opened the door and held the passenger out over the platform. He began running in the air as he had ben instructed and the train was about halfway along the station before the conductor gently lowered him down. He hit the platform and staggered but managed to stay upright, losing momentum gradually as he slowed his running legs. He managed to come to a teetering stop just before the end of the platform. Just then the last car rolled past and he was suddenly grabbed again by the collar and hauled back onto the train. Shocked, he twisted around to see the guard smiling happily at him—'Expect you thought you'd missed your train, Sir!'

High-octane travel

This is an old railway yarn told in many places:

a couple of mechanics worked together in the railway sheds servicing diesel trains in Brisbane. One day there is a stop work meeting over some issue or other and the two find themselves sitting around with nothing to do. They'd like to go to the pub, of course, but they can't leave the workplace. Then one of them, let's call him Phil, has a bright idea. 'I've heard that you can get a really good kick from drinking diesel fuel. Want to give it a go?'

His mate, we'll call him Bruce, bored out of his mind, readily agrees. They pour a sizeable glass of diesel each and get stuck in. Sure enough, they have a great day.

Next morning Phil wakes up, gets out of bed and is pleasantly surprised to find that despite yesterday's diesel spree he feels pretty good. Shortly afterwards, his phone rings. It's Bruce. He asks Phil how he is feeling. 'Great mate, no hangover at all. What about you?'

'No,' agrees Bruce, 'all good.'

That's amazing,' replies Phil, 'we should get into that diesel more often.'

'Sure mate,' says Bruce, 'but have you farted yet?'

'What?' replies Phil, a bit taken aback. 'No, I haven't.'

'Well, make sure you don't 'cause I'm in Melbourne.'

Railway birds

This tongue-in-cheek description of various railway occupations in the form of a bird-spotting guide is at least as old as the 1930s, and probably earlier. No prizes for guessing which occupational group originated this item:

Engine Drivers—Rare birds, dusky plumage. Generally useful. No song; but for a consideration will jump points, signals etc. Have been known to drink freely near the haunts of man—especially at isolated stations. Occasionally intermarry with station-master's daughters (see Station Masters). Known colloquially by such names as 'Hell Fire Jack,' 'Mad Hector,' 'Speedy Steve,' 'Whaler,' 'Smokebox,' and 'Bashes.' Great sports, often carried from their engines suffering from shock—caused by wrong information.

Cleaners—Very little is known regarding the habits of these animals. How the name originated remains a mystery.

Guards—Fairly common. Red faces. Can go a long time without water. Easily recognisable by their habit of strutting up and down. Shrill whistle, but no sense of time. Sleep between stations, hence common cry of 'Up Guards, and at 'em.' Serve no generally useful purpose, but can be trained to move light perambulators, keep an eye on unescorted females, and wave small flags.

Porters—Habits strangely variable. Sometimes seen in great numbers: sometimes not at all. Much attracted by small bright objects. No song, but have been known to hum—between trains. Naturally indolent, but will carry heavy weights if treated rightly (i.e. sufficiently). Natural enemies of passengers (see passengers). Treated with contempt by station-masters.

Station Masters—Lordly, brilliant plumage. Rarely leave their nests. Ardent sitters. Most naturalists state these birds have no song, but Railway Commissioners dispute this. Have been known to eat porters (See Porters). Female offspring occasionally intermarry with very fast Engine Drivers.

Repair Gangs—Plumage nondescript. Migratory in habit. Nests are conspicuous and usually found in clusters near railway lines. No song but passengers assert their plaintive echoing cry of 'Pa-p-er' is unmistakable.

Passengers—Very common. Varied plumage. Will stand anything as a rule, but have been known to attack porters (see Porters). Often kept in captivity under deplorable conditions by ticket inspectors, guards etc. Will greedily and rapidly devour sandwiches and buns under certain (i.e. rotten) conditions. These birds are harmless when properly treated, and should be encouraged by all nature lovers.

Rechtub klat

Butchers in Australia developed a version of a secret trade jargon, or back slang, known as 'rechtub klat'—Butcher Talk, pronounced 'rech-tub kay-lat'. This descended from the similar back slang of migrating or transported butchers from London's markets, among whom back slanging was especially rife. In Australia there was little need for trade secrets to be protected but a secret language allowed butchers to converse while others were present, perhaps commenting on the price to be charged or admiring the physical qualities of a female customer. Another valued use of this lingo was to insult troublesome customers with impunity. Butchers in France traditionally uttered a similar convolution of language; it was known there as *loucherbem*, *boucher* being French for 'butcher'. Got that?

Although now spoken by very few, rechtub klat was once a relatively well-developed language. Today its vocabulary is fairly restricted to types of meat—*feeb* for beef, *bmal* for lamb and *gip* for pig—and crude but admiring comments such as *doog tsub* (good bust) and *doog esra* (good arse), among other such constructions crafted as required. A few other slabs of butcher talk are *kool, toh lrig* (look, hot girl), *gaf* (fag, as in cigarette) and *toor*, meaning root, as in the Australian vulgarism for sexual intercourse.

As well as commenting negatively on fussy customers and admiringly on young ladies, rechtub klat could be used to let the other butchers know that a particular cut had run out. So if there were 'on steltuc ni eht pohs' they should sell something different to any a customer who wanted 'steltuc'. It was not unknown for butchers to have complete clandestine conversations among themselves, as featured in the Australian movie *The Hard Word* (2002), when the language was used by the bank-robbing main characters to securely communicate their secrets to each other.

The garbos' Christmas

A characteristically Australian Christmas occupational tradition, now probably obsolete, involved the 'garbos'. For many decades the garbage men were in the habit of leaving a Christmas message, often in verse, for their clients. The message would generally wish the household well for the coming year and was also designed as a reminder of the traditional garbos' Christmas gift. This would be bottles or tins of beer left out along with the garbage bin on the last garbage day before the season began. Here are a couple of World War I examples of some Melbourne garbo greetings:

YOUR
SANITARY ATTENDANT
WISHES YOU
A Merry Christmas

Awake, awake, all freeborn sons,
Sound your voices loud and clear.
Wishing all a Merry Christmas
Likewise a glad New Year.

While referring to the Sewerage Scheme
As the greatest in the nation,
Until completed, I hope you'll give
Us some consideration.

The mission of our life just now,
Is to cleanse and purify.
We do our duty faithfully,
Be the weather wet or dry.

So while you're spending Xmas
In mirth and melody,
And friends to friends some present give,
Just spare a thought for me.

A MERRY CHRISTMAS

In recent years this custom seems to have dwindled, with only brief messages, if any, appearing. But even as late as 1983 it was possible to receive something like the following:

CHRISTMAS GREETINGS FROM
GARBO SQUAD
(Garbologists to you)

The year from us has gone,
Now it's time to think upon
Our blessings great and small:
May they continue for us all.

Your health, we hope, like ours is fine.
May 1984 be in similar line,
And in the New Year, we pray,
We'll serve you truly every day.

To you and yours joy we wish
That Christmas be a full dish
Of gladness, content and good health,
And the New Year bring you wealth.

Brian, Neville, Wayne

A Christmas message

Always a time for over-indulgence, Christmas at the OK Mine near Norseman, Western Australia, back in the roaring days was celebrated with enthusiasm, by some at least.

It was Christmas Eve at O.K. in the days when the mine was in full swing and the local pub was the scene of a glorious general spree. In front of the building there lay many inches of thick red dust, also various stumps. On the following morning several booze-soaked individuals were slumbering in the layers of red powder after many hours of rolling and burrowing about. Waiting outside the pub for the breakfast bell to ring, the mine engineer was accosted by an aboriginal man named Jacky, who, after gazing thoughtfully for some time at the inebriated individuals sleeping in the dust, remarked, 'My word boss, white Australia all right today, eh?'

Total eclipse of communication

A favourite theme of workplace humour is communication—its failure, its absence or its distortion. One example is the shrinking memo, and the message it tried, at first, to convey. This item begins with a memo from the top levels of authority to the next level down, let's say from the managing director to the works director. The memo begins:

*M*emo: Managing Director to Works Director
Tomorrow morning there will be a total eclipse of the sun at 9 o'clock. This is something that we cannot see happen every day, so allow the workforce to line up outside in their best clothes to watch it. To mark the occasion of this rare occurrence I will personally explain it to them. If it is raining we shall not be able to see it very well and in that case the workforce should assemble in the canteen.

The next memo conveys this message down the line from the works director to the general works manager:

By order of the Managing Director there will be a total eclipse of the sun at 9 o'clock tomorrow morning.

If it is raining we shall not be able to see it very well on the site in our best clothes. In that case, the disappearance of the sun will be followed through in the canteen. This is something that we cannot see happen every day.

The general works manager then writes to the works manager an even briefer version of this rapidly disintegrating communication:

By order of the General Manager we shall follow through, in our best clothes, the disappearance of the sun in the canteen at 9 o'clock tomorrow morning.

The Managing Director will tell us whether it is going to rain. This is something which we cannot see every day.

In turn, the works manager passes this on to the foreman in another memo:

If it is raining in the canteen tomorrow morning, which is something we cannot see happening every day, our Managing Director in his best clothes, will disappear at 9 o'clock.

Finally, the foreman posts the message, or at least a ludicrous version of it, on the shop floor noticeboard. It reads:

Tomorrow morning at 9 o'clock our Managing Director will disappear. It is a pity that we cannot see this happen every day.

The laws of working life

Whatever can go wrong will go wrong. That's Murphy's Law. Even if you haven't heard of this universal truth, you'll be familiar with the general principle and the fact that whatever does go wrong at work will be at the worst possible time and in the worst possible way.

Things go wrong for us so often and with such devastating results that Murphy's Law alone cannot predict all the consequences of human error and disaster. There is a worryingly large number of similar laws, corollaries, axioms and the like, providing advice hard-won from bitter experience. You know the sort of thing. If you drop a slice of buttered bread it will unfailingly land butter-side down. And what about the curious fact that everything always seems to cost more than you happen to have in your pocket or bank account? Or, when you try to take out a loan you have to prove that you don't really need it? Here are some further helpful hints:

- The probability of a given event occurring is inversely proportional to its desirability.
- Left to themselves, things will always go from bad to worse.
- If it is possible that several things will go wrong, the one that does go wrong will do the most damage.
- Any error in any calculation will be in the area of most harm.
- A short cut is the longest distance between two points.
- Work expands to fill the time available.
- Mess expands to fill the space available.
- If you fool around with something long enough, it will eventually break.
- The most important points in any communication will be those first forgotten.
- Whatever you want to do, you have to do something else first.
- Nothing is as simple as it seems.
- Everything takes longer than expected.
- Nothing ever quite works out.
- It's easier to get into a thing than to get out of it.
- When all else fails, read the instructions.

～

Reading these little difficulties and dilemmas of work life suggests that none of us should bother getting out of bed in the morning. But of course, not everything in life goes wrong; sometimes you can have really great days when the sun shines, the birds sing and you feel on top of the world.

But next time you are having a day like this, just remind yourself of the last law of working life:

- If everything seems to be going well, you probably don't know what is going on.

Somebody else's job

Once upon a time there were four people, named Everybody, Somebody, Anybody and Nobody.

There was an important job to be done and Everybody was sure that Somebody would do it.

Anybody could have done it, but Nobody did it.

Somebody got angry about that because it was Everybody's job.

Everybody thought Anybody could do it, but Nobody realised that Everybody didn't do it.

It ended with Everybody blaming Somebody, when really, Nobody could accuse Anybody.

The basic work survival guide

This is an old favourite in Australian workplaces:

The opulence of the front office decor varies inversely with the fundamental solvency of the company.

No project ever gets built on schedule or within budget.

A meeting is an event at which minutes are kept and hours are lost.

The first myth of management is that it exists at all.

A failure will not appear until a new product has passed its final inspection.

New systems will generate new problems.

Nothing motivates a worker more than seeing the boss put in an honest day's work.

After all is said and done, a lot more is said than done.

The friendlier the client's secretary, the greater the chance that the competition has already secured the order.

Work expands to fill the time available.

In any organisation the degree of technical competence is inversely proportional to the level of management.

The grass is brown on both sides of the fence.

No matter what stage of completion the project reaches, the cost of the remainder of the project remains the same.

Most jobs are marginally better than daytime TV.

Twelve things you'll never hear an employee tell the boss

Wishful thinking is nothing new, as this list of helpful suggestions suggests:

1. Never give me work in the morning. Always wait until 5.00 and then bring it to me. The challenge of a deadline is always refreshing.
2. If it's really a 'rush job', run in and interrupt me every ten minutes to inquire how it's going. That greatly aids my efficiency.
3. Always leave without telling anyone where you're going. It gives me a chance to be creative when someone asks where you are.
4. If my arms are full of papers, boxes, books or supplies, don't open the door for me. I might need to learn how to function as a paraplegic in future and opening doors is good training.

5. If you give me more than one job to do, don't tell me which is the priority. Let me guess.

6. Do your best to keep me late. I like the office and really have nowhere to go or anything to do.

7. If a job I do pleases you, keep it a secret. Leaks like that could get me a promotion.

8. If you don't like my work, tell everyone. I like my name to be popular in conversations.

9. If you have special instructions for a job, don't write them down. If fact, save them until the job is almost done.

10. Never introduce me to the people you're with. When you refer to them later, my shrewd deductions will identify them.

11. Be nice to me only when the job I'm doing for you could really change your life.

12. Tell me all your little problems. No one else has any and it's nice to know someone is less fortunate.

Excessive absence

One of the great classics of workplace humour, this was old when it was kicking round the old Post Master General's department in the late 1960s. Versions can still be found on the internet.

*I*nternal Memo # 125
RE: EXCESSIVE ABSENCE TO ALL PERSONNEL.

Due to the excessive number of absences during the past year it has become necessary to put the following new rules into operation immediately.

SICKNESS No excuse. The Management will no longer accept your Doctor's Certificate as proof. We believe that if you are able to go to your doctor you are able to attend work.

DEATH (YOUR OWN) This will be accepted as an excuse. We would like two weeks' notice, however, since we feel it is your duty to train someone else for your job.

DEATH (OTHER THAN YOUR OWN) This is no excuse. There is nothing you can do for them and henceforth no time will be allowed off for funerals. However, in case it should cause some hardship to some of our employees, please note that on your behalf the Management has a special scheme in conjunction with the local council for lunchtime burials, thus ensuring that no time is lost from work.

LEAVE OF ABSENCE FOR AN OPERATION We wish to discourage any thoughts you may have of needing an operation and henceforth no leave of absence will be granted for hospital visits. The Management believes that as long as you are an employee here you will need what you already have and should not consider having any of it removed. We engaged you for your particular job with all your parts and having anything removed would mean that we would be getting less of you than we bargained for.

VISITS TO THE TOILETS Far too much time is spent on the practice. In future the procedure will be that all personnel shall go in alphabetical order. For example: those with the surname being 'A' will go from 9.30 to 9.45; 'B' will go from 9.45 to 10.00. Those of you who are unable to attend at your appropriate time will have to wait until the next day when your turn comes up.

Have a nice day.

THE MANAGEMENT

Running naked with the bulls

Australians like to celebrate and enjoy themselves. No surprise there. But we seem to have a particular affinity for activities that are a bit off the wall and seem to take a perverse delight in parodying pretty well everything. The Darwin Beer Can Regatta is a light-hearted make-do event involving vessels made of empty beer cans. The Henley-on-Todd Regatta in Alice Springs features homemade craft racing along the dry bed of the Todd River. Cockroach Races were established as a regular event at Kangaroo Point, Brisbane on Australia Day 1982. In a similar spirit, they like to do things a little differently in Weipa.

Beginning in 1993 and intended to mark the first rain of the wet season, the locals invented a new tradition for themselves. They called it 'Running Naked with the Bulls'. Why? Because that's exactly what they did. The first event involved 150 local miners streaking nude along a two-kilometre course at 2 a.m. Other than their joggers, the miners carried only a plastic shopping bag for donations to the Royal Flying Doctor Service.

After that, things settled down, more or less, though the running has had what they call 'a chequered history'. The event rapidly established itself on the local calendar and became an international event as well. In 1998, it was believed to have set a record for the highest number of naked people ever to be interviewed; the ABC conducted the interviews from a telephone box along the course as the runners jogged past. Not wanting to appear sexist, the organisers also allowed women to run naked with the bulls in 1999.

Sadly, the event was closed down in 2001 due to complaints about indecency. There has been recent pressure to revive it, though, as Weipa is in need of the tourist income the event attracted. Local police are said to oppose its reintroduction. The future of the Running Naked with the Bulls remains uncertain at the time of writing.

But even when a local custom like this does spring up spontaneously, the commercial world is quick off the mark. A local resident and participant was heard on ABC Radio National back in November 1998, telling of the difficulties the event had encountered with sponsorship. It was not that the locals were against sponsorship for their start of the wet-season celebration; it was just that some sponsors were inappropriate. A large brothel chain wished to sponsor the event but the participants had to decline, not because there was a moral problem, but because the brothel wanted the runners to wear a T-shirt advertising their business. Reluctantly, the runners could not oblige.

Doing business

One of Australia's prominent businessmen was the founder of the airline he characteristically named after himself. Reg Ansett was very much the self-made man. Leaving school at fourteen, he worked as an axeman in the Northern Territory to earn enough to buy a Studebaker to start a road-transport company. This allowed him to buy a Gypsy Moth aeroplane and in 1938, aged just 28, he started Ansett Airways. He continued to display his legendary stubbornness and business acumen through the rest of his life, branching into car hire and other mostly successful businesses. He was a colourful character with a considerable public profile in his day, eventually being knighted for his achievements.

Reg Ansett entered Australian folklore in various ways, but particularly in a story often told about him by friend and foe alike. According to the yarn, a young man was keen to make a name for himself in business, just like the then ageing but incredibly eminent Reg Ansett. The young bloke couldn't believe his luck when he was in a restaurant for a meeting with an important client and he spotted Reg at a table full of other prominent business people, obviously settled in for a long session. Summoning up his courage, he approached the table and nervously addressed the great man, asking for a moment of his time and for a bit of a leg up the slippery ladder of business. Magnanimously, Reg condescended to help out and asked what he could do.

'Well, Mr Ansett,' said the young man, 'I have a very important client coming to lunch with me today. I need to impress this person with my business ideas and also with my contacts. Would you be kind enough to pretend that you know me?'

'Sure,' agreed Reg, mildly amused at the effrontery of the young man and probably reminded of his own early days.

'Thank you so much,' gushed the young man. 'When I leave the restaurant with my client I'll come past your table. Would you be good enough to stand up and greet me as if I were a valued business colleague?'

Reg was bit taken aback, but he was in a good mood over his latest business deal. 'Okay, young fella,' he replied condescendingly, always happy to give a newcomer a helping hand.

Reg went back to his celebrations and the young man returned to his table to meet his client. When the meal was over, Reg and his mates were still hard at it. The young man paid the bill and carefully manoeuvred himself and his client to pass right next to Reg's table. Reg couldn't miss them and remembered that he had agreed to take part in the harmless deception. He got to his feet and enthusiastically held out his hand to the young man, saying, 'Good to see you again, how's business?'

The young man stopped, looked coldly at the great man and said, 'Piss off, Reg, you can see I'm busy.'

The end of a perfect day

Pigs do not fly, of course, but in the world of work they can—and sometimes must—be made to do so:

Another day ends . . .

All targets met
All systems in working order
All customers satisfied
All staff eager and enthusiastic
All pigs fed and ready to fly

Acknowledgements

I WOULD LIKE to acknowledge the following people and organisations for providing information, assistance, advice, guidance or permission to publish stories in their care:

Jane Diplock, Warren Fahey, June Factor, Gwenda Davey, Hugh Anderson, Maureen Seal, Peter Sutton, Mark Gregory, Peter Austin, Keith Pabai, Donald Banu, Eric Hayward, Rob Willis, Olya Willis, Phyl Lobl, Chris Woodland, Tim McCabe, Bob Reece, Peter Parkhill, Peter Ellis, Karl Neuenfeldt, Robyn Floyd, Mary Newham and the descendants of Olga Ernst (Waller), the Oral History and Folklore Collection at the National Library of Australia, the Western Australian Folklore Archive in the John Curtin Prime Ministerial Library at Curtin University of Technology, the Battye Library of Western Australian History, the Queensland State Library, La Trobe Library and the New South Wales State Library.

I would also like to thank Elizabeth Weiss of Allen & Unwin for taking on this project and the staff at A&U who helped turn manuscript into book. I am grateful to the Faculty of Humanities at Curtin University of Technology for assistance with research and pre-publication work. Finally, I hope this book honours the collectors and conservers of Australian stories, many of whose names appear in the text and notes. In particular, this book is dedicated to the legacies of Bill Wannan, Bill Scott, Roland Robinson and Ron Edwards.

Picture credits

1. STORIES IN THE HEART

Daisy Bates (standing) with Aboriginal women and children
Photograph by A.G. Bolam, 1919–1926
South Australian Museum, Bolam Collection

2. PIONEER TRADITIONS

Lost in the Bush
Samuel Calvert (engraver), Nicholas Chevalier (artist), 1864
State Library of Victoria, image no. IMP24/09/64/1

3. MAKING MONSTERS

The Bunyip
J. Macfarlane (engraver), 1890
State Library of Victoria, image no. IAN01/10/90/12

4. LEGENDS ON THE LAND

'Inland Sea' from T. J. Maslen, *The Friend of Australia: Or, a Plan for
    Exploring the Interior, and for Carrying On a Survey of the Whole
    Continent of Australia, By a Retired Officer of the Hon. East India
    Company's Service*, Hurst, Chance and Co., London, 1830.
Battye Library of Western Australian History

5. THE HAUNTED LAND

Fisher's Ghost Creek, Campbelltown, c. 1909
Campbelltown City Library, Local Studies Collection

6. TALES OF WONDER

Copy of *Children's Hour*
Photograph of painting by William Ford, 1870
State Library of Victoria, image no. H96.160/1621

7. BULLDUST

Captain Hurley spins some yarns, 1929–1931
Commander Blair, W.J. Griggs, Scout Marr, Mr Tyler, Captain Hurley
    and A.J. Hodgeman
Part of Frank Hurley B.A.N.Z. Antarctic Research Expedition
    photographs
National Library of Australia, image no. 10932811-95

8. HEROES

'Damn your explosive bullets' cartoon
From Hartt, C.L, *Humorosities*, Australian Trading & Agencies Co.
    Ltd., London, 1917

9. CHARACTERS

'Dad' (character from *On Our Selection*)
Alfred Vincent (artist) from first edition of Arthur H. Davis (Steele
    Rudd) 'On Our Selection', *Bulletin* newspaper, Sydney, 1899

10. HARD CASES

Eulo Queen, 1920
Creator unknown
John Oxley Library, State Library of Queensland, image no. 195153

11. WORKING PEOPLE

The Bullocky (postcard)
Harry John Weston (artist) 1874–19?
State Library of Victoria, image no. H87.358/15

12. WIDE, BROWN LAND

Relation ov iovrnal dv voyage de Bontekoe avx Indes Orientales
    [Relationship or log of Bontekoe's trip to the East Indies].

Separately paginated section of *Thévenot's Relations de divers voyages curieux* that comprises the accounts of the voyages of Bontekoe and Pelsaert, the latter containing the third state of the map of Australia with the line of the Tropic of Capricorn added.

John Oxley Library, State Library of Queensland, Neg: 855351

13. UPON THE FATAL SHORE

Convict love token from James Branch (undated). The engraved side features the text 'Love & Union/JAB/James Blanch/Ann Harley/ SACRED TO FRIENDSHIP' around a design of two hearts joined by a ribbon. The reverse side is the obverse of a cartwheel penny showing the bust, in profile, of a man.

National Museum of Australia

14. PLAINS OF PROMISE

Wood engraving, 1876. The Opposum-Hill rush, near Berlin, Victoria, published in *The Australian Sketcher*, June 10 1876. The upper view is of Main Street showing timber and bark buildings, the Shamrock Hotel at the left and next to it J. McLeish's store. Further along is the Bank of Victoria and another store with the sign 'Kirwan' and a Skittle Saloon at the right hand side. A sign advertising 'Mrs Sibley tonight' is on the front of the Shamrock Hotel.

State Library of Victoria

15. A FAIR GO

Show at Hammondville, 1937.

State Library of New South Wales

16. HOW WE TRAVEL THE LAND

Horse-drawn coach with passengers outside Cobb & Co. Ltd, Coach Proprietors, Booking Office. Place unknown, but probably the Eastern Goldfields.

State Library of Western Australia, 2946B/1

17. DOING IT TOUGH

Happy Valley unemployed camp, La Perouse c. 1932.

State Library of New South Wales

18. HOME OF THE WEIRD

Henry 'The Breaker' Morant (1865–1902). A drover and horseman who began contributing verse and ballads to Sydney *Bulletin* in September 1891, he becoming widely known by his pen name 'The Breaker'.
Blue Mountains City Library

19. ROMANCING THE SWAG

Studio portrait of a swagman, Melbourne, Victoria, c. 1887. (Lindt, J. W. (John William), 1845–1926, photographer).
National Library of Australia, vn4312961

20. AFTER THE KELLYS

Wood engraving, 1880. Ned Kelly (sketched as he was leaving Benalla), published in *The Illustrated Australian News*, July 3 1880.
State Library of Victoria

21. THE CHILD IN THE BUSH

Wood engraving, 1867. 'The Lost Children of Daylesford' (A. C. Cooke (Albert Charles), 1836–1902, artist; W. H. Harrison, engraver) published in *The Illustrated Australian News*, October 26 1867. Shows men finding remains of lost children in hollow of large tree.
State Library of Victoria

22. LARGER THAN LIFE

Lobby card, 1921. Playgoers Pictures, Inc. presents J.P. McGowan in *Discontented Wives*. The caption reads: 'We'll keep it a secret from Ruth until it's assayed.'
Western Silent Films Lobby Card Collection, Yale Collection of Western Americana, Beinecke Rare Book and Manuscript Library, New Haven, CT

23. WORKING FOR A LAUGH

Drawing, 1933. 'For gorsake, stop laughing: this is serious!' (Stan Cooke, artist), part of the Stan Cross Archive of cartoons and drawings, 1912–1974. Reproduced with permission of Mr Simon Cross.
National Library of Australia, vn4306283

Sources and selected references

1. STORIES IN THE HEART

Bates, D., *The Passing of the Aborigines: a lifetime spent among the natives of Australia*, John Murray, London, 1938

Berndt, R. & C., *The Speaking Land: myth and story in Aboriginal Australia*, Penguin, Ringwood VIC, 1989

Faurot, J. (editor), *Asian–Pacific Folktales and Legends*, Simon & Schuster, New York, 1995

Hassell, E., revised by Davidson, D., 'Myths and Folktales of the Wheelman Tribe of South-Western Australia', in *Folklore* vol. 45, no. 3, September 1934; vol. 45, no. 4, December 1934; vol. 46, no. 2, June 1935; vol. 46, no. 3, September 1935

Lawrie, M. (collected & translated), *Tales from Torres Strait*, University of Queensland Press, St Lucia QLD, 1972

Mathews, J. (compiler) & White, I. (editor), *The Opal That Turned Into Fire and other stories from the Wangkumara*, Magabala Books, Broome, 1994

McConchie, P. (collected & edited), *Elders: wisdom from Australia's Indigenous leaders*, Cambridge University Press, Melbourne, 2003

Palmer, K., 'Aboriginal Oral Tradition from South-west of Western Australia', in *Folklore*, vol. 87, no. 1, 1976

Parker, K. Langloh (collected & edited), *Australian Legendary Tales*, David Nutt, London, 1896

Rose, D., *Dingo Makes Us Human: life and land in an Aboriginal Australian culture*, Cambridge University Press, Melbourne, 1992

Ryan, J., 'Australia's Best-Known Folkloric Text and its Several Fates', in *Australian Folklore*, vol. 16, 2001

Spencer, B., *The Native Tribes of the Northern Territory of Australia*, Macmillan, London, 1914

2. PIONEER TRADITIONS

Darian-Smith, K., Poignant, R., Schaffer K., *Captive Lives: Australian captivity narratives*, Sir Robert Menzies Centre for Australian Studies, Institute of Commonwealth Studies, University of London, 1993

Moore, G.F., *Diary of Ten Years Eventful Life of an Early Settler in Western Australia*, with an introduction by C.T. Stannage, University of Western Australia Press, Nedlands WA, 1978

Perth Gazette, 5 July 1834, 12 July 1834, 19 July 1834, 26 July 1834, 9 August 1834, 6 September 1834, 4 October 1834

Port Phillip Herald, 10 March 1846

Torney, K., *Babes in the Bush: the making of an Australian image*, Curtin University Books, Fremantle WA, 2005

——'Jane Duff's Heroism: the last great human bush story?' in *La Trobe Journal*, vol. 63, Autumn 1999

3. MAKING MONSTERS

Bauer, N., 'A Mystery Unsolved: the story of the Min Min Light', in *Royal Geographical Society of Australasia (Queensland) Bulletin*, vol. 7, no.1, January 1982

Beatty, B., *A Treasury of Australian Folk Tales and Traditions*, Ure Smith, Sydney, 1960

Birch, R., *Wyndham Yella Fella*, Magabala Books, Broome, 2003

Clarke, P., 'Indigenous Spirit and Ghost Folklore of "settled" Australia', in *Folklore* vol. 118, no. 2, August 2007

Dixon, R., *Oceanic Mythology*, Marshall Jones Co., Boston, 1916

Dunlop, W., 'Australian Folk-Lore Stories', in *Journal of the (Royal) Anthropological Institute of Great Britain and Ireland*, vol. xxviii, 1899

Edwards, R., *Fred's Crab and Other Bush Yarns*, Rams Skull Press, Kuranda QLD, 1990

Farwell, G., *Land of Mirage: the story of men, cattle and camels on the Birdsville Track*, Cassell, London, 1950

Hassell, E., 'My Dusky Friends', undated typescript, Battye Library of Western Australian History

Henry, J., 'Pumas in the Grampians Mountains: a compelling case?', an updated report of the Deakin Puma Society, Deakin University Press, 2001

Holden, R., *Bunyips: Australia's folklore of fear*, National Library of Australia, Canberra, 2001

Journal of the Anthropological Society of South Australia, vol. 29, no. 2, 1991

Journal of the Anthropological-Institute, vol. xxx, 1900

Leeds Mercury, 25 January 1834

Massola, A., *Bunjil's Cave: myths, legends and superstitions of the Aborigines of south-east Australia*, Lansdowne Press, Melbourne, 1968

Morgan, J., *The Life and Adventures of William Buckley*, Archibald Macdougall, London, 1852

North Australian Monthly, January 1961

Parker, K. Langloh, *The Euahlayi Tribe: a study of Aboriginal life in Australia*, Archibald Constable, London, 1905

Praed, Mrs Campbell, 'The Bunyip', in *Coo-ee: tales of Australian life by Australian ladies*, Mrs Patchett Martin (editor), Griffith Farran Okeden & Welsh, London and Sydney, 1891

Robinson, R. (editor), *Aboriginal Myths and Legends*, Sun Books, Melbourne, 1966

Scott, B., *Pelicans and Chihuahuas and Other Urban Legends*, University of Queensland Press, St Lucia QLD, 1996

Short, K., *Echoes of the Clarence*, International Colour Productions, Stanthorpe QLD, 1980

Sorenson, E., *Life in the Australian Backblocks*, Whitcomb & Tombs, Melbourne, 1911

South Australian Gazette and Colonial Register, 28 November 1853, 31 January 1889

Sunday Mail Magazine, 2 March 1941

Unaipon, D., *Legendary Tales of the Australian Aborigines*, Muecke, S. &
Shoemaker, A. (editors), The Miegunyah Press, Melbourne, 2001
Walkabout, 1 April 1937

4. LEGENDS ON THE LAND

Anzac Day Commemoration Committee, Queensland, www.anzacday.
org.au, February 2009

Australian National Dictionary Centre, www.anu.edu.au/andc/
ozwords/April_2000/Anzacs.html, December 2005

Australian War Memorial, www.awm.gov.au, December 2005

Beatty, B., *A Treasury of Australian Folk Tales and Traditions*, Ure Smith,
Sydney, 1960

Committee for Geographical Names in Australia, www.icsm.gov.au/
icsm/cgna/lesson/story_001.html, September 2008

Department of Defence, www.defence.gov.au/anzacday/history.htm,
February 2009

Edwards, R., *Fred's Crab and Other Bush Yarns*, Rams Skull Press,
Kuranda QLD, 1989

Idriess, I., *Lasseter's Last Ride: an epic of central Australian gold discovery*,
Angus & Robertson, Sydney, 1931

Jack, A., 'I'd had it in mind ...', in *Wartime*, no. 46, 2009

Marshall-Stoneking, B., *Lasseter: the making of a legend*, G. Allen &
Unwin, Australia, 1985

Martin, G., Western Australian Folklore Archive, John Curtin Prime
Ministerial Library, Curtin University of Technology

Norledge, M. (editor), *Aboriginal Legends from Eastern Australia: the
Richmond–Mary River area*, Reed, Sydney, 1968

Parramatta RSL, www.parramattarsl.com.au/rsl9/DS38.htm, December
2005

Robinson, R., *The Man Who Sold his Dreaming*, Currawong Publishing,
Sydney, 1965

Trollope, Anthony, *Australia and New Zealand*, Chapman & Hall,
London, 1873

5. THE HAUNTED LAND

Anon., 'Fisher's Ghost: A legend of Campbelltown', in *Tegg's Monthly
Magazine*, vol. 1, March 1863

Beatty, B., *A Treasury of Australian Folk Tales and Traditions*, Ure Smith, Sydney, 1960

Beckett, J., 'A Death in the Family: some Torres Strait ghost stories', in Hiatt, L. (editor), *Australian Aboriginal Mythology*, Australian Institute of Aboriginal Studies, Canberra, 1975

Clarke, P., 'Indigenous Spirit and Ghost Folklore of "Settled" Australia', in *Folklore*, vol. 118, no. 2, August 2007

Cusack, F. (editor), *Australian Ghosts*, Angus & Robertson, London, 1975

Davis, R., *The Ghost Guide to Australia*, Bantam Books, Moorebank NSW, 1998

Freeman's Journal, Sydney, 1891

Emberg, B. & J., *Ghostly Tales of Tasmania*, Regal Publications, Launceston, 1991

Gale, J., *Canberra*, A.M. Fallick & Sons, Queanbeyan NSW, 1927

Hasluck, P. 'Travels in Western Australia 1870–74: extracts from the journal of Thomas Scott', in *Early Days*, vol. 2, part 15, 1934

Lang, A., 'The Truth About Fisher's Ghost', in Lang, A., *The Valet's Tragedy and Other Studies*, Longmans, London, 1903

Scott, B., *The Long and the Short and the Tall: a collection of Australian yarns*, Western Plains Publishers, Sydney, 1985

Western Australian Folklore Archive, John Curtin Prime Ministerial Library, Curtin University of Technology

6. TALES OF WONDER

Anderson, H., *Time Out of Mind: the story of Simon McDonald*, National Press, Melbourne, 1974

Bettelheim, B., *The Uses of Enchantment: the meaning and importance of fairy tales*, Knopf, New York, 1976

Briggs, K. (editor), *A Dictionary of British Folk-Tales in the English Language*, vols 1 & 2, Routledge & Kegan Paul, London, 1970–1971

Calvino, I., *Italian Folk Tales: selected and retold by Italo Calvino*, Martin, G. (translator), Harcourt Brace Jovanovich, New York, 1980

Household Words, vol. 5, no. 124, London, August 1852

Jacobs, J. (compiled and annotated), *English Fairy Tales: being the two*

collections *English Fairy Tales and More English Fairy Tales*, Bodley
Head, London & Sydney, 1968

Klipple, M., *African Folktales with Foreign Analogues*, Garland, New
York & London, 1992

Zipes, J., *Fairy Tales and the Art of Subversion: the classical genre for
children and the process of civilization*, Heinemann, London, 1983

7. BULLDUST

Brennan, M., *Reminiscences of the Goldfields, and Elsewhere in New
South Wales: covering a period of forty-eight years' service as an officer
of police*, William Brooks, Sydney, 1907

Edwards, R., *Fred's Crab and Other Bush Yarns*, Rams Skull Press,
Kuranda QLD, 1989

Fields, M., *Dinkum Aussie Yarns*, Southdown Press, Melbourne, nd
(early 1990s)

Gammage, W., *The Broken Years: Australian soldiers in the Great War*,
Penguin, Ringwood VIC, 1975

Howcroft, W., *Dungarees and Dust*, Hawthorn Press, Melbourne, 1978

Mills, F.J., *Square Dinkum: a volume of original Australian wit and
humour / by 'The Twinkler' (Fred J. Mills)*, Melville & Mullen,
Melbourne, 1917

Northern Territory News, 18 September 1997

Scott, B., *Complete Book of Australian Folklore*, PR Books, Sydney, 1988

Sydney Morning Herald, 31 August 1988

Wannan, B., *Crooked Mick of the Speewah and Other Tales*, Lansdowne
Press, Sydney, 1965

——*A Dictionary of Australian Folklore*, Lansdowne Press, Sydney, 1981

——*Come in Spinner: a treasury of popular Australian humour*, Rigby,
Adelaide, 1976

——*The Australian*, Rigby, Adelaide, 1954

Western Australian Folklore Archive, John Curtin Prime Ministerial
Library, Curtin University of Technology

8. HEROES

Anon., *Marching On: tales of the diggers*, Petersham, nd (1940s)

Anon., *Digger Aussiosities*, New Century Press, Sydney, 1927

Anzac Bulletin, vol. 64, London, 29 March 1918

Aussie, 15 April 1920, 15 June 1920, 15 October 1920

Australian Corps News Sheet, 6 November 1918

Beatty, B., *A Treasury of Australian Folk Tales and Traditions*, Ure Smith, Sydney, 1960

Bradshaw, J., *The Only True Account of Ned Kelly, Frank Gardiner, Ben Hall and Morgan*, Waverly Press, Sydney, 1911

Bryant, N. & J., 'Captain Thunderbolt', www.halenet.com.au/~-jvbryant/thunderb.html#anchor626534, August 2008

Cooper, A.H., *Character Glimpses: Australians on the Somme*, Waverly Press, Sydney, 1920

Cuttriss, G., *Over the Top with the 3rd Australian Division*, Charles H. Kelly, London, 1918

Edwards, R., *The Australian Yarn*, Rigby, Adelaide, 1978

Fair, R., *A Treasury of Anzac Humour*, Jacaranda Press, Brisbane, 1965

Gale, J., *History of and Legends Relating to the Federal Capital Territory of the Commonwealth of Australia*, A.M. Fallick & Sons, Queanbeyan NSW, 1927

Harney, W., *Tales from the Aborigines*, Rigby, Adelaide, 1959

Honk, vol. 11, 7 December 1915

Kennedy, J.J., *The Whale Oil Guards*, J. Duffy, Dublin, 1918

League Post, 1 October 1932

Longmore, C. (editor), *Carry On! The Traditions of the AIF*, Imperial Printing Co., Perth, 1940

——'Digger's Diary', in *Western Mail*, 25 September 1930

Nally, E. (compiler), *Digger Tales 1914–1918, 1939–1942*, np

——*Lest We Forget*, 1941, np

Port Hacking Cough, December 1918–January 1919

Seal, G., *The Outlaw Legend: a cultural tradition in Britain, America and Australia*, Cambridge University Press, Cambridge, 1996

'Semaphore', in *Digger Yarns (and some others) to Laugh At*, E.H. Gibbs & Sons, Melbourne, 1936

Smith's Weekly, 15 August 1925, 29 August 1925, 21 November 1925

Tenterfield Historical Society Archives, Dixon Library, University of New England, Armidale NSW

The Cacolet, journal of the Australian Camel Field Ambulance, Palestine, nd

The Digger, vol. 1, no. 6, 8 September 1918

The Karoolian, April 1919

The Listening Post, 17 August 1923

Wannan, B., *Crooked Mick of the Speewah and Other Tales*, Lansdowne Press, Sydney, 1965

——*A Dictionary of Australian Folklore*, Lansdowne Press, Sydney, 1981

——*Come in Spinner: a treasury of popular Australian humour*, Rigby, Adelaide, 1976

——*The Australian*, Rigby, Adelaide, 1954

Wells, E., *An Anzac's Experiences in Gallipoli, France and Belgium*, W.J. Anderson, Sydney, 1919

9. CHARACTERS

Aussie, 15 December 1920, reprinted from the *Third Battalion Magazine*, nd, (c. 1917)

Bean, C.E.W. (editor), *The Anzac Book*, Cassell, London, 1916

Calvert, A.F., *The Aborigines of Western Australia*, Simpkin, Marshall, Hamilton, Kent, London, 1894

Edwards, R., *The Australian Yarn*, Rigby, Adelaide, 1978

Fields, M., *Dinkum Aussie Yarns*, Southdown Press, Melbourne, nd (early 1990s)

Hardy, F. & Mulley, A., *The Needy and the Greedy: humorous stories of the racetrack*, Libra Books, Canberra, 1975

Howcroft, W., *Dungarees and Dust*, Hawthorn Press, Melbourne, 1978

Papers of Bill Wannan, manuscripts, National Library of Australia, undated (c. 1960s) letter from Mr A.H. Fisher, Camden Park SA

Parker, K.L., (collected and edited), *Australian Legendary Tales*, Melville, Mullen & Slade, London & Melbourne, 1896

Quadrant, vol. 13, Summer 1959–60

Rudd, S., *On Our Selection*, Angus & Robertson, Sydney, 1899

Salt, 8 April 1946

Seal, G., *The Hidden Culture: folklore in Australian society*, Oxford University Press, Melbourne, 1989

Seal, G. & Willis, R. (editors), *Verandah Music: roots of Australian tradition*, Curtin University Books, Fremantle, 2003

Wannan, B.,*The Folklore of the Irish in Australia*, Currey O'Neill, Melbourne, 1980

——*Come in Spinner: a treasury of popular Australian humour*, Rigby, Adelaide, 1976

——*The Australian*, Rigby, Adelaide, 1954

Weller, S., *Bastards I Have Met*, Sampal Investments, Charters Towers QLD, 1976

10. HARD CASES

Aussie, 15 December 1920, reprinted from *The Third Battalion* magazine, c. 1917

Australian Pastoralists Review, 16 July 1891

Bridge, P., *Russian Jack*, Hesperian Press, Perth, 2003

Edwards, R., *Fred's Crab and Other Bush Yarns*, Rams Skull Press, Kuranda QLD, 1990

——*The Australian Yarn*, Rigby, Adelaide, 1978

Elliot, I., *Moondyne Joe: the man and the myth*, University of Western Australia Press, Perth, 1978

Fields, M., *Dinkum Aussie Yarns*, Southdown Press, Melbourne, nd (early 1990s)

Hardy, F. & Mulley, A., *The Needy and the Greedy: humorous stories of the racetrack*, Libra Books, Canberra, 1975

Papers of Ian Turner, National Library of Australia

Wannan, B., *Come in Spinner: a treasury of popular Australian humour*, Rigby, Adelaide, 1976

——*My Kind of Country*, Rigby, Adelaide, 1967

Weller, S., *Bastards I Have Met*, Sampal Investments, Charters Towers QLD, 1976

Willis, W N., *The Life of WP Crick*, W.N. Willis, Sydney, 1909

11. WORKING PEOPLE

Adam-Smith, P., *Folklore of the Australian Railwaymen*, Rigby, Adelaide, 1976

Bean, C.E.W., *The Official History of Australia in the War of 1914–1918*, vol. 6, Angus & Robertson, Sydney, 1918

Cooper, A.H., *Character Glimpses: Australians on the Somme*, Waverly Press, Sydney, 1920

Edwards, R., *The Australian Yarn*, Rigby, Adelaide, 1978

Howcroft, W., *Dungarees and Dust*, Hawthorn Press, Melbourne, 1978

Lacy, J., *Off-Shears: the story of shearing sheds in Western Australia*, Black Swan Press, Perth, 2002

Longmore, C., 'Digger's Diary', in *Western Mail*, 2 January 1930, 30 October 1930

Marshall, A., in *Australasian Post*, 18 February 1954

Lest We Forget: digger tales 1914-18, 1939–42, Footscray VIC, nd (c. 1942), np

Scott, W., *Complete Book of Australian Folklore*, PR Books, Sydney, 1980

Seal, G., *The Bare Fax*, Angus & Robertson, Sydney, 1996

Skuthorpe, L., in *The Bulletin*, 4 August 1921

Smith's Weekly, Sydney, 6 June 1925

Stephens, J.B., in *The Australasian*, Melbourne, 8 March 1873

Stuart, Julian, in *Australian Worker*, Sydney, 31 October 1928

Tronson, M (ed.), *Ripping Good Railway Yarns*, IFH Publishing Co., Wallacia NSW, 1991

Wannan, B., *The Australian*, Rigby, Adelaide, 1954

——*Come in Spinner: a treasury of popular Australian humour*, Rigby, Adelaide, 1976

——*Crooked Mick of the Speewah and other tall tales*, Lansdowne Press, Melbourne, 1965

Western Australian Folklore Archive, John Curtin Prime Ministerial Library, Curtin University, Perth

12. WIDE, BROWN LAND

Eaglehawk and Crow: Thomas, 1923. William Jenkyn Thomas (1870–1959) was a Welsh school master who wrote *The Welsh Fairy Book* as well as some educational texts. Unfortunately, he gives no sources for the stories he includes in his book, which was intended for a general audience and probably, given his profession, as a teaching resource. See also Berndt & Berndt, 1989.

Great floods: Smith, 1930, pp. 151–68. This is Smith's edited version of a story collected and written down by Aboriginal writer, activist, inventor and man on the $50 note, David Unaipon. Unaipon gave his work to Smith, a noted anthropologist, and Smith published it under his own name without acknowledging Unaipon. Smith's version is much shorter than Unaipon's but preserves the essential details of the story. David Unaipon's original collection was finally published by Melbourne University Publishing in 2001, edited by Stephen Muecke and Adam Shoemaker, who were instrumental in uncovering the truth.

Firestick farming: Gammage, 2011.

'The landscape looked like a park': Bride, 1899.

Captain Cook's Law: K. Maddock, 'Myth, History and a Sense of Oneself' in Beckett, 1988, pp. 11–30; Redmond, 2008, pp. 255–70; D. Rose, 'The Saga of Captain Cook: Remembrance and morality', in Attwood & Magowan, 2001, pp. 61–79.

The corners: Queensland Heritage Register.

13. UPON THE FATAL SHORE

Leaden hearts: The National Museum of Australia has a large collection of convict tokens. The selected messages reproduced here have had spelling and layout regularised to some degree.

The Ring: Warung, 1891.

The melancholy death of Captain Logan: The ballad is usually credited to the convict Francis MacNamara, though research by Jeff Brownrigg (Brownrigg, 2003) suggests that MacNamara was not the author. See also Meredith & Whalan, 1979, pp. 31–8 and R. Reece, 'Frank the Poet' in Davy & Seal, 1993.

A Convict's Tour to Hell: The poem exists in various manuscript versions, probably composed c. 1839. See MacNamara, 1839.

'Make it hours instead of days': *Sydney Stock and Station Journal*, 1902, p. 3.

Captain of the push: Mitchell Library scrapbook of clippings, 1830; Lawson, 1900.

The Prince of Pickpockets: The Newgate Calendar; *Australian Dictionary of Biography*: Barrington, George (1755–1804), *Argus*, 1956.

14. PLAINS OF PROMISE

'I was not expected to survive': Moger, 1840; Sarah Brunskill quoted in Haines, 2003. Despite the popular depiction of the Australian emigrant ships as floating hells, government-chartered vessels (the main focus of Robin Haines' work) delivered more than 98 per cent of their charges to their new land in good health in the period covered by the book.

The town that drowned: *Australian Lutheran Almanac*, 1939; Flinders Ranges Research.

Wine and witches: There are various, sometimes contradictory versions of these events. See Ioannou, 1997, pp. 63ff and *Relative Thoughts*, 2009.

Phantoms of the landfall light: Cape Otway Lighthouse.

Tragedy on Lizard Island: Falkiner & Oldfield, 2000; *Australian Dictionary of Biography*: 'Watson, Mary Beatrice Phillips (1860–1881). When that site was reclaimed for Central Station in 1904, the remains were transferred to what is now Botany Bay Cemetery, where they still lie. See also McInnes, 1983; Wemyss, 1837; Lahn, 2013; Kennedy, 2011.

Who was Billy Barlow?: *Maitland Mercury and Hunter River General Advertiser*, 1843; Hildebrand, 2011 (also contains a large number of Billy Barlow ballads).

Chimney Sweeps' Day: Leech, 1989.

The dragon of Big Gold Mountain: *Bendigo Advertiser*, 1874, p. 2; *Argus*, p. 6.

15. A FAIR GO

Black Mary: Wells, 1818; Clarke, 1871.

The Tambaroora line: Beatty, 1960. It is unlikely that the song was Bill Maloney's, though; see *North Queensland Register*.

Mates: 'A Sketch of Mateship' was published in Lawson, 1907b.

A glorious spree: *South Bourke and Mornington Journal*, 1879.

The Greenhide Push waltzes Matilda: Magoffin, 1987, pp. 82ff.

The Bunuba resistance: Pederson & Woorunmurra, 1995, p. 49. See also *Aboriginal History*, 1985, p. 98, note 26; Western Australian Folklore Archive.

The bagman's gazette: *Northern Standard* (Darwin), 1931.

Homes of hope: Gibbons, 2012; *Australian Dictionary of Biography*:
'Hammond, Robert Brodribb (1870–1946)'.

16. HOW WE TRAVEL THE LAND

Rangers and rouseabouts: Fahey & Seal, 2005.

The swagman's union: *Burra Record*, 1931.

The oozlum bird: The first mention of Goodge's poem is in the
Sunday Times (Sydney), 1898. It was published a couple of months
later, so he had probably been writing it since 1897.

The Tea and Sugar train: J.D. in *Railroad*, 1928; Mail (Adelaide),
1925; *Barrier Miner* (Broken Hill), 1943.

The black stump: oral tradition

The rise and fall of Cobb & Co.: Everingham, 2007.

The Long Paddock: *Sydney Morning Herald*, 1942.

The real Red Dog: Duckett, 1993.

17. DOING IT TOUGH

Depending on the harvest: *Argus*, 1880.

'Women of the West': *Argus*, 1901

Cures!: *Argus*, 1918; Edwards, 1997; fieldwork of Rob Willis.

A seasonal guide to weather and wives: Traditional, also fieldwork of
Rob and Olya Willis; *Pageant of Humour*, 1920, but said to be
from 1842 source.

Backyard brainwaves: Australian War Memorial; Ingpen, 1982.

Sugar bag nation: *Hindsight*, 1999; Lowenstein, 1998; Seal, 1977;

Happy Valley: *Sydney Morning Herald*, 1933.

Sergeant Small: Graham Seal, 'From Texas to Tamworth via New
Zealand: Tex Morton sings an Australian song', in Dalziell &
Genoni, 2013.

The farmer's will: Author's collection.

18. HOME OF THE WEIRD

Curious discoveries: Grey, 1841.

The marble man: *Maitland Mercury & Hunter River General Advertiser*
(NSW), 1889, p. 4. Most of the Australian newspapers, large and
small, carried items on the marble man.

Was Breaker Morant the Gatton murderer?: Meredith, 1996.

Vanishing vessels: Jeffreys, 2007; Gregory, 1861, p. 482; WA Maritime Myths, referencing Busselton Historical Society; Gerritsen, 2010; Van Den Boogaerde, 2009, p. 75.

Yearning for yowies: *Queanbeyan Age*, 1903, p. 2.

19. ROMANCING THE SWAG

Introduction: *Sydney Morning Herald*, 1869, p. 4.

Lore of the track: Wannan, 1976, p. 196 (from Mr J. Robertson, North Geelong); *Townsville Daily Bulletin*, 1924, p. 9; *Nepean Times*, 1933, p. 6.

Sniffling Jimmy: *Townsville Daily Bulletin*, 1924, p. 9.

The poetic swaggie: Paterson, 1906; Henry Lawson, 'Hungerford' in *Bulletin*, 1893.

'There you have the Australian swag': Henry Lawson, 'The Romance of the Swag', in Ross, 2011.

A swagman's death: *Morning Bulletin*, 1894, p. 5.

Where the angel tarboys fly: *Capricornian*, 1908 p. 47.

Bowyang Bill and the cocky farmer: *Narromine News and Trangie Advocate*, 1934, p. 6. 'Bowyang Bill' was probably Alexander Vennard, who usually used the byline 'Bill Bowyang'.

The Mad Eight: *News* (Adelaide), 1927.

20. AFTER THE KELLYS

The saga: Seal, 2002.

A Glenrowan letter: Sutherland, 1880.

'I thought it was a circus': *Argus*, 1881.

A death in Forbes: *Illustrated Australian News*, 1880; *Forbes & Parkes Gazette*, 1898.

Living legends: *Argus*, 1902.

The stranger: *Argus*, 1878; *Ovens and Murray Advertiser*, 1979; Eastman, 1850–52.

21. THE CHILD IN THE BUSH

The beanstalk in the bush: Jacobs, 1890—'I tell this as it was told me in Australia, somewhere about the year 1860.'

Forgotten nursery rhymes: Nursery rhymes from various sources, including Howitt, 1898; *Bulletin*, 1898 & 1917.

The lost boys of Daylesford: *Daylesford Express*, 1867a, 1867b; *Sydney Morning Herald*, 1867.

Fairies in the paddock: Ernst, 1904. The *Snugglepot and Cuddlepie* gumnut baby stories were first published in 1918 and have been with us ever since.

Surviving Black Jack: *Perth Gazette and Western Australian Journal*, 1835, p. 575.

22. LARGER THAN LIFE

The fate of Captain Cadell: Nicholson, 2004.

The Fenian: Evans, 1997, p. 98. See also Sullivan, 2001; O'Reilly, 1879; Hasluck, 1959, p. 75.

The last bushranger: *Courier-Mail*, 1937, p. 13; *Keep in Touch*, 2012.

Lawson's people: Lawson & Brereton, 1931; Roderick, 1982.

The Coo-ee Lady: Richard White, 'Cooee', in White & Harper, 2010.

Australia's first Hollywood Star: McGowan, 2005.

A vision splendid: Murphy & Muller, 1998; author's collection.

The illywacker: *Clarence and Richmond Examiner*, 1902, p. 6.

23. WORKING FOR A LAUGH

Droving in a bar: Edwards, 1997, pp. 235–6.

A fine team of bullocks: Anon., author's collection.

A stump speech: *Imperial Songster*, 1907.

Working on the railway: *Railroad*, various editions.

Service!: author's collection.

High-octane travel: author's collection.

Rechtub klat: Maddox, 2002.

The garbos' Christmas: Lindesay, 1988; Scott, 1976.

A Christmas message: *Townsville Daily Bulletin*, 1924, p. 9.

Total eclipse of communication: author's collection.

The laws of working life: author's collection.

Somebody else's job: author's collection.

The basic work survival guide: author's collection.

Twelve things you'll never hear an employee tell the boss: author's
  collection.
Excessive absence: author's collection.
Running naked with the bulls: Australian Associated Press report, in
  West Australian, 2002, p. 55.
Doing business: Seal, 2001.
The end of a perfect day: author's collection.

Bibliography

BOOKS AND MANUSCRIPTS

Attwood, B. & Magowan, F. (eds), 2001, *Telling Stories: Indigenous history and memory in Australia and New Zealand*, Sydney: Allen & Unwin

Australian Dictionary of Biography, 1976, vol. 6, Melbourne: Melbourne University Press

Beatty, B., 1960, *Treasury of Australian Folk Tales and Traditions*, Sydney: Ure Smith

Beckett, J.R. (ed.), 1988, *Past and Present: The construction of Aboriginality*, Canberra: Aboriginal Studies Press

Berndt, R.M. & Berndt, C.H., 1989, *The Speaking Land*, Ringwood, Vic: Penguin

Bride, T.F. (ed.), 1899, *Letters from Victorian Pioneers: a series of papers on the early occupation of the colony, the Aborigines, etc.*, Melbourne: Brain

Brownrigg, J., 2003, *'From Bondage . . . Liberated': Frank the Poet's Dreams of Liberty*, paper given at ESCAPE (An international and interdisciplinary conference on escape and the convict experience), Strahan, Tasmania, 26–28 June

Clarke, M., 1871, *Old Tales of a Young Country*, Melbourne: Mason, Firth & M'Cutcheon

Davy, G. & Seal, G. (eds), 1993, *The Oxford Companion to Australian Folklore*, Melbourne: Oxford University Press

Dalziell, T. & Genoni, P. (eds), 2013, *Telling Stories: Australian life and literature, 1935–2012*, Clayton: Monash University Publishing

Duckett, B., 1993, *Red Dog: The Pilbara Wanderer*, Karratha: self-published

Eastman, H.M., c.1850–1852, memoirs (manuscript on microfilm), State Library of NSW, MLMSS 130, B1341

Edwards, R., 1997, *The Australian Yarn: The definitive collection*, St Lucia: University of Queensland Press

Ernst, O., 1904, *Fairytales from the Land of Wattle*, Melbourne: McCarron, Bird & Co.

Evans, A., 1997, *Fanatic Heart: A life of John Boyle O'Reilly 1844–1890*, Perth: University of Western Australia Press

Everingham, S., 2007, *Wild Ride: The rise and fall of Cobb & Co*, Sydney: Penguin Viking

Gerritsen, R., 2010, *Geomorphology and the Deadwater Wreck*, a modified form of a presentation given at the Eastern Australian Region of the Australasian Hydrographic Society Annual Symposium in Sydney on 13 September, at http://rupertgerritsen.tripod.com/pdf/unpublished/Geomorphology_and_the_Deadwater_Wreck.pdf, accessed 14 April 2014

Grey, G., 1841, *Journals of Two Expeditions of Discovery in North-West and Western Australia, During the Years 1837, 1838 and 1839*, London: T. & W. Boone

Fahey, W. & Seal, G. (eds), 2005, *Old Bush Songs: The centenary edition of Banjo Paterson's classic collection*, Sydney: ABC Books

Falkiner, S. & Oldfield, A., 2000, *Lizard Island: The story of Mary Watson*, Sydney: Allen & Unwin

Gammage, B., 2011, *The Biggest Estate on Earth*, Sydney: Allen & Unwin

Gibbons, M., 2012, *Hammondville: The first eighty years 1932–2012*, online at www.melaniegibbons.com.au/sites/default/files/content/MENAI%20HAMMONDVILLE%20BOOKLET%20NOVEMBER%202012.pdf, accessed 15 April 2014

Gregory, F.T., 1861, 'On the Geology of a Part of Western Australia', *Quarterly Journal of the Geological Society of London*, vol. 17, pp. 475–83

Haines, R. 2003, *Life and Death in the Age of Sail: The passage to Australia*, Sydney: University of New South Wales Press

Hasluck, A., 1959, *Unwilling Emigrants*, Melbourne: Oxford University Press

Hildebrand, J., 2011, *Hey Ho Raggedy-O: A Study of the Billy Barlow Phenomenon*, e-book online at http://www.warrenfahey.com/hey-ho-raggedy-o, accessed 15 April 2014

Howitt, W., 1898, 'A Boy's Adventure in the Wilds of Australia' (1854), *The Bulletin*, 12 March

Ingpen, R., 1982, *Australian Inventions and Innovations*, Adelaide: Rigby

Ioannou, N., 1997, *Barossa Journeys: Into a valley of tradition*, Kent Town: Paringa Press

Jacobs, J. (ed.), 1890, *English Fairy Tales*, London: David Nutt

Jenkins, J., 1975, *Diary of a Welsh Swagman*, Melbourne: Macmillan

Jeffreys, G., 2007, *The Stradbroke Island Galleon: The Mystery of the Ship in the Swamp*, North Stradbroke Island, QLD: Jan & Greg Publications

Kennedy, M., 2011, 'Natural History Museum returns bones of 138 Torres Strait Islanders', *The Guardian*, 10 March

Lahn, J., 2013, 'The 1836 Lewis Collection and the Torres Strait Turtle Mask of Kulka: From loss to reengagement', *The Journal of Pacific History*, vol. 48

Lawson, B.L. & Le Gay Brereton, J. (eds), 1931, *Henry Lawson by His Mates*, Sydney: Angus & Robertson

Lawson, H., 1900, *Verses Popular and Humorous*, Sydney: Angus & Robertson

——1907a, *The Romance of the Swag*, Sydney: Angus & Robertson

——1907b, *Send Round the Hat*, Sydney: Angus & Robertson

Leech, K., 1989, *Jack-in-the-Green in Tasmania 1844–73*, London: The Folklore Society

Lindesay, V., 1988, *Aussieossities*, Richmond, Victoria: Greenhouse

Lowenstein, W., 1998, *Weevils in the Flour: An oral record of the 1930s depression in Australia*, Melbourne: Scribe

MacNamara, F., 1839, 'A Convict's Tour to Hell', in Nicholas, J. (ed.) *Macquarie PEN Anthology of Australian Literature*, Sydney: Allen & Unwin, p. 83

Maddox, G., 2002, 'Behind that tray of snags, there's a rechtub talking', *Sydney Morning Herald*, 27 May

Magoffin, R., 1987, *Waltzing Matilda: The story behind the legend*, Sydney: Australian Broadcasting Corporation

McGowan, J.J., 2005, *J.P. McGowan: Biography of a Hollywood pioneer*, Jefferson, North Carolina: McFarland

McInnes, A., 1983, 'The Wreck of the Charles Easton: Read to a Meeting of the Royal Historical Society of Queensland on 24 February 1983', http://espace.library.uq.edu.au/eserv/UQ:241150/s00855804_1983_11_4_21.pdf, accessed 15 April 2014

Meredith, J., 1996, *Breaker's Mate: Will Ogilvie in Australia*, Sydney: Kangaroo Press

Meredith, J. & Whalan, R., 1979, *Frank the Poet*, Ascot Vale: Red Rooster Press

Moger, E., 1840 (28 January–18 March), letter, National Library of Australia, manuscript reference no. NLA MS 5919

Murphy, S. & Muller, A., 1997, *Fairbridge Village Interpretation Plan*, Research Institute for Cultural Heritage, Curtin University, Perth

Nicholson, J., 2004, *The Incomparable Captain Cadell*, Sydney: Allen & Unwin

O'Reilly, J.B., 1879, *Moondyne*, Boston: Pilot Publishing

Pageant of Humour, c. 1920, Sydney: Gayle Publishing Company

Paterson, A.B. (Banjo) (ed.), 1906, *Old Bush Songs*, Sydney: Angus & Robertson

Pederson, H., & Woorunmurra, B., 1995, *Jandamarra and the Bunuba Resistance*, Broome: Magabala Books

Redmond, A.J., 2008, 'Captain Cook meets General Macarthur in the Northern Kimberley: Humour and ritual in an Indigenous Australian life-world', *Anthropological Forum*, Special issue: You've got to be joking! Anthropological perspectives on humour and laughter, vol. 3, no. 18

Roderick, C., 1982, *The Real Henry Lawson*, Adelaide: Rigby

Ross, J. (ed), *The Penguin Book of Australian Bush Writing*, Camberwell, Vic: Viking

Scott, B., 1976, *Complete Book of Australian Folklore*, Dee Why West, NSW: Summit Books

Seal, G., 1977, *On the Steps of the Dole-Office Door*, (recording) Sydney: Larrikin Records

——2001, *More Urban Myths*, Sydney: HarperCollins

——2002, *Tell 'em I Died Game: The legend of Ned Kelly*, Flemington: Hyland House

Smith, W.R., 1930, *Myths and Legends of the Australian Aborigines*, London: Harrup

Sullivan, C.W. III, 2001, *Fenian Diary: Denis B. Cashman aboard the Hougoumont, 1867–1868*, Dublin: Wolfhound Press

Sutherland, D., 1880 (8 July), letter, Australian Manuscripts Collection, State Library of Victoria, manuscript reference no. MS 13713

Thomas, W.J., 1923, *Some Myths and Legends of the Australian Aborigines*, London: Whitcombe & Tombs

Van Den Boogaerde, P., 2009, *Shipwrecks of Madagascar*, New York: Strategic Book Publishing

Wannan, B., 1976, *Come in Spinner*, Melbourne: John Curry, O'Neill

Warung, P., 1891, 'The Liberation of the First Three', *The Bulletin*, vol. 11, no. 594, pp. 21–2

Wells, T.E. & Howe, M., 1818, *The Last and Worst of the Bush-Rangers of Van Diemen's Land*, Hobart: Andrew Bent

Wemyss, T., 1837, *Narrative of the Melancholy Shipwreck of the Ship Charles Eaton*, Stockton: Robinson

White, R. & Harper, M. (eds), 2010, *Symbols of Australia*, Sydney: National Museum of Australia Press/UNSW Press

JOURNALS AND PERIODICALS

Aboriginal History, vol. 9, part 1, 1985

Argus, 30 October 1878

——19 April 1880

——16 May 1881

——20 April 1892

——7 September 1901

——15 October 1902

——23 July 1918

——8 December 1956

Australian Lutheran Almanac, 1939

Barrier Miner (Broken Hill), 24 February 1943

Bendigo Advertiser, 7 April 1874

Bulletin, Christmas 1893

——March 1898

——November 1917

Burra Record, 11 February 1931

Capricornian, 14 November 1908

Clarence and Richmond Examiner, 6 December 1902

Courier-Mail, 14 January 1937

Daylesford Express, 4 July 1867a

——16 July 1867b

Forbes & Parkes Gazette, 18 October 1898

Hindsight, ABC Radio National, 1999

Illustrated Australian News, no. 29, 1 July 1880

Imperial Songster, no. 97, 1907

Keep in Touch (published by The Sisters of Charity of Australia), vol.
    13, no. 4, December 2012

Mail (Adelaide), 19 December 1925

Maitland Mercury and Hunter River General Advertiser, 2 September
    1843

——1 June 1889

Morning Bulletin, 4 September 1894

Narromine News and Trangie Advocate, 16 February 1934

Nepean Times, 1 April 1933

News (Adelaide), 28 June 1927

North Queensland Register, 18 September 1976

Northern Standard (Darwin), 29 September 1931

Ovens and Murray Advertiser, 27 February 1979

Perth Gazette and Western Australian Journal, 3 October 1835

Queanbeyan Age, 7 August 1903

Railroad, October 1928 and various editions throughout 1930s
    and 1940s

Relative Thoughts, 2009, quarterly journal of the Fleurieu Peninsula
    Family History Group Inc., vol. 13, no. 1

South Bourke and Mornington Journal, 19 March 1879

Sunday Times (Sydney), 9 October 1898
Sydney Morning Herald, 23 September 1867
——4 August 1869
——29 December 1933
——27 June 1942
Sydney Stock and Station Journal, 27 May 1902
Townsville Daily Bulletin, 4 June 1924
West Australian, 14 December 1891

WEBSITES

Australian War Memorial

The Australian War Memorial combines a shrine, a world-class museum, and an extensive archive.
http://www.awm.gov.au

Cape Otway Lighthouse

Cape Otway Lighthouse is the oldest surviving lighthouse in mainland Australia. In operation since 1848, it is perched on towering sea cliffs where Bass Strait and the Southern Ocean collide. For thousands of immigrants, after many months at sea, Cape Otway was their first sight of land after leaving Europe.
www.lightstation.com

Flinders Ranges Research

Flinders Ranges Research undertakes research, evaluates information, presents reports and writes material for publication of South Australian history.
www.southaustralianhistory.com.au/hoffnungsthal.htm.

Frank the Poet—Francis MacNamara 1811–1861

A research project by Mark Gregory.
www.frankthepoet.blogspot.com.au/2011/01/articles.html

The Legend of the Stradbroke Island Galleon

A research project by Brad Horton, Greg Jefferys and Cliff Rosendahl. See also Jefferys, 2007.
www.stradbrokeislandgalleon.com

The National Museum of Australia

The National Museum of Australia has 314 convict love tokens in its collection. These tokens were made by convicts around the time of their sentencing and were given to friends and loved ones as mementos.
www.love-tokens.nma.gov.au.

The Newgate Calendar

A searchable series of stories about criminals from the 17th century and earlier through to 1840, this is a wonderful resource for anyone interested in the criminal underworld of 18th-century Britain.
http://www.pascalbonenfant.com/18c/newgatecalendar

Queensland Heritage Register

The Department of Environment and Heritage Protection, Queensland Government, is responsible for managing the health of the environment to protect Queensland's unique ecosystems, including its landscapes and waterways, as well as its native plants and animals and biodiversity.
https://heritage-register.ehp.qld.gov.au/placeDetail.html?siteId=33360

WA Maritime Myths

A blog dealing with Western Australian wreck sites and early Dutch explorers.
http://wamaritimemyths.wordpress.com/2007/11/

Western Australian Folklore Archive

The Western Australian Folklore Archive, Curtin University of Technology, Perth, records, preserves and gives the public access to the rich folk traditions, past and present, of Western Australians.
http://john.curtin.edu.au/folklore